Confessions of an Industry Chic

VOLUME 1

———

ISBN: **099635560X**
ISBN-13: **978-0996355605**

DEDICATION

This book is dedication to every moth that is addicted to the flame.
To every woman who can't see past the handbag and designer heels.
Everything that is worth having comes with its own set of demands,
and a price that often compromises integrity. Learn how to spot the
poison in the things that are beautiful. Identify the treachery in a
heart that appears to be pure. Signs and symbols are for a conscious
mind.

Trumaine D. McClure

Part 3

ACKNOWLEDGMENTS

First, I would like to thank my mother (Jennifer Jones), who is a phenomenal poetry writer, for allowing her creative literary genius to flow through me. She is the author of two amazing poetry books: *Genuine Black Woman*, and *Genuine Black: Keep it Real* that are currently sold in Barnes in Nobles.

I will not attempt to name everyone, but I would like to give a special thanks to the following people: my big brother, Michael R. "Cut" McClure, my sisters Lashannia N. Kennedy, Nakeya Lee, Karen Artley, Stacey Ramsey, my grandmother Ada Jones, my cousins Veleria Jones, Marlin Austin, and close friends who have always been supportive of my ambitions: Dominique Walker, Laura Branch, Marlan "M.J." Johnson, Ashton "Shorty Black" Hollins, Ryan Cochran, Corey Trainer, Brian Joiner, Eddie "Wolf" Lee, Eddie Stiff, Trevor Franklin, Douglas "Fresh" McKinney, Keith "K.P." Patterson, Bad Habit, Derrick "East Side" Lowery, Abdul "Dala" Robinson, Otis "K.B" Dorsey, Derrick Triplett, Michael "Money" Davis, Terrance Byrd, Hortez "Ray" Daniels, Arturo Hudson, Jeffrey White, Jauanly Washington, David Cross, Jarvis "Jovs" Alexander, Mercedes Rodgers, and anyone else that I may have accidentally forgotten.

Thank you for your support and belief in my ability as a writer. Trust and believe that one day soon I will make you all very proud.

PROLOGUE

Present Day

Sequoia adjusted the webcam's apparatus that rested atop her laptop computer for the sixth consecutive time within the last five minutes. She sighed, frustrated, when she finally concluded that it's positioning was as precise as it was going to get.

She unenthusiastically rested her pale, thin, weary frame in a nearby chair and pulled it before the laptop with the excitement of a death row inmate who was awaiting execution. She trained her aqua blue eyes on the image that was displayed largely on the 13.3" screen and did not recognize it. It, sadly, was herself.

Her skin was deathly pale and seriously lacked the envious radiance it once possessed. Her eyes had huge dark circles around them that gave way to bags that were deeply rooted in months of stress. Her once prominent jaw line and perfect cheekbone structure now sat noticeably disfigured underneath her blotched skin. Her lips boasted a swollen scar that remained as a constant reminder from memories of that dreadful night. Her once voluminous, long, curly hair was now unkempt, damaged, and splitting at its ends.

She was in desperate need of a serious make over, but had no intention of ever following through with it, for this was the way that she wanted the world to see her: for whom she really was! The real her! There's no need to be ashamed.

Her heart's desire was not set on ruining her tainted image with things like make-up and beauty products. She wanted everyone to see her.

They need to see me like this.

She glanced at the digital clock on her computer screen and noticed it was time.

You can do this.

Her palms were sweating; a condition that her therapist long ago advised her was attributed to her anxiety. Somehow, she managed to find the strength to will herself into following through with her plan. She had to do this. The world needed to know her story, and she was about to give it to them.

The six month hiatus that she'd taken from her career and the spotlight had practically caused a frenzy within social networks, which is why she was certain that by now millions of her fans from around the world were eagerly anticipating the revelation she was set to reveal via YouTube that afternoon. She had personally taken the liberty of making use of her Twitter and Facebook accounts the previous night to ensure that a large fraction of the cyber world were perched before their PCs.

"Here goes nothing," she said aloud before setting the record option on the webcam that would send live footage of her to the viewers on YouTube.

She waved nervously at the camera. "Hi guys." She smiled weakly. "It's me, the one and only, Sequoia Ariás. YouTube sensation turned mega pop star singer and entertainer." She chuckled at the irony of her successes over such short period of time. But her energetic mood dissipated quickly and was replaced by a sea of anxiety.

"I know everyone has been wondering about my whereabouts, but I can assure you that I'm alright," she said before coughing violently.

She sighed as her mind processed what to say next. Nothing came to mind. She wanted, for the sake of her fans, to maintain some form of enthusiasm, but she saw no sense in carrying out the charade any longer. Now was the time—time for the world to know it all. Time for her to confess!

She knew that her lengthy pause was making the viewers antsy, so she decided to get it over with as quick as possible. "Look, I'm pretty sure that a lot of you may have heard a lot of rumors about me. Some are true... others... not so much. None of them I'm proud of," she said plainly, as if it really didn't matter that much to her.

"Which leads me to why I decided to broadcast my entire story for the whole world to hear, live on YouTube." She paused. "So just bear with me while I give you my confession.

CHAPTER 1

Graduation Day '08

A cool breeze from the Atlantic Ocean caressed Sequoia's skin as she frolicked feverishly alongside an ascending tide. The sun beamed brilliantly in the clear blue sky as Sequoia kicked grains of sand into the wind with the heels of her feet. She was in heaven!

She was back in her native land along the shores of Costa Rica, where life always seemed to slow to a more rational pace, where her sanity was temporarily restored and the troubles of the day were instantly cast deep into the depths of the sea.

Sequoia wished that she could dwell there for all eternity, but she knew that the very thought of it was unrealistic and that eventually reality would set in and she would have to live in the present moment.

"Sequoia?" her best friend, Desiree nudged her and spoke in a whisper, "Get ready girl. You're up next."

Sequoia nodded meekly with a weak smile as she nervously adjusted her graduation cap. She quietly recited her speech to herself as one last reminder of her lines. The last thing she wanted to do was embarrass herself in front of all the people who were in the audience.

Truthfully, she wished that she could just opt out of the whole thing, but at that point, turning back was not an option. It was just one of the obligatory duties that came along with being school Valedictorian.

Sequoia had managed to persevere successfully throughout her entire high school experience. Earning herself a 4.0 GPA, numerous certificates and awards, and two full scholarships to Harvard University (one for dance and one an academic scholarship), Sequoia was one of 96 students who were selected in the nation to receive a full academic scholarship to an Ivy League college.

Needless to say, neither of her accomplishments did anything to prepare her properly for the anxiety that came along with stage fright. She was a nervous wreck, and she was certain that if she hadn't just gotten a fresh manicure that she would've gnawed her nails down to bits by now.

"And without further adieu," she heard the dean of students say, "I would like for you to give a warm congratulatory welcome to our 2008 school valedictorian, Ms. Sequoia Ariás," she said as the crowd erupted in a round of applause.

Sequoia smoothed out the wrinkles to her gown before rising from her seat. She shot a glance back at Desiree, her one and only true friend since the fifth grade, and got a surge of confidence.

"Go get'em, girl." Desiree smiled and winked.

With that, Sequoia held her head high, tossed her shoulders back, and strutted to the podium gracefully. Suddenly she had no fear. She took a brief moment to search through the crowd for her mother's beautiful face. When she spotted her she mouthed the words, "Hi Mom." She watched a lone tear cascade her mother's cheek.

Sequoia knew it was a tear of joy. She had made her mother proud, and she had no intention of letting up anytime soon. She focused her attention on the audience and cleared her throat before making her valedictory.

"First, I would like to say that it is an honor and a privilege to carry the valedictorian title for the graduating class of 2008 at the Institute of Language and Performing Arts School. We all have worked very hard for a very long time. I know I have," she joked, which earned her a few laughs from members of the audience. "But our road to success doesn't stop here. In fact, this is only the beginning. Now, we are about to embark upon our journeys to conquer the next phase of our lives.

"Some will continue to pursue an even higher education, while others will follow their heart and life's passion, but I know that I can speak for my entire graduating class when I say that we will never forget the teachings taught to us by both our parents and our teachers sitting here throughout this assembly. We will hold true to them as we hurdle life's obstacles.

"So thank you to the parents, teachers, and faculty staff. We sincerely appreciate your commitment to us, and for preparing us for a promising future, from the bottom of our hearts. And I would especially like to thank my classmates from the graduating class for providing me with some of the most cherished memories and experiences of our young lives!

"Thank you everyone! And congratulations to the graduating class of 2008—Wooo!!!" Sequoia yelled as everyone rose to their feet to give her a standing ovation.

When Sequoia stared into the crowd and took in the plethora of parents with tear-stained faces she instantly knew she nailed it. She smiled ecstatically as the Dean of Students, Dr. Elise Sullivan, approached her and took her into her warm embrace.

Dr. Elise Sullivan spoke into the microphone, "To the graduating class of 2008!" The entire graduating class rose from their seats as if on cue. "Congratulations to you all!" she yelled ardently as everyone applauded.

Minutes later, everyone posed to take pictures. When the majority of the graduating class was able to pull themselves away from everyone, they were able to form a huge group to partake in an age-old tradition.

"1....2...3!" they all counted in unison before tossing their graduation caps into the air, commemorating the conclusion of four years of high school and welcoming the introduction to a new chapter of life.

Later 2009

The single dollar bills rained down over Butterfly's voluptuous body like confetti as she slowly gyrated her hips to Pretty Rick's "Grind with Me" song.

She inherited her stage name from the oversized colorful

butterfly tattoo that covered both of her massive ass cheeks—ass cheeks that had absolutely nothing to do with her hereditary link to Sweden and everything to do with the butt enlargement injections she received on a trip to Brazil a year ago.

Butterfly was a natural redhead and wore it proudly. So instead of shaving entirely, she always saved just enough hair on her southern lips to style with and exotic design. Today, she had three small arrows pointing south.

Her ocean-blue eyes complimented her creamy vanilla skin. She had natural 36D breasts with huge pink nipples that both bore shiny piercings, a 26" waist, and a 45" hip to ass measurement. She also had piercings on her neck, naval, lip, and vaginal lips as well.

Though, Butterfly was one of the most beautiful things walking on four-inch heels, she was only one of the diverse array of exotic beauties at SCORES Strip Club.

The place was jammed, packed to the teeth, courtesy of the New York rapper, Jewels Santiago and his entourage being in attendance, and they were being extremely generous with their money.

The stage was practically covered in bills as Butterfly danced suggestively against the stripper pole. She pulled her plumped ass cheeks apart and clasped them shut around the width of the pole. Her ass swallowed the pole until there was nothing to see but her tattoo-covered derrière. The ogling crowd of horny onlookers went wild.

Butterfly managed to pull her ass away from the pole long enough to retrieve a large black dildo from a topless waiter that was attached to a huge base. She peered at the audience seductively as she held the dildo firmly within her manicured palm. She surveyed the entire crowd for a brief moment before shoving the entire dildo into her mouth. The men and women of the audience were clapping and cheering loudly as they watched her deep throat the dildo.

She then plopped it out of her mouth and screwed it to a stationary harness that was built into the floor. It was time for her finale!

She dropped down to her knees in a smooth motion that could only be accomplished by a skilled stripper and eased her vaginal lips over the dildo. She rode the dildo slowly, picking up pace as her walls adjusted to the girth, while burying her face into the bills on the floor. The loud music was doing very little to drown out the moans of pleasure escaping from Butterfly's luscious lips.

As her pace quickened, the butterfly tattoo on her ass created the illusion that it was flapping its wings as the dildo appeared and vanished into her. Money was flying everywhere. The astonished expressions on the audience—their faces clearly said that they couldn't believe what they were seeing.

By now, Butterfly was riding the dildo so hard that her ass and thighs were plopping down rhythmically on the base, causing a loud clapping sound as seismic waves spread across her ass cheeks.

Her moans grew more vocal as she neared an orgasm. The viewers cheered boisterously as they watched a thick coat of cum form around the base of the plastic shaft. The money continued to cascade out of everywhere as Butterfly arose from the dildo and gave a bow of appreciation before gathering her money and leaving the stage.

Backstage, naked and half-naked strippers were moving about the modern decorated dressing room frantically, while others busied themselves with their hair and make-up. They all had gotten wind of the large amounts of money that the famous rapper Jewels Santiago and his entourage were throwing around and wanted to stake their claim to a piece of the pie.

"Y'all bitches betta hurry up and get out there before Butterfly's slick ass take all of them niggas money," a stripper named Cherokee said as she entered the dressing room with nothing covering her dignity but a G-string.

Cherokee was African American and Indian with features strongly resembling her Indian roots. Her hair was long and straight, and draped just above the rose and vine tattoo that covered her entire waistline. Her chestnut complexion was complimented with curves from heaven. Her high cheekbones made her face exceptionally unique and photogenic with fierce dark brown eyes. She had 38C-26"-43" measurements. At thirty-two years old,

Cherokee was the oldest stripper working at SCORES, and was often teased by the other girls as being the dinosaur of the group.

"La la la la laaaa!" Sequoia crooned in a world of her own with one of the sweetest voices ever to grace the face of the earth.

Her perfect apple bottom was perched on a short stool while she fastened the strap on her four-inch platform heels, preparing to hit the stage next.

"You need to do something with all that damn talent you got instead of shaking yo ass with us in this strip club," Cherokee said in a serious tone when she caught wind of Sequoia's voice before applying another coat of lip-gloss to her lips.

"I know that's right, Sequoia," Desiree said playfully as if she was adding her two cents.

"Shut up," Sequoia huffed at Desiree. "And what'd I tell you about using my name in here? I don't want these bitches all up in my personal business like that. Call me by my stage name—Vixen!" She rolled her eyes.

"Oops," Desiree said sarcastically. "My bad, boo. Here, give Mama a kiss," Desiree said playfully as she rushed over to Sequoia's side, bare breasts jiggling along the way. Sequoia attempted to hold her off, but Desiree was much bigger than her so her efforts were futile. Desiree planted a juicy kiss right on Sequoia's lips and rocked her in her arms. "Poor baby," she joked.

Sequoia pretended to be annoyed by Desiree's antics but they both knew that it was just a front. They could never really be mad at each other, for they had been as thick as thieves since the fifth grade. They often joked about how they were each other's "sisters from another mother."

Desiree, whose stripper name was Mocha, which derived from her genetic mixture of Italian and African American, possessed all of the desirable physical attributes of an American Next Top Model. She was 5'10" with an athletic figure. Nothing was too big or too small. Everything was just right. She had 38B perky breasts, a 27" waist, and a backside that could stop traffic. Sequoia always joked that her butt was too perfect to be real, but they both knew that

Sequoia's body was something that all women coveted and envied.

Desiree's complexion was complimented with a cute button nose, full lips, a chin that boasted a cleft, and captivating gray eyes.

"Get a room," Butterfly said to Sequoia and Desiree as she entered the room.

"Umph!" Butterfly said lustfully as she palmed one of Desiree's ass cheeks in a smooth motion without breaking her stride on the way past. "You need to let me get some of that shit. I'd turn yo young ass out," she said surely.

"Bitch, what did I tell you about keeping yo freaky-ass hands to yourself?" Desiree snapped as she turned to face a stark naked Butterfly.

"Sorry," Butterfly said with a mischievous smile. "I couldn't help it."

"Besides, you wouldn't know what to do with a bitch like me if you had the chance anyway," Desiree shot.

"Try me," Butterfly contested.

Cherokee butted in: "I see you cleaned house out there today."

"But of course," Butterfly's tone changed to a more vibrant tone. "No man can resist the Butterfly." She turned around and began making her butt clap, seemingly causing the butterfly to flap its wings. "It's fucked up that I can't keep all this money to myself because I'd be pushing my new Bentley by spring," she said as she fingered the large stack of money she'd accumulated.

"I hate going up after her," Sequoia pouted. "She get them niggas all riled up, out there fucking the stage and shit. Then when I come out there, they're looking at me like I'm supposed to do the same thing."

"I don't know why you're tripping, Vixen," Butterfly told her. "Shit, if I looked half as good as you I wouldn't have to do all of the crazy shit that I be doing to get my money."

Sequoia scoffed. "Girl, what the hell is you talkin' 'bout, you're fine! And you're Swedish so that makes you exotic," Sequoia stated seriously.

"Oh, don't get it twisted—I know I look good," Butterfly said with an air of arrogance, "but everybody in this club knows that Miss Vixen is the baddest bitch in here. Shid, every time I see yo sexy ass my pussy gets wet," she admitted.

"Well, you better dry that mother fucker out because the only thing that will even get close to this pussy is a male phallus." Everyone laughed.

"Why you always got to use them big ass words?" Butterfly rolled her eyes before finding something to do.

Sequoia knew that Butterfly's education didn't exceed the eighth grade, and that the subject alone was a delicate topic for her, but she wasn't about to feel sorry for her because she was too lazy to take her ass back to school. If she wanted to be dumb and strip for the rest of her life, then by all means, she could go right on ahead and do it, but not Sequoia. She, on the other hand, intended to use the stripping experience as a stepping-stone to help her accomplish her life goals.

Cherokee walked over to Sequoia and Desiree and spoke loud enough for only their ears to hear. "Sequoia, huh?" she asked. Vixen shot Mocha a mean askance before answering, "Yep. That's my name."

"You know that's an Indian name, right?" Cherokee asked.

"Ummhmm," Sequoia nodded. "It was an old Cherokee Indian leader, and a California tree."

"What, are you mixed with Indian or something?" Cherokee pried.

"Part," Sequoia said. "I'm Indian, Nicaraguan, Costa Rican, and Filipino. I'm a genealogical experiment, a regular modern day mutt," she joked.

"Wow!" Cherokee said astonishingly. "Well, it definitely was a perfect mix," Cherokee said as she admired her features.

"Thank you!" Sequoia said.

"Well, *Sequoia*," Cherokee enunciated her name, "take my advice: do something with your talent. Don't get caught up in this whole strip club scene. I know the money is good and to most bitches that's all it's about. But trust me when I say that this place will chew you up and shit you out!

"I started working in a strip club when I was sixteen and I've personally seen these types of places destroy more young girls' lives than the crack epidemic. So do yourselves a favor; do what you gotta do and be done with this place, because you're too beautiful, too talented, and far too intelligent for it, the both of you." She pointed at them both in a motherly fashion.

"Just make sure that you two keep that in mind. Now get up there and do your act before you miss out on all of that money them niggas is throwing around," she said before walking off.

Sequoia and Desiree studied each other's faces with a strong sense of uncertainty as if it would provide them with an answer.

"Vixen, you're up." A stripper named Cinnamon poked her head into the dressing room and spoke before either of them could utter a word.

Sequoia nodded her head meekly before rising from the stool.

"How do I look?" she asked Desiree.

"Finger licking good," Desiree joked, trying to ease the anxiety that she knew her friend was feeling.

The both hated to admit it, but the jewels that Cherokee had just dropped on them were weighing heavily on their conscience. They both graduated a year ago with honors and ambitions of conquering the world, yet here they were compromising their integrity to earn a quick buck in a strip club.

Sequoia, though both of their situations were ideally unique, would argue that hers was a bit more...complicated. She only intended to raise a set amount of money that was needed before flipping the entire lifestyle the bird. Mocha, on the other hand, was a completely different story. Because she was unable to secure a scholarship, she initially got into the lifestyle to finance her education. But as time progressed, Sequoia had noticed her warming to the lifestyle more and more. However, she was hopeful that after processing the advice that Cherokee had given her that it would have an impact on her decision making before it was too late.

Sequoia checked herself in the mirror and couldn't seem to suppress the smile that was forming at her mouth. Though she was clad in very revealing and inappropriate attire, she couldn't deny the fact that she was extremely beautiful.

She often joked to herself that God had seriously outdone Himself on her in the looks department. She was drop-dead gorgeous with a body out of this world! To simply say that she was fine would be a gross understatement, for she was beautiful!

Her long, cascading, honey highlighted curls draped over her shoulders and down her back, just gracing the imaginary line by her navel and the small of her back. She possessed deep sea, aqua-blue eyes that blended perfectly with her soft, smooth cocoa butter complexion. Her perfectly luscious lips were covered in clear lip gloss accentuating some of the whitest and straight set of thirty-two's ever to grace a dentist's office. Her nose was aesthetically perfect with her face in shape and size. Her facial beauty alone was so stunning and rare that any modeling agency would kill to photograph it.

Her inviting neckline gave way to a pair of the most succulent, perky 36's to ever fill a C cup. Her well toned abs were decorated with a diamond navel piercing, and were complimented with a small 22" waist, and hips so wide that one would swear they were made for child-bearing.

She was thick, sure enough. But she possessed no cellulite and nearly no body fat—only nice, curvaceous, shapely thighs and legs, and an ass that would put Kim Kardashian to shame. Even her feet were so mouth-wateringly decadent that, despite the French pedicure she had, she was 100% sure that she could be a successful foot model.

She was adorned in an aqua blue and black, sheer, laced, crotch-less corset, an aqua blue and black, sheer, laced thong, an aqua blue, sheer, laced halter top, and fishnet stockings covering the length of her legs and arms as she stood on four inch platform heels.

"Time to go make the donuts," she said sarcastically to Desiree, before leaving to take her position behind the stage.

Think of the beach. You are not here right now, she told herself.

Due to her anxiety issues, her therapist had long advised her to try different therapeutic remedies to help her cope with situations that may seem too overwhelming for her. Inconveniently for her, her anxiety always seemed to hit its peak whenever she neared a stage. Childhood memories of the days and nights that she'd spent on the beach in her native land, along the Atlantic Coast, always provided her with the solace she needed to make it through the troubled times.

Think of the beach.

However, ironically enough, whenever the music began to play, Sequoia would undergo an extreme metamorphosis and begin to function as if her body was no longer under her command. Which is why, when the bass began to drop for the song "In This Club" by USHER, she slipped into her element.

"And now, the moment that everyone has been waiting for: the one and only, Vixen!" the DJ announced as Usher crooned.

"I want to make love, in this club... in this club!" Sequoia graced the stage seductively eyeing the crowd as she took her position at center stage. The whooping and hollering ceased as the members of the audience took in the most captivating, beautiful woman that eyes had ever seen.

For most of the members of the audience, the beauty that the exotic dancer named Vixen possessed was a hyperbolic myth. But seeing her first-hand for themselves made it indisputably easy for everyone to put those rumors to bed. The exotic dancer Vixen was, in fact, one of the most beautiful females ever to walk the face of the earth.

Sequoia locked eyes with Jewels Santiago, who was sitting

nearly twenty feet away, in front of center stage, and immediately tuned everyone else out in the room. The look in his eyes clearly said that she had his undivided attention.

"I want to make love in this club...in this club!"

Sequoia rubbed her hands over her breasts, massaging them suggestively before caressing her stomach on down to her sheer covered pussy. Her camel toe was so fat that it looked like a balled up fist was in the crotch of her thong.

"You know all you gotta do is tell me what you're sipping on!"

Sequoia began to gyrate her hips as if they were tailor made for the beat. She eyed Jewels Santiago sexily before spinning on her heels and bending over, giving him a full view of her perfect-shaped booty and oversized, sheer-covered pussy.

She winked at him between her legs before standing upright. She watched herself in the wall-to-wall mirror that lined the back of the stage as she began to slowly shed her sheer halter top, revealing two erect, perfectly sized light brown nipples.

She turned to face the audience and dipped low in a squatting position as she grinded her hips to the beat. She dropped to her knees and locked gazes with Jewels Santiago, who was directly ahead and began riding the floor as if he were underneath her.

Her sheer and laced corset was the next piece of clothing to go. She tumbled forward, no sooner than the corset touched the floor, landing on her back. She ran her palms up the inner parts of her thighs until both of her hands were at either of her ankles. She then pulled her legs so far apart that the folds of her vaginal lips nearly swallowed her thong.

Her eyes remained on Jewels Santiago, watching him as he unconsciously gripped his erection. She further enticed him by putting her legs behind her head and clasping them together. She rubbed her waxed mound for him and blew him a kiss. The members of the audience were deathly silent as they watched her. Her beauty was simply that captivating. Instead of decorating the stage with a plethora of bills, men of all sorts simply placed their entire rubber band-wrapped stacks on the stage: a gesture that indicated she was the best bitch, and that no one could compare to her. When Sequoia rose to her feet, only her sheer, laced thong and fishnet remained. She turned to give Jewels Santiago a better view of her backside and whined, ground, dipped, popped, locked, and dropped it!

The way she moved her body made it look as if she was having sex with the song. She dropped her thong in a smooth motion and stepped one leg out of them. When she turned around to face Jewels Santiago, she kicked her thong at him. He caught it and sniffed the crotch, drawing a loud round of applause and cheers from the crowd.

She approached the stripper pole and kicked her leg up so far that her knee was at her breast. She placed the heel of her shoe on the pole and erotically licked her fishnet-covered leg.

Then, as Ludacris once said, "she worked that pole like a certified stripper." She did things on the pole that most strippers would never be able to pull off in a lifetime. She displayed moves akin to a gymnast. Putting on a personal show for Jewels Santiago, she twirled and spun on the pole before dropping to the floor in a split and grinding sexually on the flood so hard that her ass and thighs were vibrating hypnotically.

She arose from her split position just as the song was ending and was met with thunderous cheers and praises from the crowd. She bowed and waved to the crowd and was so temporarily distracted that she barely noticed Jewels Santiago approaching her until he filled her peripheral view.

"Here, Ma," he handed her two rubber banded stacks of hundred dollar bills, which she estimated was about $20,000.

She squatted on the stage before him. "Thank you!"

Jewels Santiago stared in awestruck amazement at her naked body and features.

"You know, it's rude to stare," Sequoia said flirtatiously.

"My bad, shorty. I'm just tripping yo," he said. "Why the fuck is you working in a strip club?"

She stared off as if she was suddenly embarrassed. "This is

only temporary. Trust me; I wouldn't be doing something like this if I didn't have to." She paused. "It's just...complicated."

"It wouldn't be if you was my girl," he told her seriously.

"Nigga, please. You probably say that shit to a thousand other chicks every night."

"Maybe," he said, "but I'm serious with you."

"Well, I'm sorry, but no thank you." She made a gesture like she was about to leave, but Jewels spoke so she paused.

"Well, let me be your sponsor," he told her. "Get you up outta here."

"That comes with a price," she shot.

"Just kids and a white picket fence," he joked, gaining a laugh from her.

"Sorry, but I have to pass."

"Alright shorty. Well, check it: why don't you go and grab a couple of your friends and meet us in the limo out front? I rented a floor at the Carlton-Ritz."

"And what exactly are we supposed to be doing at this hotel with you and your boys?" she quizzed with suspecting eyes.

"We can do whatever you want to, Ma." He licked his lips suggestively.

Sequoia playfully squished his face. "Wrong answer, but I'm pretty sure that a lot of these hoes around here will be looking forward to that so I'll let them know."

"So, what, you're not coming?" he asked.

Sequoia huffed. "Listen, I don't want you to get the wrong impression of me because you met me stripping in a strip club, but I'm not a hoe. I'm doing what I'm doing because I don't have any other choice, that's it!" she told him in a stern tone. "So, I'm sorry but no I won't be attending."

Sequoia was about to leave but Jewels grabbed her arm, startling her. She looked at his hand as if he'd lost his mind.

"I'm sorry," he said when he picked up on her vibe. "I didn't mean to grab you like that. I just want to tell you to think about it, Ma. We ain't gotta do nothing. I just want to chill with you; get to know you a little better," he said seriously.

Sequoia paused for a brief moment. "I'll think about it."

With that, she retrieved the large amounts of money that was on the floor before vanishing into the dressing room.

CHAPTER 2

When Sequoia entered the dressing room, several of the girls bombarded her into a huddle.

"Damn, girl!" Desiree said when she saw all of the money that her friend had. "How much is all that?"

"I don't know—but it's definitely heavy," Sequoia answered, not wanting to throw any ballpark figures around in front of the other girls.

"Shit!" Cherokee said as she eyed the stacks in Sequoia's hand. "A few more nights like that and you can retire," she joked.

Butterfly felt a tinge of jealousy towards Sequoia when she visually calculated her earnings, and surmised that it was at least quadruple the amount that she'd taken in. But she was willing to put her personal feelings to the side and focus on her true ambitions, which were to one day get Sequoia into her bed. Butterfly was sure that she could turn her out if she could only get one opportunity. She intended to make Sequoia her wife, and she was convinced up to that point that she'd been playing hard to get.

That was why whenever they encountered each other; Butterfly made it her personal business to make some form of sexual advancement towards her.

"I watched you do your thing up there, Vixen," Butterfly said sensually.

"Oh, really?" Vixen said dryly. She didn't have any idea of the angle that Butterfly was about to come at her with, but she was sure that it was going to be from left field.

"Um hmm," she practically moaned the words, "and look at what you made me do." She motioned south with her eyes. "I told you every time I see you I get wet."

Sequoia reflexively stared down and noticed the soaking wet spot on Butterfly's sheer G-string. She rolled her eyes at Butterfly before ignoring her completely. Instead, she spoke to the rest of the girls. "Anyway, Jewels Santiago says that he wants a few girls to come with him and his clique to the Carlton-Ritz. Say if y'all are coming to be outside in a few."

Before Sequoia could finish the sentence, Butterfly was nearly breaking her neck to get inside of her locker and put her street clothes on. Sadly enough, the other girls followed her lead.

Sequoia spoke. "Y'all already know to keep this whole thing on the hush, because if Big Al finds out all of us will get fired," she said, referring to the owner of the club.

"Girl, please," Cherokee said as she climbed in a pair of skin tight jeans, "all that money that we generate for the club? He wouldn't know what to do if any one of us left, especially you," she told her.

Desiree watched Sequoia as she slowly unfastened the buckle on her shoe and said, "You're going to have to move a whole lot faster than that if you want to catch this train, Vixen," she joked.

Sequoia looked at her, confused. "I'm not going with them."

"What do you mean, you're not going?" Desiree said as she pulled a pair of designer heels over her pants. "That's Jewels Santiago!"

"Yeah, I got the memo," she said sarcastically, "and what exactly does that mean? Better yet, I have a better question: what do you think they want us to do with them in a hotel?"

"I don't know, dance?"

Sequoia shook her head in disgust. "Please don't tell me you're that naïve all of a sudden."

"No," Desiree said, "but what harm could it do us to go chill with them for a couple hours? It's not like they're going to make us do something we don't want to do."

"Okay, assume that you're right," she said. "Then what would

17

be the purpose of going if you don't have any intention of doing what they want us to do?"

"I don't know," Desiree shrugged, frustrated. "To chill, I guess."

"Desiree?" Sequoia used her government name as if it would remind her of who she actually was. "We didn't get into this life for all of that. Let's leave the chilling to these other bitches. We're on a mission, so let's not lose sight of our main objective. Shit, if you want to chill, we can chill at the apartment."

Desiree chuckled. "You're too much."

"I'm serious."

"So, you gonna sit there and act like you ain't feelin' Jewels Santiago?"

"Doesn't matter what I feel. He's a rapper, which means that he probably fucks multiple groupies every night. Ain't no tellin' what that tool has, and I'm definitely not about to put myself out there to find out."

"Okay, well, look: let's go just this one and only time. We'll just go and chill and if we don't like the vibe that we get while we're there then we'll leave. Simple," she said as if she had it all figured out.

Sequoia listened to Desiree as she continued to press her into going to the hotel, despite all of the things she'd just told her. Somehow, Sequoia found herself thinking about the advice Cherokee had given her earlier: "Don't get caught up in this whole strip club scene...this place will chew you up and shit you out! I started stripping when I was sixteen and I've personally seen these types of places destroy more young girls' lives than the crack epidemic."

Sequoia hated to entertain the thought, but it was becoming painfully obvious to her that her best friend was slowly succumbing to the lifestyle. She wanted to do more, to say something that could deter her from chartering into unknown waters, but it all seemed useless at that point. She was left with only one option, and that was to be there for her friend and make sure she made it home safely.

"I'll go with you this time, but only under on condition: you have to promise me that this will be our first and last time ever doing something like this."

"I promise!" Desiree said gleefully before strolling over to Sequoia. "Now give me a kiss," she said as they engaged in a wet, brief lip lock before preparing themselves to leave.

Inside, the Carlton-Ritz Hotel was exactly the way Sequoia had expected it to be: an intolerable amount of ogling, pressed for sex, industry men who couldn't control their liquor, and seriously thought that the size of their wallet truly defined a man.

Sequoia endured their presence for as long as she could before finding the nearest exit. She did take comfort, however, in the idea that the other girls would obsequiously appease any and every sick desire that the men could think of before the night was over with. That she was sure of!

If it wasn't for Desiree wanting to be there she would've left the building altogether, but instead she found herself a nice, quiet, and secluded area by the outside pool area, which was located down the hall from the hotel rooms and held up.

Sequoia inhaled deeply, filling her lungs with the peculiarly intoxicating aroma of car emissions that only a major city like Manhattan, New York could offer. She peered hypnotically at the traffic below from the twelfth floor and marveled over the gorgeous lightshow the Manhattan skyline created at night. The night sky resembled a black velvet sheet that had been poked by tiny pins, allowing light to shine through.

She located a star in the sky and made a wish, a habit she carried with her since her childhood years. She only prayed that it would come true. Her mind continued to drift as she stared in a trance-like state at the city.

Her thoughts were interrupted by the sound of footsteps approaching from behind.

"So this is where you been hiding at," Jewels Santiago said with a mischievous smile.

He was clad in a Black label ensemble with multi-colored, limited edition Air Force Ones that Sequoia calculated to be worth a few months' rent, and couldn't be found in any common retail store. His hair was cut short in a Caesar style and his neck boasted an oversized gold chain with an eagle and a diamond encrusted name "Ditch Set" on it. His dark brown complexion was complimented with two deep dimples and a neatly trimmed goatee.

"I see you really ain't feeling the atmosphere down here, huh?" Jewels said, taking his post next to her.

"I only came to make sure that my girl Mocha isn't being taken advantage of. Because I'm quite sure that it's a freak show in there by now."

"Yeah, it is," Jewels said with knowing eyes as he rubbed his chin, "but like I said at the club; it's whatever with you, ma. I'm just trying to chill with you."

Sequoia kept her eyes trained on the city. "That's cool, we can chill," she turned to face him, "but I already told you, that's as far as this goes," she said seriously.

"Damn, shorty. Why you keep throwing me shade like that? All I'm trying to do is get to know you a little better."

"Okay. Let's start with my name. It's Sequoia, not shorty. And forgive me if I'm coming off as a bitch. It's not you," she said, "it's your lifestyle."

Jewels processed what she said. "Sequoia, huh?" He eyed her intently. "I like that. That's a nice name."

"Thank you."

Like every other man that she'd encountered in her life, Jewels Santiago found himself mesmerized by her captivating beauty. He took in her taupe cashmere, Dolce and Gabbana dress with the plunging neckline and her matching taupe Dolce and Gabbana open-toed platform heels. Her wrist bore a diamond encrusted Dolce and Gabbana wristwatch and two carat diamond earrings. She had an intoxicating amount of Dolce and Gabbana perfume on that filled Jewels' nostrils as he stared deeply into her aqua-blue eyes.

"Are those real?" Jewels asked as he stared inquisitively into her eyes.

"I'm one hundred percent authentic. Nothing is paid for or added on," she assured him.

"DAMN," he said, shaking his head in disbelief. "Sequoia, you bad as fuck! I bet you'd make some beautiful kids."

Sequoia rolled her eyes, knowing full well what he was hinting at.

"I'm just saying." He showed her his palms playfully, gaining a slight chuckle from her, which he joined in on.

The mood was right. The ice had been broken, and just as things were picking up between them, they were interrupted. Desiree poked her head inside the entrance door that led to the hotel floor. "I hope I'm not interrupting anything, but Jewels, one of your boys wants you in here," she said.

"Tell him I'll be there in a minute," he made an attempt to brush her off.

"He said to tell you that it was important if you said that," Desiree retorted.

Jewels sighed irritably. "Don't go anywhere, Sequoia. I'll be right back."

"You alright out here?" Desiree asked Sequoia as Jewels squeezed past her through the doorway.

Sequoia nodded. "You ready to go?

"Give me a few minutes and I'll be back, then we can leave."

Sequoia didn't respond. She simply turned and stared back out into the night, where she fantasized about the life that she intended to create for herself when she finished law school. Her plan was to finish law school first before going on to work with a prominent firm, where she would ultimately prove herself in the courtroom. She then intended to branch off and establish her own firm with a fierce team of civil and criminal lawyers. That was the plan, at least.

She was positively certain that whenever that day came, her mother, along with the rest of her supporting cast, would pop bottles of champagne to celebrate her success. Though she would never say it, that day would also be the commemoration of one of the biggest regrets she would have in her life.

The truth was her heart was never settled on becoming a lawyer. She only pursued the career because she thought that it would make her mother proud. Though she would never say it, her true heart's passion was to become a singer and entertainer.

She possessed dancing skills of various styles that were second to none, unique songwriting capabilities, and a voice that was as heavenly as a road paved with gold. Her confidence in her talent made her second guess her pursuit of a higher education. If it weren't for the high probability that her mother would blow a gasket, she would strongly consider dropping out to pursue her dream.

However, as the old adage goes, "one bird in the hand is worth two in the bush," so even though Sequoia toyed with the idea in her head, she wasn't fool enough to sacrifice her scholarship at Harvard University for the idea that should could land a record deal. So for the sake of common sense she would stick with her current situation, even if she dreaded to do so.

Sequoia didn't like discussing her true feelings, not even with Desiree, so she buried them deep inside and prayed that they would never surface. She was doing pretty well until the conversation she had with Cherokee earlier: "Do something with your talent... Don't get caught up in this whole strip club scene." She wanted to do something with her talent so badly, but the reality of her situation kept her in her comfort zone.

To her surprise, she had even considered showcasing her talent to Jewels Santiago. It was a desperate move that would be completely out of character for her, but she was certain that he would be interested in exploiting her talent for his benefit— something she wouldn't stand for or allow, even though she knew he had more connections than an interstate railroad.

Sequoia checked her watch and realized that twenty minutes had elapsed since Jewels and Desiree said they would return. The heels were killing her feet and the midnight breeze blowing in off the coast was giving her goose bumps, so she decided that it was time to find Desiree so they could leave.

She entered the opulent hallway that was lined with plush Carlton Ritz monogrammed carpeting, imported oak furniture, and costly paintings, and approached one of the doors that had been rented. There were four rooms in total that the clique owned for the night, which made it more difficult to determine where to find Desiree. Thus, she had to bear the annoying responsibility of playing musical doors in order to find her. She started with the nearest door, and the closer she got to the door, the more she could hear the muffled cacophony of voices and loud music from behind the door. She knocked loud enough to be heard, and a man from Jewels' entourage cracked the door slightly and eyed her suspiciously.

"Is Mocha in there?" Sequoia asked.

He opened the door a little wider, causing a huge plume of Kush smoke to hit her in the face.

"Shid, I don't know none of those hoes' name. You wanna check for yourself?" he said curtly, before walking back to the miniature freak show that was going on in the room without waiting for a response.

Sequoia began coughing uncontrollably as she fanned the smoke away from her face. When she was able to see clearly she nearly jumped out of her skin. Before her were four men with their jeans down to their ankles, forming a circle around a stripper named Strawberry as she gave all of them mouth and lip service simultaneously. Another stripper named Candy was snorting a line of cocaine from another man's erect penis before cleaning off the residue with her wet mouth.

Sequoia suddenly felt as if she was looking at train wreck: she just couldn't seem to turn away from it. She quickly shook off the fixation when everyone looked at her. However, none of the women were Desiree, so she backed out of the door and closed it behind her

23

with a great deal of appreciation.

Sequoia tried to shake off the mental images from her mind as she approached the next door, but they continued to play over and over in her mind as if it were on instant replay. Sadly, none of what she'd seen was surprising of unexpected. In fact, it was exactly what she thought it would be. The part that disturbed her the most about it all was why Desiree would want it to be part of her.

She didn't want to admit it, but her girl was slipping, big time. The minute she discovered her whereabouts she intended to have a serious sit-down with her.

Sequoia approached the next door a bit more apprehensive than the first. She figured the quicker she located Desiree, the quicker they could get out of here, so she mentally prepared herself for what may lie behind door number two and knocked loud enough to be heard over the loud music.

The door swung open almost instantly and a dark-skinned man with a Caesar cut, humungous "Ditch Set" chain, and a protruding belly filled the doorway. He was wearing boxers, socks, and a white wife beater.

"Ahhh. Okay, alright," he said while eyeing her lustfully as he took a swig from a crystal bottle. "So you decided to come back and join the party, huh? I'll never forget that face. You that bad ass bitch that was on the stage, right?"

Sequoia scoffed as she stared at him like a venereal disease. "No, I'm just looking for my girl, Mocha, so we can leave. You seen her?"

"I don't know who the fuck that is, but why're you trying to leave? The party's just getting started. And those bitches in here is about to get oil changes so it's really about to get crackin," he said animatedly.

"Oil changes?" Sequoia asked, baffled. "What the hell is that?"

The man stepped aside so Sequoia could get a better view inside the room, which was something she quickly wished he hadn't done. She saw a naked man holding a camera pointed in the direction of the bed while simultaneously stroking his penis. On the foot of the bed was a butt-naked Butterfly and Cherokee in the doggie-style position.

Butterfly's face was buried between the legs of a stripper named Gemini while Cherokee's head bobbed up and down in the lap of one of the "Ditch Set" members who lay before her. Two men were standing at the foot of the bed, meticulously lubing the end of two black funnels before delicately sticking them in their ass holes. They then grabbed two shot glasses full of a diluted liquid and prepared to pour it into the funnel.

"An oil change is something that we made up," the man told her. "We crunch up a few X pills and mix it with a shot of Patrón and Red Bull, and we pour it in they ass so it can go straight to they system." He paused. "Talk about being fucked up!" he laughed. "Those bitches is gonna be fucked up more than they've ever been in they life in less than two minutes."

Sequoia couldn't believe what she was hearing, and even mores o, what she was seeing with her own eyes. It was insane! The fact that Cherokee was degrading herself to such a low level had destroyed any type of respect that she had for her. "This life will chew you up and shit you out! ...I've been stripping since I was sixteen and I've personally seen this type of place destroy more young women's lives than the crack epidemic." She could hear Cherokee's words ringing an eerie truth in her head. Suddenly, it all made sense to her. Cherokee was speaking to her out of experience—out of *her* experience. She was trapped in a spiraling cycle that only went down.

One thing was for sure, after tonight she had some serious reevaluating to do about a career change in the more immediate future.

"What's up, shorty? You tryin' to get an oil change and do something with a nigga or what?" he asked casually, as if he was asking for the time.

Sequoia didn't feel the need to respond to his ignorant ass. She excused herself from the room and closed the door behind her. She paused for a brief moment to consider her emotions. Her first thought was to simply leave Desiree so she could get away from all the madness, but she was a true friend, so leaving her was not an option.

Besides, she was sure that if the roles were reversed that Desiree wouldn't even consider it. Desiree may've been a lot of things, but disloyal wasn't one of them. For the sake of affirming her loyalty to Desiree, she would bear through it and see what was behind door number three.

She knocked on the door and a distant voice yelled, "Come in!"

Sequoia was reluctant at first, but mustered up enough courage to open it. Inside was another live porno scene. She recognized the man, Freaky Teaky from "Ditch Set," holding a champagne bottle of Cristal in the Jacuzzi to the east wall as a stripper named Asia rode his erection. He completely ignored Sequoia's presence as he poured the champagne all over Asia's bare breasts before hungrily sucking the remainder off. He glanced at Sequoia like a newborn baby who was being breast fed.

"Hey, ain't you that bitch that was dancing—"

Sequoia slammed the door shut on him mid-sentence. She felt no need to dignify his remark with a response. Besides, Desiree wasn't in that room either.

When she approached the next door her heart nearly dropped to the pit of her stomach. She overheard a woman's voice pleading for help on the other side of the door. Sequoia's heart began to beat violently in her chest as she placed her ear to the door and heard the muffled cries: "Stop! No...please! Uhh awww! You're hurting me!"

Tears began to fill Sequoia's eyes when she realized that the woman's voice that she was hearing was Desiree's. Sequoia began to kick and bang on the door, feeling as if Desiree's life depended on it.

"Get off of her!" Sequoia pounded on the door.

"Hol' up," a man yelled before saying to Desiree, "Shorty, shut the fuck up. I'm almost finished. Uggghh!!"

Sequoia continued to bang on the door for what felt like an

eternity, though it was really only twenty seconds. Suddenly the moans and pleas ceased, followed by the sound of footsteps approaching. The door swung open.

"Yo, what the fuck is you—"

Jewels Santiago stopped himself mid-sentence when he realized who he was talking to.

Sequoia was taken aback. She stared at him incredulously. She wanted to believe that this wasn't happening, that this was some type of misunderstanding. That Jewels Santiago was nothing like the rest of the boys in his entourage, but his sweaty face, unbuckled pants, and the small bloodstain that was on the hem of his shirt was just too much evidence to ignore.

He avoided eye contact with her as his countenance shifted to embarrassment.

"You grimy mother fucker!" Sequoia slapped him so hard that is stung her palm before shoving her way past him.

Jewels Santiago took off to assemble the members of his entourage. He knew that things could get ugly for him if he stuck around.

Sequoia shrieked and cupped her mouth when she saw the huge bloodstain on the hotel's comforter that had formed near Desiree's backside as she lay in the fetal position with her dress pulled halfway up her back. She ran to her whimpering friend's side and kneeled.

"Desi, it's going to be okay. I'm going to take you to the hospital and call the police."

Desiree's eyes went dark. "No! Please, no," she cried. "No one can know about this!"

Sequoia looked at her in disbelief. "Desi, he just raped you. What's wrong with you? We have to go to the police." Sequoia tried to talk some sense into her.

"I know, but..." Desiree was struggling to find the right words to say. "I... I invited him here."

"You what?" Sequoia snapped. "What do you mean, 'you invited him?'" Desiree had a noticeable amount of betrayal in her that Sequoia had picked up on.

"I'm sorry, Sequoia," she cried, "but no one never really wanted him. I... I lied to get him to come here with me. I knew that you wouldn't, so I—"

"You fucked him," Sequoia finished for her.

Desiree nodded her head.

Sequoia was quiet for a brief moment. She wanted to be mad at Desiree for her act of betrayal, but she knew that now was not the time or place. She had to focus on getting her to a hospital.

"Well, don't worry about none of that right now. We'll talk about it later. Let's worry about getting you to a hospital."

"No, Sequoia!" she pleaded. "I don't want anyone to find out about this."

Sequoia ignored Desiree, assuming that she was in some state of shock. Instead, she went to inspect the damages. Upon first glance, she noticed that there was a huge split in the skin where her rectum and pussy was, and blood was leaking from it.

"You let him fuck you in the ass?" Sequoia said as more of a statement than a question.

"I didn't know he was going to be so rough," she said regretfully.

"You didn't know he was going to be so rough?" Sequoia repeated. "Well, I seriously hope that you learned your lesson. And, I hate to say this now, but I told you we shouldn't have come here."

Desiree wept.

"From the looks of things you don't have a choice in the matter of going to a hospital because you're going to need stitches. So I'm taking you and that's the end of that," Sequoia said authoritatively.

Desiree remained silent as Sequoia made the necessary preparations to take her to the hospital. She found Desiree's purse in a chair nearby and found an unused tampon and some baby wipes. She cleaned Desiree off before taping the cotton tampon on her wound.

Sequoia had obviously spoken too soon about Desiree's loyalty, because she was sure if she would've gotten away with her sexual tryst with Jewels Santiago she would've never told her about it. Even if she had started dating him, it would've been their little secret.

Still, it wasn't enough to make her turn her back on her. They had been friends since fifth grade and as far as she was concerned no man would ever come between them. She only wished that Desiree could take a page out of her book, because judging by the current situation, she was reading another book altogether—one that neglected to mention the code of ethics between best friends.

"Oh, and you can continue this stripping shit if you want to but I'm going to take Cherokee's advice and quit stripping. It's not the life for me. Hopefully this experience that you just had will provide you with enough clarity to see that it's not for you either."

CHAPTER 3

If there were two places that Sequoia hated being it was funeral homes and hospitals. To her, they were both spine-chillingly cold and reeked of death. She figured that most would argue that a funeral home was a considerably worse place to be over a hospital any day, but not Sequoia. She felt that they were one and the same.

She always figured that a hospital was a sort of proverbial purgatory where people went before eventually being carted off to a funeral home, which is why she always avoided them at all costs. Until now, that is.

Sequoia had long ago confided in her therapist about her phobia of hospitals, and after much digging her therapist concluded that her troubled past is what triggered her phobia and anxiety disorder. Sequoia initially disagreed with her assessment, but before long she had to face reality, and that was that her anxiety disorder stemmed from post traumatic stress. Post traumatic stress that had stemmed from one of the worst days of her life.

Sequoia hated to think about that day, that dreadful day! Suddenly, her mind was instantly invaded with thoughts of that day. *Think of the beach*, Sequoia told herself.

There was so much blood... Blood was everywhere!

Think of the beach!

Blood covered her hands, her blouse, her pants, her shoes...

The knife in her hand...

No!

Sequoia's heart began to race as her lungs expanded; an early indicator that she was on the brink of an anxiety attack. *Just breathe Sequoia!*

"Miss Ariás?" An Arabian-descent doctor in a white overcoat

approached Sequoia, breaking her from her momentary trance.

"Yes?" Sequoia rose from the waiting room chair.

"Good evening, my name is Dr. Muhummad," he said cordially, reeking of Old Spice deodorant and aftershave. "Miss James told me to advise you of her condition," he said. "She's going to be fine. We've given her thirteen stitches and have put her on a liquid diet, which she'll have to continue for the next three weeks.

"The liquid diet is to ensure that her waste isn't solid during bowel movements, so it doesn't threaten to tear at the stitches. We want to keep her a few days to make sure that her bowel movement has a consistent liquid flow.

"She'll be given pain pills, bacterial ointment, and dressing to prevent infection. She may need some help changing the dressing and cleaning after bowel movement, but she has assured us that you would help her with that."

"I'm sure she did," Sequoia said sarcastically.

Dr. Muhummad picked up on her lack of enthusiasm. "This won't be a problem for you, will it Miss Ariás?"

"Oh, no, Dr. Muhummad. I'm just a little tired, and this whole... situation... is beginning to give me a headache," she said honestly.

"I understand." Dr. Muhummad was empathic. "If you like, I can prescribe you some Tylenol."

"Oh no, thank you," she said. "I'm sure that I'll be fine when I get to my bed and get some rest. Considering that I have to be at school tomorrow, I really need to get going. Is it alright if I see her before I leave?"

"Oh yes, absolutely." He looked around to make sure that no one could hear what he was about to say and spoke lowly, "And Miss Ariás? Could you please tell Miss James that anal sex with her boyfriend is never a good idea?"

Sequoia immediately concluded that Desiree had given him her version of what happened, so she knew to play along. "I'm sure she gets the point, but I'll make it my business to remind her."

"Thank you," Dr. Muhummad said. "Now, follow me."

Dr. Muhummad led Sequoia to Desiree's room and excused himself so the two could talk in private.

When Sequoia saw Desiree she was laying on her side, facing her, with an IV stuck in her arm, while various other cords ran from her body to different machines. Sequoia nearly freaked out.

"Hey, Desi," Sequoia tried to sound ardent.

Desiree smiled weakly, but it waned quickly.

"How you feeling?" Sequoia asked with genuine concern.

Desiree grimaced as she attempted to move into a more comfortable position. "I feel like the pain medication is dragging its feet."

Sequoia hated seeing her best friend like this. Sure, it had all been self created and could have easily been avoided if she had simply displayed some form of loyalty to her, but either way, she was still her best friend, and she didn't deserve this. If it were her in Desiree's position, she would have pressed charges against Jewels Santiago, because whether she initially agreed to have consensual sex with him was irrelevant to the fact that he did not stop when she begged him to.

"Try not to worry about it. Just relax as much as you can and everything will be alright," Sequoia encouraged her. "I'll contact your school tomorrow morning and let them know that you'll be out for at least a week."

"Thanks," Desiree said. "I'm pretty sure that I can get my professors to email me the lectures and assignments."

"Well, you know I have a long drive back to campus so I can get some sleep and go to school, but I'll be here as soon as I finish my appointment. Do you want me to bring you something?" Sequoia asked.

Desiree pulled a folded piece of paper from underneath her

pillow and handed it to Sequoia. "I thought you'd never ask." She smiled.

Sequoia glanced at her weirdly before looking over the paper. "Desi, you don't need all of this stuff. You're only gonna be here for a few days."

"I know, and I want to be comfortable while I'm here," she said in a spoiled manner.

Sequoia shook her head as she looked over the list. "You are too much," she paused, "and what the hell do you need curling irons for?"

"You have to ask?" Desiree asked in disbelief. "A girl's gotta keep her 'do intact," she said while patting her hair. They both laughed.

"You're crazy," Sequoia chuckled, "and, oh, I'm not brining you no damn Twinkies, so you can forget that!"

"C'mon Sequoia, please!" she begged.

Sequoia checked the door to make sure no one was there and whispered, "Okay, but don't tell nobody." They both giggled like school girls. "Well, I'm going to get out of here so I can be up for school tomorrow."

"Okay." Desiree paused. "I just want to thank you. For forgiving me, and not judging me," she said emotionally.

"That's what friends are for," Sequoia told her. "Now give me a kiss so I can leave."

When Sequoia moved in for a kiss, Desiree cupped the back of her neck sensually and held her in a lip lock longer than she was comfortable with. When they finally broke their union, Sequoia peered at Desiree in confusion, but instead of saying anything she walked out of the room, leaving behind a lingering sense of uncertainty.

CHAPTER 4

Cambridge, MA – Harvard University

Sequoia buried her face underneath the hot shower faucet in a vain attempt to wake herself up completely from the useless three hours of sleep she'd gotten last night. Days like this really made her regret the caffeine diet that she vowed to uphold until her dying day.

Still, she managed to drag herself out of the bed, contact Desiree's school, and work on preparing herself for school. Luckily for her she had decided to retire to her Harvard University dorm room, instead of her off campus apartment. If that had not been the case, she seriously doubted that she would be making it to school that day.

She really wished that she could just sleep the day away and forget about all that had happened over the weekend, but that was out of the question. It was simply too much to forget, especially the part where Desiree betrayed her trust, which resulted in her being hospitalized for sodomy.

True enough, she and Jewels Santiago didn't actually have any real ties to each other. It wasn't like they were an item or anything, but it was more than obvious that he had expressed a genuine interest in her from the jump. For Desiree to go behind her back like that and actually seduce him into sleeping with her really said a lot about her. It was painfully apparent to her that she did not know Desiree like she thought she did!

To say that she would be addressing the situation when the time was right went without saying, but for now, like every other week, she had to put the skeletons in the closet where they belonged and focus on her school work.

Midterms were only two weeks away, and she had been hardly hitting the books like she needed to, which was highly unusual for her. Nevertheless, it didn't stop her from maintaining her 4.0 GPA, which she knew would be in jeopardy of declining as the semester continued if she slacked off. Now that she intended to quit working at SCORES Strip Club she figured that she would have all the time in the world to get caught back up.

Like most people in this world, Sequoia loved to sing in the shower. She often joked to herself that it was her private little vocal booth where she could display her talents for her imaginary crowd to hear. Considering how much she loved the artist Mariah Carey as a vocalist, she always sang her songs to test the limits of her own vocals. Today was no different. Her song of choice was from Mariah Carey's "Emancipation of MiMi" album.

"You got me running around in circles over you!" she crooned.

She sang the entire song, hitting every note as if her voice was tailor-made for the song. When she was finished, she turned the shower off and dried off her beautiful body. She wrapped a dry towel around her body and used another to wrap around her wet hair.

She exited the bathroom and immediately took in the disturbing view of her roommate, Jade, in one of her many contortionist positions on the floor. Jade's chin and forearms rested on her yoga mat while her legs dangled freely over her head. She looked like a human pretzel, a pretty painful image from where Sequoia was standing.

The girl was very talented though, Sequoia though. She somehow managed to hold her position while talking on her phone, which reminded Sequoia of the time when they first met. The day Jade nearly gave her mother a heart attack.

Five months earlier...

"Ma, don't worry about that, I'll get it," Sequoia hurriedly snatched the brown box of miscellaneous items from the trunk before her mother could fully get her hands around it. Sequoia had been going beyond the call of duty lately to make life as easy as she could for her mother. Especially since her diagnosis, she didn't want her using any unnecessary strength on anything frivolous. She wanted to help her conserve as much energy as possible so she could focus on fighting her illness.

Her mother frowned at her, annoyed. "Sequoia, you can stop treating me like a child. I can be of help, you know," she said in a strong Spanish accent with her hands on her hips.

Sequoia played dumb. "What are you talking about?"

"You know exactly what I'm talking about," she said sternly.

"Don't sweat it, Ma," Sequoia moved in closer and planted a kiss on her cheek. "I'm just trying to be a big girl."

"Umm hmm," her mother said, unconvinced, as she closed the trunk of her late model Nissan Maxima.

They both oohed and ahhed at the sights along the way to Sequoia's dorm room. Upon their brief inspection, it wasn't hard to deduce that the campus was extremely diverse; a true melting pot, akin to a morning trek in Madison Square in the Big Apple.

Honor of prestige filled Sequoia as she looked her peers over. Everyone was cordial and peaceful, making it their personal business to speak or wave to Sequoia and her mother as they passed. Sequoia knew that she was going to like it there. Everything about it just felt so right, and figuring that she intended on being there for several years or more, that's exactly the way she hoped it would be.

The both entered the dorm where Sequoia had been assigned and traversed through a sea of college students before making it to Sequoia's room. "This is it," Sequoia said, gaining an ecstatic smile from her mother.

Instead of using the key that she had been given, Sequoia decided to knock first. Considering that this was her first time living with someone she didn't know, she didn't want to get off on the wrong foot with them by just barging in. So she rapped on the door lightly.

"Come in," a woman's voice said.

Sequoia smiled graciously at her mother before opening the

door. However, they both stopped dead in their tracks when they took in the sight of Jade doing a one-armed handstand, on her forearm, while balancing an apple between both of her feet by her face as she held her bent over backwards position.

"What the—?" Rosa, Sequoia's mother, gasped while clutching her chest when she saw Sequoia's roommate in the spine-bending position.

"Hey roommate," Jade said, oblivious to the heart attack that she nearly gave Rosa.

Sequoia just stared in a state of awe.

Jade rolled the apple from one foot to another before kicking the apple in the air towards the ceiling, springing to her feet, and catching it. She took a huge bite out of it and bowed to her audience of two.

Sequoia and Rosa stared at each other astonishingly. Words wouldn't help a moment like that, but even in their silence, they both knew that being roommates with Jade would be extremely interesting.

Present day...

"Here she is," Jade said into the phone before holding it out for Sequoia to grab. "It's your mom."

Sequoia grabbed the phone from her, not bothering to ask her why she'd picked it up and answered it from her charger. Her relationship with Jade had long ago flourished into a loving bond. Jade was like a sister to her.

"Bueno, Madré?" Sequoia spoke into the phone. "Oh, you were calling me last night? Sorry, I must've had my phone off." Sequoia made small talk with her mother, catching up on a few things that had happened since they last spoke. Of course, Sequoia was sure to withhold the details about her weekend as Vixen the stripper. It was just one of those things that she vowed to take to her grave.

They covered bases in all the formal issues before moving along to the really pressing matters. "So, what did the doctors say?" Sequoia asked in an apprehensive tone.

Rosa had been diagnosed with a rare form of leukemia over a year ago, and as a result she now had to endure the painstaking process of chemotherapy. She also had to get a bone marrow transplant, which was proving to be a difficult feat, considering that her blood type was type O, a rare and uncommon blood type to find a donor for.

Things may not have been so difficult if she was able to get some help from her insurance company, but after fifteen years of loyalty to the company they decided to drop her when she got ill, citing that she had a pre-existing condition. It all could not have happened at a worst time, figuring that she had lost her job due to a company down-size and that Sequoia was away at college.

Sequoia wasn't one to disappoint, though. She understood loud and clear that she had to come up with some serious money, and fast! Not only to cover the cost of medical expenses, but also to cover the cost of court fees that would be needed to sue the insurance company: hence, the reason why she was stripping.

That didn't matter to Sequoia though. She would travel to Mars if it meant that she could save her mother's life. Rosa was all that she had, and Sequoia practically worshiped the ground that she walked on, which is why it was killing Sequoia to hear that her mother had just been given a timeline to live. According to the doctors, if she didn't find a donor within the next four months, her chance for surviving would be very slim.

"Well, I do have some good news," Sequoia told her. "I got a hold of some more money. It's pretty close to $40,000... You know what? I just came up with an idea," she told her, "but I'm going to have to run it by you later because I have to head out to school."

The two said their goodbyes before ending the call. Tears filled Sequoia's eyes as she tried to process the idea of her mother being given a timeline to live. None of it made sense to her.

Ever since she was little she had been taught never to question God's will, but she just couldn't understand why He was allowing her to suffer like this. For as long as she could remember, her mother had always been a good person. She was a devout Catholic who had always been active in the church. She was a faithful wife before the divorce, who had never done anything bad to anyone, but somehow her good deeds weren't enough to spare her the anguish of one of the rarest forms of leukemia. None of it made any sense to her!

"So, how's she doing?" Jade asked, now standing in an upright position as she began rolling up her yoga mat.

Sequoia shrugged. "Alright, I guess," Sequoia wasn't about to repeat what she heard about the timeline, "but knowing her, she doesn't want me to worry about her."

"Well, me neither," Jade said, "so try not to, because I'm pretty sure that she'll pull through everything alright."

Sequoia nodded as she pulled her medicine bottle out of her purse and chased two pills with a half-full bottle of Dasani water. She sifted through her dresser for her blow-dryer and after retrieving it, went to dry her hair in the washroom.

"On another note," Jade said before Sequoia turned the hair dryer on, "you must've had a real interesting night."

"What are you talking about?" Sequoia asked in a clueless manner.

"I'm talking about you roaming in at 4:30 in the morning," Jade said. "Must've been nice," she winked.

"Oh, I can assure you that it was everything but that," Sequoia stated sarcastically.

Jade picked up on her tone. "Is everything alright?"

"Yeah, I'm good," Sequoia lied, "I just want to forget about it and get back into my studies so I can be prepared for the upcoming midterms."

Though Sequoia loved Jade like a sister, she never made the

mistake of telling her anything that would come back to bite her in the ass. It wasn't that she didn't trust her, in fact, it was the complete opposite. To her, it was just that some things held no benefit in discussing, much like her secret life as a stripper. That was why she never made the mistake of letting the information leave her mouth, and she was grateful that Jade never pressed her for it.

Jade lowered her eyes nervously. "Well, I was thinking, maybe we could hang out sometime after midterms?" she said. "Just the two of us?"

"Are you asking me on a date?" Sequoia joked.

Jade laughed. "No, it's not a date. I just want to hang out with you."

Sequoia's heart warmed at the idea of Jade wanting to hang out with her. She knew that Jade had practically been sheltered her entire life and had no idea what it was like to go out and have fun—much like the majority of the students at Harvard University.

Their childhoods, like Jade's, were filled with all work and no play, a lifestyle that Sequoia could partially relate to considering that she and Desiree had always made time to go hang out at the movies or a party on the weekends.

Jade was Japanese, but she spoke perfect English. She was a ten-year-old sophomore trapped inside a twenty-year-old's body. She also maintained a 4.0 GPA and was in America on an academic scholarship and foreign visa. She was in pursuit of a business major, but secretly entertained the fantasy of performing as a contortionist in the circus, not to mention her strong desire to pursue photography and film. To say that she was a big 1 7 (sic) was an understatement!

Jade was very short, 4'11" to be exact, with a well sculpted, petite frame. She weighed 110 pounds, which was packaged nicely. She had a nice butt and large B-cups. She had slanted green eyes and long, jet black hair that she usually wore in a ponytail. Simply put, she was adorable, which made her virtually impossible to say no to.

"Of course we can hang out," Sequoia said, "as soon as we finish our midterms."

Jade smiled ardently as she hugged her. "Thank you Sequoia! You won't regret this! I promise!" she said ecstatically.

Jade was about to exit the bathroom but stopped. "Oh, one more thing," she said, gaining Sequoia's undivided attention.

"What's up?"

"I never like to force my opinion on anyone, but I just have to say this," Jade said. "You have the most amazing voice of anyone I've ever heard. It's like...unreal!" she told her. "I just really think that you should do something with it. I know you'd make it! Just... think about it," Jade said before leaving the bathroom.

Sequoia took a long moment to process what Jade had said. She understood exactly where Jade was coming from, but it wasn't like she was going to drop everything to pursue a singing career. That would be stupid!

So, entertaining the thought any longer was only serving as a distraction for the moment, and the last thing she needed was a distraction. What she needed was to finish blow-drying her hair so she could get to school, and that's exactly what she was about to do.

CHAPTER 5

Sequoia received the text message three minutes before her dance class ended. The message was from her good friend, Sasha Guiliani, reminding her of the lunch date that she'd promised to have with her a week ago.

The time couldn't have been worse. Sequoia wanted to call the thing off and provide Sasha with a rain check, but she knew that decision would only hurt her in the long run. It wasn't a good idea to tell Sasha Guiliani no, plus the text message that she'd send left very little room to wiggle out of.

SASHA: Meet me out front. Lunch is on me. :)

Sasha Guiliani was the daughter of one of the most successful defense attorneys ever to grace the East Coast. He was also the founder of one of the most prominent firms in America.

Due to her father's clout and connections in the corporate world, Sasha had been able to live a relatively lavish and privileged life, one filled with all of the amenities and luxuries that a young girl could ever dream to have at their manicured fingertips. Not to mention that she was also the would-be heiress of the empire that her father had built over the past two decades.

Sasha was the kind of girl that all of the other girls envied, a sad reality that she was more than privy to, but never let go to her head. She was always as cool and collected as the best of them, which is what Sequoia discovered to be so magnetic about her personality: she was never egotistical or pretentions, but still managed to carry herself with a level of class and prestige that was uncommon in most spoiled, rich kids. That made her extremely easy to get along with. They were traits that Sequoia learned to cherish, especially considering that her friendship with Sasha wasn't solely based on friendship, but business as well.

Sasha had promised Sequoia a position at her father's firm

upon completion of her law degree. Though they both had many more years until they actually graduated, Sequoia's heart warmed at the idea of knowing that she had a great job to go to when she graduation. The gesture had all but made the two inseparable.

Sequoia emerged from the building to find Sasha stabbing the keypad on her Blackberry under a nearby tree.

"Hey, you," Sequoia said as she neared her.

"Hey!" Sasha said ardently, placing her phone in her purse without bothering to finish her text message.

Though Sasha wasn't arrogant in the least bit, she did have a strong personality, which she expressed with her impeccable sense of fashion. Because of her daddy's dime, she was able to spare no expense on her threads, which gave her the creative edge that she needed to never mix name brands that she wore.

Today, she was donned in Marc Jacobs, from her sunglasses, black stretch-pants, gray loose-neck sweater to her black leather pumps.

Sasha was 100% Italian with roots that could be traced back to Sicily. She maintained a healthy shade of tan over her olive skin. She was 5'6", with dark brown eyes and shoulder-length, blonde hair that she wore straight. She possessed a firmly toned body, which she maintained with a three-day-a-week religious work-out regimen. She had 32D breasts, wide hips, nice, shapely legs, and a petite butt.

"Wow," Sasha said as she fingered a loose strand of Sequoia's hair away from her face. "You look exhausted."

"I am," Sequoia said seriously as she sighed heavily.

"You sure you're feeling up to lunch?" Sasha asked with concerned eyes. "I wouldn't mind if you took a rain check; you could always retreat to your quarters and catch up on some R and R."

"No, no, no," Sequoia shook her head. "A lunch date you were promised, so a lunch date is what you're going to get," she said, though she was feeling the complete opposite. "Besides, I got too many things to do today to be lying around catching z's," Sequoia joked.

Sasha shrugged, "Works for me." She made a gesture that suggested they walk. "Shall we?"

They both headed in the direction of the campus parking lot, turning heads effortlessly as the strutted sexily through the campus.

All eyes were on them, which in their case was pretty normal—unwanted, but normal. Neither of them ever complained about the extra attention that they received in public. They knew that they were both beautiful women who were as down to earth as gravity itself, so they took it all in stride.

"You must've had a pretty wild night yesterday," Sasha said knowingly.

Sequoia exhaled a chest full of hot air. "You don't know the half of it."

"Care to share?" Sasha made an attempt to pry.

"I'd rather not," Sequoia said truthfully. Although Sequoia held Sasha in the highest regard and had genuine love for her, she would never truly feel comfortable enough to let her into her world. Simply put, there were just some things that she didn't need to know.

"I understand," Sasha said, "but I will say this: midterms are only weeks away, and if you intend to maintain that attractive GPA you have, you'll really need to put an end to your late night rendezvous and get some sleep."

Sequoia knew that Sasha was right, so she didn't protest. She only nodded her head in agreement.

"Yes, mother," Sequoia joked.

They both shared a laugh as Sasha playfully pushed her. "How is your mother, by the way?" she asked cautiously. "Is her situation improving any?"

"I don't believe so," Sequoia said plainly. "We're basically waiting on a genetic match for the bone marrow transplant in between trying to meet the outrageous demands of medical expenses that the hospital is asking for to cover the cost of chemotherapy."

Sasha shook her head in disbelief. "And you say that her insurance company dropped her, claiming that she had a pre-existing condition?"

"After fifteen years!" Sequoia said with a serious sense of indignation in her tone.

"I spoke with my father about your mother's situation and he assured me that he has a close colleague that will help her pursue a civil suit."

"Really?" Sequoia exclaimed enthusiastically. "Thank you!" She hugged her lovingly.

"Don't worry about it," Sasha managed to say as Sequoia nearly choked the life out of her. "Let's give it a week or so and everything should be in place."

"You're the best!" Sequoia said jovially as they continued on toward the parking lot.

"Anything I can do to help," Sasha said, "and quite frankly, I'm sick of these huge corporate companies taking advantage of the underdogs. It's time that we actually did something about it, and helping your mother out is the perfect place to start."

"Damn straight!" Sequoia agreed. "Those assholes are lucky that I don't have my degree yet. Otherwise, I'd be hands on with this thing myself."

"Hold it there, Mayweather," Sasha said. "Let's leave the handling to the big dogs for now and focus on our studies. You'll get your chance to litigate your life away in no time."

Sequoia nodded. "Ditto."

They both laughed.

"So how is Professor Einhert's class coming along?" Sasha asked.

"Physics?" Sequoia said with a traceable amount of trepidation in her tone.

"That's the one."

"There's nothing like the theory of relativity to get my neurons going," Sequoia said sarcastically.

Sasha laughed at Sequoia's sarcasm. "It'll get better, I promise."

Sasha was in her sophomore year at Harvard, so she pretty much knew all of ins and outs of the freshman year a lot better than Sequoia did, and she held no qualms about sharing her experiences with Sequoia to save her from unnecessary mishaps along the way.

"Oh, I almost forgot," Sasha said with a surge of energy, "I got us two V.I.P. backstage and after-party passes to the Horror Squad concert this weekend."

"No thanks," Sequoia said, disinterested and remembering the last twenty-four hours. "I'll pass."

Sasha shot her an incredulous look. "Sequoia? Do you know how much I had to beg my father to get me these things? You can't just leave me out here to dry."

Sequoia understood that Sasha may have used her father's clout to procure the tickets, but she was sure that if Sasha had experienced what Desiree and she had the night before with Jewels Santiago and his entourage, the idea of spending a weekend in the company of entertainers wouldn't be so appealing. On the other hand, Sequoia didn't want to just leave her friend out there, especially considering that she was currently pulling the strings that could ultimately decide the fate of her mother's medical outcome.

Though Sasha would never say it, a request such as the one that she had just made was not to be denied. Secretly, it was one of many recorded determining factors to the longevity of their relationship, and would be judged accordingly.

Though Sequoia was wise to this unspoken truth, she couldn't possibly forget the way that Jewels Santiago treated Desiree last night. He had taken complete advantage of her, and had done it seemingly with a clear conscience. Therefore, Sequoia knew that attending a backstage and after-party with the members of the

Horror Squad would be no different.

At this point, they were all one and the same to her. They had absolutely no respect for women and would practically do anything to satisfy whatever sick, sadistic fantasy that they'd conjured up in their minds at the expense of a woman's dignity.

However, Sequoia was sure that Sasha wouldn't understand it if she tried to explain it to her. She had never truly been exposed to men from the hood before, and the closest that she'd ever come to a rapper was from her front row seat at a concert. She simply wouldn't understand, and Sequoia had no desire to twist her arm to get her to see things her way. Even though she knew that she could easily sway her decision by confiding in her the details about her "rendezvous" from the night before that was something she wasn't going to do. That story was going to her grave.

Still, Sequoia also realized how easy it was to compromise her future plans with Sasha by simply declining to attend a friendly outing with her, so she figured that the best way to handle the situation was to talk her out of it.

"Look, Sasha, you're my girl and I love you to death, but trust me when I say this: those backstage and after-parties aren't what you think they are," she said seriously as the both came to a halt at the front of Sasha's truck. "It's nothing more than a bunch of wild, sex-depraved men, who look to take advantage of young women who don't know any better."

"Wow! You're way too subjective about this, Sequoia," Sasha eyed her skeptically. "As if it's personal or something. Jesus Christ! I just thought that we could catch a concert, hang out a little bit, and go home. Nothing more!" Sasha chuckled.

"I know, I know. It's just… Something happened to a close friend of mine… something terrible." Sequoia's eyes began to water, so she avoided eye contact.

"At one of those parties?" Sasha asked worriedly. Sequoia nodded.

Sasha could see that Sequoia wasn't feeling the idea in the least bit, and she knew her well enough to know that the reason had to be a serious one; otherwise she'd be all in. She could visibly see that the subject had gotten too emotional for Sequoia, so she decided not to pry any further.

However, there still lay the problem with the free tickets to the Horror Squad concert. Sasha was sure that she had come up with the perfect alternative solution to the problem.

"Okay, Sequoia, I've got an idea," Sasha said. "How about we go to the concert, but no backstage or V.I.P. after-party? And we leave immediately after. That way the tickets won't be totally wasted."

Sequoia saw nothing wrong with Sasha's new plan so she seconded the notion, "Okay."

"So, now that that's settled," Sasha said as she exhaled a sigh of relief, "we can focus on satisfying our taste buds." Sasha climbed into the driver's side of her Audi truck and unlocked the door for Sequoia to climb in. "You got any place in mind?" Sasha asked Sequoia as she climbed in the truck and pulled the passenger door closed.

"Not really," Sequoia said. "All I know is that I'm starving!"

"Very well. Fasten your seat belt," Sasha said. "I've got the perfect place in mind."

CHAPTER 6

Sequoia pulled her midnight blue Dodge Charger into an empty parking space at her therapist's office minutes before her five o'clock appointment.

She sucked her teeth and tasted the lingering flavor on her taste buds from the fried shrimp and French fries she'd eaten at Joe's Crabshack.

Secretly, the entree was one of her guilty pleasures, but that did not mean that she wanted the entire world to know that every time she opened her mouth. If there was one thing she knew, there was nothing more unattractive than an attractive woman with horrible breath!

Sequoia cupped her hand over her mouth and exhaled deeply, and inhaled through her nose. She wasn't impressed.

"Damn, I nearly incinerated my nose hairs," she joked aloud at her own expense.

She sifted through her purse and extracted a box of dissolvable Listerine strips. She placed two of them on her tongue, and when they had dissolved she repeated the cupped hand over her nose and mouth process until it warranted her approval.

Seconds later, she emerged from her car and entered the building. She had a brief conversation with the receptionist Amanda before receiving the word from her therapist to come to her office.

When Sequoia entered the office, her nostrils were instantly filled with the delightful aroma of herbal scented candles. The soothing sound of a waterfall filled the backdrop from the stereo system. The room was dimly lit as a flickering silhouette from the candle light was cast upon the wall.

Sequoia saw her therapist sitting Indian style on a pillow

with a pair of meditative beads in her hand. Sequoia smiled at the customary scene before her as she pulled the door closed behind her.

Like always, Sequoia removed her shoes and made her way over to the pillow that was adjacent to the one her therapist was sitting on. Without speaking, her therapist handed her a pair of meditation beads before inaudibly mouthing a mantra with her eyes closed in deep concentration.

Sequoia followed her lead, closing her eyes and concentrating on her breathing as she'd been instructed to do many times before. In... Out...

Her lungs expanded and contracted slowly as she allowed all earthly thoughts to flee her mind. She began to slowly feel the tension in her body transitioning into a relaxed state of being.

"Focus on your breathing," Dr. Victoria Lee said in a relaxed tone with her eyes closed. "Allow all thoughts to flee your mind."

Sequoia did as instructed, or at least that's what she tried to do. For some strange reason, she couldn't seem to resist the urge to furtively glance at Dr. Lee.

As always, the woman was as beautiful as ever. She was a forty-two year old Filipino who didn't look a day over twenty-five. She had long, jet black hair and rich olive skin over slanted eyes. She was the epitome of forty being the new thirty.

Dr. Lee was donned in a silk blouse and black, straight-leg pants.

"Concentrate, Sequoia," she said without opening her eyes, which startled Sequoia.

Sequoia's face flushed beet red from embarrassment. She had no clue how Dr. Lee was able to detect her movements, but she most certainly picked up on it every time Sequoia's eyes began to wander off. It was as if she learned how to do astral projection and had the ability to watch the room around her while her eyes remained closed.

"Connect with your chi," Dr. Lee told her.

Dr. Lee had a very unique form of administering therapy to her patients. Instead of immediately delving into a patient's problems of past from the jump, she'd encourage her patients to participate with her in a twenty minute meditation session before their actual therapy session.

She stressed how meditation has been clinically and scientifically proven to reduce stress, ailments, and in some cases, even cancer. The ultimate purpose, she'd say, is "to obtain a higher state of consciousness that would allow one to disregard the problems that everyday life hurls at us and accept everything whether good or not as what is."

Sequoia knew that the basis of Dr. Lee's teachings derived from spiritual texts such as Yoga Sutras and the *Bhagavad Gita*. She was a devout Buddhist, and though Sequoia was raised as a Baptist, she couldn't deny the tranquil state she dwelled in after meditating. Thus, she took it in stride.

Twenty minutes later the two concluded their meditation and proceeded with the therapy session. Sequoia took her seat in the leather chaise lounge chair that was in front of her desk.

"So, how's everything Sequoia?" Dr. Lee asked as she plopped down in her huge leather seat behind her mahogany wood desk.

Sequoia exhaled a chest full of hot air. "I'm making it."

Dr. Lee held a perturbed look on her face. "That sounds assuring," she said sarcastically.

"I'm sorry," Sequoia said sincerely. "It's just this thing with my mom."

"Is her condition improving any?" Dr. Lee asked as she rose from her chair and made her way over to an electric coffee pot on a nearby mahogany table.

"We're still searching for a donor who has her blood type," Sequoia said dryly as she watched Dr. Lee pour the brewing water from the coffee pot into two green ceramic mugs.

Dr. Lee handed her one of the mugs. "It's herbal tea," she said before taking her seat. "Cinnamon."

They both sat in silence for a brief moment as they took sips from their mugs.

"Thank you," Sequoia said.

"Don't mention it." Dr. Lee placed her mug onto the table. "Well, let's just continue to stay positive about your mother's condition, and I'm pretty confident that she'll pull through."

Sequoia nodded somberly as she took another sip of her tea. "This is good," she said.

"I know." Dr. Lee smiled.

Sequoia smiled.

Moments later, Dr. Lee spoke in a more serious tone. "Have you been experiencing any attacks lately?"

Sequoia recollected for a moment. "Not really."

"I don't understand your answer, Sequoia."

"That's because it's improving."

"Well that's good," Dr. Lee said. "You just have to remember to take your medication, and don't forget to—"

"Remove myself form potentially aggravating factors," Sequoia finished the sentence for her. "I know, I know." Dr. Lee smiled. "It's just my stage fright, and—"

"So you're still doing that, huh?" Dr. Lee asked, seemingly in a judgmental tone not commonly found in a shrink.

"Not anymore," Sequoia said seriously. "It's too much," she admitted emotionally.

"Well, that's good, right?" Dr. Lee asked and Sequoia nodded. Dr. Lee took another sip. "Have you come up with any alternative solutions for paying for your mother's medical expenses?"

"Not yet, but I am open to suggestions," Sequoia hinted.

Dr. Lee chuckled. "I'll reach out to a few colleagues of mine, see what I can come up with. Anything to keep you out of that place."

"Thank you!"

Dr. Lee nodded as she nursed her tea. "No problem. So, besides the obvious, how's things going in your personal life?"

Sequoia took another sip. "How's things in my personal life?" she repeated. "Well, my best friend was sexually assaulted yesterday night by a famous rapper, but other than that I guess I'm pretty peachy." Sequoia forced a smile.

"Oh my God, Sequoia! Are you serious?" Dr. Lee placed the mug on her desk and sat on the edge of her seat. Sequoia nodded. "Well, where is she? Did she contact the police?" she asked with genuine concern.

"She's in the hospital right now, and no, she did not contact the police," Sequoia said matter-of-factly. "In fact, she won't even acknowledge the ordeal as actually being a rape."

"So she's in denial?"

"Call it what you want," Sequoia shrugged, "but I personally know that that was not the case!"

"So why won't you go to the authorities for her?" Dr. Lee quizzed.

"Because she'd never talk to me again," Sequoia said surely. "I have to respect her wishes to keep things between us two."

"Loyal girl."

"I try to be."

"Well, I will say this," Dr. Lee said, "nearly two out of five women who have been victims of sexual abuse eventually contemplate suicide at some point after the attack. So, if she ever needs someone to talk to, I'll counsel her free of charge. Just tell her to give me a call."

"That's sweet of you," Sequoia said. "I'll be sure to pass it on to her."

Dr. Lee sighed. "On another note, have you been experiencing any more nightmares?"

Sequoia spoke after a short moment; "Not really, but I did have a slight problem coping with being in a hospital. It nearly reminded me of that day—nearly triggered an attack."

"Sequoia, you have to face that demon. You can't continue to allow what happened in the past to stand in the way of your future."

"I know," Sequoia agreed.

"I hate to say it, Sequoia, but we have to go from the top again."

"Again?" Sequoia whined.

"I'm sorry Sequoia, but if you ever want this thing to truly be behind you, then you're going to have to face it."

Sequoia sucked her teeth before saying dryly, "Where do you want me to start?"

"The top will be fine."

"Alright," Sequoia said unenthusiastically.

Sequoia replayed the ordeal in her head as she mustered the courage to start. It was the day that had changed the lives of her family forever.

Ten years ago...

"Sequoia, help me with this bag please," her mother, Rosa, told her as she struggled to balance the large grocery bag with putting the key into the front door of their house. Sequoia complied without protest. She wasn't one to have any qualms about assisting her mother when she asked her to do something—a rather unique quality uncommonly found in adolescents.

"Do you think we're still going to be able to make it to the movie in time?" Sequoia asked.

Rosa glanced at her white gold Rolex wristwatch, a gift that was given to her by her husband for their twelve year anniversary. "Yeah, but we gotta hurry," she said with a strong Spanish accent.

"We probably should've went grocery shopping after the movie," Sequoia said.

"Probably so," Rosa said, "but since we didn't, I need to make this pit stop to put the ice cream away before it melts."

Rose and Sequoia entered their plush Long Beach home, which had five bedrooms, three and a half bathrooms, and a three-car garage. The house was a wedding present to Rosa from her husband before Sequoia was born. According to him, they were going to need the extra space for the large family he intended to build, even though over ten years had passed and the only offspring they'd produced was Sequoia.

Manuel Ariás, Rosa's husband and Sequoia's father, wanted to continue his pursuit to achieve the parental goals that he'd set out for himself, but he temporarily postponed them to expand the distribution of his coffee import business. It had continued to thrive over the years, according to the company's annual income statement.

Albeit, he hadn't fully fulfilled his patriarchal promises; he compensated by providing handsomely for the wife and child that he did have, and it was for that reason (along with his ability to be monogamous) that the two practically worshipped the ground that he walked on.

"Let's just worry about putting the ice cream away for now. We can put the rest away later," Rosa said. "That way we still have twenty minutes to make it to the show."

The plan was perfect, like music to Sequoia's ears. She had been all but clicking her heels since the previews of *Toy Story* had surfaced, but unfortunately for her she wouldn't get the opportunity. Within a matter of seconds, Sequoia's life was about to change forever.

Sequoia could sense that something was seriously off when

55

she first entered their house—she just couldn't quite put her finger on it. Call it a woman's intuition, either way, she was right.

Her mother's face was the first indicator, and whether or not it was the genetic link that they shared Sequoia wasn't sure, but without her mother ever uttering a word she was able to read her body language and facial expression. The next indicator was her nose. Rose followed her nose over the marble tile foyer up the small flight of stairs toward the kitchen.

However, it wasn't until Rosa and Sequoia were within earshot of the kitchen that their worst fears had become a harsh reality. Soft, sensual moans and audible grunts escaped from the kitchen.

Apprehension enveloped Sequoia as she watched her mother enter the kitchen. "Ahh!" Rosa shrieked.

Sequoia's heart began to pound violently in her chest as she got closer to the kitchen's threshold. Nothing in the world could've prepared her for what she was about to see. She saw her father hurriedly snatching up his pants over his bare erect shaft as a half-naked woman stood upright from the bent over position she was in over the granite countertop.

Sequoia's heart skipped another beat when she noticed who the woman was. It was their next door neighbor, Iyanna, a woman whom Rosa had befriended nearly seven years ago. She'd introduced her to her husband, given her an exclusive, all access pass to their home, and this was how she repaid her: by fucking her husband!

Rosa flung the bag of groceries to the ground aggressively. "Oh no!" She snatched her earrings off and kicked her heels off. "Bitch, you picked the wrong man to fuck! Sequoia, go wait in your room!"

Sequoia heard her mother loud and clear, but she couldn't bring her body to comply. Instead, she watched the entire ordeal unfold.

"Rosa, I am so sorry!" Iyanna pleaded with so much fear in her eyes that Sequoia nearly felt sorry for her. "Rosa, please!" Iyanna said as she hurriedly pulled up her panties before Rosa landed a powerful punch to her nose. Iyanna lost her footing as she toppled clumsily over a stool.

"Bitch, get yo sorry ass up!" Rosa vehemently said with hate in her voice.

Sequoia had never seen her mother like this before. Her once loving, passive nature had undergone an extreme metamorphosis. Now, only a rage-filled she-devil remained. Blood was pouring from Iyanna's face and tears were coming from her eyes and she struggled to make it to her feet.

"Yeah, get yo ass up!" Rosa was rolling up her sleeves.

"Rosa, stop!" Manuel grabbed her in a bear hug. "That's enough!"

Iyanna used the opportunity as if it were a ruse for her to escape. Sequoia nervously moved out of her way to avoid contact.

"Yeah, you better run!" Rosa said. "And get your mother fuckin' hands off of me," Rosa said before sinking her teeth into her husband's arm and biting a plug out of it.

"Ow!" Manuel yelled in a pained tone.

Unable to bear the pain any longer, Manuel bashed Rosa over the back of the head, causing her to stumble over the counter. Rosa managed to shake the dizziness from the blow off relatively quick.

Rosa snatched a huge skillet from the overhead pot and pan rack and swung it at his head with the might of Barry Bonds.

He managed to block it just in time, and reflexively responded with a powerful right-hand hook that caught Rosa square on the mouth. He hit her so hard that both her nose and mouth started bleeding.

"STOP!" Sequoia yelled as she stared on in a state of shock.

For the first time in her life, her breathing was slightly labored and her heart seemed to be beating ferociously in her chest as she began to feel light-headed. She would later discover that she was experiencing her first anxiety attack.

Sequoia couldn't believe that her father had the gall to put his hands on her mother like that, especially considering that they'd just caught him cheating on her inside of their own house.

"Sequoia, please go to your room!" her father said, winded.

Sequoia couldn't tell if he was winded from the fight with her mother or the sexual tryst he just had in their house with Iyanna. Either way, she wasn't budging.

"Not until you two stop fighting!" Sequoia demanded. Manuel attempted to respond, but was cut short by a swift kick to his groin from Rosa's heel. He nearly keeled over, but he caught his balance.

What happened next terrified Sequoia to her core. Her father began punching and kicking her mother violently all over her head and body, and she tried to curl up into the fetal position in an attempt to shield herself from the barrage of punches.

Sequoia couldn't watch it any longer. She jumped onto her father's back and tried to pull him off.

"Get off of her! You're going to kill her!"

He didn't stop. He was too far gone to hear anything that she said. He flung her off of his back like a rag doll, making her head hit a nearby cabinet. Sequoia was slightly shaken by the impact, but when she heard her mother screaming for help she quickly shook it off.

"Help! Help!" Rosa screamed as she endured blow after devastating blow from Manuel.

From where Sequoia was sitting her mother seemed to be losing consciousness, which Sequoia interpreted to mean that she was dying—and she most definitely wasn't about to let that happen.

Sequoia sprang to her feet with a feeling stirring inside her that was completely foreign. She couldn't describe the feeling if she tried, but what she did know was that it had everything to do with witnessing her father having sex with another woman in their house, and him putting his hands on her mother. Not to mention that he had tossed her into the cabinet and made her hit her head.

The feeling that continuously mounted in her with each

passing second had all but carried her to the knife drawer to extract a large butcher's knife. She wrapped her tiny hand around its handle and, on complete impulse, she plunged the knife into her father's back several times.

The entire motion was mechanical. She watched him with a surging sense of anxiety as he collapsed to the floor and struggled for air to breathe. Sequoia studied the blood-covered knife in her hand as if she had no idea where it came from. She tossed it from her clutch as if it was a thousand degrees Fahrenheit.

Instinctively, Sequoia scurried to her mother's side and tried to jostle her awake, but she was unresponsive. She saw her father bleeding from his mouth while wheezing heavily. She knew that if she didn't act, and soon, both of her parents could die.

Present day...

"And that's when I called 911," Sequoia told Dr. Lee, who had her hands clasped over her stomach as she listened intently.

"What happened next?" Dr. Lee asked.

Sequoia sighed heavily. "The ambulance and the police showed up and we were all transported to a nearby hospital."

"And was it that particular hospital visit that you would say your anxiety attacks stem from?"

Sequoia nodded. "It was just seeing all that blood and my mom laying on the ground unconscious...and my father... It was just—Argh!" Sequoia cringed.

"How about we stop right there," Dr. Lee said, "but I would like to commend you for your strength and courage. Not only for that day, but because of how well you've managed to progress and the things you've accomplished since then."

"Thank you," Sequoia said nobly.

"Just know that you were not at fault. You were young and scared and you did what you had to do to protect your mother," Dr. Lee told her seriously. "There's no telling what would've happened to her if you didn't."

There was a timely pause.

"I want you to continue to find twenty minutes a day to meditate, and remember to remove yourself from any situation that may prove to galvanize you stress level."

"Alrighty," Sequoia said before rising from the chaise lounge.

"And we'll pick up where we left off next Monday to see how everything is going," Dr. Lee said before rising from her seat also.

She maneuvered around her desk and embraced Sequoia. "Give your mother my blessing, alright?" Dr. Lee said, rubbing Sequoia's back maternally.

"Alright. I'll tell her," Sequoia assured her.

The two broke their embrace and Sequoia prepared to make her exit. When she reached the door, Dr. Lee called out to her.

"Uh, Sequoia?" she said apprehensively.

Sequoia stopped in her tracks. "Yes?"

"How's that other medication been?" she asked. "Has it helped any?"

"Um hmm," Sequoia nodded. "It's been working just fine actually."

Dr. Lee nodded somberly. "Alright then. Drive safe, and call me on my personal line if you need me."

"Will do." Sequoia waved. "Bye," she said before exiting the room.

CHAPTER 7

Desiree was happy to finally be back in the privacy of her own bedroom. The whole hospital thing was really beginning to cramp her style. Something about heart rate monitors and defibrillators gave her the heebie-jeebies.

She took a sip of her liquid veggie smoothie, scowled at the taste, before stabbing the keys on her laptop. She was putting the finishing touches on a sociology paper that was to be included in her midterm that her professor emailed her.

Thankfully, Sequoia had made it her responsibility to advise her instructors that she'd been hospitalized and would require a couple of weeks of convalescing before she returned; otherwise she wouldn't be able to procure her assignments for that period of time.

That was why it had been practically haunting her that she'd actually betrayed her trust the way she had with Jewels Santiago. She knew that Sequoia would never do a thing like that to her, and through it all Sequoia had stuck by her side, never judging her for one minute. To say that the experience had made her love her all the more was an understatement.

"Ow!" Desiree grimaced as Sequoia blotted her rectum area clean with a soft sponge and anti-bacterial soap-water that the doctor had given her.

It was a formidable task that the doctor insisted on being done whenever Desiree had a bowel movement, to prevent a bacterial build-up that would potentially lead to infection.

"What an asshole," Sequoia unconsciously said aloud, referring to Jewels Santiago.

"What'd you say?" Desiree asked as she lay propped on her side in nothing but a t-shirt. Her entire bottom half was exposed and rested atop a huge throw-towel to prevent the bed from getting wet as Sequoia cleaned her.

"Who me?" Sequoia dried her off. "Oh, nothing. Don't worry about it."

Desiree grimaced. "Shit, Sequoia."

"Hey, I told you not to eat that damn pizza," Sequoia said matter-of-factly, "but little miss know-it-all doesn't want to listen."

"I was hungry," Desiree whined. "I'm tired of eating all of my food through a damn straw." She sucked the last bit of her veggie smoothie from the plastic cup, making the annoying noise that soft drinks make when nothing else is in the cup.

"Well, I hope that you'll at least consider my newly appointed position when you think about eating something like that again," Sequoia said, referring to the shit that she literally had to clean up every time Desiree's bowels moved. She applied a thin coat of Neosporin to the stitches before taping small gauze over it.

"Ow!" Desiree said as she taped it up.

"Big baby," Sequoia said jokingly before removing the latex gloves and placing them in a plastic bag, along with the rest of the disposable medical utensils. "I wouldn't wear a thong for a least another week if I was you."

Desiree scoffed. "Yeah, that's going to happen," she said sarcastically.

Sequoia gathered the plastic bag with the disposable items and the tub filled with soap-water and headed to the washroom.

"You should probably wear some silk panties," Sequoia told her. "Cotton will only snag at the gauze."

Desiree watched Sequoia as she exited the room. She knew that she was lucky to have a friend like her. Most women wouldn't acknowledge her presence, let alone assist her in the way in which Sequoia was doing after she'd been caught betraying her red-handed.

Moments later Sequoia entered the room. "I'm going to make a run to Blockbuster to get us some movies for the night. You need anything?"

"Naw, I'm cool. Thank you!" Desiree said with a noticeable amount of emotion in her voice. The unconditional love that Sequoia was showing her despite her treachery made her view her in a whole new light, a light filled with admiration and respect.

"Alright then, I'll be back." Sequoia turned to leave.

"Hold up, wait, Sequoia," Desiree said, causing Sequoia to stop and face her. "Look, I just want to say that I'm sorry, and that I really do appreciate everything that you're doing for me."

Sequoia walked over to the bed and sat down before her. "Desi, you don't have to keep apologizing to me. You're my best friend and I love you, and I would never wish something like what happened to you on anybody in the world. I just want you to grow from this, and for you to realize that it's a whole other world out there. One that neither of us had no business being a part of to begin with."

"I know, I know. You're right," Desiree admitted. "We got in way over our heads."

"But we don't have to continue, Desi," Sequoia said. "I don't know about you, but I'm done with SCORES. I'm taking Cherokee's advice and I'm leaving it alone. Hopefully you'll do the same."

"I will Sequoia," Desiree said solemnly. "I promise."

"I sure hope so, because if I have to go through something like this again with you I'll definitely have a heart attack," she joked.

Desiree nodded weakly.

"Don't be getting all depressed on me." Sequoia rubbed her back in a sisterly fashion. "Give me a kiss so I can leave."

The two shared a peck on the lips before Sequoia exited the room, grabbed her car keys, and headed out of their apartment.

CHAPTER 8

Sequoia agreed to meet her mother at the hospital the next morning so she could undergo treatment. She would've preferred it if Rosa would have simply waited for her to arrive at her apartment so they could carpool there together, but Rosa saw right through her like a sequin.

Sequoia hated that her mother knew her so well. She tried to convince her mother that she only wanted to be more eco-friendly and take the initiative to personally contribute to as much reduction of CO_2 emissions being pumped into the ozone layer as possible, but Rosa was no fool.

She knew Sequoia like her very own menstrual cycle, which is why she knew that the whole eco-friendly trip was nothing more than a ploy to get her to accompany her to the hospital to help her with her phobia of hospitals. Sequoia also knew her mother well enough to know that she would never knowingly enable her in any situation.

She would just have to be a big girl and apply the advice that Dr. Lee had been giving her over the past couple of years. Sequoia spent an extra twenty minutes in her car in pure silence after she arrived at the treatment center to meditate, and to her surprise, it actually worked. She made it all the way to the room in which her mother was being treated before she actually noted that she was in a hospital. For the first time in years, she was finally able to admit that it wasn't all that bad.

Sequoia smiled warmly when she saw her mother sitting patiently on her hospital bed. Normally, Rosa would be packed in a room with several other patients who were also undergoing chemotherapy, but considering the level of toxins that were being pumped into her system she now requested a room with a bed to compensate for her weary body.

Sequoia entered the room. "Hey mom."

"Hey to you too, stranger." Rosa smiled as she took Sequoia into her loving embrace.

"Don't do that mom." Sequoia drew back and eyed Rosa defensively.

"Don't pay me any mind, Sequoia, I'm only teasing you," Rosa said as she pulled Sequoia back into her arms.

On the outside, Sequoia was a grown woman—a woman with confidence, humility, and stunningly beautiful features—but deep down inside, she was still her mother's little girl.

That was why it was killing her to see her mother in the condition she was in, for more reasons than she could count. The one reason that took precedence was how rare the condition was. The odds of contraction were one in ten million.

Rosa was diagnosed with Acute Myeloid Leukemia, or AML as it's most commonly referred to as. According to the specialist, AML is a disease that usually hits two age groups: the first group ranges from ages twenty to thirty, and the second group is usually ages seventy and up.

Rosa was thirty-nine and knocking on forty within a few short months, so technically she didn't fit the criteria for either age group, and considering that AML was most commonly found in Caucasians, specifically those of Jewish descent, Rosa's diagnosis raised a lot of eyebrows. It also usually infected more men than women.

Every specialist who had the opportunity to review Rosa's case all unanimously and unequivocally stated that her case was a medical mystery that would go down in the books.

Before the discovery of her ailment, neither Sequoia nor Rosa fully grasped the scope or significance of bone marrow and its affect on the body. Now, they both knew enough about it to write a book.

They both learned that the body manufactures its blood in the bone marrow and that is where AML strikes. The white blood cells, which are in charge of fighting off infection, become malignant in acute leukemia and the white cell count often rises to one hundred times normal. Red blood cells are suppressed when this occurs, making the patient pale, weak, and anemic. As the white blood cells grow uncontrollably, they also choke off the normal production of platelets, the third kind of cell found in the bone marrow. This leads to easy bruising, bleeding, and headaches.

Today, Rosa was undergoing treatment, referred to also as induction therapy. The idea behind the intensive induction therapy was to kill every cell in the bone marrow and hopefully create an environment where normal cells could grow back faster than leukemic cells

Sequoia hated to watch the treatment take place. It made her stomach turn, so she usually stayed for a short while before retreating to the waiting room until it was over. She only stomached the entire process one time, and in no way did she intend on compromising her digestive system for the unwanted view again. You couldn't pay her to do it. It was just something about seeing her mother injected with large tubes and doped up with medicines that even she couldn't pronounce that wasn't all that appealing to the untrained eye.

The doctor would place what he called a catheter into a large vein under her mother's collarbone. The first induction of chemotherapy would be a drug called Aro-C, which goes into the body for twenty-four hours a day, seven days straight. The next drug, Idarubein, would be given during the first three days. Next would be Allopurinol, and anti-gout agent, because gout is common whenever large amounts of blood cells are killed. Additionally, Rosa received intensive intravenous fluids to flush the by-products out of her kidneys. She was also given antibiotics and antifungal treatments because she would be susceptible to infection.

The extensive induction treatment that Rosa underwent usually lasted anywhere from four to six hours and often times rendered her exhausted. Sequoia would usually park it in the chair adjacent to Rosa's bed after treatment and catch up on some reading or studying, but to her surprise, Rosa was feeling the complete opposite today. She was alert and seemed to be in good spirits.

She was sitting upright and was donned in a hospital gown, and on her head was a colorful silk scarf that she used to hide the hair loss she'd suffered from chemotherapy.

"Not tired today, huh?" Sequoia said as she sat down in the chair.

"Nope." Rosa rubbed her hand over her thighs. "I think I'm developing an immunity to this stuff. Besides, I'll have plenty of time to rest when I'm deceased."

Sequoia shot her a mean scowl. "Don't say that."

"Sorry Sequoia, but if we don't find a donor within the next ninety days and come up with $80,000, then the doctor said that the treatments would no longer be of any use."

Silence filled the room.

Sequoia understood her mother loud and clear. It was just one of those things that required no further dialogue, but in no way did that mean that they had to accept it.

"You just reminded me," Sequoia began to dig through her Coach purse. "Here," she handed Rosa an envelope filled with money.

Rosa examined the contents as if they were a foreign object. "Where do you keep getting all this money from?"

"It's better if you didn't know that," Sequoia said seriously.

Rosa didn't pry, even though she wanted to, for fear of what she may find out. "Well, how much is it?"

"Twenty-six thousand."

"What? But how did—!" Rosa stopped herself before she could finish the sentence. "Well, thank you!"

"Don't mention it. Just try not to worry yourself about it. I know that everything will work itself out soon," Sequoia said even though she was beginning to have a hard time believing her own words.

After a brief moment Rosa spoke. "So how's Dr. Lee doing?"

"She'd good, she'd good." Sequoia was glad that she took the initiative to change the subject.

"Do you like her more than the other ones?" Sequoia's phone began to vibrate in her purse, so she pulled it out and checked her text message. "Sequoia, do you hear me talking to you?" Rosa asked in an irritated manner as she watched the cell phone steal all of Sequoia's attention.

"Huh? Uh, yeah. I mean yes," Sequoia said as she began to stab away at the keypad. "She's the only one who actually treats me like a human being instead of a case study."

"Well, that's good, isn't it?"

"Of course it is."

"Well... is it working?"

Sequoia shrugged as she kept her eyes trained on the cell phone. "I don't know. I guess. She did give me some pretty good pointers on meditation, says that it reduces stress and helps prevent ailments. She even said that it adds years to your life."

"Really?" Rosa angled her neck so she could see what Sequoia was texting. "Who is that?"

"Humph?" Sequoia finally pried her eyes away from the device long enough to see the annoyed expression on her mother's face. "Oh, sorry," she giggled. "It's Desiree. She says to tell you hello and that she misses and loves you, that she's been praying for you and that she'll be to see you soon."

"Oh, that's sweet. I'm surprised that she didn't come out here with you. You two have practically been joined at the hip since you met." She chuckled.

Sequoia laughed awkwardly all the while avoiding eye contact as she thought about the real reason why she wasn't there. Considering how terrible she was at keeping secrets, and how easy it was for Rosa to read her, she knew to quickly change the subject to prevent from spilling the beans.

She placed the phone back in her purse. "I told her you love her too and that you're looking forward to seeing her soon," she said. "Now, what's on the agenda for today?"

"Well, first we need to get out of here. Then maybe we can figure it out over lunch. My treat." Rosa smiled while waving the envelope filled with money.

"You're crazy," Sequoia smiled. "How much longer will it be?"

Rosa checked her watch. "Another forty-five minutes."

Sequoia sighed heavily as she removed a Sudoku book from her purse and flipped it to the extremely hard section. "Well, I'll just stay put until then."

CHAPTER 9

Saturday night rolled around before Sequoia knew it, and to her surprise she was actually looking forward to attending the concert with Sasha. She was dressed to kill in a black, tight-fitting, curve-hugging Prada dress that rose four inches above the knee. It was trimmed with black alligator at the seams. Her toes boasted a fresh French pedicure that was adorned inside 4.5" black Vera Wang alligator open-toe heels with black tassels along the backside of them. Her hair was pulled into a bun that rested on the crown of her head. Not a strand of her hair was out of place.

She set her GPS to the address that Sasha had given her, and forty-five minutes later she arrived at East Manhattan, New York at the Tribeca Tower. A very upscale and costly residential building of condominiums and lofts, the building was rumored to have a number of successful celebrities as tenants taking up space inside—big names along the lines of Jay-Z and the Kardashians.

Sequoia had no idea that Sasha held residency up in the Tribeca, because up to this point she had only been to the spacious and lavish apartment that she was renting close by the campus. It didn't surprise her however, considering who her father was. One thing was for certain though: she would purposely take as long as she possibly could to make it to Sasha's loft in hopes that she would have an encounter with someone famous. Not that she was a groupie or anything like that—she just felt that is was something special about people who actually made it in the entertainment business. Maybe they could give her a few key pointers if she ever did decide to pursue a career as a singer/entertainer.

Sequoia received valet parking out front before entering the building, which she quickly discovered was like entering Fort Knox.

For a moment, she actually thought that she would have to produce her birth certificate and Social Security Card to confirm her citizenship.

After experiencing Gestapo-like treatment from the

concierge in the lobby, Sequoia was permitted to board the elevator and ascend to the thirteenth floor. She wasn't fortunate enough to have a run-in with anyone popular, but the experience being in the Tribeca was exhilarating and memorable nonetheless.

To Sequoia's surprise, the elevator opened on the thirteenth floor into Sasha's apartment. When she exited the elevator, Sasha was nowhere to be found, so she took the liberty to embark upon a brief tour. Astonishingly, her enthusiasm waned when she took the place in: she wasn't impressed.

Sure, the place was nice and had some obviously expensive furniture and exclusive accessories but she saw nothing to click her heels about. She did, however, fall in love with the three hundred and sixty degree view of East Manhattan that the loft provided. The place was unbelievably small, even for one person, so on account of the view she rated the place a six.

"Hey!" Sasha exclaimed ardently as the descended the spiral stairs. "What's up girl? Damn, you look good!"

"Hey to you too, and thank you!" Sequoia said with a confused expression. "You ready to go?" she asked when she noticed that Sasha was in nothing but a laced panty and bra set and a pair of the most adorable heels that Sequoia had ever set eyes on. "Where are your clothes?" Sequoia asked.

"What are you talking about? I am dressed," Sasha said with a serious look on her face.

Sequoia was caught off-guard by Sasha's response.

"I'm just playing with you girl!" Sasha joked. "The show doesn't start for another hour so we got plenty of time. If you like I can give you a quick tour of the place.

"Figuring that I already started that sounds like a pretty good idea," Sequoia chuckled.

"Oh, you did?" Sasha exclaimed with a shocked expression.

Sequoia nodded. "Yep, but I only made it this far."

"Okay, well, follow me."

Sasha started her tour in the kitchen. The countertops were granite and the cabinets, according to Sasha, were handmade bamboo-wood that was imported from South America. The staircase was uniquely designed from a rare tile that had a name that she couldn't pronounce and that was imported from Greece.

The loft, as Sequoia noticed, had a three hundred and sixty degree view of downtown Manhattan. One lavishly decorated master bedroom, bathroom and arguably large walk-in closet covered the top floor.

When the tour was over Sequoia and Sasha ensconced themselves in the master bedroom. Sequoia took her position by the sliding glass door that led from the bedroom to a patio that also overlooked Manhattan.

"Have you ever run into any celebrities in here?" Sequoia asked, as if she was anticipating some juicy details.

"Actually, this is my first time really staying here," Sasha told her as she put on a pair of black diamond earrings. "This is supposed to be my father's 'bachelor pad,'" Sasha made fictitious quotation marks with her index and middle finger while rolling her eyes at the thought, "but he has a timeshare that he's decided to put to use in San Diego. So I'm only babysitting this place until he gets homesick."

"Oh, poor you," Sequoia said sarcastically with a sneer.

"I know, right?" Sasha smiled. "But it is nice, right?"

"Definitely," Sequoia assured her. "How much does a place like this cost?"

"Uh, I believe that he said he knew the realtor so he only paid $16,800."

"Total?!" Sequoia exclaimed unbelievingly.

"Of course not! What, are you crazy?" Sasha laughed. "A month."

"A month?!"

"Um hmm."

Sequoia overlooked the loft in her immediate proximity. Suddenly, the place wasn't all that attractive to her anymore. Now, there seemed to be a number of things that was wrong with the place that she would need more fingers than the ones attached to her hands to point out.

"There's no way I'd ever pay that type of money for this little ass apartment," Sequoia said seriously.

"It was $20,000 a month, so he actually got a deal," Sasha said, "but you're basically paying for the location and the view over Manhattan."

"Not me. I'm much rather pocket that $16,000 and overlook the view of Manhattan in a ten dollar magazine." They both laughed.

"You're crazy," Sasha said as she applied a light coat of make-up to her face. "So how's your mother doing?"

Sequoia sighed heavily. "Not so good. The doctor told her that she needs to find a donor within the next ninety days or she'll be past the point of getting help. She could die." Sequoia got choked up.

Sasha's eyes grew misty as she came to Sequoia and took her into her arms. "Please try not to cry, Sequoia. I promise you she'll be okay," she said as she pulled back and looked into her eyes. "Which reminds me, I have a surprise for you. Well, I've been working on it."

"Really?" Sequoia said. "What is it?"

"I talked to my father about your mother's situation and he promised me that he would get a close colleague of his who specializes in these types of civil suits to handle your mother's case on a contingency. He says that they'll have to file an injunction immediately to get the insurance company to cover all of her medical expenses and whenever the payout comes from the suit he'll take his cut along with the expenses that were procured over the course of the suit.

"So try not to worry about it. Everything is about to work out," Sasha said. "Besides, if you start crying then I will too, and if I do that then I'm going to ruin my make-up, and if I ruin my make-up me and you are fighting." They both laughed.

"I had no idea that you ever asked him. Wow!" Sequoia was baffled. "Thank you, Sasha! That means the world to me."

Sasha scoffed. "Of course I asked him, so please stop worrying."

"You're probably right," Sequoia said as they broke their embrace.

"You bet I'm right. Trust me," Sasha said sincerely. "Now, let me finish getting dressed so we can leave—and no more crying out of you! Okay, young lady? I mean it."

"Alright, damn!" Sequoia laughed.

"That's my girl."

If there was one thing that Sequoia loved about Sasha, it was her sense of humor. She always knew how to make light of the most serious situations and put a smile on everyone's face. That made spending time with her something worth looking forward to and less of a chore, and that's exactly what she needed right now: to laugh and have fun.

"And since we're handing out memos, tell me what's with the lingerie set? And what kinda shoes are those? They are so cute!"

"Oh, these old things," Sasha joked, stirring up another laugh from them both. "This lingerie set is from La Pearla and those shoes are suede and glitter open-toe shoes by Miu Miu."

"Sounds like they cost a grip," Sequoia said.

"Just a down payment on a late model Buick."

"That's ridiculous."

"What can I say?" Sasha said. "I'm my Daddy's favorite girl."

"I thought you were your Daddy's only girl?"

Sasha shrugged, "Same difference."

Sequoia shook her head. "Sometimes, I don't know what to do with you."

74

"You know, I tell myself the same thing at times," Sasha said, "and you're one to talk. That outfit doesn't look like you got it from the thrift store." She strutted away sexily and retrieved her dress from the king size bed.

"What can I say," Sequoia said. "Neiman Marcus had a clearance sale."

"Mm hmm," Sasha said in an unbelieving tone.

Sequoia admired Sasha's body as she climbed into her dress. Her body was toned, tanned, and firm, and rested on a pair of some of the longest legs that she was sure every man wanted to climb. She had a nice-sized butt—not too big, but not small—and breasts that would assuredly serve as a distraction to everyone in the courtroom one day.

Sasha slipped into a tight-fitting Miu Miu sheer and polka-dot dress that left very little to the imagination. A huge, sheer V-shape covered eighty percent of the front of the dress, blatantly displaying a desirable amount of her breasts all the way down to her southern lips.

"Wow!" Sequoia was astonished. She'd never seen this side of Sasha before. She always took her for the conservative type. Little did she knew, she was about to learn a lot more about her.

"You like it?" Sasha twirled on her heels, allowing Sequoia to see the back of the dress was an upside-down V-shape that exposed a large portion of her back and her thong-sporting backside. She sprayed a shot of Balenciaga perfume on.

"That smells good."

"Balenciaga."

"Oh!" Sequoia exclaimed. "You're looking good, smelling good... Somebody might be getting lucky tonight."

"Maybe," Sasha said with a wicked smile. "Just one more thing, then we can head out."

Sasha retrieved an expensive-looking pen from the oak dresser. After fiddling with it for a moment, she took a powerful sniff out of the back end of it. She wiped her nose repeatedly as she drifted into another realm of consciousness. She giggled in a disoriented manner.

"Are you alright, Sasha?" Sequoia asked, not wanting to believe her eyes.

Sasha nodded. "Awesome dude!" She laughed before taking another sniff.

"Sasha, what the hell are you doing?" Sequoia was taken aback with a disgusted scowl.

"Coke," she answered plainly. "Want some?"

"Hell no!" Sequoia closed the distance between them, "And I'm surprised that you actually mess with that stuff."

"What? Coke?" Sasha fanned her off. "I've been doing coke since I was fifteen."

"Well that makes all the difference in the world," Sequoia said sarcastically.

Sasha sighed. "Since when did you get so self-righteous? You're going to sit here and act like you never did something that you don't regret doing."

It suddenly dawned on Sequoia that she was treading in dangerous water. Of course she'd done things that she regretted. Who was she to judge someone? She didn't mean to be so overt in disrespecting her, but it was apparent to her that she succeeded in doing just that.

"Sasha, I'm sorry—"

"No, Sequoia," Sasha said aggressively. "Like you're so fucking perfect! You don't know shit about me!"

"Sasha, I didn't mean it like that." Sequoia tried to embrace Sasha but she yanked away.

"Don't touch me!" She was fuming. She was extremely irritated.

Sequoia immediately guessed that Sasha's cocaine usage was the biggest contributing factor to her reaction, so she kept her distance long enough to figure out how to handle the situation.

"You think I wanted to use this shit?" she said as tears began to stain her face. She paused for a lengthy moment, long enough to blot her eyes dry with a nearby towel and collect herself.

"You okay?" Sequoia asked, not knowing what else to do. She had never seen Sasha act like this before.

Sasha gave Sequoia her back as she placed her palms on the dresser. Her shoulders were slumped.

"My father was the first person to ever give me coke." She spoke in an even tone. "Said that he stopped doing it after college, but started back after he and my mother separated." Sasha wiped her eyes. "I guess I was just as vulnerable as he was at the time, seeing as how she was like my best friend. She lost custody of me to my father, and not because he was the better parent of the two. I mean—obviously," she scoffed. "It was simply because the judge was a close colleague of his, and that he needed me as a bargaining chip to keep leverage and control of her."

Sequoia was at a loss for words. She had no idea that Sasha harbored so many internal conflicts. She'd always pegged her as the spoiled rich kid who lived the fairy tale lifestyle that was usually depicted in movies. It was now apparent to her that that was far from the truth. Considering how devastating and costly her mother's divorce was with her father, she could relate.

"I'm sorry, Sasha. I never knew that you felt this way inside."

"Don't be sorry, Sequoia," she sniffed. "Just know that everything that glitters ain't gold, and I know that sounds a bit cliché but it's the truth. Just remember this Sequoia, whenever the world is handed to you on a silver platter: it always comes with a huge price."

Sequoia didn't realize, at that moment, but what Sasha had just told her would soon make all the sense in the world to her. The revelation did, however, change any preconceived notions that she may have had about her father. What type of man would purposely expose their adolescent daughter to cocaine?

"You know what Sasha? Let's not ruin our night before it starts, okay? Let's just go out and enjoy ourselves, and whenever you feel that time is right we can revisit this subject. Or not. Okay?"

Sasha nodded. "I'm sorry for yelling at you, Sequoia. I was just—"

"Don't worry about it Sasha." Sequoia hugged her. "You just hurry up and get ready so I can teach you how to PAR-TAY!"

They both laughed.

"Will do. Just a few more minutes," Sasha said before re-doing her make-up.

CHAPTER 10

Roseland Ballroom

Sequoia was trying her hardest to ignore the obvious change in Sasha's behavior, but it was becoming more and more intolerable with each passing second. For the past thirty seconds she had been practically laying all of her weight on the steering wheel, and it was beginning to give Sequoia a headache.

Sequoia feared that this would happen. She knew that it was only a matter of time before the effects of the cocaine would begin to mount. The result would be a sudden and dramatic change in Sasha's behavior. She was anxious, jittery, and extremely impatient, a conclusive mixture that she was suddenly convinced would ruin their night. Nonetheless, Sequoia remained positive.

"Sasha, we've got another forty-five minutes until the concert starts, so do us both a favor and lay off the horn. Please!" Sequoia massaged her temples.

"Sorry!" Sasha smiled irritatingly. "Force of habit."

Sequoia rolled her eyes and sucked her teeth while trying her hardest to ignore Sasha.

Fifteen minutes later, after frustratingly navigating through the frantic crowd of anxious concert spectators, Sasha was surprised to find their V.I.P. parking spot empty. She parked the platinum Maserati Quattrato Sport and she and Sequoia exited the car. The car was one of many toys in her father's extensive car collection — a toy that she temporarily had the luxury of playing with until he returned.

"Please don't tell me we're going to have to wait in this long ass line," Sequoia complained.

"Well, I could tell you that," Sasha paused for dramatic effect, "but I'd be lying." She smiled. "Just stay close and follow me."

Sequoia followed Sasha to the front of the line.

"Sasha, Sasha, Sasha," an Italian bouncer the size of a refrigerator, who had enough mousse in his hair for six Guidos, said. He held a mischievous smile that revealed more than it disguised.

"Hey Tony," Sasha said as she hugged him. "Sorry for being so impatient, but you know me and long lines have a bad relationship."

"Don't mention it," Tony said. "Besides, you know you got it like that." He winked at her.

Sequoia became annoyed when she caught a glimpse of how openly flattered Sasha was, so she nudged her in the rib in a vain attempt to move things along more quickly. "Ow!" she said animatedly before mumbling, "What was that for?"

Sequoia mumbled back through clenched teeth, "Could you hurry this up?"

Sequoia flashed a fake smile at the bouncer, which he mistakenly took as an invitation to have a conversation.

"And who is this lovely young lady?" he asked in a strong New York accent.

Sasha took it as her cue to introduce Sequoia. "Oh this is my best friend, Sequoia. Sequoia, Tony. Tony, Sequoia."

Sequoia offered Tony a fake smile as she reluctantly offered Tony her hand. Sequoia immediately noticed that he had so much mousse in his hair that the smell drowned out his cologne.

He kissed Sequoia's hand and eyed her lustfully. "You let me know if anyone gives you a hard time. I'll be on the first thing smoking."

"That's comforting to know," Sequoia lied.

Sasha handed Tony their tickets and he gave them back after tearing off the stub. He then wrapped a neon pink bracelet around both of their wrists. One displayed the location of the concert and the performers—Horror Squad. The other displayed V.I.P. BACKSTAGE PASS boldly on it.

"Thank you!" Sasha said. "We'll catch you on the way out, Tony."

"Alright, but just in case I'm not around, remember to tell your father I asked about him."

"Will do!" she shot back before entering the establishment with Sequoia.

No sooner did Sasha and Sequoia leave Tony's eyesight than his demeanor changed. He folded his massive arms across his chest and stared down a few spectators who were in the line vocally expressing their disdain for Tony allowing the two women to cut the line like they weren't standing there.

Inside, Sequoia and Sasha entered the lobby area of the concert hall to a captivated crowd. Men and women alike couldn't seem to resist the temptation to affix their gazes upon the two. It was something about the way their designer dresses clung to their curvaceous bodies that demanded the undivided attention of everyone in their immediate proximity, especially Sequoia. Her beauty was second to none, and always required a double-take. Every inch of her frame, from the crown of her head to her pedicure-covered feet, was uniquely note-worthy of a cover page layout, and she carried it all with a sense of pride and confidence that wouldn't easily be mistaken for arrogance.

Judging by the way that the ogling crowd gawked at them, you would swear that everyone was there to see them.

"Damn, it's jam-packed in here." Sasha was thinking out loud as they waited in a line to get through the congested doorways that let into the concert hall.

"Tell me about it." Sequoia's eyes roamed the crowded entrance while simultaneously trying to avoid eye contact with the ogling stares that were coming from the men and women in their vicinity.

"Sounds like someone wants to minimize the crowd." Sasha waved the V.I.P. bracelet that was on her wrist in Sequoia's face, her way of hinting that they could easily go backstage when they desired.

Sequoia sucked her teeth. "Sasha, I thought we'd discussed this already." Sequoia was slightly annoyed by Sasha's relentlessness.

"I'm just asking, Sequoia."

"What's good, Ma?" a light-skinned black man covered in Louis Vuitton denim and black diamond jewels interrupted their conversation. To Sequoia he said, "Is it cool if I can speak to you for a moment?"

Sequoia held and annoyed smile. "Sure. Go right ahead."

The man scoffed when he picked up on Sequoia's sarcasm. "I apologize for interrupting you and your friend here. I just wanted to introduce myself."

"Oh, that's alright. We're not here to make any friends," Sequoia said curtly.

"Sequoia?" Sasha interrupted the interruption. "Go easy on him, he's only speaking."

Sequoia rolled her eyes with much attitude. "Whatever."

Secretly, Sequoia was attracted to the man, and despite his initial intrusion, she was enjoying how well he articulated and how clean cut he was. However, this was not social for her. She came here simply to accompany Sasha, and from the way things were turning out it seemed more like she was babysitting.

The man looked between the two women. "Hold up. Don't tell me this is one of those bi-relationships?"

"What? Hell no! You know what?" Sasha snapped.

Sequoia dropped her head.

"I'm sorry," the man said. "You know what? Just forget that I said anything. Enjoy the show," he said before removing himself from their presence.

Sasha sighed. "Do you believe him?"

"Look, let's just go watch the show so we can leave."

"Alright." Sasha attempted to go through the entrance but was violently shoved out of the way by a group of women.

"Hey, watch where the fuck you're going!" Sasha vehemently stated.

"Bitch, what the fuck you say?" said a blonde-haired black woman with multiple face piercings. She spun around in her Air Force Ones, along with her three friends.

The four women each possessed menacing demeanors that could only be acquired through lengthy prison stints, or an upbringing in one of the roughest projects in New York. From where Sequoia was standing, she deduced that it was probably both.

They each had enough tattoos and piercing between the entourage to fill an entire issue of *Urban Ink* magazine.

"YOU HEARD WHAT I SAID!" Sasha shouted. "Watch where the fuck you're going!"

Sequoia wasn't sure if it was the cocaine that was giving Sasha the balls she suddenly had, or if she thought that her father's clout held any weight amid this pack of wild dogs, but she was certain that if she didn't act quickly they both would be leaving there tonight with scars on their faces that plastic surgery couldn't fix.

"Don't pay her no mind, she's been drinking tonight, that's all." Sequoia tossed herself in front of Sasha, in harm's way.

"No, Sequoia, don't try to—"

"Sh!" Sequoia turned to face Sasha and spoke low, "What the hell is wrong with you? Are you trying to get us killed?" Sequoia eyed her seriously.

The blonde woman spoke up. "You really need to keep a leash on that bitch." She extracted a razor blade from underneath. "I'd hate to have to cut that pretty little tongue of hers out."

"And we wouldn't want that now would we?" Sequoia laughed awkwardly in plain fear.

"Cocoa, what the fuck is you doing? Put that shit away. This is my peeps right here," Cherokee said in an angelic fashion as she materialized out of nowhere.

Cocoa reluctantly placed her razor back into her mouth, but not before pointing a threatening finger at Sasha. "You's a lucky bitch." She then spoke to Cherokee. "We'll be inside. Y'all bitches, c'mon."

Cocoa kept her eyes trained on Sasha as she, along with her entourage, entered the door.

"Don't pay her no mind, Vixen," Cherokee said. "Her crazy ass just got out the joint two weeks ago.

"You two know each other?" Sasha said as she eyed Cherokee and all of her Southern thickness.

"Yes," was all that Sequoia was willing to say.

Cherokee placed her hands on her hips sexily. "I heard about what happened to Mocha that night. Is she alright?"

Sequoia could all but smell the curiosity seeping out of Sasha's pores, but she intended to deal with that later.

"Yeah, she's doing pretty good."

"Doesn't look like you plan on coming back anytime soon," Cherokee replied. "Is that temporary or permanent?"

"It's permanent," Sequoia assured her. "I'm taking your advice."

Cherokee smiled before taking Sequoia into her embrace. "I knew you were too smart for us. Just promise me that you'll go off to pursue your dreams and that you'll never look back."

"I promise," Sequoia said seriously.

"That's my girl." Cherokee released her. "Well, if you need me, you know where to find me." Cherokee allowed her eyes to land on Sasha's. "And you need to stop doing coke if you don't know how to handle the shit, cause that girl would've did plastic surgery on your face if I wouldn't have been here to stop her."

Sasha's face flushed red from embarrassment as Cherokee walked inside. Sasha looked at Sequoia and whispered, "How does she know I did coke?"

Sequoia paused before responding. "Let's just say that she knows."

Sequoia and Sasha managed to make it all the way to the front of the show without further incident, and twenty minutes later, during the opening act, Sasha and Sequoia discovered that the man who approached them in the lobby was actually a local, New York rapper named Torrey Guns. He was performing a song called "Midnight."

Suddenly, Sequoia found herself entertaining the thought that the young, underground star, who was on the rise, had earned himself a few points with her. That was, until he shouted her out and pointed in the direction of "the FINEST GIRL IN THE ENTIRE ROOM TONIGHT" and embarrassed the hell out of her.

Her embarrassment quickly went out the window when she heard him spit. His word-play was ridiculous, in a good way. He was an impeccable lyricist that she figured would go real far if he stuck with it. She did, however, have a few words that she wanted to share with him for putting her on the spot like that if they ever encountered again.

Shortly after Torrey Guns exited the stage, the Horror Squad clique seized it. They were all clad in popular designer clothes and either Timberland boots or Jordan gym shoes. Every member had a diamond encrusted platinum chain with the huge symbol "HS" dangling from their necks.

No sooner than the beat dropped did the entire crowd get amped up as the bass from an old popular club banger resonated throughout the room. The song was a radio and club hit called "Fall Back," and it had made it all the way to number nine on the Billboard 100 list.

Sequoia thought that the idea to open with that particular song was genius. It was a perfect way to get the crowd on your side, and since her and Sasha had a front row seat to the entire show, there were able to get the full effect of the experience.

According to Sequoia, everything had changed for the worse by the time the second song came on. That was when Fat John introduced his surprise guest K. Holliday, a rhythm and blues singer who developed a significantly sized fan base with the ladies with a few hit singles and a debut album. All of the ladies in the audience exclaimed their enthusiasm for the R and B singer.

The DJ dropped the beat to their new smash single, "Baby I won't talk." The entire crowd went wild. Sequoia shot a glance at Sasha just in time to catch her inconspicuously taking a sniff of coke from her father's pen.

Their eyes met for all of half a second, but it was long enough for Sequoia to conclude that their night was about to take a dramatic turn for the worse in the next few minutes. It all started when Fat John and K. Holliday announced that they would need a sexy young lady from the audience to come on stage and help them with their song. Of course, Sasha took that as her cue, because (apart from Sequoia) Sasha thought that no chick on heels could hold a candle to her when it came to being sexy.

So she joined the crowd of boisterous heifers who were bucking for Fat John and K. Holliday's attention. Despite all of the yelling and screaming that the entire crowd was doing, K. Holliday set his sights on Sequoia. He signaled for her to come on stage, but she nervously lowered her head in embarrassment.

Sequoia had no intention of going on the stage, or even acknowledging his request, but Sasha didn't seem to pick up on the hint.

Sasha nudged her in the side. "Get up there girl! He's talking to you!" she exclaimed excitedly.

With her had shielding her face, Sequoia said, "I'm good."

Sasha didn't try to convince her any further. Instead, she simply used what she would call Sequoia's missed opportunity as an opportunity for herself. She waved her arms and shouted frantically until K. Holliday and Fat John called her onto the stage.

Sequoia didn't know if they picked her out of empathy, or what the cause was. Either way, it worked for her, and she was obviously taking advantage of the experience.

Sasha was bumping pelvises with K. Holliday as she sang the hook of the song. "Baby I won't talk if you don't!"

Sequoia watched her friend dance suggestively alongside the rapper and R and B singer and stared on in sheer embarrassment. All the while she wondered if anyone in the audience could tell that Sasha was as high as she was.

Sasha swayed her hips to the beat and ground pelvises with K. Holliday until the song was over, and when it was over, he introduced her to the audience before exiting to the backstage with her.

"Oh, shit!" Sequoia said aloud as she watched Sasha vanish into backstage. "Where the hell does she think she's going?"

Sequoia sucked her teeth and sighed as the beat dropped for Fat John's next song. She concluded that the night was going to get far more interesting than she had hoped before the night was over.

CHAPTER 11

The concert had ended over thirty minutes ago, but there was still no sign of Sasha. Sequoia felt that it was inconsiderate and selfish of her to just leave her out there to fend for herself amid the sea of frantic wolves. It was as if she'd forgotten that she was her transportation back home. It was safe to say that Sequoia had it up to her MAC lip gloss with the behavior that Sasha was displaying that night, and if she didn't return within the next five minutes Sequoia was strongly considering hailing a cab home and severing her ties with her.

Being in the crowded lobby filled with ogling strangers was doing absolutely nothing to suppress her anxiety issues, so she found a secluded area to isolate herself by the wall and set up camp. She folded her arms defensively across her chest and forced her face to contort into a glare, giving passers by the impression that this was not the time, nor the place. To her surprise, it was actually working.

Unfortunately for her, it was short-lived, figuring that this was, however, New York. No one actually respected anyone's wishes, let alone space and privacy.

"Please tell me that you're a damsel in distress."

Sequoia rolled her eyes when she saw that it was the rapper, Torrey Guns.

He obviously had poor comprehension when it came to reading other people's body language, because he wasted no time in closing the distance between them with total disregard for whether she wanted him to or not.

"Still not talking, huh?" he smiled, which Sequoia turned her head to avoid him noticing the attraction she had for him. "It's all good. I just wanted to give you this." He handed her a business card which she reluctantly accepted. "For whenever you decided to talk: give me a call." He winked at her before slowly walking away. He turned and asked when he was near the door, "You wouldn't happen to need a ride or anything, do you?"

His timing was perfect, and there was something uniquely alluring about his person that made Sequoia feel that she could trust him. However, unlike Sasha, she wasn't one to just leave her friends for a random guy without offering her the common courtesy to let her know where she was going. For that reason, and that reason alone, she would stay put.

"Naw, I'm good, but thanks anyway."

Torrey Guns smiled. "Oh, so you do speak. For a minute there I thought you was catatonic or something."

Sequoia giggled. "Of course I can talk."

"Don't trip, I get it," Torrey Guns said. "Defensive mechanism, right?"

Sequoia nodded.

"Well, I won't hold that against you. Just make sure you keep that same attitude towards niggas when I make you my girl."

Sequoia sucked her teeth and looked at him like he lost his mind.

Torrey Guns laughed. "I'm just fucking with you. But seriously though, the whole trying to look upset thing don't suit you. Just makes you look crazy. Like an angry angel. Shit don't work."

Sequoia couldn't help but laugh at that one. "You're crazy."

Torrey Guns made the universal phone gesture with his thumb and pinky. "Call me, alright?"

"We'll see," Sequoia said in a non-promising tone, "and I don't appreciate the way you embarrassed me in front of everyone."

Torrey Guns smiled and paused. "We'll talk about it over dinner," he said before exiting the building.

Sequoia shook her head at his silliness, even though deep down she was attracted to him. That didn't mean that she suddenly lowered her defenses though. She posted herself back on the wall and surveyed the room just in time to see the blonde from earlier leading her pack of ex-cons out the door.

Sequoia was almost fortunate enough to avoid any interaction with her until she caught a glimpse of Sequoia from her peripheral vision. Sequoia immediately noticed that Cherokee wasn't with the crew and this made her nervous. Sequoia thought about pepper spray, but realized that it was in her designer clutch inside of the Maserati.

Hoping that the women would remain cordial seemed pretty far-fetched, but it was all that she could bank on at this point. Sequoia had never been in a fight in her entire life, so defending herself against an attack by the women would prove futile. She did what anyone in her situation would do.

"Look, I don't want any trouble."

Blondie scoffed at Sequoia's obvious fear. "Oh, I know," she said confidently, "I just wanted to know if you're loud mouth ass friend left you stranded to go chase that industry dick."

Sequoia lowered her head and remained silent.

"Guess so," Blondie said. "Well, you could come and kick it with us if you want. We got enough room for one more."

"Naw, I'm good," Sequoia tried to let her down easy. "My friend should be out here any minute now."

"She's probably just dragging her feet because she knows that I'm out here. Shid, she's lucky I ain't got no backstage pass cause I was definitely looking forward to bumping heads with her again."

Sequoia wasn't quite sure exactly what Blondie meant by 'bumping heads' with Sasha, but she was sure that whatever it was couldn't be good. However, the entire conversation turned out to be more useful than she could've hoped, figuring that Blondie had just reminded her of the backstage pass that she had.

"You're right, my backstage pass," Sequoia respectfully navigated past them. "How could I forget? Excuse me, excuse me, excuse me." Sequoia practically ran away from them. "Talk to you later!"

"Damn!" Blondie yelled angrily.

"You let her get away!" one of her friends said.

"Shut the fuck up!" Blondie snapped. "It's all good though, because the next time we meet I'm turning her ass out. That's gonna be my bitch," she said surely.

"Yeah, whatever," another member of their entourage said before finding the exit. The remaining women followed her lead, leaving Blondie to collect her lesbian fixation of the girl whose name she didn't even know.

Sequoia hated to think that she was correct, but it seemed as if Blondie was hitting on her. She saw how her eyes incessantly roamed all over her body. It made her uncomfortable. God only knew what that woman was thinking. She was just happy that she didn't have to find out.

She managed to charm the security guard into letting her backstage to find Sasha, even though he was pretty adamant that he could lose his job because the artists were surely squared away on the bus and ready to roll. To appease his worried conscious, she allowed him to accompany her backstage as she searched for Sasha. It was a feat that he insisted on making as formidable as possible by complaining the entire way.

"Listen, we have to hurry up," the security guard said in a voice just above a whisper. "If my boss catches me I'm dead."

"Gotcha," Sequoia said, but inside she was laughing insanely, not simply because of how scared the man was acting but because the man strongly resembled former rapper Biz Markie.

He was sweating bullets as his eyes scanned the crowded backstage. "I can't believe I'm doing this. I got child support up the ass. My P.O.'s breathing down my neck just waiting for me to slip up so he can violate my black ass, and—"

"Hey," Sequoia said, stopping in her tracks. "Relax. You're beginning to make me nervous and I don't even work here." The man dropped his head in shame.

"You're right. I'm so sorry. It's just—"

"It's okay," Sequoia told him with a genuine smile. "Let's just find her and get the hell out of here before anyone knows we're here."

The man nodded.

The two traversed the arteries of the Roseland Ballroom in silence until Sequoia spotted Sasha giggling flirtatiously along a wall with K. Holliday. Their faces were just inches away from each other, and from where Sequoia was standing Sasha didn't seem to have a problem with it.

"Here she is," Sequoia said to the security guard as she neared Sasha. "Sasha? Sasha!"

Sasha looked at Sequoia as if she'd done five more lines of coke since the last time they'd seen each other, and spoke with an enthusiasm that irritated her.

"HEY, Sequoia! What took you so long to get back here? We were just about to leave."

"Leave?" Sequoia repeated in disbelief. "What do you mean, leave? Did you forget that you just climbed on the stage and left me out there all by myself? My purse is in your car and you're the one with the keys, not to mention I could have just got jumped by the girls that you started shit with."

Sasha shot K. Holliday a knowing glare and they both started laughing. Sasha whispered loudly. "I told you she was crazy."

"You what?" Sequoia looked at the security guard, who was just as clueless as she was. "We can hear you, you know."

Sequoia had never been a violent person in her life, unless you penciled in the incident with her father. Of course she would argue that was different, and that she was simply acting in defense of her mother, but now it was suddenly taking everything in her to not land a hard right hook on Sasha's chin.

"Look," Sequoia said in frustration with her hands on her hips, "just give me the keys and I'll wait for you in the car."

"Huh!" Sasha sighed dramatically. She searched her person for the keys before saying, "Shit, I think I left them on the bus."

"What bus?" Sequoia was getting more and more agitated with every word that left her mouth.

"Oh. K. Holliday showed me around the tour bus earlier. I guess I must've left the keys behind."

Sequoia didn't need any further explanation for what Sasha meant by K. Holliday 'showing her around the tour bus.' In fact, she was repulsed by the behavior Sasha was displaying tonight, even despite the sentimental anecdote she gave before leaving the loft. At this point, all she wanted to do was get her purse and get to her car so she could drive back to the campus, even if that meant she had to ditch Sasha and use a cab.

"Well, can you just hurry up and get the keys so we can leave?" Sequoia was aggravated.

"So are you good?" the guard asked as he scanned the corridor for his boss.

"Yeah, she's good," Sasha answered for her.

Sequoia thought to say something but found the strength to hold her tongue. When the Biz Markie look-a-like made himself scarce she signaled for Sasha to speak to her in private for a moment, which she reluctantly complied with.

"Sasha, what's up with you?" Sequoia spoke softly. "I thought we agreed that we're only coming to see the show and leave, not to be backstage hugged up with entertainers doing God knows what."

Sasha sucked her teeth and pouted. "I know, but... I was just trying to have a little fun. That's all."

Sequoia covered her nose. "Damn girl! How much have you had to drink?"

Sasha nervously bounced from leg to leg as she folded her arms across her chest. "Just a couple of shots."

Sequoia shot her a knowing glare.

"Okay! Twelve! I had twelve shots. But I—"

"Twelve shots?" Sequoia repeated dramatically. "C'mon, let's go get the keys. I'm taking you home."

Sasha didn't offer any protest and K. Holliday had heard her comment so he simply led the way. They navigated the corridors until they arrived at an oversized tour bus that was parked at the curb of a congested underground parkway.

Sequoia allowed K. Holliday to lead the way into the bus. She entered the bus to a plume of Kush smoke so thick that she had to fan away the lingering smog just to see in front of her. When she managed to adjust her eyes she immediately took in the view of a plush interior that was filled with groupies and entourage members. Music was blasting from a custom surround-sound system, which a member of the entourage muted to hear K. Holliday speak.

"Did any of y'all see some keys lying around here?"

"Yeah, there's some in the back room," a light brown man with a Caesar cut who was covered in jewels spoke up. He eyed Sequoia lustfully, which made her uncomfortable.

"Wait right here," K. Holliday told Sequoia before saying to Sasha, "C'mon."

K. Holliday and Sasha went to the back room and closed the door behind themselves, and as if on cue, Fat John entered the tour bus with a couple of oversized goons in tow. She figured they were probably body guards.

Fat John paused to take in the lovely view that was Sequoia before telling the driver that they were ready to roll.

"Uh, excuse me, Mr. Fat John," Sequoia said as Fat John neared her. She knew that she sounded really corny. "But I'm not here to stay. I was just waiting on my best friend to get her keys from the back with K. Holliday, and then we're leaving."

"Leaving already?" Fat John sounded disappointed. "That's fucked up, Ma. I would've really looked forward to getting to know you a little better." He licked his thick Puerto Rican lips hungrily as he allowed his eyes to roam Sequoia's body.

Sequoia barely noticed because her eyes were settled on the large bag of ecstasy pills that one of the men was brandishing about as if it were a badge of honor.

"Dig in," she told everyone, and everyone greedily reached inside the bag and began popping pills.

Sequoia noticed one more from the entourage grab a few pills from the bag and walk to the back room that Sasha and K. Holliday went into. No sooner did the door close than memories of the night with Desiree flooded her mind. On impulse, she followed him in fear that they were about to take advantage of Sasha in her inebriated state, but when she reached the door she found it to be locked.

She began to try to break in, but was shocked when she was forcefully shoved into a nearby bathroom.

"What the fuck are you doing?" she snapped when she saw that it was Fat John and he was locking the door behind himself.

"Girl, stop tripping. You know what's up." He advanced on her, groping her inappropriately. "I seen how you was looking at me out there."

"Are you fucking CRAZY? And get—" She slapped his hands away aggressively. "Get your fucking hands off of me!"

Sequoia knew that she was yelling loud enough to be heard over the music, but no one was coming to her rescue. She suddenly felt helpless against the bigger, stronger Fat John, who was easily overpowering her. That alone was beginning to trigger an anxiety attack, which she fought hard to suppress so she could focus her energy on fending off Fat John's advances.

"Damn, Ma! Why you tripping?" Fat John asked her. "I know you ain't just come on this bus to wait for your girl to get no keys."

"GET THE FUCK OFF OF ME!" Tears began to fill Sequoia's eyes as she tried to keep Fat John's hand from going underneath her dress. When she felt his fingers on the outer folds of her pussy over her panties, she knew she was fighting a losing battle. She felt his fingers slip inside her panties before penetrating her folds.

"Please! I'm begging you, please don't do this!"

Fat John smiled arrogantly as he pulled his fingers out of her panties, sniffed, and tasted them. "Damn that's good! Tastes like you're ready to me," he said before kissing her neck.

Sequoia tried to push him away but he was too strong. Lucky for her, divine intervention had other plans. They both felt a massive jolt as the bus screeched to a crashing halt. Both Fat John and Sequoia were flung violently into a wall.

Sequoia quickly clamored to her feet and dashed to the door, but was startled when someone began banging on the door before she could get it open.

"John, bring yo ass outta there man! This stupid mother fucker just hit a police car!" a man from his entourage said as Sequoia slipped past him.

Fat John scrambled to his feet. "Fuck, you mean he hit the police?" Fat John suddenly seemed to have completely forgotten about the fact that he tried to rape Sequoia less than ten seconds ago.

Sequoia had a completely different agenda. She used the opportunity to find Sasha so they could put as many miles as possible between them and the Roseland Ballroom. Unfortunately, when she entered the room that Sasha and K. Holliday walked in earlier she nearly regurgitated her lunch.

Sequoia stared in complete shock, and if it weren't for the cacophony in the background or everyone bustling as quickly as possible to dispose of drugs, guns, and Kush smoke, there's no telling how much longer she would've stood there.

Meanwhile, Sasha managed to extract K. Holliday's dick out of her mouth long enough to convince the unknown entourage member who was banging her back end to get off of her. He reluctantly complied with her until he overheard all of the commotion transpiring in the background, along with the words "cops" and "are coming" in the same sentence. Only then the he and K. Holliday climb back into their clothes and exit the room to see what was going on.

Sequoia shook her head in disgust and for more than the obvious reasons. Sadly, it was because not only did Sasha degrade herself by letting two men run a train on her, but also because she allowed them to do it without wearing protection. Stupid bitch!

Sequoia turned to face the door to give Sasha some privacy, which did very little for the photographic memory she had. Sequoia couldn't seem to shake the vulnerable image that Sasha had etched on her face as she searched the room for her lone dress. It was a very sobering look.

No words were spoken between the two until Sasha was fully dressed and ready to leave. It was then that Sequoia stepped up and slapped Sasha.

"I should snap your fucking neck, you know that?" Sequoia threatened in a low but aggressive tone. "First, you leave me behind to fend for myself with no phone, no cab fare, and for what? For what, huh? So you can go off and get fucked and suck the dick of somebody you don't even know on a tour bus?

"Well, let me tell you what the fuck happened to me while you was back here getting a train ran on you. I almost got mobbed by them bitches that you started a beef with. Not to mention that Mr. fat mother fucker Fat John just tried to rape me!" Sequoia snapped.

"He WHAT?" Sasha exclaimed emotionally with pain in her eyes. "Sequoia I am so sorry!" She buried her face in her palms.

"Ladies, I'm going to need you to stay where you are and show me some I.D." a middle-aged, white male officer with a bald head said authoritatively in a drill sergeant manner as he probed the dark room with his flashlight.

"Both of our I.D.'s are in the car in the parking lot, sir," Sasha explained. "All we have is our ticket stubs and backstage passes."

The officer flipped the light switch on and the girls squinted. He turned his flashlight off and placed it in its holster while simultaneously studying the girls. He maintained a sense of professionalism, but it was clear to see that he was strong attracted to the two women before him—especially Sequoia.

"How old are you two?" he asked.

"Nineteen," Sequoia said.

"I'm twenty," Sasha said.

"Have either of you been drinking or doing drugs?" he asked as he studied both of their pupils before removing his flashlight again.

"No," Sequoia answered as he flashed the light in her pupils.

"What about you?" he asked Sasha.

"No," she hurriedly responded.

He studied her pupils. "Well, that's one god-damn lie you've told me so far, now isn't it? Your pupils are as big as saucers. What'd you do, stick your face in a bowl of coke?"

"No," Sasha said shamefully.

"Well, I'm going to need to search both of you. You ladies don't have anything on you, do you?" They both shook their heads. "You sure?" he asked Sasha once more.

"Yes, I'm sure," she sighed.

"Alright, I'm going to call a female officer in here," the officer said, before stepping into the doorway to signal for another officer's assistance. Sequoia distracted him but calling for his attention.

"Yes, Miss...?"

"Sequoia. Sequoia Ariás."

"Pretty name," he said. "What's the problem?"

"I only came on this bus with my friend because she left her car keys behind the first time she was here, and while I was waiting for her to return I was forced in this washroom right here," she pointed outside the door, "by the rapper Fat John and he attempted to rape me."

"Rape?" the officer scoffed as if he didn't believe her. "You mean to tell me that someone as rich and famous as Fat John actually tried to rape you?" he asked just as a female officer entered the room.

"Who was raped?" the female officer asked. "One of you girls was raped?" she asked, initially expressing her concern.

The male officer spoke. "This one here says that Fat John *tried* to rape her."

The female officer flashed Sequoia an unbelieving look. "I find that kinda hard to believe."

"What is with you people?" Sasha spoke up on Sequoia's behalf. "My friend just made a very serious allegation and here you are violating her equal protection and due process rights by not taking a more proactive approach to investigate the matter!"

The two officers looked at each other before the male officer spoke. "What, are you a lawyer now?"

"Almost." She folded her arms across her chest defensively. "We're both Harvard law students," she said as a matter-of-fact, "but my father is—does the name Anthony Guiliani mean anything to you two?"

The sudden change in expression on their faces clearly said it did.

"Yeah, you know what Sequoia? Maybe we should just give my dad a call and see why we can't file a suit on these officers and their department."

"Hold up," the male officer said with a weak smile.

"There's no need to do any of that. All I'm trying to say is that you wouldn't believe how many young women try to use the opportunity to be with an entertainer as a way to cash in. I'm sorry, but it happens more that you'll ever know, and both of you women are young, beautiful girls who are dressed... suggestively. And you," he said to Sasha, "you're high as shit right now. Not exactly the criteria of a Harvard Law student. If you know what I mean." Sasha nodded. "But, if you're serious about filing charges, we're going to need you to come down to the station to take your statement."

"No problem," Sequoia said.

"I'll come with here," Sasha offered.

"Okay, we just need to get you girls searched, then we can be on our way." He signaled for his partner.

The woman searched Sequoia first and came up empty-handed. She search Sasha and found the silver pen that contained the coke. Sasha and Sequoia's eyes both locked on the pen, but luckily for Sasha the officer disregarded the pen in its entirety and finished the search.

"We're going to escort you two women off the bus and to your car so we can see I.D. and to make sure that you two get there safely. Don't worry about what's happening here. It's Fat John's problem," the male officer said.

"Can't forget these," Sasha scooped the car keys off the dresser, "and this," she grabbed her pen and locked eyes with Sequoia once more.

They exited the room to what looked like a federal bust. Two automatic handguns, along with a Ziploc bag filled halfway with Kush, and what remained of the ecstasy pills that looked to have nearly made it down the toilet were on a wood grain and gold table.

Three officers on one side of the bus were interrogating the women while all of the men were in restraints on the other side.

While Sequoia was being herded by the police past Fat John their eyes locked momentarily—long enough for Sequoia to see the arrogantly smug look he was wearing.

"You might as well wipe that stupid ass look off your fucking face because I'm on the way to the station to press charges on your fat ass!" She slapped him, and the officers grabbed her before she could do it again. "No means no!" She tried to kick him.

Sasha was surprised at how violent Sequoia was. She had already ended up on the business end of her wrath, and she wasn't planning on experiencing it ever again. The part about it all that was so difficult to accept was that she knew that she was responsible for the whole ordeal—and that was killing her.

"Shorty, what the fuck is you talking about? Ain't nobody do shit to you," Fat John snapped.

"Okay, Miss Ariás." The male officer pulled her in the direction of the door. He briefly offered his officers an explanation for Sequoia's behavior. "She says the guy tried to rape her, so we're going down to the station to take a statement."

A Mexican officer whistled woefully while eyeing Fat John disapprovingly. "Looks like you've got more problems than a gun and some drugs."

If Fat John was worried about it, he didn't show it. He only made one statement before shutting his mouth entirely. "I want to call my lawyer."

"Smart man," a black officer said, "because you're going to need him."

CHAPTER 12

It was no surprise to Sequoia that she actually followed up her allegations with a formal statement to the NYPD. "If" charges would be filed against Fat John, then they—according to the police—would come after the investigation. She was then told that if any additional information was needed that she would be contacted for it.

She really wished that the ordeal could've ended back at the station with the statement, but the knowledge that she acquired as a law student suggested otherwise. She knew that the statement was only the beginning of the process. Next would come the preliminary investigation, which would result in more questions (and hopefully charges), and ultimately a trial. None of which she was actually looking forward to.

It was an annoying inconvenience, but she felt it was perfectly necessary to make. She considered it her contribution to the hip hop community, her way of helping to rid the industry of the large number of chauvinistic womanizers who took advantage of women at every opportunity that presented itself.

Sadly, she knew that she couldn't blame Fat John entirely, not when there were groupie-like women like Sasha that gave entertainers the wrong impression—that all women were looking to be exploited as sexual objects.

The very thought of Sasha at this point was raising her blood pressure, and it was giving her mixed feelings. She only tolerated a silence-filled car long enough to make it back to the Tribeca to get some sleep, but when nightmares of the incident with Fat John continued to haunt her and she was unable to sleep, she found herself on the nearest turnpike to Massachusetts. She didn't offer Sasha as much as a goodbye. To her surprise, she drove the entire six hours without blinking.

She bypassed her off campus apartment and crashed at her dorm room for a few hours before pulling herself out of bed. Jade usually slept in on the weekends so she did her best to stay quiet.

Sasha had sent her several text messages, but she was still on Sequoia's "shit list" so she felt no need to respond. She did, however, call Desiree and her mother to respond to the number of messages that had been left on her voicemail. Desiree assured her that everything was okay and that she no longer needed her assistance, and that she would not have to stop by her place before going back to campus. Her mother's message was considerably worse. According to the doctors, her situation was growing direr by the day. Now, she had to be admitted into the hospital for reasons that she didn't want to get into on the phone.

The entire phone call was stressful, so when it was over Sequoia decided to do what she always did when she was stressed out: she danced! She climbed into a pair of black leggings, halter top, and tennis shoes and went to the dance hall.

By the time she made it to the dance hall she discovered that it was empty. Sequoia watched herself in the room-length mirror the encompassed the entire wall. She did some light stretches before going into a routine she'd recently created. It was a combination of ballet, reggae ton, salsa, and crumping. Her motions were executed so effortlessly that one would assume that she was the originator of the dances. She was flexible beyond belief, so splits and high kicks were incorporated and carried out smoothly as well. Dance was always a passion that Sequoia loved, so she exposed herself long ago to different forms of dance styles, cultures, and the history of the dances.

She often joked that in another life, she would've pursued a career as a choreographer, because deep down she really wanted to be an entertainer.

She wrapped up her routine just as the hip hop song she was dancing to came to an end. She blotted her face dry with a towel from her gym bag and nearly had a heart attack when she realized that someone was standing in the doorway, recording her every move with a camcorder. She gasped a sigh of relief, however, when she noticed that it was her roommate, Jade.

"Damn it, Jade! You scared the shit out of me!" she snapped, hurling her towel into her gym bag aggressively.

"I'm sorry, Sequoia, I didn't mean to," she lowered the camcorder as she timidly spoke. "It's just... I thought you would be here and I... I just love watching you dance, and I wanted to ask you if we were still going to hang out today, but don't... don't worry about it." Jade looked as if she were about to cry as she hung her head and walked off.

Sequoia knew that she was wrong. She had no right to talk to Jade that way. She knew that Jade had the purest intentions out of everyone that she knew outside or her mother, and that she was now allowing her personal life issues to affect her social life.

"Jade, wait!" Sequoia called out to her. "Hold up." She knew Jade was fragile.

Jade sheepishly returned to the doorway.

"I'm sorry, Jade," Sequoia said in a sincere tone. "It's just this thing with my mother... Look, I'm sorry!"

Jade nodded.

"So what's up?" Sequoia asked.

Jade shuffled her feet. "I just love watching you dance, you know? You're so talented. I really wish you'd pursue a career as an entertaining artist so you can send me some free tickets."

Sequoia shook her head at Jade's naïveté and smiled, but she paused long enough to consider something Jade had said. "What did you mean by you 'love watching me dance?' You've never seen me dance."

Jade's face flushed red. "That's not entirely true," she said. "I've come here from time to time and watched you, but I never stuck around when you were finished."

Sequoia didn't know how to feel about Jade secretly spying on her, but she felt that it was unnecessary to address. "Okay, well, is that all that you came here for?"

"Not really," Jade said. "I also wanted to know if you were still going to hang out with me today like you promised."

Sequoia smacked herself in the forehead. "Damn it! I knew I forgot something," she said. "Can I have a rain check? I'm very tired and I just came back from New York."

Jade didn't hide her disappointment. "Okay, whatever."

She suddenly seemed disinterested in finishing the conversation with Sequoia and basically walked off without so much as uttering a word.

"Shit." Sequoia was suddenly hit with a stream of guilt. She knew how Jade looked up to her. Why? She had no clue, but her affinity for Sequoia meant that she needed to be handled with kid gloves.

"Jade?" Sequoia chased after her. "Jade?"

"Yes?" Jade asked in a distant voice.

"Just give me some time to take a shower and we can roll."

"Are you serious?" Jade exclaimed ardently as she hugged Sequoia tightly around the neck, as if Sequoia had told her that she had won the lottery.

"Okay." Sequoia managed to pry Jade from her neck. "You can come with me to change if you want to."

"Change?" Jade was lost. "For what? I'm already dressed."

Sequoia looked her over as she stood before her in a greed tweed jacket, brown skirt, knee-high multi-colored socks, patent leather penny loafers, and an orange beret.

"You know what?" She knew that Jade was weird and that she had absolutely no sense of fashion, so she figured it best to put off making a big deal about it. "Don't worry about it. Just give me a little while so I can take a shower."

Sequoia took a fifteen minute shower before packing an emergency bag that enclosed a change of clothes, tampons, toiletries, another pair of shoes, and her medication. She was seriously feeling the effects of hanging out all night before driving the six hours back to campus, so Jade agreed to drive the entire way to New York while she caught up on some sleep.

A camera's flash woke Sequoia from her nap. She was slightly disoriented and the bright rays of light from the sun required her sun visor, which she immediately made use of. When she shielded herself from the sun's rays, Jade's camera was going off again, which made her squint.

"Jade?" She covered her face. "What are you doing?"

"Sorry, Sequoia," she said enthusiastically, "but you should've seen your face. You looked so angelic."

Sequoia flipped the visor mirror open and studied her face. "What are you talking about? I look like crap."

Jade sucked her teeth and shot Sequoia a disapproving look. "Don't say that. You look absolutely beautiful."

"Well, thank you." She closed the visor and noticed for the first time that they were coming up on the Brooklyn Bridge. "How long have I been asleep, Jade?"

Jade checked her watch. "About four hours."

"Four hours?" Sequoia repeated. "How did you get here so fast?"

"Oh, it wasn't too hard. I had plenty of help." She patted the dashboard: "Hemi." She smiled. "Here, take the steering wheel," she said without waiting for a response.

"What the hell?" She grabbed the wheel before they veered into a semi truck as Jade snapped shots of the Stature of Liberty from the oversized camera that was hanging from her neck.

"Oh, sorry," Jade said as she continued to snap away on the flash button.

Sequoia shook her head in disbelief as she realized that the day with Jade in New York would surely be unforgettable.

An arctic breeze licked the coast of New York, just off the Hudson River, creating a relatively uncomfortable day for sight-seers and tourists alike. Jade didn't mind though. She was all smiles, with an attitude so positive and zealous that it was almost painful for Sequoia to watch, and she had a front row seat.

Nevertheless, Sequoia was enjoying her company and she intended on making the most out of the day, especially considering it was halfway gone already.

The first thing on the menu was to satisfy their grumbling stomachs, so Sequoia suggested a popular Cajun restaurant in the heart of Brooklyn. She watched Jade as she feverishly devoured her Cajun chicken and stir fry rice, and ordered the exact same thing before she even had an opportunity to sink her teeth into her meal.

When the two had finally satisfied their cravings, Jade revealed her to-do list to Sequoia of all the things she intended to do while in New York. Sequoia had no idea why Jade would put the list together, but she found it to be a bit amusing. Unfortunately, she had to inform her that they would have to put off ice skating in Central Park for another day because it was too late. Instead, they agreed on visiting Times Square. Sequoia played chaperone along the way, giving her a complete tour of Brooklyn and Manhattan before making it to Times Square.

Sequoia had lived in New York long enough to know that it would take a lifetime to find a parking space in downtown Manhattan, and nearly an arm and a leg to cover the cost of parking, so she convinced Jade to ride the subway to Times Square. It was a trip she would never forget.

Jade felt as if she were a director to a documentary film when her foot set on 7th and 45th in Times Square. She held her camcorder higher than the euphoria she was having at that moment. She twirled on her heels in a complete circle as she took in all of the electric lights.

Bright billboards displaying various models and advertisements filled Jade's camcorder's lens, as did the sea of multiracial people that covered the streets. From this experience, Jade truly understood the meaning of the words "melting pot."

Though Sequoia wasn't a stranger to Times Square, revisiting with Jade would undoubtedly be one of the fond memories she would hold dear to her heart for many years to come.

At every corner, Jade was like a kid in a candy store. Her face was lit up like the Christmas tree in front of Rockefeller Plaza, and it warmed Sequoia's heart to know that she was directly responsible for it.

The two window-shopped in downtown Manhattan until Sequoia was able to convince Jade that they should retire their tour until the next day. They hailed a cab to the subway and rode it back to Sequoia's car that was parked in East Manhattan.

Initially, Sequoia planned on renting a hotel room for the night (considering that the following day was a holiday and therefore they didn't have to go to school), but since she hadn't been by Desiree's to check on her in nearly a week she figured it would be better to spend the night at her place to do some catching up.

So, after placing a call to her and letting her know that she was bringing Jade along, Sequoia made a pit stop at the hospital to check on her mother. She was only able to stay for thirty minutes. It was either that or spend the night, but the good news was that she would be released the following day.

She assured her mother that she would be back in the morning to assist her, then stopped by a popular pizza place in Brooklyn and ordered two extra large pizzas, then to a Blockbuster to rent a movie, before finally going to Desiree's apartment.

When Sequoia let herself in, Desiree was sitting Indian-style on the couch with her laptop in her lap. Desiree tossed the laptop to the side and sprang from the couch as soon as Sequoia's foot crossed the threshold.

"Hey Quoy!" Desiree exclaimed excitedly as she hugged Sequoia around her neck.

Sequoia could barely breathe as she struggled with the bag of orange Crush soda, Doritos, DVD's, and her overnight bag.

"I can't breathe," she muttered into Desiree's shoulder.

"Oh, I'm sorry, Quoy." She stepped back to allow her to enter. "And you must be Jade." She offered her hand. "I'm Desiree."

Jade awkwardly balanced the two pizzas in her left arm while extending her right. "That's me. Thank you for having me on such short notice."

"Don't mention it. Any friend of Sequoia's is a friend of mine."

"I see that you're doing a lot better," Sequoia said, and Desiree immediately picked up on what she was saying.

"Thanks to our friends at the FDA, vicodin has made the recuperation process something worth looking forward to."

"Hold up." Sequoia placed the bags on the living room table. "You're not getting high off that stuff, are you?"

Desiree folded her arms across her chest. "No, Sequoia." She paused. "Maybe."

"Desiree?"

"I'm just kidding." She laughed as she pushed the door closed. "I got first dibs on the pepperoni."

"Don't worry, there's plenty to go around," Sequoia told her. "So, what have you been up to?"

Desiree sashayed over to the couch and hopped onto it. "I haven't left the house much this week. I've just been studying for my midterm exam and watching cartoons in between."

Sequoia rolled her eyes and scoffed. "Cartoons?" She knew that Desiree had been a cartoon fanatic since they were little kids. Sequoia thought that she would've grown out of it by now, but it was becoming apparent to her that Tom and Jerry, Scooby Doo, and the entire ACME family were here to stay.

"Whatever." Sequoia changed the topic. "We just came from the hospital: had to see my mother."

"The hospital?" Desiree said, confused.

"Yes, Desi. She's getting worse," Sequoia said, "but she's also going to be released tomorrow, so we're going to have to pick her up."

A long, eerie silence ensued before Desiree said, "She's going to be alright, Quoy. Trust me."

Sequoia nodded. She was obviously perturbed. "I sure hope so," she said. "Tell you what. How about we set these pizzas in the oven while I take a quick shower? Jade, you can go after me if you want to. That way we can just sit back, relax, and enjoy each others' company."

"Sounds good to me," Desiree said.

"Me too," Jade offered.

"Alrighty then." Sequoia retrieved her things from her bag. "I'll be back."

CHAPTER 13

"So…" Desiree said, "Jade, is it?" Desiree looked her over. "You're Japanese, right?"

Jade nodded as she sat on the couch beside Desiree. "Yes, but I've been living in the States for nearly ten years."

"I guess that explains your perfect English." Desiree smiled. "So you and Sequoia are roommates in the dorm, right?"

Jade nodded again. "Yes, she's the absolute best roommate that I could've asked for. I look up to her."

"You and me both," Desiree said ostensibly.

"You go to school out here?" Jade asked her.

"Yep." She tugged at the shirt she was wearing that displayed the letters 'NYU.' "I go to NYU; Communications major," she said. "I didn't fit the academic criteria to make it into Harvard, but that's alright. I like it at NYU. It keeps me closer to home. Jade nodded but remained silent.

Desiree kept her eyes on Jade. She was finding it hard to ignore the weird taste in attire that she was wearing.

"Can I ask you a personal question, Jade?"

"Go ahead."

"What's with the clothes?" She wanted to laugh, but she didn't want to offend her. "Excuse me for saying this, but they're weird."

"I know," she said plainly. "Matches my personality. I've always been considered sort of an enigma so it fits."

"Well, you're a beautiful woman, so it's easy for you to pull it off."

"You think I'm beautiful?" Jade asked, as if she'd never heard it before.

"You don't?"

"Not really," she answered honestly. "I've always looked at myself as the girl that nobody wants."

"So you mean to tell me that none of the boys at Harvard are drooling over you?"

She shook her head. "It they have, I haven't noticed, and to tell you the truth I've never really been into boys like that."

Desiree looked at her strangely, trying to pinpoint exactly what she meant. "What do you mean? Like, you're not attracted to them?"

"No, it's not that. It's just that no one has ever paid me any attention, so I've kinda just lived in my own little world and focused on things I actually have control over. Like my education."

Desiree considered what she said for a moment before asking, "Well, are you attracted to women?"

Jade figured that it was a fair question; an honest question that she'd been asking herself for a long time now. "I don't know. I mean, I definitely find them to be attractive, but I always figured that was a natural thing among all women."

Desiree studied her as she nodded distantly. "Well, there are ways to find out how you feel. I mean, that is part of the college experience. That is, of course, if you choose to partake in it."

"Have you?" Jade asked.

"Mm hmm," Desiree nodded.

"Well, what did you think?"

Desiree shrugged. "Let me just say that nothing will ever replace a man, but it was definitely fun. It's even better when a man and a woman are there."

"A three-some?" Jade asked in an anxious tone.

Desiree nodded.

"Wow!" Jade seemed to have traveled off into her head, something that Desiree deduced she did more often than she should. "Can I be honest with you?"

"That's what I prefer."

"I'm a virgin."

Desiree looked at her in disbelief. "Are you serious?" She nodded sheepishly. "Well, that's nothing to be ashamed of. In fact, I commend you for it."

"But it's not like I'm trying to be."

"Listen, don't worry about that." Desiree paused. "So where did you get your name from?" Desiree asked, changing the topic.

"Because my eyes are jade green," she replied. "Why'd you ask that?"

"Can I look?"

Jade removed her glasses and Desiree closed the distance between them to get a closer look. Instead of focusing on her eyes she planted a juicy kiss on Jade's lips. Jade's body tensed up, but she didn't show any signs of resistance. Desiree took her silence as an invitation to continue.

Desiree focused her attention on each lip, sucking on them gently before forcing her tongue into Jade's mouth. Jade was a novice, no doubt, but she was also a quick learner, so with Desiree's assistance she quickly developed a rhythm.

Desiree moved from her mouth to her neck, while using her free hand to massage Jade's B-cup breast. Soft moans escaped Jade's lips as Desiree slowly worked her hand up Jade's skirt. She wrestled with her panties hungrily before gaining access in which she began massaging her clit. When Jade's legs parted wider she knew that she was loving it. She dipped two fingers into her and Jade moaned hard. It was so loud that Desiree had to muffle her by kissing her passionately.

Desiree fingered her, working her G-spot, causing her to buck wildly on the couch before cumming hard. She covered Jade's mouth with her palm and peered over her shoulder to make sure Sequoia wasn't coming.

A lone tear worked its way down Jade's cheek as she tried to understand the surge of ecstasy permeating her anatomy.

Desiree pulled her fingers out of her and sucked on them. "Mm," she said, before putting them into Jade's mouth. "Taste it."

Jade looked at her fingers unsurely, but welcomed them into her mouth nonetheless. She sucked her fingers clean of any evidence.

"How does it taste?"

She shrugged with a smile. "Like strawberries."

"One day I'll let you taste mine," Desiree said just as Sequoia came out of the bathroom humming an R and B tune.

Desiree and Jade immediately jumped to either side of the couch. Jade tried to wipe the guilty look off of her face as she gathered her things to take a shower. It all went unnoticed by Sequoia—everything but the weird way Jade was suddenly acting. She nearly pushed her to the ground to get to the bathroom.

"What's gotten into her?" Sequoia asked Desiree.

Desiree shrugged. "Hell if I know," Desiree said, smiling devilishly to herself.

Sequoia was about to press it but the sound of her phone ringing distracted her. As she answered, all of the memories from the previous night came flooding back into her mind: the embarrassment, the hurt, and the helplessness. All of it came back when she heard the man's voice on the other end of the line. It was Fat John's lawyer, and he wanted to talk.

The two agreed to meet in a public area the next day, where

they could discuss something "extremely important," according to him. They met at a local Starbucks in Brooklyn. Sequoia slipped out of the apartment before either Jade or Desiree had a chance to wake up. The plan was to get back before either of them did. It was a fairly simply task, figuring that Jade and Desiree shared a bed in Desiree's room last night. Sequoia felt that was a pretty noble gesture from Desiree, considering that the two had just met and all.

Desiree had a two bedroom apartment, so Sequoia slept in the other room, and to her surprise is was some of the best sleep she had gotten in years. She made it her business to peek inside Desiree's room before leaving and saw that they both were cuddled up next to each other sleeping peacefully.

Desiree didn't know how good it made her feel that she'd accepted Jade with welcoming arms the way that she did. She intended to let her know it whenever the opportunity presented itself.

It was a quarter past eight on a Monday morning, and Sequoia was baffled to discover that Starbucks wasn't crowded. She figured it was probably because it was a holiday, one that she couldn't tell you if her life depended on it.

When she made it inside, Fat John's lawyer was already there and situated at a table near a window that overlooked the entrance and parking lot. Sequoia wore a huge pair of Chanel glasses and a black fedora that matched her black Chanel leather jacket, True Religion jeans, and quarter length black Timberland boots.

Fat John's lawyer introduced himself as Ted Silverman as they shook hands.

"Miss Ariás, I presume?" he said as he offered her a seat, which she accepted.

"The one and only," she said. "You wanted to speak to me?"

"Yes, Miss Ariás—"

"Please, call me Sequoia," she told him. "Miss Ariás makes me feel so old."

"Forgive me."

"It's alright."

"Well, I'm going to get straight to the point." He interlocked his fingers over a manila envelope on the table. He was donned in a gray blazer over an Oxford white shirt. His hair was styled like George Clooney's, and was graying at the temples. Sequoia thought he was every bit of fifty. "First, let me start by saying that my client sends his apologies. He was intoxicated last night—"

"With all due respect, Mr. Silverman, that is no excuse for the way he behaved last night. He tried to rape me. There is no excuse for that. So, no, I do not accept his apology."

Attorney Silverman squirmed in his seat nervously. "Understandable."

"So if that's all, sir, I'll be leaving." She began to gather her things.

"Actually, it's not all," he said solemnly. "This is really what I'm here for." He slid the envelope that was under his hands to her.

Sequoia eyed him suspiciously before reluctantly flipping the envelope open and reading over the contents. She read over a few sentences before having a clear understanding of what this meeting was all about. She scoffed, "So this is what this is about. You want to pay me for silence."

Attorney Silverman made a weird gesture with his face. "More like compensate you for a misunderstanding."

Sequoia chuckled in an unbelieving fashion. "Sir, with all due respect this isn't a situation that's open to interpretation. Your client tried to rape me," she said seriously, "and if Kismet wouldn't have allowed that bus driver to have an accident when he did, he would have succeeded." Tears began to build in her eyes.

"So, what, I'm supposed to just compromise my integrity and let bygones be bygones? What about the girls that are too scared to come forward who he's probably done this to before? Or the girls who may come after me?"

"Well, we can't deal with hypothetical," Attorney Silverman told her, "but what I will tell you is that this is real." He tapped the file. "This is something you can actually say that you were able to get out of this terrible experience."

Sequoia folded her arms across her chest and sighed. "No thank you," she said seriously.

"Sequoia, I sincerely think you should reconsider my client's generous offer."

"I'm sorry, Mr. Silverman, but I can't accept this," she told him. "I'm not some money-hungry groupie who's trying to con your client out of some money. I only went on that bus because my friend left her keys behind when she first visited, and she was pretty drunk, so I figured—"

"Miss Sequoia, forgive me for interrupting, but I feel that it's necessary to offer you a bit of personal advice."

Sequoia's posture said that she was all ears.

"You're in school for law at Harvard University, am I correct?"

"Yes."

"So, your brief exposure to the way the law works should have clearly shown you by now that you don't have a case."

"I what?" she repeated incredulously.

"You don't have a case," he said again. "Think about it. You're alleging that my client attempted to sexually assault you, but there's no evidence to support your claim.

"You both were in the privacy of a washroom together, according to you. So no one witnessed the incident in question. A DNA test wasn't necessary, but according to the police report you refused it anyway. Even if any bodily fluids were on you, or my client, they're long gone by now. It basically comes down to your word against his.

"And I can assure you that I am 100% confident that I could convince a judge or jury that my client was targeted by a groupie with an ulterior motive who is trying to sabotage him because he is an entertainer. He'd be the victim, and in the end you'd be the black sheep. Remember, it's not what you know; it's what you can prove.

"So this," he tapped the file again. "It's not because we're scared to take this thing to court, but simply because we want to avoid the bad press. My client won't be able to avoid being charged with the drugs and gun charges, because the bus was in his name, but you know—like I do—that sort of press will only further solidify his reputation as a gangster rapper. This is all off the record that I'm telling you; my client wouldn't approve of this conversation we're having."

Sequoia was hearing him loud and clear. Though the revelation wasn't sitting well with her, she knew she had to be realistic with herself. It wasn't what you know, it was what you could prove, and in a court of law the allegations that she was trying to bring on Fat John didn't have a leg to stand on.

In the end, she would only be bringing embarrassment and shame to herself by going public, which would be counter-productive to her true objective: to expose Fat John as the disrespectful, perverted rapist he was. She sighed heavily as she raked her brain for answers.

On one hand, she didn't want to make it seem as if it was all about money, but on the other hand she could take the $250,000 that he was offering to help her mother and use it towards bills, or God knows what.

"Sequoia, I don't mean to rush you, but I will be needing an answer before this meeting is over, or the deal will be off the table," he told her. "And if you do agree to the offer, then I will also need you to sign a confidentiality form and never speak about the incident to no one."

"A confidentiality form?" she asked.

Attorney Silverman nodded.

"And that goes both ways, right? Will he be able to bring up having paid me for my silence?"

He shook his head.

Sequoia sighed heavily before acquiescing to his offering. "Alright, Mr. Silverman. Let me look this over for a moment."

She studied the contractual agreement, reading over each sentence very carefully. When she concluded that everything was alright, she sighed on the dotted line.

Attorney Silverman made the deal official when he presented Sequoia with a check in the sum of $250,000, which she accepted apprehensively. He also gave her a carbon copy of the contract, and told her that if she ever spoke about said incident in public, the contract would be void.

Once Sequoia fully understood the ramifications of their agreement, the two concluded their meeting with a professional handshake.

"You're a smart woman, Sequoia," Mr. Silverman said before placing his card onto the table. "One that I'm pretty sure our firm could benefit from one day."

He rose from his seat and gathered his things before exiting the establishment. Sequoia sat in silence for a short while after Attorney Silverman had left, blankly staring at the check.

"So this is what my silence is worth?" Sequoia said aloud.

Though Sequoia had mixed feelings about the entire situation, she couldn't negate the fact that its timing was so peculiarly perfect that it had to be heaven-sent. She seriously needed the money to cover her mother's medical expenses, so all things considered Sequoia was able to find solace in that alone.

The thought of her mother, lying inside of a hospital, had her on the phone calling to see if she was ready to leave. Sadly, she discovered that she was actually feeling worse than the previous day and that she would not be leaving the hospital. The news was depressing, but Sequoia promised to come visit her with good news. She deposited the check at a local Citibank and headed back to Desiree's place.

Desiree and Jade were still sleeping when Sequoia made it back to the apartment, so she took her shower and dressed before waking them up. She gave them all of thirty minutes to dress, so they could get some breakfast and start the day: her treat!

The trio did lunch at Joe's Crab Shack before going ice skating at Rockefeller Park. Next, they went to the Brooklyn Zoo. Sequoia then gave Jade a more thorough tour of downtown Manhattan, moonlighting as a tour guide along the way. Sequoia was feeling exceptionally well so she took the girls on a shopping spree at Macy's, maxing out two of her credit cards. It was a move that raised a lot of questions and eyebrows between Desiree and Jade, but she managed to convince them both that she was alright without disclosing anything too personal.

Sadly, Sequoia and Jade and to get on the road to embark upon their six hour journey back to Harvard, and they had to stop by the hospital on the way. Sequoia picked her mother up some toiletries, fast food, portable DVD player and DVDs, and multiple changes of clothes.

Desiree promised to check on her everyday and to assist her with anything she could while Sequoia was away. When it was time for Jade and Sequoia to leave, Desiree was noticeably upset. However, she knew that they had to get back, so she made it her personal business to give Jade all of her contact information—which Sequoia thought was sweet of her.

Sequoia and Jade bid Desiree farewell, promising to call her when they arrived before they hopped on the interstate back to Cambridge, Massachusetts.

Sequoia had downloaded several new songs from Desiree's laptop for the long ride. They stopped at a rest area to switch drivers and to eat McDonald's. They'd listened to five different albums by the time they made it back to the campus.

They made it back to the dorm at 12:12am. Sequoia was dead tired, so she took a shower before attempting to retire to her bed. Little did she know, Jade had other plans for her.

"Really, Jade," Sequoia said dryly in an annoyed tone as she ran a dry towel over her wet, curly hair.

"Pay me no mind," Jade said, holding the video camera in her face. "Pretend that we're filming a reality show."

"C'mon, Jade. It's too late for that." She fanned the camera away. "I need to get some sleep. I'm tired."

"Aww, you're no fun." Jade lowered the video camera. "Tell you what, I've got thirteen minutes worth of film left, and I got one request. I promise if you do it I won't ask you for anything else the entire time we're in college."

Sequoia stared at her blankly.

"Your enthusiasm is infectious."

Sequoia chuckled before hurling one of her pillows at her. Jade sidestepped.

"What's the request?" Sequoia asked.

"First, you have to promise me that you're going to do it."

"Jade? You can't seriously expect for me to agree to something without knowing the terms."

"Please?" she begged.

"What is it?" Sequoia was growing impatient.

"One song."

"No." Sequoia pulled the covers back.

"C'mon Sequoia," she begged. "You promised."

"No, I did not." She sat down on her bed and continued drying her hair.

"Pleeaase!" she begged.

"Jade, it's too late, and I'm tired, and I really don't feel like it."

"C'mon," she pouted.

"Don't try that face with me. I'm not caving today," Sequoia said, sticking to her guns.

Jade continued to display her puppy dog eyes.

Sequoia turned her head. "Not today, nope. I'm not falling for it today." Sequoia was trying to be true to her words, but it was something about the way that Jade stared at her that always seemed to lower her defenses and made her want to comply with whatever request she dreamed up.

"Damn it!" Sequoia shouted. "Okay, one song, but that's it!"

"Thank you!" Jade hugged Sequoia with her free arm before shoving the video recorder back into her face.

"Okay, I'm ready," Jade told her.

"What song?"

"Do that one that I like by Beyoncé," she said eagerly.

Sequoia rolled her eyes before clearing her throat. Jade was an absolute die-hard fan of Beyoncé's music. Sequoia had no intention of disrespecting the Diva's music, so she prepared her vocals to make it a moment to remember. If only she knew what Jade's true intentions were behind her request, she would've certainly never agreed to do it.

CHAPTER 14

Sequoia practically spent the entire following week in complete solitude, using the time wisely and buckling down on her studies. Her midterms were only a week away and she absolutely needed to ace them, and for more reasons than one. Unlike the majority of the alumni and undergrads who were attending the prestigious college, whose careers were practically mapped out and financed by their rich parents before their conception, Sequoia had to earn her keep.

She didn't have the luxury of slacking up, not even for one minute. It was imperative for her to maintain a GPA of 3.0 or higher, or she would easily run the risk of being on academic probation. Even worse, she could lose her academic scholarship—something that she couldn't let happen by any means.

That was why it was a blessing in disguise for her to receive financial compensation for the whole "misunderstanding" that she had with Fat John. Now, she was able to stress less and focus more, not to mention that she was able to assume some more financial responsibility for her mother's medical expenses, pay off her car, and stash the rest away for a rainy day: all $237,800 of it.

Though she still had mixed feelings about receiving her newfound inheritance the way she did, it did manage to remove the bitter taste from her mouth when she saw Fat John on Fox News being booked on weapons and drug charges. Even though she now struggled with the idea of her being a sellout, and that the only thing that Fat John would learn from this experience was that whatever situation he got himself in, his money could fix it. That was something that she was having a hard time digesting.

She really wanted to teach him a lesson, one that would require the assistance of four concrete walls and years of isolation. She figured that maybe then, and only then, would she be able to prevent something like this from happening again to someone else.

Sequoia was a strong believer in fate, which stemmed from her Catholic roots, so even though she didn't agree with the experience that she had with Fat John, she found comfort in the idea that part of the money was going to be used to help her mother.

To her surprise, Sasha actually came through for her with the lawyer. His name was Chuck Schurenberg, and after meeting up with him and providing him with the necessary information that he needed, he immediately filed an injunction in court that forced the insurance company to pay for Rosa's medical expenses until everything got sorted out in court.

Surprisingly, after the injunction was enforced, Rosa and Sequoia received the news that they'd been dying to hear four days later: Rosa had a donor! Coincidence? Probably not.

Either way, Sequoia was now able to breathe a sigh of relief. She was indebted to Sasha and her father for their altruistic gesture, even though she had yet to call her or her father to thank either of them.

Sequoia wanted to be with Rosa, but she couldn't afford to miss her midterm, so Desiree checked on her every day until she was able to do so while she underwent her convalescent period.

A week later Sequoia received more good news when she learned that she had aced all of her midterm exams. She had studied hard and it had paid off. Now that the hard part was behind her and she had more than one reason to smile, she felt that she had earned the right to celebrate. Considering how much tighter her bond had grown with Jade over the past few weeks, she figured that she'd be the perfect person to celebrate with.

Her watch read 11:12 am, which meant that Jade was more than likely in the cafeteria, so that's where she headed.

Along the way, Sequoia was getting the weirdest vibe from the students on the campus. Everyone was being extremely cordial with her for reasons that were completely foreign to her. It made no sense to her, considering that she had never expressed any desire to be social with anyway. She had always been cordial enough to speak to her peers, but nothing that would warrant the attention she was getting.

She exited the academic building to a crowd of her peers, who all acknowledged her presence as if she were a pop star who had been spotted at a local mall. The unexpected attention nearly triggered a panic attack.

"There she is!" a man whom she had never seen before alerted his entourage, pointing in Sequoia's direction. Within seconds the entire herd of college students had surrounded Sequoia and began saying the most ridiculous statements that she'd ever heard.

"Oh my God, you look even better in person!" said a weird looking man, who was wearing a prehistoric, service-issue Army fatigue outfit, thick glasses, black boots that were laced to the shin, and a blonde mushroom-style hairdo.

Sequoia was confused by the way they were acting, but she wasn't delusional. She was sure that she was undergoing a serious case of mistaken identity.

"Who me?" she asked, looking around to make sure that no one was behind her. "I'm sorry, but I believe you have me mistaken with someone else," she attempted to pass but the man cut her off.

"Wait!" the man exclaimed energetically. "You're Sequoia, right?"

"Yes," Sequoia answered apprehensively, all the while trying to compute where these people could have possibly come from and how they knew her name.

"We just wanted to get an opportunity to meet you before your career actually takes off. We were hoping that we could get some autographs," the man said.

"Before my career takes off?" Sequoia repeated with an annoyed scoff. "Listen, I don't have the slightest clue what you're talking about, so if you'll excuse me." She maneuvered her way past them and did everything shy of breaking out into a full sprint to put as much distance as she could between herself and the weird people.

"We'll be waiting for you when you come back," an Irish woman with orange-red hair and an honest accent yelled at the departing Sequoia.

"Damn it Kate!" one of the men snapped at the Irish woman.

"What'd you have to say that for? Now she may never come back."

Sequoia was moving as fast as she could to get to the cafeteria, and with every step that she took it seemed as if someone whom she had never met before was going out of their way to speak to here. Even odder, they were congratulating her. She was beginning to think that she was in the Twilight Zone.

She entered the cafeteria and surveyed the room with just enough time to lock her eyes on Sasha's: the one person whom she had purposely been avoiding.

Sequoia attempted to exit the cafeteria before Sasha had an opportunity to fix her mouth to call her, but she apparently moved too slowly.

"Sequoia, wait!" Sasha ditched the group of girls she was sitting with, bringing her laptop along with her.

Sequoia reluctantly halted her stride and turned to face her with serious disinterest. Instead of speaking, she stood there in silence with body language that would run a bear off. That didn't stop Sasha from taking her chances.

Sasha seemed tense and apprehensive as she approached Sequoia. "Why have you been avoiding me, Sequoia? I've been trying to talk to you for over a week now."

Sequoia sucked her teeth. "You don't really want to go there, do you Sasha?" she responded defensively. "You know exactly why I've been avoiding you."

"Sequoia, I'm sorry! I had no idea that Fat John would try some shit like that with you, but you can't shut me out. I'm your friend."

"Oh, are you?" Sequoia placed her hand on her hip.

Sasha stared at her in shock. "Yes."

"Let me tell you something, Sasha. My friends—" she made question marks with her fingers—"wouldn't have knowingly brought me into an uncomfortable and potentially dangerous situation, and for what? Because you wanted to let a few industry niggas run a train on you."

"I was drunk and high off pills!" Sasha said with tears building in her eyes. Sequoia's words had obviously hurt her.

"And that's an excuse? Because you were drunk and high?" Sequoia retorted incredulously. "I'm sorry Sasha, but I've always held you in the highest regard. Maybe I was wrong though. Maybe you never deserved that kind of respect from me."

"Don't say that, Sequoia." Sasha wiped the tears from her eyes. "I'm sorry."

Sequoia held a lot of resentment towards Sasha and the way that she had behaved the other night, but she didn't have the heart to spit in her face and knowingly inflict pain on her. She wasn't wired that way, especially after considering what she had talked her father into doing for her mother. Sasha deserved better than that.

"Sasha, stop crying. Please!" Sequoia took her into her embrace. "Tell you what; just give me some more time to process everything and I'll give you a call."

Sasha shook her head solemnly. "Okay." She wiped her eyes. "I also wanted to tell you that a lawyer has been assigned to your mother's case."

"We know, and we thank you," Sequoia said seriously. "He filed an injunction immediately and now the insurance company has to pay for her medical expenses. And, get this," Sequoia said, "they've found a donor."

"Really?" Sasha exclaimed and Sequoia nodded. "Well, that's great!"

"Yes it is, and we owe it all to you."

"Well, my father actually," Sasha said, "but it's the same difference. So, see, I'm not that bad after all."

"Mmm hmm," Sequoia said in a motherly fashion. "Anyway, the lawyer did say that he would work on a contingency."

"Right, I know," Sasha said. "He'll deal with all of the court expenses now, but he'll take a third of the settlement when it comes, along with whatever court costs."

"That's what he said." Sequoia smiled. She wanted to let Sasha completely off the hook because of that act of altruism that she showed her, but she had learned long ago from her mother that "you are the company that you keep." So, despite how grand the favor was that Sasha had done for her she wasn't going to allow it to impair her judgment when it came to the company she kept. However, she would speak to her about that later, because she knew that Sasha would eventually begin questioning her about the events that transpired after the police report that she filed.

"So how did—"

"Hey, have you seen my roommate Jade around today?"

Sequoia slyly switched the topic for fear that the conversation could lead down corridors that she'd never intended on traversing.

"As a matter of fact, I spoke to her about thirty minutes ago. She was headed to the dorms. Oh, and before I forget I wanted to personally congratulate you on your video. You were amazing! I always said that you were a natural. You should really pursue a career—"

"What the hell are you talking about, Sasha?" Sequoia was confused. "You're like the tenth person who has said something along those lines today and I don't have any idea what you're talking about."

"I'm talking about the video that you posted on YouTube."

"Video? I never posted a video on YouTube."

Before Sasha could respond, Sequoia's phone rang. "Hello," she answered quickly, holding up the traditional index finger asking Sasha to wait a minute.

"Hey girl, I saw you on YouTube doing your thing. I just wanted to tell you that you were looking good, and oh thanks for the cameo!" Desiree said enthusiastically.

"Desi, I'm going to have to call you back." Sequoia hung up before she had an opportunity to respond. "Let me see the clip." Sequoia nodded towards Sasha's laptop.

They found a nearby table to set up shop, and within a few short minutes Sequoia was viewing the online video footage of herself.

The YouTube video included various pictures, some of which she recognized taking several months ago, and more recent footage that included her and Desiree from her last visit to New York a little over a week ago.

The footage had been edited perfectly and contained ongoing vocals from her rendition of Beyoncé, which she performed for one person in a relatively personal and intimate setting: her dorm room.

The video was conservative and sexy, but too intimate for her liking—especially figuring that, until now, she had no clue that the video existed.

"You mean to tell me that you had nothing to do with this?" Sasha asked.

Sequoia shook her head.

"Wow! Well, do you have any idea of who it may've been?"

"Not a doubt," Sequoia said curtly.

"I don't think there's nothing to be upset about," Sasha said when she picked up on Sequoia's vibe. "Just this morning you had over two hundred thousand hits, but now look." She pointed at the screen.

"Four hundred seventy-three thousand and twelve!" Sequoia read off in surprise. "Is that for real?"

"You seem surprised."

"And you're not?"

"Hell no!" Sasha said seriously. "You're star quality, Sequoia. You look better than any super model I've ever seen. You have a body that Kim Kardashian would dream of, and you have the most amazing voice that I've ever heard in my life," she said. "I've actually always found it a pity that you would waste all of that talent on law school."

"Well, thank you, but this is more realistic," she said, referring to school.

"I hear you, but there are obviously a half a million viewers who strongly disagree with you. This video hasn't even been posted for a full seventy-two hours, so kudos to whoever it was that put this on YouTube."

Sequoia gathered her things and headed towards the nearest exit.

"Where are you going?" Sasha asked.

"To see the person who put that video on YouTube. I'll call you later," she said without halting her stride.

Once outside, Sequoia hung her head low to avoid eye contact with anyone. She didn't want to run the risk of being recognized again. Her unexpected fifteen minutes of fame was bringing all of the wrong attention.

That gave her an inkling of a glimpse into the life of someone who was really famous. She almost made it to the dorm room without being spotted, but a young male student—an economics major sporting a varsity jacket and crew cut—was sitting on the bench outside, seemingly awaiting her arrival.

"Sequoia, right?" He rose as she neared the entrance, offering her his hand. "The name's Ted Miller."

"Sorry Ted, but I'm in a rush. I can't talk right now." She ignored his hand.

"Wait!" he said. "I just wanted to give you this." He handed her a business card. "My father is an executive at Virgin Records. He's expecting a call from you at your earliest convenience."

"Your father?" Sequoia repeated in disbelief. "But why would he want to talk to me?"

"Don't be naïve Sequoia. We've both seen the video that you posted on YouTube. You have star potential, and my father wants to be the first of the many labels to offer you a deal."

"A deal?" she said in shock.

"You got it." He began to walk away. "Just call him."

Sequoia stared at the card for a moment, taking the man's advice under strong consideration. She wondered for a brief moment where this road could lead her. She figured that it wouldn't hurt to at least think about it.

When she entered the dorm room Jade was practically glued to her laptop, sitting on her bed.

"We need to talk," Sequoia said sternly as she slammed the door behind herself.

"I take it you've seen the site," Jade said casually, as if she'd been waiting for this conversation. She closed her laptop and rose to her feet.

"Yeah, I seen it," Sequoia said heatedly. "Me and nearly half a million people."

"Yeah, I know. I just got finished looking at it. Well, actually, I was just engaging in some Q and A with a few people about it on the Facebook page I made for you."

Jade laughed at the thought of it, but Sequoia didn't find it funny at all. "Jade, this isn't funny. You never asked me how I felt about you putting this video on the internet."

"That's because I knew you would say no."

"Well, why would—"

"I'm not finished," Jade said firmly, cutting her off and shocking Sequoia. "Look, you're either the most clueless person in the world, or you just don't believe in yourself, but you're good. And not any kind of good, but you may be one of the best dancers and singers that this world has to offer and you're doing nothing with it. And frankly, I'm tired of it.

"So I made an executive decision, and I know that you might be upset with me right now, but I can promise you that you'll be thanking me for this soon. So, just focus on keeping your vocals in order because you'll undoubtedly be getting some calls next week."

Sequoia was shocked that Jade had responded the way she did. She did it with such conviction that Sequoia felt that she no longer had a dog in the fight. Jade climbed back into her bed and continued typing on her laptop—as if Sequoia wasn't even standing there. *Well, I guess she told me,* Sequoia thought to herself after she picked her jaw up off the floor. She slowly strolled to her bed. She reached in her pocket and removed the card that Ted Miller had given her. Was this the first of what would be more cards and calls to come?

Oddly enough, the fact that Ted Miller had given her the card did support Jade's theory. However, that didn't mean that she suddenly had a desire to abandon her education for some pipe dream that probably didn't have two legs to stand on.

If Jade wanted to waste her time creating web pages and hanging out on YouTube all day then it was just fine by her. She intended to concentrate her efforts on something a little more down to earth, like going out to celebrate her latest good news. Whether Jade knew it or not, she would be riding shotgun.

"Okay Jade, I forgive you. Now get ready to leave. I'm taking you to celebrate."

CHAPTER 15

Manhattan, New York

8 am

Big Boy Records was located on the 11th floor of a downtown New York City skyscraper. The record label had sold over eighty million records to date, grossing the company over a billion dollars since its conception in the early '90s.

The company's success was due hugely in part to the tenacity of its C.E.O., T. Bibby. His vision for the record label, along with his ability to spot a star a mile away had made it possible for him to sign and produce some of the hottest rappers and rhythm and blues artists ever to grace the globe for over a decade and a half. It had also made him a fortune and helped open multiple doors in the business world, which he ingeniously used to expand his portfolio—adding fashion, acting, and a liquor brand, and many more expenditures to the fold.

As with any success, there were significantly low points, much like the rumors that had been circulating for over a decade that suggested he was a dictator who legally bound all of his clients to bogus contracts so he could steal millions of dollars from them. There were also the attempted first degree murder charges he faced in 2001 that nearly ended his career.

T. Bibby was no fool though. He capitalized on the tumultuous period in his life, and used the rumors and bad publicity to establish an ambiguous form of reputation, which ironically served as a catalyst to catapult his career to new heights never before imagined. Now he was worth nearly a half a billion dollars and could afford the luxury of tickling his funny bone and the expense of someone else's dignity.

This was obvious in the scene before him, which consisted of his office being filled with a camera crew and a group of obsequious contestants who were competing for an assistant position on his reality T.V. show.

He realized that he was single-handedly responsible for humiliating the small cast in front of the entire nation, but he strongly felt that the reward of working for him would be worth it in the end. He intended to make the show as amusing and entertaining for the viewers, and himself, as possible.

"Okay, this is what I want," he said from behind his glass desk, to the four remaining contestants. "Now, this will be the last assignment. Whoever does it first will win it all and will have a chance to work for me. Now, here's what I want you to do."

He handed each of them a paper with instructions on it. "My auntie made some peach cobbler for me yesterday, and for anyone who's been following my career, you know how much I love my auntie's peach cobbler. It's the best in the world. So don't even think of trying to switch with some bullshit at a bakery, because I'll know.

"Now, on each list I've given you are clues that are placed throughout the city and will lead you to my auntie's location. The first one to bring me the peach cobbler will have the assistant position. And to make matters even more interesting, I'll say this: I mentioned the location she's at in a 2006 *Source* magazine, in the April issue. The only thing is that the issue sold out."

"I remember that issue," one of the male contestants said. "Didn't you say that she stayed in a Brooklyn project?"

T. Bibby nodded with an ambiguous smile. "Now go. You've got eight hours."

Each of the contestants looked at each other in confusion over the daunting task they'd just be instructed to do. The apprehension slightly annoyed the mogul, so he figured they needed an extra push.

He looked at his watch. "You now have seven hours and fifty-eight minutes."

Upon being reminded of the looming time constraints, they all scurried to their feet and filed out of the door. They nearly knocked the company's A and R, Marvin Stone, over, knocking the open laptop he was carrying.

"Hey, y'all need to watch where y'all are going," he snarled angrily before moving slightly to allow the camera crew to pass.

"Please, tell me that they're gonna be finished shooting this reality TV shit soon."

"Next week," T. Bibby said.

"Good."

Marvin Stone was a 5'10", 265 pound man of a linebacker build. It was courtesy of his athletic career as a linebacker throughout high school that led to his athletic scholarship at LSU. He was dressed in a black Prada jogging outfit and Prada boots. His full beard was razor-lined, and his short afro was tapered.

He maneuvered around T. Bibby's desk and placed the laptop in front of him and stood over his shoulder.

"What's this?" T. Bibby asked curiously.

"Man, you gotta see this," he said energetically. "This, my friend, is the promotion and increase in salary I've been begging you for," he said surely. "This is the next international star."

He played the YouTube video of Sequoia for T. Bibby, periodically gazing from the screen to T. Bibby's face to study his reaction.

The video started off with a close-up of Sequoia as she exited the shower, bashfully batting away the camera. T. Bibby was so enthralled and floored by how strikingly beautiful she was that he was sold before he had an opportunity to hear her voice. The video's backdrop was immediately filled with some instrumentals from a hit single by a Beyoncé, which Sequoia's vocals began to play over the instrumentals. The video then showed Sequoia dancing freestyle hip hop.

Though T. Bibby did manage to notice how effortlessly she carried out her dance moves, he couldn't take his mind off of her well-sculpted figure. Watching the way she moved and gyrated her hips was giving him an erection, unlike any he'd ever received from anyone else, and that's the exact affect that he was sure she would have on the public.

T. Bibby managed to ignore her suggestive dance moves long enough to concentrate on her vocals and was amazed at how beautiful her voice was. She was hitting notes that would make Whitney Houston proud.

There were various other clips of her and a few of her friends, but T. Bibby hardly noticed. He couldn't bring himself to take his eyes off of her.

"Would you believe this chick is an undergraduate law student at Harvard right now?" Marvin Stone said.

Wow, beautiful and intelligent, T. Bibby thought. *She's definitely a winner!*

"So what do you think?" Marvin asked T. Bibby even though he already knew the answer.

T. Bibby paused a long while before responding. He kept his eyes fixed on the laptop screen in front of him before responding. "I think we need to find you a bigger office."

T. Bibby rose from his seat with a wide grin and embraced Marvin with a friendly pound and a hug.

"Look, I need you to get the jet gassed up, and have a Phantom awaiting our arrival when we land in Boston. We're gonna take a ride to Cambridge."

Marvin Stone looked at him as if he had a pound of shit on his tongue. "Nigga, you tripping. You better get one of your flunkies to do that shit. I just got a promotion."

He flipped T. Bibby his middle fingers before exiting the office. It was a privilege that he alone was able to do because of their friendship, which dated back to their childhood years.

T. Bibby ignored him and rushed to his phone to tell his assistant to get the car ready. He was going to Boston!

CHAPTER 16

Cambridge, MA

Harvard University

11:39 am

"Sir Issac Newton invented the theory of gravity when an apple fell from a tree and hit him in the head; a theory that Albert Einstein enhanced with his theory of relativity, which states that large bodies of mass generate and create gravity. Basically, the bigger the object, the more gravity it exerts. Who can give me an example of this?" Professor Steinberg asked from the front of the class.

Sequoia sighed irritably as she tried to avoid eye contact with the instructor by keeping her eyes trained on her writing pad. She knew that if she attempted to look in his direction, he would call on her like he always did.

"No one wants to volunteer?" He searched the sea of students for a hand. When he couldn't find one he volunteered someone else's services.

"Alrighty then," he paused. "Sequoia?"

Sequoia looked up from her writing pad, baffled. "Oh, I'm sorry, but I didn't have my hand up," she said curtly before fixing her eyes back onto her pad.

"I know, Miss Ariás, I was actually hoping that you could grace this classroom with your lovely voice and answer this question for us," he said, which made the entire classroom snicker.

Call me crazy, but it seems like he's flirting.

Sequoia was about to make a response, but upon noticing

that the entire classroom had directed their attention toward the doorway she also redirected her attention.

When she realized what all of the fuss was about she nearly fell out of her chair.

"Oh my GOD! It's T. BIBBY!" a female voice shouted as T. Bibby descended down the aisle with two massive body guards in tow.

Professor Steinberg smiled graciously. "Mr. T. Bibby, to what do we owe this privilege?" He closed the distance between them so they could shake hands.

"Actually, you have a student here who I would like to talk to. Uh, Sequoia Ariás?"

Professor Steinberg offered T. Bibby his famous smile before making a motion in Sequoia's direction. "There's the lovely Miss Ariás right there. Sequoia?" Professor Steinberg singled her out. "Mr. T. Bibby would like to speak with you for a moment. You're welcome to leave if you like."

Sequoia looked around nervously and noticed that everyone was staring at her supportively, as if they all knew what the meeting was about.

"Me?" Sequoia said, confused. "Why...? Why would he want to talk to me?" she uttered nervously as she apprehensively rose from her chair and gathered her things.

T. Bibby closed the distance between them both and began assisting her with her things. His cologne was intoxicating and she immediately took notice that he was donned in his own very popular clothing brand, Deshawn Juan. It was a two-tone gray on gray sweatshirt over a crisp pair of white Air Force Ones. He had a pair of designer sunglasses over his neatly trimmed goatee. His hair boasted some thick, neat waves over a Caesar style haircut that Sequoia had never seen. To say that she thought that he looked a lot better in person was an understatement.

He handed her the notepad to place into her shoulder bag. "I wanted to come down here personally to ask you if you were interested in a five million dollar recording contract that comes along with a million dollar advance."

The words nearly triggered a panic attack as soon as they'd left his mouth. Sequoia's breathing began to grow labored. She felt as if she would begin hyperventilating. Her palms were beginning to sweat, as did her forehead, but she managed to hold it all together long enough to take in the reaction of the classroom.

"Do it!" a female's voice yelled.

"Put it in writing," a male student added.

"So what do you think, Sequoia?" T. Bibby asked her, drawing the attention back on himself. "Could you see yourself signing with Big Boy Records?"

Sequoia smiled nervously as she considered her response. She looked to the crowd of students to gain some form of reassurance, and found plenty. She opened her mouth and uttered the first words that came to mind.

Hours later...

"You said what?" Desiree demanded to know as she stared at Sequoia on the laptop screen via Skype. Desiree was on a split screen with her mother, Rosa.

"I told him that I would think about it," Sequoia answered coyly.

"What's there to think about?" Desiree continued to badger her.

"Desi, calm down," Rosa told Desiree authoritatively, whom she considered just as much her daughter as Sequoia.

"But mama," Desiree pleaded with Rosa, "this is the opportunity of a lifetime. She may never get an opportunity like this again in her life. She'll be a star! Something she's always wanted to be."

"Correction," Rosa said. "She's always wanted to be a lawyer. Right, Sequoia?" Rosa said surely.

Sequoia began scratching her head and avoiding eye contact with her mother while dodging the question—something that seriously annoyed her.

"Right, Sequoia?" Rosa asked more sternly.

"Huh?"

"If you can 'huh' you can hear," Rosa said matter-of-factly.

Sequoia knew that her mother was about to be upset with her answer, but she blurted it out nonetheless.

"Well, I never really wanted to be an attorney, per se. I only wanted to do it because of the way the courts treated us after the divorce, not to mention the way the insurance company intended to treat you. I guess I just wanted to defend the underdog for a change. Maybe do some pro bono work from time to time."

Rosa was surprised, and it was visible on her expression. "Wow! Well, you sure fooled me," she said in a sarcastic manner.

"Mom? Could you just help me? Please?" Sequoia was looking for advice, not attitude.

"Help with what?" Desiree responded for Rosa. "This is such a no-brainer to me that I don't understand why we're having this discussion."

"What is she supposed to do, Desi? Just throw her education away to chase some fairy tale dream?" Rosa posed.

"Throw it away?" Desiree said incredulously. "Mom, if she accepts this deal, she'll have more money within a year's time then she would probably get in the next forty years as a lawyer. Think about it, mom. This is the whole purpose for going to school all these years, isn't it? To make money?"

"Excuse me, but if I may," Jade butting in standing over

Sequoia's shoulder. "I have to agree with Desiree on this one as well. Sequoia is great, and the fact that she's had over ten million views on YouTube suggests just that. In essence, she already has a fan base, and with a five million dollar contract it wouldn't be long before she got the exposure she needed to expand her fan base."

"And hello to you too, Jade," Rosa said.

Jade smiled. "Hi mom, how have you been feeling?"

"I'm doing a lot better Jade. They released me from the hospital yesterday."

"We'll be out there to see you shortly."

"I can't wait."

"Hey Jade," Desiree winked.

"Hey Desiree," Jade waved flirtatiously, which went unnoticed by Sequoia and Rosa.

"You know what, Sequoia?" Rosa said. "I know you usually consult with me before making and serious decisions, and that is something that I've always loved about you. But you're a grown woman now. You're on your own, and you're even helping to take care of me. So it's not about what I think. The decision is entirely up to you, and whatever you choose to do, I and your friends will support you."

"You got it," Jade said.

"You know I'm here for you," Desiree added.

"So what do *you* think, Sequoia? What do *you* think you should do?"

Sequoia pondered her response. "Honestly?"

"Yes, of course honestly," Rosa said.

"I want to do it," Sequoia admitted.

Jade rubbed Sequoia's shoulders encouragingly as Desiree grinned from ear to ear.

"Well, there's your answer. Just promise me you won't just walk away from your studies?" Rosa negotiated.

"You've got yourself a promise." Sequoia smiled.

"And make sure that I get backstage passes when you have your first sold out show," Rosa joked.

Everyone laughed in unison.

"Sure thing," Sequoia said.

CHAPTER 17

Manhattan, New York

"Sequoia?" Desiree whispered, with a sense of urgency in her tone.

Sequoia looked at her nervously, barely able to contain her trembling leg from bouncing. "Hm?"

"Could you at least try to relax? All of that twitching you're doing is making me nervous too," Desiree told her. "Just breathe. Everything is going to be fine. I promise."

They had been waiting patiently in the lobby area of the eleventh floor, down the hall from the office of Mr. T. Bibby himself. Just five minutes had elapsed since they'd entered the office and received instructions to wait briefly as T. Bibby finished wrapping up a meeting.

That was perfectly fine by Desiree, but Sequoia on the other hand was a completely different story. Her nerves were shot to shit. She tried to take some form of comfort in the ambience of what could potentially be her new employer's establishment.

The décor was very upscale and modern, and the phones had been ringing incessantly since the moment they'd set foot in the office—a key indicator to anyone with eyes and ears that business was booming. Her only fears now lay with the many rumors she'd heard about the underhand business dealings he'd allegedly been doing for years.

Rumor had it that T. Bibby was notorious for robbing his artists blind with bogus contracts and ditching them after he made off with their money. That was why Sequoia had taken all of the necessary precautions to ensure that she would not become a victim as well. Jade, along with the entertainment lawyer she'd hired, had agreed to help her with her feat. Jade opted to moonlight as the operating manager until further notice.

Jade sat stone-faced next to the entertainment lawyer, Phillip Snow. She was wearing a Calvin Klein two-piece, navy blue business suit next to Desiree and Sequoia. She hadn't said a word since she'd gotten there, which everyone understood to mean she was focused. Neither Sequoia nor Desiree wanted to distract her from her mode, so they both agreed to simply let her be. Jade completed her ensemble with a leather briefcase that was fitted with some miscellaneous papers.

"Mr. Bibby will see you now," the young black female clerical aide said as she hung up the phone.

"Go knock'em dead," Desiree told Sequoia. "I'll be out here waiting for you."

"She will," Phillip Snow said confidently flashing his winning smile. He was dressed in a gray Hugo Boss suit that complimented his olive skin and gray hair.

Sequoia smiled. "Show time Jade."

Before they could reach the door, they were nearly knocked over by security guards as they rushed into T. Bibby's office.

Five minutes earlier...

"But T. Bibby, I did manage to find the old magazine that you were talking about, and there wasn't an address in it. You only made reference about your aunt's place that you visited now and then," Sherell, one of the four finalists that were left, said.

The other remaining three finalists were nodding their heads in agreement.

Sherell continued, "You did, however, mention that it was a project in the Bronx. So, I went to the Bronx, but there were entirely too many projects for me to figure it out. I asked a lot of people if they knew where you grew up, and no one could give me an answer.

"So, I took the liberty of purchasing you three different peach cobblers from three different bakeries."

"You sure that the address isn't in that article?" T. Bibby asked, as if he was shocked by the news.

Sherell grabbed the magazine from her seat and flipped to the page that his article was on. She pointed to a section on the page that was highlighted.

"Q and A right there." Sherell pointed.

T. Bibby scanned the page briefly and concluded that she was telling the truth.

"Tell you what." He tossed the magazine in a nearby garbage can. "I think it's obvious that somebody made a mistake here. So, to refrain from pointing fingers and anyone in particular in this room, how about we all take some accountability for this?"

Everyone exchanged confused glances among themselves.

"So, with that said, I can only pick one of you, and considering that I can't draw any conclusions from the final competition, I'll just have to pick the person who I believe is best suited for the job." He paused for a millisecond. "Issa. You got the job. The rest of you can let yourselves out," he said curtly before grabbing the phone to place a call.

"Yes!" Issa, the Brazilian bombshell exclaimed excitedly. "Thank you! Thank you! Thank you!" she said energetically. "You won't regret this. I promise."

"This is some bullshit!" Sherell snapped as the other losers expressed their disdain with muffled complaints.

Sherell immediately deduced that Issa's victory had nothing to do with her ability to function in the capacity of a reliable assistant, and everything to do with her 38D-26-42 measurements. That was not only an insult to all of the embarrassment and humiliation that she'd suffered throughout the entire competition process, but it also undermined her work ethic and skills.

Knowing that her dark skin, short hair, and slightly overweight figure had everything to do with it only added insult to injury.

Surely T. Bibby never stated those feelings out of his mouth, but it was fairly easy at this point for Sherell to draw her own conclusion. Sherell dismissed any ounce of professionalism she once displayed. Now it was time to get angry.

"Oh hell naw!" she snapped. "How in the fuck is you gonna give this bitch the job over me? Over any one of us?" She motioned toward the black and white males behind her, while Issa rolled her eyes and scoffed.

"Send her in," T. Bibby said into the receiver before hanging up. "Hey Sherell, you really need to calm down with all that, yo."

"Fuck that!" she vehemently stated. "I've been calm throughout this whole fucking process. I was calm when I broke my heel on my stilettos doing that stupid ass obstacle course you had us doing. I was calm when those two pit bulls trying to get that dumb ass sweater of yours chased me. And I was calm when I was running around the God-damn projects trying to find your fucking aunt's famous fucking peach cobbler!

"And after all of that, you go and give the job to Issa?" she said incredulously. "She's never even completed one of the challenges that you've given us, let alone won any of them. So tell me, how could you have possibly picked her over us three?"

"Sherell, I don't have to explain myself to you. The contest is over. You lost, along with the rest of them." He pointed at the other two losers. "Now, please, leave my office. I have an important meeting to conduct. Oh, and leave the peach cobbler behind."

He picked up the phone and was about to attempt to place a call to his assistant so she could alert security to remove the three losers to his office, but before he could finish dialing her extension Sherell had come across the table and began choking him. Sherell's actions shocked everyone in the room.

The two male losers, along with a male member of the camera crew, tried to pull Sherell off of him, but breaking the alligator-like grip that she had on his neck proved to be futile.

Luckily for T. Bibby, his assistant was able to deduce that something was wrong by all of the commotion she overheard coming from the direction of his office, and alerted security to go provide some assistance.

When security arrived, the scene looked like a clip from old "Three Stooges" footage. The two burly security guards rushed over, and after a fierce struggle they managed to pry her off of him.

They dragged Sherell out of the room kicking and screaming as she yelled threats and obscenities.

"Don't let me catch yo ass on the streets, you shiesty mother fucker! Let me go!" She struggled to get loose. "You betta watch yo back!" she threatened.

"Get her outta here!" T. Bibby managed to say between hyperventilating. "All of y'all get the fuck outta my office! And leave the fucking peach cobbler behind!"

Everyone moved quickly to get out of his office, as if the school bell just rang and they were in grade school. No one offered T. Bibby so much as a goodbye.

Sequoia, Jade, and Phillip Snow walked into the tail end of the commotion as they neared the office. Sequoia and Jade poked their heads inside of the doorway.

"Uh, excuse me, Mr. T. Bibby, is this a bad time?" Sequoia asked as she stared at a distraught T. Bibby from behind his desk.

His entire demeanor changed instantly when he set eyes on Sequoia. "Uh, yeah. Everything is good." He rose from his chair and maneuvered around his desk so he could greet her properly.

He shook Sequoia's hand. "She's just upset because she lost the competition in the reality show we were filming."

"Wow!" Sequoia said. "Well, that was unprofessional."

"Very." Bibby extended his hand for Jade to shake. "And who is this?"

"How are you, Mr. T. Bibby? I'm Jade, her manager, and this is Phillip Snow, her entertainment lawyer," she said. Bibby shook Snow's hand as well.

After greeting them all graciously, he offered them a seat. He then contacted his lawyer and told him to get his ass over there within the next ten minutes or he'd be in the unemployment line by tomorrow.

"He'll be here shortly." He hung up the phone. "Until then, why don't you tell me a little bit more about yourself?"

Sequoia blushed and chuckled nervously. "Like what?"

"Are you nervous?" Bibby noticed a slight change in her demeanor.

"Kinda," she admitted.

"Don't be. It's all love up in here. I know a lot of people try to depict me in a negative light, but I'ma be completely honest with you: what you see is what you get with me. You be straight up with me and I'll be straight up with you."

"That's good to know." Sequoia felt herself loosening up. "Well, as you know, I'm an undergrad at Harvard, and I'm studying law."

"Of course, Harvard," Bibby said before sinking further into his leather seat. "That's a pretty prestigious school."

"Yes, it is." Sequoia picked up on his implications. "But I don't come from money, if that's what you're thinking. In fact, it's been pretty hard on my mom since my parents got divorced," she said. "But I managed to stay focused and worked hard, and was fortunate enough to earn myself a four year scholarship at Harvard as part of an exclusive national selection program.

"So, you're a genius?" Bibby speculated.

"That she is," Jade added her two cents.

"No, I'm not," Sequoia blushed, downplaying her academic achievements.

"Modest?" Bibby said. "I can feel that. It's an admirable trait." He reclined in his chair. "But I can tell you what: how 'bout we put off all of the personal stuff for a later time, and focus on why you're really here?"

Sequoia nodded. "Okay."

"So, what do you intend to accomplish over, say, the next five years?" he asked her.

The look on Sequoia's face clearly stated that she had put very little or no thought at all into the idea. "Five years? Um... wow. I never really thought about that as it pertains to a career in entertainment. I've had practically all of my attention focused on getting my law degree."

"Worked for me," Phillip Snow chimed, which drew a mild laugh.

"Well, how about I answer it for you?" Bibby interjected. "In five years you'll have been on every magazine cover, from the *Source* to *Rolling Stone*. You will have sold tens of millions of albums. You'll be a world renowned pop star and a household name, which will open the market for you to create a clothing line, fragrances, jewelry, modeling, and acting.

"Sequoia, what I'm saying is that the possibilities are endless, and I guarantee you, with respect to your academic achievements, that you'll never need to consider working for anyone ever again.

"I'm willing to bet the house on you, but you have to share at least a fraction of the passion that I have for this, or else it won't work."

"Oh, I can assure you, she's extremely passionate about the opportunity you're willing to give her," Jade said.

"Oh, yeah?" Bibby needed reassurance. "Convince me. No, tell you what: do me one better. Impress me," he said before sinking back into his chair.

Sequoia was confused. "What do you mean? Sing? Now?"

Bibby nodded. "Absolutely. You got the stage. Blow me away."

Sequoia rose from her seat and placed her purse inside of it. She was nervous, but not enough to let it distract her from showcasing her talent.

He pondered his response briefly. "How 'bout you do that song that you did on YouTube? The one by Beyoncé?"

Sequoia cleared her throat and proceeded with letting the tunes flow. The melody flowed from her vocal cords sensually.

Bibby was captivated within seconds of having the opportunity to have a first-hand experience of what type of talent he was about to fund. To say that he was impressed would be a serious understatement. He no longer needed confirmation.

Throughout his career, he'd had the wonderful and unforgettable privilege of discovering and producing some of hip hop and R and B's most iconic figures. If there was anything that he'd learned from working with such people, it was knowing how to spot talent, and the woman standing before him had all the makings of a mega pop star if she was marketed correctly. As fate would have it, marketing was his middle name.

Bibby suddenly realized that he'd heard enough. "Sequoia, you can stop right there. I don't need to hear anything else."

Sequoia complied, all the while trying to compute whether or not this was a good or a bad thing.

"That was absolutely amazing," Bibby said seriously, which instantly calmed her fears. "Mark my words," he said, eyeing her intently, "I'm gonna make you rich far beyond your wildest dreams."

Sequoia glanced at Jade, who was as excited as she was, and smiled eagerly.

"I was hoping we could've had this deal written in stone by now," Bibby said, glancing at his Rolex, "but it looks like I'm going to have to replace my lawyer with someone who can get here on time!"

Bibby reached for the phone, but seeing his office door burst open and his lawyer barging through recklessly made him release it.

"You're two minutes late," Bibby said simply.

His lawyer was panting heavily with a briefcase hanging from his clutch by a nub. His pants leg had a huge water stain on it as if he'd stepped in a puddle. His dark hair was wild and frayed, and his tie hung loosely around his collar.

"Sorry about that," Attorney Nicholas Schuman uttered through labored breaths, "but I got here as fast as I could. I would've made it here sooner, but I had to make an unexpected detour." He began fixing his tie. "Apparently it's illegal to run atop cars that are waiting for the light to change—which reminds me: if anyone asks, I've been with you guys all morning. Now just give me a second to get myself together over here and we can get started."

Within minutes the meeting had officially begun, and Phillip Snow, along with Jade, were given a single copy of the legally binding document to review. The three of them scanned its contents with a fine-tooth comb until they reached a unanimous decision that very little negotiation had to be done.

To everyone's surprise, Bibby was extremely generous when it came to his offer for Sequoia. The contract outlined the details of a two album deal. She would receive thirty-three percent of the gross sales profit per album sold, have full control over her masters with fifteen years, receive sixty-five percent of the revenue generated from live touring, executive control and ownership over her publishing and subsidiary rights, and she would have one hundred percent control over any movie deals or merchandise that may stem from her music career.

The deal was too good to be true, which usually meant that it was, yet nothing seemed out of place or underhanded. When Bibby asked if she needed more time to think about the deal, she quickly dismissed the notion and signed on the dotted line.

Attorney Schuman looked over the contracts before giving Bibby the thumbs up and giving Sequoia and Snow a copy of the contract.

Bibby rose from his chair and extended his hand to Sequoia. "Welcome to Big Boy Records."

"Thank you!" Sequoia accepted his hand with an appreciative grin.

Bibby then shook hands with Jade and Phillip Snow. "I'm looking forward to working with you."

Jade, Sequoia, and Snow exchanged handshakes with his attorney, Nicholas Schuman.

"I would offer you guys drinks," Bibby said, "but that would be solicitation of alcohol to an underage drinker."

"That's alright," Sequoia said. "We don't drink anyway."

"That's good," Bibby said. "It's a bad habit anyway. How about, for the sake of tradition, we pretend we have glasses so I can propose a toast?"

Everyone raised their imaginary glasses and Bibby said, "I would like to propose a toast to the industry's next iconic pop star, Sequoia Ariás!"

Everyone laughed as they pretended to clank their imaginary glasses with one another.

"So, do you have an idea of when my first studio session will be?" Sequoia asked.

"It's ironic that you asked that," Bibby said before looking at his watch. "If it's alright with you, I'd like to get into the studio as soon as possible, introduce you to a producer and songwriter who has some records that he feels will be a hit."

Sequoia was beaming. "When exactly are you talking about?"

Bibby smiled. "How about... twenty minutes?"

Sequoia swallowed hard. "Twenty minutes?"

"Absolutely," he said seriously. "That is, assuming that you don't have anything more important to do?"

Sequoia considered her answer momentarily before responding. "Nope. I'm free until five o'clock tonight."

"That's what's up. So let's get to it," Bibby said as he exchanged a lengthy gaze with Sequoia.

CHAPTER 18

Sequoia had placed her signature on the dotted line over an hour ago, setting in stone the dawn of a new age and turning a new page to a new chapter in the book that was her life. Not to mention that inking the deal had officially propelled her to a higher social class, sort of like winning the lottery.

Initially Sequoia felt as if she was floating on a cloud of pure bliss, but her enthusiasm quickly dissipated when she considered her fear of heights. She became overwhelmed by the thought of how dramatically her life was about to change.

Everything from the scrutiny of the paparazzi to performing in front of a packed stadium crossed her mind. She was trying like hell to suppress the thoughts, which were becoming more and more frightening by the second, but she still somehow found herself hiding in the company's washroom, trying to control an imminently mounting anxiety attack.

Jade and Desiree were right outside the stall door, pleading for Sequoia to let them in.

"Come on, Sequoia. Open up," Desiree said in a frustrated fashion.

"Remember to breathe," Jade added. "Just calm down and breathe."

Sequoia had her palms pressed against the stall walls with her waist bent at a forty-five degree angle over the toilet. She felt as if she was choking, and needed to hurl to clear her airways, but nothing was coming out.

Jade and Desiree's heads turned in the direction of the door when Bibby's female assistant poked her head inside. "Is she going to be alright?" she asked, concerned.

"Yeah," Desiree responded. "She just got overwhelmed by the news, that's all."

"I can't say that I blame her. That was a pretty hefty deal she just made," she said. "Just let me know if she needs anything. I'll be at my desk," she said before exiting the washroom.

Jade and Desiree directed their attention back toward the stall door. "Sequoia, do you need anything? The lady just offered to get it," Desiree said.

Sequoia remained silent.

"Sequoia, if this has anything to do with that imaginary champagne you drank, then don't worry about it. The real thing is probably better."

"Jade?" Desiree nudged her in the side.

"Ow!" Jade rubbed her side. "What?"

Both Jade and Desiree flinched when they heard the toilet flush, followed by a rustling of the stall's door knob. Sequoia emerged wearing a flushed look. The girls remained silent, but maintain their supportive edge.

Sequoia very quietly and calmly uttered, "I'm alright. I just got a little overwhelmed by it all."

"Well, did you take your medication this morning?" Desiree asked in a concerned tone.

Sequoia nodded. "I did, but sometimes it's not that affective," she said. "Really depends on the severity of the attack."

"Well, you need to get it under control, because this is only the beginning. You're about to be a celebrity! A mega pop star! Now, get your head in the game," Jade said.

"I'm dying to see who Bibby is about to introduce you to so you can make your first hit," Desiree exclaimed enthusiastically.

Sequoia forced a weak smile before leading the way out of the washroom. She walked right into a sea of concerned staff members at Big Boy Records, who were offering her everything shy of the earth itself. The feeling was exhilarating, but she was humble.

After declining everyone's generous offers, she, along with

Desiree and Jade, were led to the studio located on the fifth floor. It was an experience that she intended to absorb fully, and not taint with her mental health issues.

Bibby indicated that she would really look forward to working with the anonymous songwriter/producer she was scheduled to meet. She wanted to remain humble, but a huge part of her would be lying if she said that all of the hype wasn't piquing her interest—that, along with the idea of entering a state-of-the-art studio for the first time in her life.

Figuring that she had never been to one before, she really didn't know what to expect, but when she entered the room she somehow found herself in her element. It was as if she'd frequented the place in her former life.

She allowed her eyes to roam the $1.5 million dollar studio, taking in all of the expensive equipment and gadgets that it had to offer. All of the equipment in the world couldn't have prepared her for the person who was in the studio apparently awaiting her arrival.

"Oh my God!" Sequoia exclaimed nervously, attempting to conceal her coy smile with her hands.

"Is that who I think it is?" Desiree whispered.

Standing beside Bibby was the multi-platinum R and B artist, songwriter, and producer Neon. He had just released his sophomore album, "The Year of Chivalry," which was already climbing the charts. He currently had two smash hit singles that were on Billboard's Top 100.

Bibby introduced everyone. "I'm quite sure you all know this is R and B singer, Neon. He's one of the writers who is going to help you make your first hit single.

"Neon, this is Sequoia, who I was telling you about," Bibby said, "and these other lovely young ladies are her manager and friend, Jade and Desiree, I believe it is?"

"That's correct," Desiree said, "I'm Desiree." She shook both of their hands, while grinning from ear to ear. It was taking her every bit of restraint not to cream in her pants right there. She didn't want to come off like an obsequious groupie, so she said, "I just want to say that you two guys are amazing," before tucking herself away behind Sequoia and Jade.

Jade shook Neon's hand. "Pleasure to meet you, sir. I love your music."

"The pleasure is all mine, and thank you for the compliment," Neon responded cordially before taking Sequoia's hand and kissing it. "And let me just say that I'm really looking forward to working with you, and that no compliment that anyone has ever made on your behalf has done you any justice. You're a very beautiful woman."

"And I say that being both modest and as professional as I can be."

Sequoia blushed.

"With that said, why don't we sit down and discuss some ideas so I can get a mental picture of the sound we're trying to make, so the song can fit your personality and character. That cool with you?"

"Absolutely," Sequoia said, "and thanks, for the compliment."

"You're welcome."

"Well, I'll let you two exchange ideas for a bit while I go check on a few things. I'll be back shortly," Bibby said as he maneuvered around everyone in pursuit of the door. "If you need anything just tell him, and he'll contact my assistant." He pointed to the engineer, who sat behind the boards and PC, before exiting.

"So," Neon said, "If it's alright with you two, I need to steal her away from you for a little while."

Desiree and Jade both giggled bashfully.

Desiree responded, "Fine by us. We'll just find us a seat over there and stay out of your way." She pointed at the plush leather sofa.

Neon helped Sequoia into a leather recliner seat in front of the boards and pulled one up for himself. "So, Miss Sequoia, what kind of sound are you going for exactly?" he asked.

Sequoia pondered the thought briefly and shrugged. "I don't really know. To be completely honest with you, I didn't expect any of this," she leveled with him with deep sincerity. "All of this is new to me. I wasn't expecting any of this, especially today." She illustrated with her hands around the studio.

Neon contorted his features into a puzzled look. "So does that mean that you don't want any of this? I... I don't understand what you're saying."

"No," Sequoia patted his thigh platonically. "No, I'm not saying that. This is a dream come true for me. It's just...unexpected."

"Understandable. I remember when I first got signed. I must've undergone an out-of-body experience for nearly two weeks."

"Oh my God!" Sequoia exclaimed. "That's exactly how I feel."

He nodded his head. "Don't worry about it. It'll fade."

"I hope so," Sequoia said unsurely.

"Well, my advice to you is to accept your new role. Embrace it, and get focused on the work." Sequoia nodded. "Because this opportunity could easily be squandered if your head's not in the game."

"So the idea is to first decide the way that you want to be perceived. Like, are you trying to have a gimmick, or do you want to be received as a down-to-earth person whose music translates that type of persona to the world?"

"Wait. So you're about to write the song now?" Sequoia asked. "Because I was under the impression that you had some songs you wanted me to hear already."

"I do, and we will hear them at some point, but I figured since you was here it would probably be better to see if we could come up with something right now."

"Okay, so break it down to me one more time. What exactly is it that you need from me?" Sequoia said.

Neon paused briefly to consider a new approach. "Okay, think about it like this: when you think of an artist like Prince, you think of tight leather pants, silk, and polyester shirts, with high heel shoes. While an artist like Brian McKnight may prefer a simple suit and tie."

"Oh, I see what you mean," Sequoia said. "Well, in that case I'd like to keep it simple and stay true to myself. I don't know how well I'll be able to do portraying a role that's not me."

"Great answer," Neon said, "so in that case, who are you?"

"Excuse me?" Sequoia didn't quite understand his line of questioning.

"You say that you want to stay true to who you are and not, in essence, portray an image that isn't you. Well, I need you to tell me who you are. The real you. I need to understand who I'm writing for, so we can give the people the one person in the world that they're dying to meet.

"Like, have you ever been in love before? What struggles have you overcome, endured, or are currently going through? What are your beliefs, values, motivations? These are the things that people are concerned with. They want to be able to relate to you, to identify with you, and feel your pain.

"That's what the people can relate to. That's what the people want to hear from you, and that's what we're going to give them, but I'm going to need your help to do just that."

Sequoia understood what he was saying, and she wanted to be of some help to him, but there was something about divulging personal information about herself to a complete stranger, even if that stranger was Neon. It just didn't sit well with her, regardless of whether or not he was a multi-platinum selling artist.

"I can sense some trepidation on your end, which is understandable," Neon told her, "so let me say this: I'm not trying to psycho-analyze you, Sequoia. I just need to understand you, and who you are as a person. That's all. I'm afraid that if you can't do something as simple as confide something personal with me, then I'm not gonna be able to work with you."

"I'm sorry, I'm just having a hard time trusting you with my personal information like that."

Neon considered her reply for a moment. "I feel you," he said, "so how about we do it like this: I'll tell you something about me that I've never told anyone, and I may add that I have a lot more to lose at this point, so I'm practically taking a huge gamble with me career right now.

"But, I'll tell you something very personal that you can use a leverage over me in the event I betray you, but first you have to pinky swear that neither of us will rat each other out to the tabloids, or anybody else," he said with his pinky finger extended.

Sequoia laughed at the thought of making a pinky swear; something that she hadn't done since Desiree and she were kids. "Pinky swear." She interlocked her pinky with his.

"Okay," he said, "when I was in high school I was kinda confused about my sexual preference, so I did something that I'm not too proud of with a friend of mine. "

Sequoia didn't need to say a word, because her facial expression said it all. "Wow!"

"Okay, now it's your turn."

"Okay… Well, for starters, I'm multi-racial, but I was born in Costa Rica."

"So, what are you exactly? Because if I were to be completely honest with you, you're the most exotic, beautiful woman that I've ever met. No B.S."

"Anyway," she disregarded his comment, "I'm Costa Rican, Native American, Filipino, and Nicaraguan."

"Damn!" he said. "Well, I will say this. This mix makes for a perfect combination."

"Whatever." She rolled her eyes. "I came from Costa Rica when I was four with my parents. My father exported coffee and had strong political ties to the U.S., so we were able to gain dual citizenship pretty easily. My mother was a former beauty queen in the island.

"I've gotta admit that we were living a relatively privileged life. That was until my mother and I caught my father cheating in our home one day. And, when my mother became violent, and so did my father towards her.

"And though I was young," Sequoia wiped a tear from her eye, "I knew that it was wrong for a man to hit a woman, especially the way he was hitting her. So I came to her defense. I can't really remember clearly what happened detail for detail. All I know is that when I came back to I was holding a butcher's knife, and my father was sprawled out on the floor covered in blood."

Neon cringed. "Damn! Is he alive?" He began to understand why she didn't feel comfortable disclosing her personal business. "Yeah, physically," she said, "but he's pretty much dead to my mother and I." She paused and sighed hard. "My therapist blames my anxiety issues on the traumatic experience, so I take medication for that now. Is there anything else you want to know?"

Neon wasn't sure at that point that he wanted to know more, but he asked, "Have you ever been in love?"

"Love?" Sequoia frowned. "I was in love once. His name was Calvin Gold. He was a football jock and an honor roll student. He took my virginity," Sequoia said, not minding that she was confiding in Neon about her personal business. "We both had this fairy tale life planned out for ourselves, but things just don't work out like that in the real world.

"He was a senior, I was a sophomore, and I finally got the memo that we weren't such the hot item everyone mistook us for when he very casually opted to take his secret lover Becky Bluestreak to the prom instead of me." The pain in Sequoia's eyes said that she still hadn't fully gotten over the experience.

Neon nodded. "I think you've given me more than enough to work with."

"At the expense of these tears." She wiped her face and chuckled.

"You ever write a song before?" Neon asked.

"I have, but I don't have my notebook with—"

"Don't worry about that. We're going to start anew."

"'We're'?"

"Yeah, 'we're'," Neon said, as he grabbed two blank tablets and two ink pens from a nearby drawer. "I feel like you have a unique story to tell that the world will fall in love with. The only thing is, I won't be able to do it any justice without your help. So, you're going to help me write it."

"Me?" Sequoia was unsure.

"Yup," Neon said, "and I've got the perfect concept and beat."

CHAPTER 19

Bronx, New York

"Ma, you really need to sit down. You're supposed to be resting anyway," Sequoia said as she watched Rosa work her magic in the kitchen.

"No, what I need is for you to stop telling me what I need to do," Rosa said in a thick, Spanish accented form of English as she point the spatula she was using to mix the herbs and spices into the Spanish rice.

"I just don't want you overworking yourself, you know. The doctor said you should rest," she tried to reason with her.

Rosa placed her hand on her hip and shot Sequoia an annoyed stare. "Sequoia, I'm not bench-pressing a Mack truck, just cooking dinner. And in my book the timing couldn't be better," she said. "Besides, what does the doctor know anyway? According to him, I was supposed to be dead by now."

Sequoia sucked her teeth and stared at her with angst in her eyes. "Ma, don't talk like that."

"I'm just saying," she mumbled, "but never mind that. Tell me more about this deal you just signed!" she said with a surge of enthusiasm.

"Well, I—"

"Hold up," Rosa interrupted her before she could get started. "Let me get you some water. You look thirsty." She buried her head in the fridge before coming out with two bottled waters. "Figi or Dasani?"

"Mom—no. I'm not thirsty." Sequoia began messaging her temples.

"What about yogurt? You always loved your yogurt. And I got some really good flavors." She buried her head back inside the fridge.

Rosa was dressed in a violet Liz Claiborne blouse and tan Liz Claiborne pants with house shoes, and a colorful silk scarf wrapped around her head.

"Mom…no…what? I of course I don't want any yogurt… Have you forgotten that you're cooking?" Sequoia was growing more and more irritated with the way everyone had been acting with her of late. It was almost as if the deal she had just signed was making everyone around her crazy.

"Mom? Mom? Could you please come over here and sit down with me for a moment?"

Rosa ditched the yogurt she was holding back into the fridge and bolted to Sequoia's side. "What's wrong baby? You're not ill, are you?" She began patting Sequoia's forehead, checking to see if she had a fever. "Oh, God! Please tell me you're not sick." Rosa began to panic.

"Sick?" Sequoia managed to pry her hands off of her long enough to get a word in. "No, I'm not sick. I just want to talk to you."

"Oh, okay." Rosa apprehensively sat in the chair. "Que pasa?"

Sequoia sighed as she pondered the approach she should take. She didn't want to offend her mother. "Look, I just watched you go through one of the most difficult times in the both of our lives. I could've lost you." Both Rosa and Sequoia's eyes began to develop tears.

"And now we've been blessed with an opportunity to not only spend more time together with each other, but for you to also live to see me get the opportunity to live out my dream. And yes, our way of living is about to change dramatically." She chuckled while wiping away her tears. "But I've watched you sacrifice your entire way of living to ensure that I can be successful. And it's happened. So now what I want you to do is kick back and let me take care of you— starting with a new place." They both laughed.

"Just give me some time to manage my money correctly.

Because the last thing I want to do is dig myself into a hole before I've ever produced a hit."

"Smart girl," Rosa said before rising to give Sequoia a hug. "I know you're going to overachieve at whatever you do." Sequoia wanted to savor the moment for all eternity, but a thick plume of smoke rising from the pan of Spanish rice served as a bit of a distraction.

"Uh, mom. Mom?"

"Yes baby?" Rosa responded with a huge smile on her face.

"The food's on fire," Sequoia said plainly.

"What?" Rosa said, releasing her loving grasp on Sequoia before rushing to the disaster on the stove. Seconds later the smoke detector was blaring its annoying alarm, so Sequoia assisted her mother by fanning it clear of smoke.

When they both managed to contain the inferno, the food had already been burnt beyond recognition—leaving Sequoia with only one option.

"You know what," she said, "how about I take a rain check on this meal for a later date? How about we go out and get something a little less... crispy?" she chuckled. "My treat."

Rosa sighed and nodded meekly. "Sounds like a good idea," she said. "It definitely trumps my poor excuse of a Cajun dish anyway."

They both laughed.

CHAPTER 20

The dress was a vintage Vera Wang piece with matching three inch leather heels that were accessorized with a tassel on the back. It was a piece from Vera Wang's exclusive collection. It was a one strap, lavender colored satin, leather and polyester piece that would easily set a consumer back a lot of money. The shoes were open-toed and leather with a lavender hue as well. It was a gift from Bibby to her, complete with a hairstylist, make-up artist, and a nail technician. There was also an appointment at the Bath and Body Works Spa at 2 pm.

Sequoia received the package from Bibby's new assistant, Issa, on her way to the studio, which was a shock to her considering how pricey the items were. It was certainly nothing she intended to turn a blind eye to. She'd never been a huge fan of selective treatment, especially when she was on the receiving end and the giver was her boss.

The gesture made it hard to resist entertaining certain questions that were now in her head, questions about Bibby's true intentions, because in her book—boss or not—he was still a man, and that was all the reason that she needed to feel suspicious.

However, she was able to breathe a lot easier when she discovered what the dress was for: he wanted her to accompany him to a promotional party for new liquor that he recently signed an endorsement deal for Siróc.

Apparently, he felt that her attendance would not only give her an opportunity to gain some form of notoriety and exposure, but that it would also give her a chance to rub elbows with the elite of the entertainment business. It was a chance to get her feet wet, so to speak (in his words).

In the end, she welcomed the experience with an open mind and totally looked forward to gaining some form of popularity with what Bibby dubbed to be the "in" crowd. Because she was smart enough to know that the entertainment industry was ten percent talent and ninety percent politics, and to succeed she would have to administer her own line of diplomacy. That wouldn't be too hard for her, considering how diplomatic she felt at the moment.

If Sequoia thought that the ensemble and spa meant something, then she wasn't remotely prepared for all of the stops that Bubby had pulled out for the night. Bibby spared no expense. Sequoia had heard plenty of rumors in the past about the wild parties Bibby were known for throwing, and now she was about to experience it first-hand.

Sequoia agreed to carpool in his ivory white Maybach to the event. Bibby was sporting an all white Armani tuxedo trimmed in black with matching leather shoes. His Caesar-styled haircut boasted a deep three hundred sixty degree wave pattern. His Frank Mueller watch complimented his shiny gold cufflinks.

They arrived promptly to the event, with an ogling crowd of on-lookers. Everyone in the crowd had their eyes fixed on the luxury sedan. The car was practically sound-proof, so neither Sequoia no Bibby could overhear the crowd announcing Bibby's arrival to the entertainment mogul.

"You nervous?" Bibby asked Sequoia when he noticed her leg bouncing incessantly.

"Hmm?" Sequoia came out of her temporary daze. She finally noticed her own leg bouncing for the first time. "Kinda," she smiled nervously.

Bibby touched her hand sensually. "Don't be. I'ma take good care of you."

He reached into his tuxedo pocket and pulled out an elongated jewelry case. "I got this for you."

Sequoia reluctantly accepted it. "What's this?" she said with mixed emotions. She opened the case to find a twenty carat diamond necklace. She stared him down skeptically. "What is this? I mean really? First, you get me this expensive dress and shoes, then you tell me that you want me to attend this function with you, and now you're giving me this necklace. What's really going on here? Huh? What are you up to?" she asked, wearing a suspecting look.

"Correction," he said, before pulling out a smaller case from another pocket. "Necklace and earrings to match." He smiled as he handed them over.

Sequoia ignored the gesture completely and allowed the earring case to remain in his hand, but she never broke eye contact. She wanted answers, and she wanted them now.

"I'm sorry, but I can't accept this. I don't feel comfortable taking expensive gifts from any man, let alone my boss," she said seriously. "It makes me feel as if you're trying to buy me."

Bibby sighed hard and shook his head. "Ma, you're reading this situation all wrong, and to be completely honest, it's admirable. It lets me know that you have integrity, and that you won't let anyone take advantage of you," he said sincerely. "Keep that attitude when dealing with these niggas in this game, because the minute they set their eyes on you they're going to be all over you.

"But when it comes to me, you don't have to have your guard up. We're both on the same team, and whether you like it or not, I'm a representation of you just as you're a representation of me.

"Now, we're about to walk into a room filled with billionaires and millionaires and press, and you have on a Vera Wang gown and shoes, but no bling. I know this may sound a bit grandiose, but that raises eyebrows with these fools. They want to see the complete package in you, and that's what I intend to give them. So please, put this on, and let's go in there and kill it."

Hearing Bibby's explanation made a lot more sense to her, so she caved to the request.

Bibby assisted her with her necklace and watched her with captivated eyes as she put her earrings on.

"Damn, ma, you bad as shit!" he said seriously. "You ain't got shit to feel nervous about. Leave that to all these other chicks in the game for when they see you. Besides, this is my city, and I have you under my wing, so you know I gots you."

Sequoia nodded.

"Now let's get in here and make you famous."

Though she always attracted a lot of it, Sequoia had never been a fond ally of attention, so navigating a sea of paparazzi and answering the most insignificant questions they could think of was going to take some getting used to. Besides, who really cared what she thought about a man's tie?

She'd like to say that she was thankful to disappear off of the red carpet and into the crowd inside the event, but after taking in the room filled with celebrities her stomach began to fill with butterflies. It didn't help that everyone in attendance suddenly began to stare at her.

Safe to say, Bibby was right, so after replaying the conversation that she had with Bibby she gained a bolt of confidence. She had absolutely nothing to be nervous about. She was a very beautiful woman with the voice of an angel, not to mention that she had just signed a five million dollar deal with one of the hottest and most dominant labels in the game. She was also practically killing the Vera Wang dress that she was wearing, and her long, curly hair had been pressed straight down her back, barely licking at her plush backside. Her hair was pulled behind her ears so the diamond earrings Bibby had bought her could get their time to shine.

She agreed if anyone needed to be nervous, it was them.

On the strength of Bibby's popularity and fame, Sequoia was receiving a lot of attention and stares. She silently marveled to herself over it all, basking in the moment. Though Sequoia's confidence was through the roof, she remained silent and observant. She was paying close attention to the eye movements, hand gestures, and jargon of the elite. They all suddenly seemed to be focusing around the idea of her presence.

Being introduced to the many people that she'd either looked up to or admired on the screen was slightly unnerving, and in some cases downright frightening, but Sequoia took pride in her privilege from drawing strength from her newly appointed mentor. His reputation was second to none and he always maintained his confident edge.

Some would say that he carried himself in an arrogant manner, and that he was extremely cocky, but Sequoia saw it differently. She saw him as a man who had grown into the role he had created for himself, and he finally understood the power that he held. He literally conducted himself as if he owed the city, and to a huge degree Sequoia found that characteristic admirable and certainly demanding of respect.

Bibby introduced her to many different men and women alike, all of whom were success stories in their respective careers. Some she recognized right off the bat, others not so much so, but all were equally important and pivotal to her establishing a more efficient and solid networking system.

She met filmmakers, business executives, movie stars, and entertainers, all of whom expressed a strong desire to work with her in some way in the future—and the night was still young.

A tuxedo-sporting maitre d' carried a silver platter filled with hors d'oeuvres and expensive champagne as smooth R and B filled the backdrop from a live D.J.

Sequoia remained close by Bibby's side since they arrived at the event, so when Bibby saw one of the largest producers in the game (and a popular New York multiplatinum artist), he hurried to introduce them.

"Sequoia, I want to introduce you to a few close friends of mine, so just stay close."

Sequoia nodded while secretly blushing as they neared the two entertainers—both of whom Sequoia knew all too well.

"Fellas, fellas," Bibby greeted them both with a warm embrace. "Thanks for coming out to support the event."

"Cut it out," producer Dr. J. said, waving Bibby off. "You know we gonna follow you to the end of the earth whenever you throw a party."

"Yeah," Famous said, dressed in an all black tux with dark shades and diamond earrings the size of cantaloupes. "You sho' know how to get it cracking, and this Siróc is pretty decent too," he said before taking a sip from a medium sized glass. He eyed Sequoia seductively. "She with you?"

"Yeah, this is my new artist. She's about to kill the game! So, my advice to y'all is to make an appointment, and get ready to put some working hours in with her, 'cause shorty's the truth!"

"Oh yeah?" Dr. J. said, becoming more interested in her.

"That's what's up."

"She got a name?" Famous asked, as he continued to nurse his drink.

"Absolutely, but we can credit my mother for that," Sequoia said in one of the sexiest octaves that they'd ever heard. "I'm Sequoia." She shook both of their hands.

"Wow," Dr. J. shot Bibby an approving look, "beautiful and a sense of humor! Well, Miss Sequoia, I'm looking forward to working with you," he said sincerely. "If you're even half as good as Bibby says you are, then you're going to be an absolute success."

"Oh, I am," Sequoia said confidently, "and I appreciate what you said—that means the world to me coming from you."

"Hey, aren't you that girl that has the rendition of Beyoncé on YouTube?" Famous asked.

"The one and only," Sequoia said.

"Yeah, she's super dope," Famous said seriously. "You got my vote, ma. Whenever you're ready, I'm in. T. Bibby knows exactly how to reach me."

"She's like that?" Dr. J. asked in an investigative tone.

"The truth!" was all Famous said.

"I'm feeling that," Dr. J. said. "The name, the look—the look is crazy! You on some straight exotic shit; hands down ain't none of these females touching you on the look. You shouldn't have no problem taking over the game, and I'll be honored to be one of the people who've helped you climb to the top."

"Thank you! Thank you both!" Sequoia was so ecstatic she was on the verge of tears. "That means so much to me coming from you both."

Everyone's train of thought was broken when an Italian, balding man with an expensive tuxedo and a five o'clock shadow whispered something in Bibby's ear.

Bibby nodded and turned his attention back towards them. "They need me over there for a minute. Sequoia, are you going to be alright over here until I get back?"

"Don't worry, dog, she's in good hands," Dr. J. said.

Sequoia nodded. "Yeah, I'm good."

"Alright, I'll be back in a minute," he said before vanishing into a crowd of people.

Moments later, T. Bibby's voice boomed over the floor speakers. "Everybody! Let me get your attention for a moment please!" he said, which silenced the room and gained everyone's attention. "First, I want to thank you all for supporting my new drink, Siróc! It means a lot to me, and I also want to take this opportunity to introduce my newest artist to Big Boy Records: Sequoia Ariás! Sequoia, could you please come up here for a second?"

"What is he doing?" Sequoia said, embarrassed.

"Don't be shy," Famous said. "This is all part of building your brand."

"He could've at least have given me a heads up," she said before making her way towards him.

When Sequoia neared his side, he continued. "Now, I just want all of you to get a good look at her, because she is the future for pop and R and B music! She is officially the baddest chick in the game, and within a year's time the entire world is going to know her! So let's give her a round of applause!"

Everyone joined Bibby on the applause. Some members of the audience could even be heard whistling extremely loud. The moment was surreal to Sequoia, as if she'd won Miss Universe. Though the unexpected attention was all welcome, it was unfortunately short lived when she set her sights on a man whom she thought she'd never be in a room with again in her life: Fat John!

"I'm sorry, T. Bibby, but I gotta go." Sequoia rushed her way through the crowd in pursuit of the exit doors, leaving behind a confused crowd.

CHAPTER 21

Sequoia hadn't spoken much to T. Bibby about her abrupt departure from his promotional function a few night ago, even though he pressed her to know what was going on. She avoided him as much as she could, but the time was steadily approaching in which their paths would collide. However, she didn't intend to face that music until she absolutely had to, and not a minute sooner.

He had been very patient with her, this she knew, but his patience has obviously been running thin. The incessant texts and phone calls that she'd been receiving from him over the past few days was a testament to that fact.

Still, Sequoia avoided all of his calls regardless, opting to bury herself right under his nose in a place she was certain her would never check.

"That was amazing, Sequoia," Neon said into Sequoia's headphones from the producer's board.

She had just completed the first song of her recording career, a song that she co-wrote with Neon over music that he produced and sung with her angelic voice.

Sequoia was smiling from ear to ear. "Thank you so much, Neon."

"Don't thank me, girl! You killed it!" Neon said.

"Oh, did she?" T. Bibby said from over Neon's shoulder. Neon had been so caught up in the moment that he had failed to see him enter the room.

Bibby was dressed in a tight fitting black Gucci shirt that was tucked into his black Gucci pants, showing off his Gucci belt and black Gucci tennis shoes. His waves were complimented with sharp razor lines.

"Oh snapped. What's up my dude?" Neon gave Bibby a pound

from his seat.

Neon was freshly clean-shaven on his bald head. He was sporting a tight fitting white Locaste polo shirt and tan Locaste khaki pants, and white Air Force One gym shoes.

Sequoia tried to avoid the firm stare that Bibby was giving her through the glass partition in the recording booth, but they managed to lock eyes.

"What are y'all working on?" Bibby asked, keeping his gaze fixed on Sequoia.

"Yo!" Neon exclaimed with animated emotion. "She just killed it! Your girl just laid her vocals down to the song we co-wrote and it's a straight hit!" he said seriously. "I still can't believe what I just heard."

"Word?" Bibby said.

"Definitely."

"Alright then, play it back for me."

Neon sprang into action, fiddling with the mouse on the computer and stabbing the keys. "I haven't had a chance to clean it up, but here's what we got so far."

The song started with a click of the mouse, and not soon after Neon and Bibby began to bob their heads to the rhythmic tune. The beat was a mixture of heavy percussions, drums, and a compilation of melodic tunes from wind instruments.

Bibby was impressed—the mile-wide grin he was wearing testified to just that. When the song was complete, Bibby nodded his head approvingly.

"That shit was hot!" he exclaimed. "Do whatever it is you need to do with this by tomorrow. I want the world to hear this immediately," he said with a sense of urgency in his voice.

"I got you," Neon told him. "I just want to go over a few things with her first, get some more vocals, maybe some ad-libs."

"Alright, give me a minute with her first." Bibby pressed a button on the board that allowed him to speak with Sequoia into her headphones. "Sequoia, I need to talk to you for a minute. I'll be in my office."

Sequoia nodded before reluctantly placing the headphones she was wearing around the microphone.

She took the elevator to his office floor and went to his office. She helped herself to a seat.

"First, I would like to say congratulations on your first song. I think it's hot, it's a hit, and I'ma do everything in my power to make sure it lands at number one on the Billboard charts. Also, you look very beautiful today."

Sequoia was donned in Michael Kors ensemble: a long sleeved button up white shirt with dark blue jeans, and Marc Jacobs pumps. She also had on red frame Michael Kors eyeglasses and red lipstick. Her long, curly hair was cascading over her shoulders.

"Thank you!" she said.

"But," he paused, "I want to know what's going on with you. First, you run out on me a few days ago. Then, you won't return or accept any of my calls, and that's something that never happens to me. So what's up?"

Sequoia shrugged. "I'm sorry, really, I am, but it's complicated."

Bibby sighed in frustration. "Sequoia, I'm about to say something and I want you take it at face value." He paused as if he were waiting for a response.

Sequoia picked up on the hint and nodded. "Umm hmm."

"When I told you that you were under my wing, I meant that I'm not going to let no one do anything to you. I'm not going to take advantage of you. But I need to know who I'm dealing with, and the more that I'm around you, the more it seems as if you've got a lot more going on then you're letting on."

"And what does that mean?" Sequoia felt kind of wary about

his choice of words.

"Look, I'm not trying to offend you, but you running out on an event while I'm trying to introduce you to the people that matter is both offensive to me and suspicious in nature to that entire room."

"So, in between me placing a million unanswered calls to your phone, I've spent the bulk of my past few days doing damage control on your behalf."

"I'm sorry," Sequoia said sincerely. "You have to believe that I would never do anything that could potentially damage your investment in me."

"And I believe you," he said genuinely, "but we both know that it wasn't stage fright or nervousness that made you bail like that. Either way, it doesn't matter. All I'm trying to get you to see is that I'm here for you. If it was somebody in there that you may've had a problem with, just let me know and I'll deal with it," he said seriously.

Sequoia had no idea what Bibby meant when he said he'd "deal with it," but she found the statement a bit unnerving. The underlying implication behind the phrase sounded more like a classic line out of a mob movie she'd seen before. It was certainly not something that she would want to hear from someone like Bibby. Until now, she always pegged him as a successful, college-educated business man, not some industry underworld mob boss with a Suge Knight persona.

In any event, the classic line, the supportive monologue, nor the neatly Caesar styled hair were enough to make her compromise the confidentiality clause the encompassed the contract she signed. However, she knew that Bibby wasn't going to drop this topic anytime soon, so she figured that the best thing she could do for now was buy herself some more time.

"Look, I know you have a lot of unanswered questions that you really want to get to the bottom of, and I intend to answer all of them... eventually," she paused, "but can you please just suppress the third degree until later."

Bibby nodded reluctantly. "Alright, but I'ma need you to be

honest with me from now on. Deal?"

Sequoia nodded violently. "Absolutely."

"Okay," he said. "Now, turns out that your little exit yesterday created a serious buzz among the right crowd. There's some people that think what happened last night was a publicity stunt, and that's cool, because they're talking. Everyone thinks you're an exotic mystery now. Taboo even.

"So, I'm gonna call in a few favors to get some of the hottest producers and writers in the game to work with you, because we need to ride this wave of speculation all the way to the top—starting with that new single you just finished."

"Sounds good to me!" Sequoia was enthused.

"Good, because we're going to try to set a date to do a shoot and figure out a budget. Do you have any concepts or locations in mind?" he asked her.

Sequoia pondered for a moment before responding. "How about Costa Rica?"

Bibby thought briefly. "I like that. That's a great idea. Let me make a couple of calls to see if we can get a few permits. We'll probably need to narrow down a few locations so we can know what we need permits for, but I like it."

"So, is that it? I mean, what do we do next?"

"What do we do next?" he repeated as if he didn't understand her. "We do everything. ITunes, talk shows, radio stations, interviews, magazines, and if you're comfortable with it: modeling and layouts."

Sequoia giggled in disbelief. "Wow!"

"What... What's wrong?" he asked, concerned.

"Nothing! Nothing. It's just... everything is happening so fast."

"Well, you better put a seat belt on, because it's not going to let up anytime soon. In fact, this is only the beginning. You see," he rose from his seat with sincere passion in his tone, and sat in front of her on his desk, "I intend to make you the biggest star since the late king of pop, but you have to be able to function in that role to its full capacity. That means no more running out on promotional events and no more keeping secrets that could damage our business relationship. Like I told you before, I want you to win, but I'ma need you to be one hunnit with me if we're going to do that.

"So here's what we're going to do first. After Neon is finished with the production on the track you just did, I'm going to send it to my girl who's a top forty choreographer and see what we can come up with.

"So let me make these calls and see what I can come up with. You can go back to the studio if you like," he said, before maneuvering back around his desk to claim his chair and wrapping his hand around the phone handle.

Sequoia rose from her chair. "Okay then. I'll be in the studio if you need me." She neared the door. "And I just want to say thank you for giving me this opportunity, and thank you for believing in me!"

"Don't mention it, girl. You're a talented, beautiful woman, and you deserve it. Just do me a favor?" he paused.

"What's that?"

"Turn your damn phone on." She smiled.

Sequoia chuckled. "I can do that," she said before closing the door behind her.

CHAPTER 22

Sequoia and Rosa gazed in satisfaction at the two story apartment in brick in Upper East Manhattan.

"Nice, isn't it?" Sequoia asked Rosa.

Rosa covered her mouth with her hand in an attempt to suppress her muffled cries of joy. "Mm hmm," she nodded.

"Great! And wait until you see the inside," Sequoia said ardently.

"Excuse us, miss," an oversized black man said as he and his partner carefully navigated up the steps past Sequoia and Rosa with Rosa's new, exclusively hand-picked furniture.

"Oh, excuse me." Sequoia made room for them to pass.

"Do you have anywhere in particular that you'd like us to put this?" the other mover, who was slightly smaller than his coworker and of European descent, asked.

"Yes, please," Sequoia said as the men carefully mounted the stairs with the couch. "Can you put it in the living room, facing this window right here that's overlooking this street? Thank you."

"Sure thing," he said before they vanished into the doorway.

"Oh my God, Sequoia," Rosa said as she wrapped her arms around Sequoia's neck. "Thank you so much."

"Don't mention it," Sequoia struggled to say, considering the vise-like grip Rosa had around her windpipe.

Once Rosa realized what she was doing she released her. "Oh, sorry!" She smoothed Sequoia's silk designer blouse out with the palms of her hands.

"Don't worry about it," Sequoia told her. "C'mon, let's go take a look inside."

When Rosa and Sequoia made it inside, the movers assured them that they would be finished within the next fifteen minutes. That was good news to Sequoia because she was beginning to grow uncomfortable with all of the ogling the two men were doing at her and her mother.

Nevertheless, Sequoia made good use of the time and began to give Rosa a tour of the place. The apartment was modern and opulent in nature. Everything, from the oak wood floor to the stainless steel appliances, reeked of lavish taste. The master bedroom had an elegant bathroom with a huge whirlpool Jacuzzi tub that could easily fit four people and a walk in shower with a glass door, stainless steel knobs and an overhead faucet. A gourmet kitchen had stainless steel Kenmore appliances, granite counter- and tabletops, and marble floors. There was also a walk in closet, a huge master bedroom, and a guest room.

Needless to say, Rosa was happy. Her daughter's altruistic deeds had provided her with all her medical expenses paid in full, lots of love and support, and now a new apartment in an upscale community, all without her having to pay so much as the garbage bill. She felt that she was truly blessed.

"This place is absolutely wonderful." Rosa's eyes welled up. "I'm so happy…and thankful…and proud!" She wiped her eyes.

"Aww!" Sequoia began to cry as well. "Could you please stop crying, mom? You're making me cry too." She chuckled.

"I'm sorry," she giggled, "it's just… I am so proud of you, and I am honored to have given birth to you." They both embraced.

"Don't worry about it, madre. You just kick your heels back from now on and let me take care of you."

Rosa shook her head in disbelief. "How did I get so lucky?" she said rhetorically. "Have you even bought yourself anything yet?"

Sequoia pondered it and shrugged. "Some green tea."

"You're too much!" Rosa laughed. "I'm actually surprised that you found time in your busy schedule to find this place, with all that's been going on lately."

"Oh, I didn't have time," Sequoia assured her. "I had a realtor do it for me."

"Well, excuse me," Rosa said jokingly with her strong Spanish accent.

"Cut it out," Sequoia laughed. "It's just one of the perks of being a newly signed artist."

"But what about you?" Rosa asked. "Have you begun looking for another place to stay yet?"

"No, I figure that my dorm room will do until I finish this year out."

"Are you serious?" Rosa seemed concerned. "Sequoia, you have to understand your new status. You can't just be laying around a campus or in an apartment building thinking that by downplaying your new found wealth and career that people won't know who you are. It's dangerous!

"I think you may need to invest in a place to stay, a place with security, so you can rest comfortably at night. You may also want to consider taking off of school for awhile, until you're more established in your career."

"Wow!" Sequoia exclaimed in a surprised tone. "I never thought I'd live to see the day where you'd encourage me to not go to school."

"Sequoia, I'm not saying that," Rosa corrected her. "All I'm saying is you have to be honest with yourself. Your new career is about to get extremely demanding very soon, and I think that you may need to be prepared for the transition.

Sequoia nodded. "I know what you mean, and I have been thinking about it. I just don't want to put all of my eggs in one basket and later realize that I don't have anything to fall back on."

Rosa placed her palms on the kitchen counter. "I think you're going at this with the wrong attitude. When I think back to as far as I can remember, I see the little girl who used to dress up in my make-up and heels and sing song after song into my curling irons."

Sequoia covered her face with her hands in a childish fashion. "Oh my God. You saw me."

Rosa rolled her eyes. "More times that I like to remember."

"Why didn't you say anything?"

"And stop you in the middle of one of Selena's hit songs? Are you crazy? I love her music!"

They both laughed.

"But even then I knew where your true passion and heart lay. Although I wanted to be more supportive of your talents, I had to be realistic when it came to the odds of you getting a record deal. I wanted you to have a career that would be obtainable because of the degrees you have, but now everything is different. You've made it. You've been given the perfect opportunity to do exactly what you've always dreamed of. So just focus on it. Give it your all and have fun doing it. "

Sequoia remained silent as she listened to the words of wisdom that her mother gave her. She didn't protest one bit. Rosa was right. She was looking at the entire experience all wrong. She had dream of this, prayed for it silently for years now, and now her time had come. In no way did she intend to blow it.

Sequoia's cell phone vibrating in her True Religion jeans distracted her from responding. She checked it and saw that it was from T. Bibby, saying that she needed to get to the studio A.S.A.P.

"My boss," Sequoia joked, holding up her phone, "says he wants me in the studio."

"T. Bibby?" Rosa asked. "What is he like, by the way?"

"Very cool, overprotective, slightly narcissistic, but overall pretty down to earth and easy to get along with," Sequoia told her. "But enough about him. When's your next appointment?"

"Tomorrow, actually."

"And how have you been feeling lately?"

"I feel like a new woman, thank you!" she said gleefully.

"Good. I'm coming with you tomorrow, so be ready for me to pick you up tomorrow morning. Okay?"

"Alright."

"Good. Now let's get these guys out of here so I can leave."

CHAPTER 23

Three weeks later

Manhattan, New York

"So, have you found a place to stay yet?" Desiree asked Sequoia from the backseat of the company-provided S.U.V.

"No, I've been thinking about putting it off until I finish the semester," Sequoia said while gazing at the pedestrians strolling New York's inner city streets.

"That's a terrible idea," Jade offered, sitting to Sequoia's immediate right.

"What's wrong with everybody?" Sequoia said rhetorically. "I said the same thing to my mother and she nearly ripped my head off."

"That's because, though you're the smartest girl I've ever met, you can be extremely naïve at times," Desiree added her two cents.

Sequoia scoffed. "And how is that?"

"Because you're famous now."

"Correction," Sequoia interjected, "I just got signed. That does not constitute me being famous in the least bit."

"Oh my God!" Desiree said in frustration. "You are so delusional. F.Y.I., over twenty million people have seen your face on YouTube, and so far you've had over two hundred thousand downloads on ITunes for your new single. People know who you are. Newsflash—your secret's out," she said sarcastically.

"She's right, you know," Jade spoke up as she scrolled through her IPhone. "You really need to start thinking about making some adjustments, just to play it safe."

"Yes, mothers," Sequoia joked. "No, but seriously, I'm going to look into it as soon as possible."

"Yeah, whatever." Desiree waved her off. "Yo ass will learn when some weirdo tries to turn you into his personal sex slave." Desiree flipped through the pages of the latest *Source* magazine.

"Must you be so negative?" Sequoia shook her head.

"I'm just saying," Desiree said.

"Could you two please put your claws away?" Jade butted in. "At least until we're done with the interview and photo shoot?"

"Right. Game face." Sequoia displayed a serious face, which made the girls laugh.

"C'mon, Sequoia, I need you to be focused," Jade said. "This is your first interview, and we need you to leave a lasting impression."

"And which interview are we doing first?" Sequoia asked.

"Uh, we're doing the *Source*, and then we have to do *XXL*." Jade looked out of the window and noticed that they were within a block of the building. "We're almost here."

When they arrived, the bodyguard who T. Bibby provided Sequoia with emerged from the front passenger seat of the S.U.V. and opened the door for the ladies. They all filed out into the brisk February morning and wasted no time entering the skyscraper.

They were all dressed casually but professionally. Everyone except Jade, that is: Jade was simply...dressed. Jade was wearing gray Ugg boots, purple Seven jeans, a tan trench coat, a bright orange scarf, and a lime green knitted skull cap.

Desiree was donned in Donna Karan straight leg black pants, red knit cardigan sweater, red snake skin calf-high boots, and a blue London fog pea coat. Her hair was pulled back into a ponytail, her succulent lips were covered with Mac lip gloss, and she carried a red snake skin clutch.

Sequoia hand-picked a cream, floral embroidered, Salvatore Ferragamo dress that accented her 36C's and tied at the neck from a high-end boutique yesterday. The dress had whipstitch detail along either side. Sequoia's long, curly hair draped graciously over one side of her shoulder. The cream and black, Salvatore Ferragamo open-toed stilettos she was wearing matched her leather cream and black Salvatore Ferragamo clutch. She wore a cream, cotton and silk, duchess satin Burberry Prosum coat.

They were instructed by a receptionist to wait momentarily before being advised to board the elevator and go to the eleventh floor.

The experience was surreal to all of them, especially Sequoia. Ever since Jade posted that viral video on YouTube, her entire life had changed dramatically, so much so that she was barely able to keep up with the changes.

Her Facebook and Twitter accounts were mounting ridiculously in numbers, and her popularity in the streets was growing at an alarming rate. There was even an incident yesterday, when she, Desiree, and Jade, were swarmed by a wild pack of thugs in a Chili's restaurant. She was practically held hostage until she agreed to autograph various items: napkins, and someone's neck. The man assured her that he would be visiting the nearest tattoo shop so he could get her name permanently inked on his neck (which was news that she found about as comforting as swapping out her Sealy Posturepedic mattress for one with nails and razors).

Needless to say, it was taking her some time fitting into the shoes that were all but thrown into her closet, but she intended to fill them with grace and humility.

Sequoia managed to finish the shoot and the interview in less than two hours, which was a shock to everyone considering how much work needed to be done and the fact that Sequoia was unfamiliar with the entire process. However, she handled herself like a professional and the photographer told her that she was a natural in front of the lens. He also mentioned that she should strongly consider tackling modeling at some point in her career.

Overall, Sequoia walked away from the exclusive interview with additional wisdom on how to handle herself during such interviews in the future. She quickly realized where their focus lay, and what was practically insignificant to them. For example, the fact that she was a national genius who currently attends one of the top Ivy League colleges paled in comparison to the mystery that was her dating and sex life.

She thought that was much too intimate, much too personal, and certainly not something that she would divulge to the entire world via a popular urban magazine—even if it would increase their sales.

So, she kept that experience in mind before she went to do the interview with *XXL*, and before long she had wrapped up everything and was ready to get a bite to eat before going to the choreography session T. Bibby had arranged for her.

Because of her unfortunate experience from the day before, she feared that she would encounter another group of wild supporters that could possibly be inside any restaurant, so they settled for the drive through at McDonald's.

While eating, the trio realized that times like these were going to be far and few in between in the months to come, so they figured it best if they used every opportunity to savor each moment when they could.

That was also Desiree's justification for talking while stuffing her face with a fist full of fries.

"So, Sequoia," she struggled to say. "Where are you heading to after this?"

Sequoia took a huge bit into her quarter pounder and spoke through the food, "I've gotta go ta co-ra-og-go-fy..."

"English," Jade said with an annoyed scowl.

Sequoia swallowed her food and chased it with her Sprite. "I said, I have to go to choreography, to learn some moves for this video shoot I'm supposed to be doing."

"Really?" Desiree exclaimed in excitement. "You're shooting a video already?"

Sequoia nodded as she filled her mouth with fries. "That's what I said."

"This is for that new single, right?" Desiree asked.

"Mm hmm," Sequoia nodded, "the one I co-wrote with Neon."

Desiree shook her head in disbelief with a silly grin on her face. "I still can't believe all of this is happening. I'm so proud of you."

"You should be proud of Jade—or have you already forgotten that if it weren't for her none of this would be happening?"

"Of course not. How could I forget?" She winked at Jade. "She's a genius, one of Harvard's best. That reminds me: you should probably let her direct a video of yours in the future."

"Oh my God!" Sequoia exclaimed. "That's a great idea! What do you think, Jade?"

Jade shrugged and smiled nervously. "I don't know. I guess I'd like to do it. I would probably have to learn how to use the equipment and cameras, but I would definitely be up for it in the future."

"Good, because I want you guys to be as active in my music career as your school schedules will allow. There's no sense in shelling money out to a bunch of unfamiliar people."

"You know what?" Desiree said before shoving a handful of fries into mouth. "I love your attitude about this. That makes perfectly good sense." She paused to swallow her food. "So what do you think I can do?"

"I don't know," Sequoia said. "Maybe dance for right now?"

"Oh, that's cool. When do you think I can do it?"

"I don't know. Maybe I can squeeze you in with this shoot we're about to do in Costa Rica."

"Wow! You're going to Costa Rica to shoot your first video?" Desiree was excited.

"Well, it's not written in stone just yet, but I'd have to assume that we'll be able to get the permits we need to do it."

Desiree blushed. "That would be like a dream come true for me Sequoia."

"And I'm quite sure we'll be able to make it come true." Sequoia finished her burger and balled the bag up. "Now let's get to the dance studio—don't want to be late on the first day."

CHAPTER 24

"Thank you!" Sequoia said to T. Bibby's chauffer as she climbed into his silver Rolls Royce Phantom. The chauffer closed the door behind her and she sat patiently while Bibby dished out executive order left and right to some unfortunately chap on the receiving end.

Sequoia fixed her sights on the Rolls Royce's opulent interior in a futile attempt to distract herself from eavesdropping on Bibby's conversation. It was impressive, to say the least, but not nearly as captivating as overhearing Bibby chew someone out on the phone. Somehow, she found herself feeling sorry for whoever may be on the phone.

"I don't care who's responsible. If the order's not right by the time I review it, somebody's getting fired!" He ended the call before the person on the other end had a chance to respond.

"And good morning to you," Sequoia said with a hint of sarcasm in her voice.

"Sorry 'bout that," he made a gesture in the phone's direction, "but I hate dealing with incompetence."

"So I see."

"Don't mind that though. It's just business." He leaned over and gave her a peck on the cheek. "But what's good with you?"

Sequoia didn't respond initially. It was taking her a moment to process Bibby's intent behind him putting his lips on her. She didn't want to jump to conclusions and make meritless assumptions, but she also didn't want to give Bibby the wrong impression that this was a business relationship—strictly platonic!

Regardless of how attractive she thought he was, or how rich and famous he may be, that's exactly how the relationship would stay. She did, however, entertain the idea that it may be presumptuous to draw conclusions from something as small as a peck on the cheek. She figured that it was probably best to just ignore it.

"I'm good," Sequoia said in a noticeably tired tone.

"Word?" Bibby eyed her through his dark designer lenses. "You sound tired."

"I am," Sequoia admitted while rubbing her hands over her thighs nervously.

Though she tried to contain herself in the company of the mogul producer, she was finding it to be a more difficult task that she initially assumed.

"I was studying last night."

"And how's that working out for you?" Bibby asked, which sounded more challenging than it did questioning.

"What do you mean?" Sequoia asked unsurely.

"What I mean is, eventually you're going to have to decide what is more important to you: your new career or your education. And try not to take offense to the way I'm putting it, because I'm all for education. I have a B.A. in Communications myself, but in my defense, I didn't have nothing to worry about but my studies. You have a full plate."

Sequoia sighed heavily. "I know. I see exactly what you're saying. I'm just not ready to walk out on my education like that."

"I'm not saying that at all, but what I will say is this: you're a very, very beautiful woman, and you're about to be very successful. So you have to understand that it can be very dangerous for you to actually go to school and maintain your anonymity.

"Just think about it," Bibby said before handing her a tabloid magazine from underneath his armpit, "because you're already the talk of the town."

Sequoia gazed over the cover of *Star Magazine* and nearly shattered when she saw herself in an oversized picture outlined by several smaller pictures. The headline read, "The Caribbean beauty with the voice from heaven! Why did she run out on T. Bibby during his big night? Our cover story on page eight!"

Sequoia could not believe that she was actually looking at herself on the front cover of a popular magazine. It was a bittersweet moment, one that was short lived. Her enthusiasm quickly waned when she began to fully process what drew the tabloid to report the story in the first place. The stark reality suddenly had her stomach feeling acrobatic and had her seething with embarrassment.

"You alright?" Bibby asked, as if he had picked up on her sudden change in mood.

"I'm sorry," Sequoia said emotionally, "but this just reminded me of how bad I embarrassed you the other night."

T. Bibby laughed. "Embarrassed me? No. See, you've got it all wrong," he assured her. "This is perfect. This is what you call 'free publicity.'

"Now, let's assume that this magazine has a circulation of a million plus. That means that a million plus more people who never knew who you were will be interested in finding out more about you now. This is how you establish your fan base, and this is how you sell albums."

Sequoia was beginning to understand as he spoke. She knew enough about him to know that he had this game all figured out. His record label had sold over eighty million records to date, and if she wanted a piece of that action she knew that it would be in her best interest to pay close attention and work very hard.

"I figured that you might want to check that out. You can read it later though," Bibby said. "You hungry?"

"Starving," Sequoia said dramatically.

"What do you gotta taste for?"

"It doesn't matter. Breakfast is good, I guess."

"Freddie, swing by Micky D's so we can get something to eat."

Sequoia laughed. "Are you serious?"

"What?" he asked with a genuinely confused expression.

"Nope. Nothing. I didn't mean anything by that." She giggled.

"The hell you didn't. What's up? What's so funny?"

Sequoia gathered herself. "It's just... You're worth nearly a billion dollars and you still eat McDonald's. I mean, I guess I would've thought that you were more of an organic veggie and fruit type of guy."

"Hell naw!" He couldn't believe her. "I'm more of a sirloin steak, junk food, and alcohol type of guy. And occasionally a Micky D's type of guy too. Besides, it's a recession out here. Shit, I grew up on fast food restaurants. Call it a guilty pleasure or whatever you want to call it, but I'm not giving it up."

They both laughed.

"That's my bad for making assumptions," Sequoia said.

They both grew silent when Bibby's phone began to ring.

He answered. "Yeah... No, we're stopping to get something to eat first... Well, tell them to wait. We'll be there." T. Bibby continued on, but Sequoia wasn't paying his conversation any attention.

Sequoia was finding it hard to believe how successful T. Bibby was. Here he was creeping up on the entry lane of a billion dollars, and he was dressed in a pair of Air Jordan's, gray jeans, and a leather jacket from his Urban Street collection. He single-handedly epitomized what it meant to be a true hustler.

Though she intended to maintain a platonic relationship with him, she had to admit to herself that he possessed some of the most attractive qualities that any woman would love to find in a man.

He ended his call and sat silently for a moment before speaking. "You killing that 'fit. What is that, Louie?"

"As a matter of fact it is."

Sequoia was sporting a pair of rhinestone-studded, red bottom Louis Vuitton heels; black, leather studded leggings, and a leather studded Louis Vuitton jacket over a gray Louis Vuitton blouse with a plunging neckline.

"I see you invested in a new wardrobe," Bibby said. "Now all you have to do is find you a better place to stay instead of a hotel and I'll be able to sleep better at night."

"Actually, outside of purchasing my mother a place, I haven't bought myself anything with my advancement."

"Word?" Bibby asked astonishingly.

"Umm hmm," Sequoia nodded. "It's only an advancement, one that I intend to work hard and actually earn before I get to spending it all crazy.

"That's the smartest shit that I've ever heard a new artist say." Bibby was impressed. He wanted to commend her for the business approach she was taking until something dawned on him. "But it that's the case, where did you get all of these expensive clothes?"

Sequoia chuckled. "Excuse me, I did have a wardrobe before you signed me."

"And I get that. All I'm saying is, you're a Harvard law student with bills and obligations. What kind of job could you have possibly been working that would allow you to afford all of these fancy clothes. Where were you working at?"

"Hunh? I... I was working at—"

Bibby's phone rang again and he answered it.

Sequoia couldn't have been more thankful. She had no idea that they were going to play twenty questions at her expense.

He was off the phone in less than sixty seconds. "What was I saying?" He paused, but Sequoia didn't offer him any assistance. "I can't remember. But what I did want to tell you was; try not to make it a habit of buying too many clothes. Before long, you're going to receive some endorsements, and fashion designers will more than likely send you a load of their newest items to model at events, or just to wear in public.

"It's crazy, because when you're broke you can't pay somebody to look out for you, or give you a deal on something, and when you're rich you either get everything for free or half price."

"That is crazy," Sequoia had to admit.

"Where are you from? Like, where did you grow up at?" Bibby asked.

"I was born in Costa Rica, but we moved to the States when I was one. My mother, father, and I have dual citizenship. I grew up in Buffalo, but when my parents divorced we had to downsize, so we moved to Brooklyn for awhile."

Bibby nodded but said nothing initially. He switched the subject. "I'll know something about the permit to film in Costa Rica by tomorrow," Bibby said. "Any of your friends going with you?"

"I know Desiree will. She's the one who rehearsed for the dance session, and she already has a passport. I'll have to check with Jade though. I'm not sure if she has something important to do in class."

"And how does that work for you? What, do you email your work to your instructor?"

"Yep. I spoke with all of my instructors, and to my surprise every last one of them was extremely supportive and willing to be flexible. They are all going to work with me and make sure that I get everything I need to stay caught up."

Bibby nodded. "That's cool for now, but I'm already working on establishing you some tour dates sometime in the late summer, going into the fall season. Though I don't want to say it, you may have to choose what's more important to you in the long run. Your tour dates are going to be hectic, and being honest, it's gonna be nearly impossible to be successful with both," he said seriously. "Don't worry about it right now, but I do want you to think about it."

They pulled into the McDonald's drive through a short while later and were greeted by an ogling crowd of pedestrians who couldn't resist the urge to swarm the lavish limo and attempt to peer through the tinted windows.

Bibby paid them no mind, but Sequoia was nervous as shit. They both placed their orders and were suckered into signing autographs for what seemed like an entire football team's roster before receiving their food.

They both devoured their meals before going to the photo shoot and interview for *Complex Magazine*. Everyone that was there in attendance was extremely professional, so hair, make-up, and wardrobe didn't take long. Before long she was in front of the photographer's lens working her magic.

The shoot lasted for forty-five minutes at the most, and the question and answer was about the same. In total, they wrapped up their business with *Complex Magazine* in a little over two hours.

The next stop was Hot.97 with Funk Flexer. It was a bit more nerve-wracking for Sequoia at first, but being under the wing of T. Bibby had served as the perfect shade for her.

The interview lasted for all of twenty-five minutes, which led to an introduction of her new song to the public. Shortly after, brief but cordial exchanges of well-wishes were said by Funk Flexer, T. Bibby, and Sequoia. Before long Sequoia and Bibby were exiting the premises and back inside the comforts of T. Bibby's Phantom.

He advised Sequoia that he had a prior obligation that he needed to attend to while simultaneously checking his text messages. He said that she was welcome to come along for the ride, but Sequoia declined, stating that she had to use all of her free time to hit the books. He agreed to drop her back off at the hotel.

When they were within a mile of the hotel, Bibby told her that he had some good news.

"Guess what?" Bibby asked.

"What?" Sequoia asked with a nervous smile.

"We got clearance to shoot the video in Costa Rica."

"Really?" she exclaimed enthusiastically.

"Yep. Got the club, the beach, and you'll have a suite at the hotel," he told her, "and since this is your first video I'll be coming along to walk you through it, and also to bring along a few people I know for cameo shots."

"Are you serious?" Sequoia was nearly in tears with excitement. "You'll do all that for me?"

"I told you before, I got you," he said seriously.

Sequoia hugged T. Bibby out of sheer excitement. She broke her embrace when the chauffer stopped in front of the hotel.

She was about to express her appreciation, but was caught off guard when he attempted to follow up her embrace by shoving his tongue down her throat.

When their lips locked, Sequoia forcefully pushed him off of her. She shot him a look before exiting the car.

"Sequoia! Sequoia, wait! I—"

She slammed the door behind herself and nearly broke down in tears when she walked into the hotel. She didn't want to acknowledge his pleas, or the fact that he even existed, so she never turned back. Her heart was broken. She slowly began to process the fact that her mentor, the man who had given her a unique opportunity, the man she looked up to, was just like the rest of them. He was supposed to be different than the men in the industry!

CHAPTER 25

A week later, Sequoia was on T. Bibby's G5 jet on her way to Costa Rica. She hadn't spoken a word to him since the day he attempted to force himself her. Sequoia was contacted by his assistant, who then relayed the message to her. It was a spineless move from Sequoia's vantage point, but it was nothing she intended to lose sleep over.

She did, however, want to know what the hell was going through his mind at the time. What was it about her that gave him the impression that she would be even remotely interested in anything other than a business relationship with him?

She entertained a plethora of scenarios in her mind, but nothing made sense so she avoided addressing the issue altogether until Bibby decided to grow big enough balls to give her the apology she deserved. Until that time came, she intended to simply avoid him at all costs—which would prove to be problematic considering that he was within arm's reach.

"Is everything alright?" Desiree asked as she stared at Sequoia's bouncing leg.

Sequoia pulled herself out of her daze long enough to acknowledge her dear friend. "Umm hmm. Why you ask that?"

"Gee, I don't know," Desiree said sarcastically, "but it probably has something to do with the fact that your leg has been twitching for the past thirty minutes. And from the looks of it, you've been going out of your way to avoid any contact with T. Bibby."

Sequoia wanted to protest, but when her eyes locked with Desiree's she decided against it. She knew that Desiree could read her better than a sex novel by Zane, so she came clean. She lowered her voice to a whisper from her hunkered position in the back of the plane.

"He tried to kiss me."

"He who?" Desiree asked.

"T. Bibby."

"Are you serious?" Desiree said in disbelief.

"Of course I'm serious!" Sequoia snapped. "I think I would know whether or not someone tried to kiss me."

Desiree dropped her head into her lap. She was disappointed in T. Bibby, so much so that she couldn't put it in words. She had a great deal of respect for him and all that he accomplished over his career, but now she had no idea what to think. If she had to guess, she would unfortunately presume that he was no different than the rest of the men in the industry.

Desiree trained her piercing gray eyes on the back of Bibby's head while he yapped away on the phone.

"Desiree, could you please stop staring at him like that?" Sequoia said. "Somebody's gonna be able to put two and two together if you don't."

"Sorry," Desiree said, "but these niggas in the industry made me sick."

Desiree had been voicing her disdain for the "niggas in the industry" ever since her degrading incident with Jewels Santiago. She still bore the scar of that painful memory every time she wiped her ass.

"So what are you gonna do?" Desiree asked her.

"Nothing, for now," Sequoia told her. "I'll just continue to torture him with the silent treatment until he works up enough balls to apologize to me. Until that time comes, we'll just pretend that this little conversation we just had never happened."

"Right," Desiree agreed. "But if he starts tripping when we got out of here, I'm sticking these Prada's all up his ass," she said, making Sequoia laugh. "Now, I'm about to get my free load on with all this expensive champagne that's floating around here."

Sequoia shook her head as she fixed her eyes on the screen of her laptop and concentrated on a report that her professor was expecting to be emailed within the next forty-eight hours.

When the G5 came within view of the Costa Rican landing strip, Sequoia's eyes were practically glued to the window. For a moment, she actually forgot about her fear of landing as she took in the sight of all that beautiful blue water surrounding the landing strip. A private beach was a half mile away from the landing strip. All in all, the sight was absolutely beautiful—just the way she remembered it.

They arrived at 9:15 AM Costa Rica time, and were immediately chauffeured to a local hotel. There were only two limos awaiting their arrival on the tarmac to transport them to the hotel, which wouldn't have been too hard to manage if it weren't for the amount of luggage that everyone was transporting.

There were ten people in total: two hair stylists, two make-up and nail technicians, two stylists, T. Bibby's assistant, T. Bibby, Desiree, and Sequoia. When you factored in the collective amount of luggage and equipment that was brought along the ride to the hotel it only assured that the ride would be an unforgettable one. T. Bibby seemed hardly fazed by it, seeing as he had yet to detach his ear from his cell phone long enough to complain.

Sequoia found herself entertaining the idea that a cyclone could hit the limo at that very moment, and he would still be on the phone. It would more than likely provide pathologists with his identity after they surgically removed it from his hand.

Everything about him seemed to irritate Sequoia suddenly. She figured that it had something to do with the idea of him not extending her the common courtesy of a well-deserved apology for practically forcing himself on her. If not for moral reasons, she figured that he should at least do it for the sake of their business relationship.

Nevertheless, she wasn't about to let it stand in the way of her money. If he wanted to play the silent game, then fine; that's how they would play it. She would simply swallow her pride, deal with the discomfort of having luggage piled up to her eyes, and remain cordial until they made it to the hotel.

When everyone arrived at the hotel, Sequoia was dealt a hard dose of the truth: they would be working shortly, once the camera crew, dancers, directors, and a few cameramen that already possessed passports set up.

Sequoia and Desiree were informed that they were to be prepped by hair and make-up while T. Bibby went to secure the necessary paperwork from local town officials and to make sure that security would be provided while they filmed the video.

Bibby's assistant, Yoni, was the messenger, and despite her feelings towards Bibby, she thought that Yoni was amazing—definitely too good to be bossed around by the likes of him.

Needless to say, there would be no lounging by the pools, shopping, or sight-seeing like Desiree and she anticipated, which really put a damper on her mood. But business was business, and after all, business was the sole purpose for them being there. Therefore, she intended to give it one hundred percent!

Everyone assembled on a nearby beach several hours later to start filming. The director had long since arrived, along with the dancers, camera crew, security, and a few famous friends of T. Bibby's, who were set to provide cameos in the video (including another one of T. Bibby's artists, Sassy, the Caribbean bombshell that he was rumored to be sexually involved with).

Despite her exotic looks and wonderful voice, Sassy had yet to reach the heights in her career that paralleled all of the hype built around her, so the rumors came as no surprise to anyone who knew T. Bibby that sex would definitely serve as an effective bargaining chip to prevent him from dropping her from the label.

The unfortunate thing for T. Bibby was that subtlety was not Sassy's strong suit, and if he did have any prior intentions of keeping their private dealings a secret Sassy was threatening to compromise that agreement.

Ever since she arrived in Costa Rica, she'd been practically glued to his hip—which, judging by Bibby's body language, was the complete opposite of what he wanted. Even crazier was the motive that lay behind her actions; she seemed to be more interested in asserting some form of proclamation over T. Bibby and less concerned with public opinion. The cold stares that she'd been shooting in Sequoia's direction since her arrival was starting to make her feel as if all of the open affection she was displaying was nothing more than a ploy to make her jealous. Luckily Sequoia knew better than to pay her any mind.

They were nearly done wrapping up the shoot on the beach. The shoot had lasted nearly twelve hours, and darkness had long since claimed the backdrop.

Instead of calling it a night, the director thought it would be best to get a few shots in during the night, and everyone agreed. Sequoia went inside her trailer to change her wardrobe for the next shoot. She was sharing a trailer with Desiree, for Desiree's convenience.

However, seeing as though she would only be shooting a solo shot, she hurriedly changed into another bikini set—a two piece, magenta, Dolce and Gabbana set that she covered with a white, floral embroidered, oversized, fishnet poncho—and exited the trailer.

To her surprise, T. Bibby was standing at the foot of the stairs of her trailer. He removed his shades when she trained her eyes on him.

"We need to talk," he said in a no-nonsense tone.

Sequoia folded her arms across her chest defensively. "Talk."

He mounted on stair before Sequoia stopped him. "No, you're good right there."

Bibby exhaled a sigh of frustration. "Sequoia, please! Alright. I know that was some dumb shit on my part, and I apologize for it, but this…" He gestured between himself and her, "This Cold-War-silent-treatment shit is bad for business. We need to be able to communicate."

"Oh, you want to communicate." Sequoia rolled her eyes just enough to see everyone in the background that was staring in their direction.

Everyone was staring, from the director and the film crew who were on the beach at least fifty yards away, to Sassy and several popular artists who were there as cameos. In any event, Sequoia had no desire to give anyone the wrong impression about her and T. Bibby's relationship, so she eased her body language to give a more relaxed state and spoke to Bibby in a professional tone.

"T. Bibby, I want you to understand something about me," she said. "First, I am a woman who respects herself, and it's because of the respect that I have for myself that allows me to demand respect from others."

Bibby attempted to speak, but Sequoia silenced him with an open palm. "Wait, wait. Let me speak," she said, and he held his tongue. "Like most women who read tabloids, experience personally, or hear about the ways guys in this industry treat women, I have my own preconceived notions about industry men. And what you did to me was not only disrespectful to our employer/employee relationship, but also to me as a woman. But I forgive you, and I'll put this behind me and move on."

"You done?" Bibby asked curtly. Sequoia nodded before he continued. "You're right. What I did was very disrespectful, and I've been trying to come up with an explanation for my actions...but to be completely honest with you, I don't have any.

"I guess I was reading you wrong, and I apologize for that," he said sincerely. "But, in my defense, you're a bad ass woman Sequoia! And it's hard for any man, I'd assume, to be in your presence without being attracted to you. I mean, I know that I'm your boss and all, but I'm still a man."

Sequoia had no clue if she was supposed to be offended by his comment or flattered, but either way, his honesty was amusing to her, so she laughed it off, breaking the tension between them.

"Just try not to let your little girlfriend over there hear your little comment. She looks like she's just seconds away from causing a big scene."

Bibby shot a glance at her over his shoulder and locked eyes with her. She wore a noticeable amount of attitude.

"That's the past," he said. "I don't even know how she got here, because I sure as hell didn't invite her."

Sequoia saw the director, Hype Wilson, motioning for her to come back to the set.

"Well, looks as if I'm being summoned. I think I need to do a touch-up on hair and make-up, so let me get out of here before your little girlfriend gets the wrong impression and decides to attack me." She giggled.

Bibby shook his head. "I just told you what it is."

"Well, it looks like me and you are the only ones who know what it is. You should probably tell her now so she can stop ice-grilling me."

"She ain't ice-grilling—" Bibby began, before he caught a glance of Sassy staring in their direction.

"Excuse me," Sequoia walked past him. "I'll talk to you later." Sequoia kept her eyes trained on Sassy.

"I've been meaning to tell you that you're doing a phenomenal job. Keep it up."

"I will." Sequoia smiled as she made her way to the make-up artist's chair.

The final shoot for the night was wrapped up in less than ninety minutes, and everyone agreed to call it a night so that they could continue shooting the following afternoon.

Everyone who was in attendance congratulated Sequoia on a job well done as she made her way to her trailer. Sequoia had left her cell phone behind in the trailer accidentally, and told Desiree to wait for her while she retrieved it.

Sequoia had intended to get in and out as quickly as possible, but the looming presences that had suddenly entered the trailer behind her suggested otherwise.

Sequoia turned to see an angst-stricken Sassy standing in the doorway of the trailer.

"Well, well, well," Sassy began her monologue in a dark and evil tone. "Miss Sequoia. We finally meet."

"Can I ask you what you're doing in my trailer?" Sequoia asked.

"Oh, don't worry, I won't be here long," she told her surely. "I just wanted to have an opportunity to meet the new artist on the Big Boy label, and take this brief moment to introduce myself."

There was a serious sense of insincerity in her words, and Sequoia picked up on it immediately, but she intended to play along long enough to figure out Sassy's angle.

"I'm Sassy, and I understand that you're Sequoia." They both shook hands.

"That's it?" Sequoia asked as Sassy turned to leave.

"Umm hmm," Sassy nodded. "Why? What were you expecting?" she asked with an evil grin.

"Nothing. Never mind," Sequoia responded. She wasn't enjoying this in the least bit, so she decided to abruptly end their conversation and put as much distance as she could between them. "It was nice meeting you."

"You too. Guess I'll see you around," Sassy said with one of the most fake smiles Sequoia had ever seen. She turned as if she was about to leave before deciding to leave Sequoia with a strong word of advice. "Oh, there is one more thing." Her voice was suddenly as cold as ice. "Stay the fuck away from T. Bibby. If I even think for one minute that you're trying to impose on what we've built together, the medical examiner will be digging my Jimmy Choo's out of your pretty little ass!" She stared Sequoia down before exiting the trailer.

Sequoia exhaled a sigh of relief when she disappeared. She had never been, nor did she ever plan to be, the confrontational type, especially at the expense of some guy she had no interest in or relationship with. Needless to say, she didn't need the unnecessary drama in her life, so it would be no big deal to her to simply keep a respectable distance between her and Bibby to avoid a future altercation with Sassy. The last thing she needed was to engage in a cat fight with a more than willing Sassy over T. Bibby. It would undoubtedly be one of those early career moments that would define her.

Sequoia finished filming the rest of the video over the course of the following day. The entire shoot was done in a local club called Caliente, and they managed to wrap everything up in less than twelve hours.

Sequoia had taken Sassy's threatening advice at face value and had kept her distance from Bibby. With all that was going on at the set, it was relatively easy for her to pull it off without stirring much curiosity amongst everyone—especially T. Bibby.

Sequoia did, however, fill Desiree in on the details of the interesting conversations that she'd had with both Sassy and T. Bibby—conversations that they both agreed to discuss in further detail when they arrived back in the States.

Despite the negativity that originally threatened to cripple the joy from what would be her first video shoot, she would have to say that it was a total success.

Sequoia had been given the non-traditional privilege by Hype Wilson to look over the majority of the video footage after it hit the editing stage. To say that she was impressed would be doing her feelings an injustice. She was so proud of herself. Just seeing herself on the video footage, along with her best friend Desiree, was a dream come true. It was an incomprehensible euphoria that she hoped would never wane.

It was certainly a favorable distraction from the B.S. she had to endure since she'd arrived there.

The flight back to the States was no different. She bragged to whoever wanted to listen, which was ultimately narrowed down to Desiree, her mother, or Jade. She also posted her first tweet on Twitter, complete with a few pictures of her experience with her first video.

She was in a great mood, one that neither T. Bibby's drama, nor Sassy's cold stares, could pull her out of. She intended to remain that way throughout the duration of her successes and failures, and savor whatever moments of joy that her new career had to offer.

CHAPTER 26

By the time that Sequoia made it back to Boston, she was experiencing one of the worst cases of jetlag imaginable. She arrived on a private airstrip, courtesy of T. Bibby's pilot, at 1:43 AM, and made it back inside her Harvard dormitory at 2:27 AM.

When she made it back to her dorm room, Jade was sleeping, so she quietly showered and undressed before stumbling into bed. She wanted to catch as many Z's as she could before classes started.

She woke to the sound of Jade scurrying about the dorm room, what felt like moments after closing her eyes.

She groggily pulled her head from underneath the covers and forced her eyes open. The clock read 4:03, which meant that she had only been asleep for just over an hour's time. She buried her head underneath her pillow and spoke; "Why are you up so early, Jade? We don't have school for another four hours."

Jade scoffed before making her way over to Sequoia's bed. She sat down beside her and raised the pillow. "Sequoia, you really have to get back in touch with reality."

"What are you talking about? I'm perfectly in touch with reality," she said as she tried to pull the pillow back over her head.

Jade snatched it up again and watched her squint. "Sequoia, it is four o'clock in the afternoon. I've been at school all day."

Sequoia jumped out of her bed dramatically and pulled the blinds back to see if there was any truth to what Jade was saying.

Jade watched her. "I just got back. I tried to wake you up, but you were sleeping so hard, and I know that you were filming that video, so I figured that you needed the sleep. How was Desiree, by the way? I should call her," Jade said, thinking out loud.

Sequoia sighed and turned to face Jade. "You're right, Jade. I never knew it would be so hard," she admitted, before burying her head into her palms. "What am I gonna do?"

"Well, for starters, you may wanna consider taking some time off from school. Effective immediately," Jade told her.

"I know, I know," Sequoia said, exasperated. "But I don't want to lose my scholarship."

"Maybe you don't have to lose your scholarship," she speculated. "Maybe you can talk to the Dean and explain your situation in full detail. Who knows, he may be able to pull some strings and allow you to take some time off to get your career together," she suggested.

Sequoia paused to consider Jade's opinion. "You think they'll let me do that?"

"Won't hurt to try," Jade said, "but one thing's for sure; you need to make some adjustments quickly. Things aren't going to get any easier, and in all truth, it's just not safe anymore. You're too popular to be in here now."

"I'm not that popular," Sequoia said naively.

"Tell that to the entire student body who has been constantly asking me for your whereabouts every day," Jade retorted.

"Are you serious?"

"Unfortunately, yes," she admitted. "And to be honest with you, it's getting pretty annoying."

"Well, I'm sorry if it's getting 'pretty annoying,'" Sequoia quoted Jade, "but I'd be lying if I said that I haven't been having fun. I just finished my first new video," Sequoia bragged, "and I gotta tell you that it was AMAZING! I really wish you could've been there."

"I know. I'm sorry, Sequoia," Jade said emotionally, "but I had no idea that my parents would be coming to town, and the whole Visa thing was crazy."

"Don't worry about it though. I'm looking forward to making plenty more, so you'll get another opportunity," Sequoia said while turning her phone on. She checked her text messages and missed calls and discovered that nearly the entire world had been looking for her. "So how were your parents?" Sequoia scrolled through the messages as she sat on her bed.

"They're so proud of you—of us both, actually." She sat beside her.

"Really?" Sequoia exclaimed excitedly.

"Oh yeah." Jade rolled her eyes dramatically and sighed. "They just love them some Sequoia."

"Aw!" Sequoia said. "Have you told them how significant you've been in making everything possible?"

Jade shook her head. "Now, you know I would never do that."

"And why not?" Sequoia demanded to know.

Jade shrugged. "It's not my shine. I mean, I may have hinted at the idea of my being remotely involved, but let's be honest; I hate the attention. Plus, you're such a talented and beautiful person that I felt that you'd be cheating the world out of some of the best talent that the world may have to offer."

Sequoia got misty-eyed. "Thank you for believing in me Jade! If it wasn't for you, none of this would be happening."

Jade hugged her. "You're going to make me cry."

"Don't cry," Sequoia said as her phone rang, signaling that someone was texting her.

She read it and saw that it was from T. Bibby. He told her that she was expected to be in the dance studio for choreography lessons in New York at 7:15 tomorrow.

"Ugh!" Sequoia exclaimed dramatically.

"What is it?" Jade pried.

"It's T. Bibby," she said enthusiastically. "He says that I have to go to dance rehearsal tomorrow in New York."

Jade forced a smile. "Duty calls."

"That reminds me, I almost got beat up in Costa Rica," Sequoia said jokingly.

"What?" Jade exclaimed in shock. "By whom?"

"By T. Bibby's girlfriend, Sassy," Sequoia told her. "Apparently, she thinks I'm trying to move in on her territory."

"Wow!" Jade was floored. "I heard rumors about them, but I never knew that there was any truth to it."

"Well, to hear him tell it, they're old news—as if I cared to know that much. But it doesn't matter to me either way, because I intend to just stay away from him to alleviate any unnecessary drama."

"I hear that."

"But never mind them. I'm starving," Sequoia said as she rose from her bed wearing a gray wife beater and pink boy shorts. "How about we grab something to eat at that diner across the street, and I'll let you know all the details about the trip? My treat."

Forty-five minutes later, Sequoia was sinking her teeth into a grilled double cheeseburger with extra onions, while Jade devoured a handful of onion rings. Neither Jade nor Sequoia consumed the unhealthy, greasy food on a regular basis, but every now and again they couldn't resist the urge to indulge themselves.

What they didn't count on was a small army of fans and well-wishers of Sequoia stalking her every move while they ate.

A crowd of nearly fifty people had assembled outside of the diner when they received word that Sequoia was there, and the number was gradually growing at a steady pace.

Initially Sequoia thought that the idea of so many people going out of their way to show their support and love for her rising career was wonderful. However, the more the crowd continued to grow, the less civil they became, and the more brazen and demanding they were becoming.

When the crowd continued to grow to a more unmanageable rate, Sequoia began to weigh in on her personal safety. She was suddenly beginning to understand exactly why people had been feeling so pessimistic about her attending college with her new status, and if the scene before her—with the sea of frantic students who were filming her and waving at her hysterically—wasn't enough confirmation of the dangers that could lay in wait for her, then the Indian foreign exchange student Dhuram Patel most certainly did.

After very forcefully and vocally working his way through the crowd of autograph- and picture-demanding people, he dropped to his knees in a very dramatic and disturbing fashion and pleaded with Sequoia to go out on a date with him.

Under common circumstances, Sequoia would've found the gesture flattering, but when her eyes settled on the fresh tattoo on his neck she knew something was seriously wrong with him. He had a very large face portrait of her on the left side of his neck with the words "The one and only for me" in cursive letters beneath it.

Sequoia and Jade exchanged uncomfortable, yet knowing, glances between each other before making a hasty departure.

They ditched their food and hot-tailed it back to the dorm room with an anxious crowd in tow. In a matter of minutes, their dorm room had transformed from living quarters to a safe haven, a refugee camp where asylum was sought.

The entire scenario was surreal and frightening to both Sequoia and Jade, to say the least. Campus security had to be contacted to see the crowd off of their doorstep.

When the crowd thinned down to no more than a few loiterers who were residents of the dorm, Jade and Sequoia went into a sort of Gestapo-esque mode. They put heavy surveillance on the dorm room by taking alternating shifts as patrolwomen. Somewhere in the better part of the second hour of standing patrol, Jade spoke as she peered into the peephole.

"Still think that it's such a good idea to be attending college at a time like this?" Jade asked with a heavy sense of sarcasm in her tone.

Sequoia shot Jade an irritated look from her Indian-style position on her bed. "Don't start," she said in a no-nonsense tone as she continued to stab away at the keys of her laptop.

Jade shrugged as she slowly walked away from her post. "I'm just saying... Who's to say how someone from that crowd could've responded to you being there tonight," she said. "Like the guy who put your face on his neck. What was that?" she said rhetorically. "I'm telling you, we got out of there safely today, but the next time... Who knows?"

Sequoia sighed. "I hear you." She stared at the screen blankly for a moment. "I just really wanted to finish this semester first."

"Well, at the rate things are going, that may not be possible."

"I see." Sequoia's ring tone when off and she took it off the charger to scan the caller I.D. She had never seen the number before and was surprised when she heard the voice on the other end.

"How did you get this number?" Sequoia asked as Jade pleaded to know who it was in the backdrop.

"Doesn't sound like you're too happy to hear from me," Sasha said.

"It's Sasha," Sequoia said with her hand over the speaker of the phone. "I'll be right back." She exited the dorm room.

"Be careful," Jade said apprehensively as the door shut in her face.

The hallway of the dormitory was practically vacant, except for one lone female Gothic computer nerd who was sitting beside her door with her laptop in her lap. The dramatically vocal one-night stand that was power-driving her roommate clearly indicated the reason why she was sitting there. The noise was serving as a bit of a distraction for Sequoia so she excused herself.

Jade and Sequoia's dorm room was only a few doors away from the exit/entrance door of the dormitory, so Sequoia decided to step out into the brisk night air.

"What's up Sasha?" Sequoia was moody.

"What's up?" Sasha seemed surprised by her tone. "Did I call at a bad time?"

"I was studying," Sequoia responded curtly. "How did you get this number? I haven't had it for more than a week yet."

"I have my ways," she said jokingly, "but never mind that. How have you been doing? I heard your new single. Is it true that you just came back from Costa Rica?" Sasha rambled on.

Sequoia stared at the phone as if it sucked her earlobe. She scoffed in disbelief before speaking. "Are you serious? I can't believe—"

Sequoia stopped mid-sentence when she took in the view of Dhuram Patel approaching her. She could hear Sasha screaming through the receiver for her in the background.

Dhuram Patel had a deranged look in his eyes, and he had traded in his North Face jacket form earlier for a gray, hooded sweatshirt. The hood of the oversized sweater draped over his bearded face. Sequoia was dressed in gray Harvard University sweats with her curly hair pulled back into a ponytail and a pair of Nike tennis shoes.

She locked eyes with him for all of a split second before Sequoia tried to make a run for the door into the dormitory.

"Wait, Sequoia! PLEASE!" He was right on her heels.

Sequoia tried to pull the door open, but Dhuram shut it will his open palm before she could open it. "HELP!" Sequoia screamed fearfully before Dhuram placed his hand over her mouth to silence her.

"Sequoia, please! I don't want to hurt you," he said frantically. "I love you. I want you to be my wife—"

Sequoia kneed him in the nuts and shoved him to the ground. She tried to run into the dormitory, but he grabbed her leg and pulled her to the ground forcefully.

"HELP! SOMEBODY HELP ME!" she screamed, but no one seemed to hear her. She struggled underneath Dhuram's weight as he climbed on top of her.

Sequoia began to fear the worst as he mounted her.

"STOP FIGHTING ME!" he yelled as spittle flew from his mouth. "All I want to do is love you!" He tried to plant kisses all over her face, but Sequoia continued to squirm beneath him.

"HELP!" Sequoia yelled.

He was staring at the woman beneath, the woman he'd been dreaming about since he first laid eyes on her in the school's cafeteria. Dhuram began to get aroused. He could feel the blood in his body rushing south. He was filled with lust, and he knew that he would never get another opportunity like this in his life so he intended to make the best out of it. He began to fondle her breast greedily.

Dhuram had become so blinded by his lustful desires that he negated to see Jade exit the dormitory until it was too late. He looked up just in time to catch the toe of her Cross-Trainer Nikes across his chin. He was out cold instantly.

Sequoia pushed him off of her and Jade helped her to her feet.

"Are you alright?" Jade asked, concerned.

Tears flowed from Sequoia's face. "I think so."

By now, two white, middle-aged security guards were running toward the dormitory, probing the night's darkness with their flashlights.

"What's going on over here?" they asked as they approached the scene. "We got a call from a young lady that said someone was being attacked."

"I came out and this guy was trying to rape my friend," Jade told them. "I kicked him in the head and knocked him out cold."

The security guards called for the real police on their walkie-talkie. By now a crowd had formed. "Aren't you the young lady who called us earlier about people camping outside of your dorm room?"

Sequoia nodded.

"Well, are you alright miss?" the other security guard asked her.

"Yeah, I'm okay," Sequoia told him. "I'm just a little shaken up."

More and more students were coming outside of the dorm room to see what all the commotion was about.

"Sequoia? Sequoia?" Sasha could be seen running up the walkway in pajamas, tennis shoes, and a North Face coat. She had apparently driven to the dorm from her apartment.

"I'm right here," Sequoia said before embracing her.

Sasha hugged her tightly as Sequoia cried on her shoulder.

"I called the security guards when I heard you scream. I figured that someone was trying to attack you."

Jade retrieved Sequoia's phone from the ground. Her entire screen was cracked, but it was the least of her worries at the moment.

"Miss, the police will probably want you to make a statement. You think you can handle that?" one of the guards asked her.

Sequoia nodded.

The police arrived a short while later and hauled Dhuram off to jail. Thanks to everyone with a camera phone the aftermath of the ordeal had already gone viral.

Local and national news broadcasters had set up shop, and journalists and reporters were itching to sink their teeth into the story.

Sequoia avoided them as best she could and allowed Jade to do as much damage control as she could while she answered the police's questions.

When the police were confident that they had all that they

needed to charge Dhuram, they exchanged information with Sequoia, told her to contact them if she had any questions, and took Dhuram to jail.

The incident had shaken Sequoia to the core, so she thought it would be best if she took Sasha up on her offer to spend the night at her off campus condo. Sequoia assured Jade that she would call her in the morning.

The situation only played along to the tune that everyone had been singing for awhile now. It was naïve of her to think that she could attend school and go about her life routinely as if nothing had changed. She had received a rude awakening that day.

If she had any doubts about the true power that lay behind her celebrity status, she was thoroughly convinced now. She realized that from this day forth she would have to do things completely different. No longer would she be able to walk in the street carelessly, or socialize among the general public like before, and even worst, the sad truth was that she would have to leave her schooling behind and simply focus on her career.

There was no getting around it anymore: it was simply too dangerous!

CHAPTER 27

"Sequoia, you need to see this," Sasha barged into the guest room where she was sleeping with her laptop in hand. "Look at this." She showed her the clip that was running on CNN.

The footage showed her being attacked by Dhuram last night. Someone, at an angle that she could vaguely pinpoint, had sat there and watched the whole thing and hadn't thought to intervene. Though Sequoia knew that she wasn't as popular as most A- and B-list celebrities, she was certain that the footage would earn someone enough money to cover a percentage of their student loans.

"That's fucking crazy!" Sequoia snapped at the screen in total disbelief. "Anything to make a fucking buck. What if he would've hurt me? Or even worse..."

"I know," Sasha agreed sympathetically. "And that's not all."

Sasha had Sequoia's undivided attention. "What? What else could it be?"

"The police released a report saying that Dhuram is contending that you guys were an item, and that you were simply having an altercation."

"They what?" Sequoia couldn't believe what she was hearing. "Do they believe that?"

"I doubt it," Sasha responded, "but I'm sure that they'll want to talk to you again about it. The thing that did sound strange was that he supposedly has a large tattoo of you on his neck with the words 'The Love of My Life,'" Sasha said with an inquisitive connotation behind her words, something that Sequoia picked up on immediately.

"Are you insinuating that I was actually dating him?"

"No. God, no!" Sasha said unconvincingly. "I was just letting you know what was being said."

"Well, yesterday while Jade and I were at the diner, that kid

Dhuram comes in scaring the hell out of us, professing his love for me with a tattoo of me on his neck and asking me on a date."

"That's crazy," Sasha said.

"I know. And when you called, I was in the dorm, so I stepped outside to talk to you in private, and he pops out of nowhere on me, wearing a hooded sweater over his face..." Sequoia was getting emotional just thinking about it.

"I'm sorry, Sequoia!" Sasha hugged her. "As long as you're okay."

"I'm alright." Sequoia wiped her face.

"Look," Sasha drew her attention to the screen of the laptop.

It was Jade's interview with a CNN reporter from last night. Sasha and Sequoia were trying to tune in to hear Jade give her account of the incident, but Sasha's doorbell broke their concentration.

"You expecting somebody?" Sequoia asked.

"No," Sasha said as she went to answer the door.

She returned moments later with Jade. Jade tossed Sequoia an overnight bag that was filled with a pair of faded Seven jeans, Rachel Zoe patent leather boots, and a white cotton Brand sweater, not to mention hygiene products and toiletries.

"T. Bibby, your mother, Desiree, and the rest of the world are looking for you."

"My phone's broke," Sequoia retorted.

"I told them." Jade handed her a new IPhone that had a number taped across the back of it. "I bought you a phone this morning. It's on my plan. You should call T. Bibby back first because he's been calling me all morning."

"Have you slept at all since yesterday?" Sequoia noticed the dark rings around her eyes despite the fact that she was wearing her glasses.

"Not really," she admitted. "I've been on Twitter, Facebook, and moonlighting as a PR to various tabloids and journalists to make sure this things works to our benefit."

"Good luck with that," Sequoia said. "You need some rest."

Jade sat on the bed beside Sequoia and saw the screen of the laptop with CNN running a loop of the footage that was shot of Sequoia's attack. Jade respectfully shut the laptop before speaking to Sequoia in an even tone.

"Sequoia, you need to take off of school for a while. Maybe even consider some online schooling, because incidents like the one from last night will only become more frequent."

"Okay," Sequoia said simply.

"Okay?" Jade repeated, which drew Sasha from her position in the doorway into the room.

"Sequoia, are you sure you want to do this?" Sasha asked. "You'll be dropping everything that you worked hard for, sacrificing your scholarship along with your college experience for your dream."

"Yes, I'm sure this is what I want to do. I thought about it long and hard last night. I've been secretly dreaming about pursuing an entertainment career since I was a child, and now I have the perfect opportunity, on the perfect label, with enough capital to make several mistakes and bounce back. Yeah, I'm pretty serious, and the way I see it, I have grounds for a civil claim right now," Sequoia said seriously. "Because security was contacted earlier that night about people camping outside of our dorm room, stalking me, and they failed to see to it that I was provided adequate security even though I asked for it.

"So, in my eyes, that's leverage to take to Harvard's president to keep from losing my scholarship, and to be able to exercise it if I ever decided to return in the next few years."

"Sounds like blackmail to me," Jade said.

"Definitely," Sasha agreed.

"No, it's not," Sequoia defended her idea. "It's more political than anything."

"Okay, that's a terrible reference. Everything in politics is corrupt," Jade said.

"I'd have to second that too," Sasha added.

"Well, if it doesn't work, then I'll pay for it myself. I have five million dollars at my discretion, and I'm already beginning to generate money from my sales on ITunes. I intend to take all of the energy that I've been dividing between school and work and focus it solely on my career."

"Sounds perfect to me," Jade said.

"Same here," Sasha agreed.

"Good, because my mind is made up." Sequoia rose from the bed. "So don't try to change it."

"No, I think it's good," Jade said, "and since we're on the topic—T. Bibby has scheduled a date for you in a few days to open up a concert for Famous, and he needs you back in New York by six to go over some choreography."

Sequoia was dialing T. Bibby's number before Jade could finish her sentence. Her mind was made up. She would put her education on the back burner for the moment and focus on her career.

There wasn't a doubt in her mind that she was making the right decision. Everything felt so right. In all truth, she felt as if she should've made the decision awhile ago. She felt that if she had, she could've saved herself a lot of unwanted stress. Nevertheless, she intended on turning the pages to the book that was her life to a new chapter, one that would begin with her placing a call to T. Bibby and end with her conducting a meeting with Harvard's president.

The phone rang twice and T. Bibby picked up. "Hello, T. Bibby? This is Sequoia. As of today I'll be leaving school."

CHAPTER 28

Three Days Later...

To Sequoia's surprise, she was able to arrange a brief meeting with the school's president upon request to address a breach in security that nearly permitted an obsessed psychopath to come within seconds of sexually assaulting her on his campus.

What she didn't expect was for her newfound celebrity status factoring into the president's decision to mutually agree with Sequoia that her residency on campus had become too dangerous, and that it was beginning to serve as a distraction to the students, faculty, and staff. That, in his terms, was also a breach in her scholarship, but instead of terminating her for reasons that were both unforeseen and out of her control, he agreed to give her the time off that she desired with the option to exercise her scholarship within the next three years.

That was three days ago, and ever since then she had been practically chained to T. Bibby's wrist. He hovered over her like a guardian angel.

Initially, she thought that his over-protective antics were comforting, but after twenty-four hours of the security detail equivalent of the Secret Service tailing her, including Bibby himself, it was beginning to get annoying.

Nevertheless, Sequoia went along with it for the sake of his peace of mind. Her mother and Desiree didn't help the situation either, but Sequoia had attributed their fears to the exacerbation of the incident by the media with the continuous looping of the video footage of her attack on campus. To her surprise the both exhaled sighs of relief when she revealed that she would be focusing on her music career and taking time off of school for awhile.

Though she had previously spoken to her mother about giving school a break for awhile, she had no idea how supportive she would actually be when she did decided to do it.

Needless to say, Rosa's support meant the world to her, and for it, she did not intend to let her down.

Bibby had allowed Sequoia to use his private jet to go back to Boston to attend the meeting with the president, and when she returned he gave her keys to a condo in East Manhattan that he owned—until she was able to work out her living arrangements. She attended choreography with Desiree and hit the studio after to work on a song. That was yesterday.

Now, she was in the Highline Ballroom going over rehearsal with her dancers to do an opening performance for the rapper Famous later on that night. Famous had been very vocal to Bibby about his desire to do a collaboration with Sequoia, but because of their conflicting schedules, no official date had been set to create the magic.

Sequoia was sure that they would encounter each other some time that night, but that wasn't the only reason she was nervous. They were expecting a full house in a place that seated nearly ten thousand. She had never performed for any crowd outside of a strip club, and surely the spectators there didn't come close to a crowd of ten thousand.

Safe to say, Sequoia would be taking an extra dose of Xanax before performing.

After rehearsal, Sequoia agreed to do lunch with Desiree. Bibby had to attend a meeting so he sent one of his goons to keep her company, a gesture that was greatly appreciated but considerably annoying nonetheless. The trip made a pit stop at her dressing room, which was no bigger than a hornet's nest, so Desiree and Sequoia could change.

Sequoia tossed on a pair of faded True Religion denims, black number four Air Jordan's, a black Express sweater, North Face jacket, and a Bulls snapback hat. Desiree had on a pair of wheat Timberlands, light blue Bebe jeans, long sleeved vanilla Bebe shirt, a studded Pelle Belle jacket, and a brown custom New York Knicks snapback.

224

Shortly after, they navigated the throes of the Highline Ballroom to the exit door, where T. Bibby allocated a black S.U.V. and chauffer for their personal use.

The oversized goon, whose name they discovered was Sean Oniwakue, accompanied them to the Olive Garden restaurant. It was one of Desiree and Sequoia's favorite restaurants ever since they were young.

Instead of stuffing their gorgeous faces with decadent dishes, they decided to eat light to prevent themselves from feeling sluggish during the performance that night. They both ordered garlic and butter smothered breadsticks, Caesar salad, and pasta. Sequoia offered to buy Sean something to eat, but he declined. So, she took it upon herself to order him a steak and baked potato dish.

"You nervous, Quoy?" Desiree asked as she poked at her pasta before shoving a forkful into her mouth.

Sequoia swallowed. "Not as much as I'm gonna be tonight."

"I know, right?" Desiree smiled eagerly. "I can only imagine how you feel, because I'm nervous as hell." They both laughed.

"I hope I don't freeze up or something," Sequoia joked with a hint of seriousness in her voice.

Desiree waved her off. "You're a natural for the stage. Shit, I intend to follow your lead, so don't get all scared on me now." Desiree bit off a piece of garlic bread.

"Wow!" Sequoia exclaimed. "I sure do appreciate you for not adding any extra pressure on me," she said sarcastically. "But anyway, when is the last time you talked to Momma?" Sequoia asked, referring to Desiree's mother.

Desiree's face revealed that it had been awhile, as she apparently searched her memory back for answers. "Maybe the fifth or sixth, I believe."

"Oh, that's not so bad," Sequoia said, before stabbing her salad with the fork and shoving it in her mouth.

"Of November," Desiree rolled her eyes and continued to eat

as if she wasn't affected by it, but her body language and eyes betrayed her feelings.

Sequoia made a pained expression, as if she wished she had never brought it up. She realized long ago that Desiree's relationship had become strained over the past few years.

Desiree was an only child to Denise and Marlon James, but unfortunately for Desiree, she never got the opportunity to experience a father-daughter relationship with her dad. He was killed in the line of duty during the Desert Storm war in Kuwait, leaving her fatherless and her mother a widow.

Marlon James's unexpected absence in the household created a rippling affect that resonated vastly into Desiree and Denise's standard of living.

Because her mother and father married so young, and conceived Desiree within the first year of their marriage, they never had an opportunity to experience the wonders of the world like they planned to. They were high school sweethearts, young and naïve. They married at nineteen, and within a year Desiree was born. Neither of them went to college, or had stable jobs, so Marlon enlisted in the service in an attempt to establish a career in the American armed forces. However, when he was killed in battle he only succeeded in leaving behind a shattered home.

The picture perfect life that Denise had always dreamed of with Marlon had been broken to pieces. Instead of traveling the world, Denise now traveled to the public aid office. Instead of a house with a white picket fence, Denise had to settle for a project building.

The daily sacrifices that Denise had to make on Desiree's behalf had more than just a financial affect. Secretly, Denise began to resent Desiree. She secretly blamed her, and her unexpected arrival, as the driving force behind her father's decision to enlist, and ultimately to his demise.

Over the years Denise felt as if she had been sentenced to eighteen years of imprisonment with Desiree. The moment she was old enough to fend for herself, Denise went to travel the world working at a travel agency in Italy.

She had left when Desiree was sixteen, leaving her grandmother to take care of her. Now that Desiree was grown, however, and her grandmother was in a retirement home, she was on her own. Denise didn't even bother to attend her graduation. The alienated approached that Denise had taken towards Desiree had created an emotional void in her—one that Rosa, Sequoia's mother, filled completely. She treated her like her own, and Desiree loved Sequoia and her mother for it. To her, they were her sister and mother.

"She'll come around soon," Sequoia said. "Let's just focus on tonight's performance for now."

"You'll do fine," Sean said in a deep baritone as he vigilantly studied the patrons who were moving about the crowded restaurant.

Sean was 6'3", built like a linebacker, and was bald. He had yet to grow any real facial hair, so his true age remained a mystery to anyone who tried to guess. He was wearing Ralph Lauren Polo from head to toe: from his blue bubble down coat with matching knitted sweater that both bore huge while Polo insignias on them, to his blue jeans and blue Polo boots.

Sequoia and Desiree exchanged knowing glances before giggling. They both had been in Sean's company for all of three hours and he hadn't spoken one word until now. They had long ago concluded that he was a mute, and had thereby decided to disengage from any communicative efforts with him.

"So he does speak," Desiree said as she picked over her garlic bread while eyeing him. "You mind eating something now? I'll feel a whole lot more comfortable knowing that the guy protecting me won't be distracted by hunger pains in the event something does go down," she joked. "We need you on your toes."

Sean smiled before unfolding the napkin that contained his silverware and placed it in his lap. "It would be terrible manners for me to simply let this meal go to waste, now wouldn't it?" he said while cutting a piece of the sirloin and forking it into his mouth. "Mmm. Not bad," he said with more personality than they both expected.

"So, what was it that you saying when you rudely

interjected?" Sequoia said to Sean almost flirtatiously.

Sean shot Sequoia a warm look. "I was saying that you'll be fine," he said sincerely. "I have total faith in that. I've been to hundreds of rehearsals and live shows, and between me and you, there are people who are vastly popular and iconic who can't move or sing like you."

Sequoia drew back as she stared in shock at Sean. "Well, thank you Sean!"

"Wow!" Desiree said. "He talks AND compliments. Can we keep him Quoy?"

Everyone laughed.

"Please tell me you can be domesticated?"

Sean blushed as he took a sip of water.

"What took you so long to say something to us?" Desiree asked. "What? Don't tell me you were intimidated by al-l-l-l of this," she said animatedly, drawing out the L as she motioned with her hands over her entire body.

Sean ignored the gesture. "Because, unlike you, I'm here to work. It's hard enough staying focused as it is, and that's part of the reason why I try not to engage with my clients. But you ladies are such great hosts, I figured what the hell."

"So Sean," Sequoia said, "since you're protecting me, what are your credentials?"

Sean downed another piece of steak and chased it with water. "I'm a golden gloves boxer, a former Olympic wrestling gold medalist, a former Special Ops Navy Seal veteran, and I have a black belt in Jiu Jitsu," he said modestly. "But now, I'm currently studying mixed martial arts and am an amateur fighter in the UFC."

"Really?" Sequoia was floored.

Desiree asked, "And how old are you?"

"Twenty-seven."

"That's an impressive resume, Sean," Sequoia said.

"Not nearly as impressive as yours," he retorted.

"Tell that to the thousands of troops who're overseas defending this country."

"Oh, trust me; they need what women like you have to offer in those places. It gives them something to relate to, something to provide solace, and even something worth fighting to get back to."

With that, everyone finished eating their meals.

Desiree wiped her mouth with a napkin and finished her glass of pink lemonade.

"So, are you dating, Sean?" Desiree asked in a flirtatious manner.

Sequoia stared at Desiree defensively. "Desi!" she snapped.

"What?" she asked as if she was confused.

Sequoia said to Sean, "I'm sorry Sean." She looked at Desiree. "What are you doing? You can't just ask someone a question like that."

"Why not?" Desiree asked. "I'm just curious."

"It's no big deal, Sequoia," Sean said. "I'm not currently involved with anyone," he told Desiree.

"You want to be?" Desiree teased.

Sean blushed, but didn't respond.

Sequoia shook her head. "You're terrible."

"Sequoia, I'm just playing with him," Desiree said. "But you gotta admit he's cute."

"CHECK PLEASE!" Sequoia said to the waitress as she walked past the table while simultaneously responding to a text from T. Bibby. "I have to go to T. Bibby's office for a short meeting."

Though Desiree was speaking in a joking manner, she was dead serious. She figured that all people were tied to a certain type of parson, and hers was tall, dark, with a muscular build and a college boy attitude. The description fit Sean Oniwakue perfectly, but she had no desire to scare him off by being too aggressive, so she decided to relent. But only after one more question.

"I'm sorry," Desiree said, "but do you carry a gun?"

Sean rose from his chair and helped Desiree to her feet. "A Sig Sauer," he answered as he helped Sequoia to her feet as well. "Thank you for the meal."

"Don't mention it," Sequoia said.

"Oh," Desiree crooned, "I don't know what that is but it sounds intimidating."

Sequoia left a hundred dollar bill to cover the cost of the meal. She was sure that the meals did not exceed sixty dollars, but she couldn't stand another minute of Desiree drooling over her protector, not to mention that she wanted to leave the waitress a generous tip.

Sequoia brushed Desiree aggressively as she made her way out of the establishment, a gesture that Desiree understood as meaning that she was seriously annoyed with her.

"She looks upset," Sean said.

"She'll be alright," Desiree assured him. "Especially when you get up there and protect her," she smiled derisively.

"We need a sound check on this mic," a female audio technician said as she placed the audio apparatus onto the back of Sequoia's wardrobe and attached it to the microphone and earpiece that went to her headpiece.

Her earpiece would deliver the music to her song to her so she could stay on rhythm.

Sequoia was dressed in a black, embroidered, stretch

material, cat suit that was sheer along the length of either side of her body. Her wardrobe was complimented with a pair of black, closed-toe, three inch Chanel heels. Her hair was curly and draping over her shoulders.

Desiree, along with two other dancers, was dressed in black leather, high-riding shorts, with a sheer and leather laced top, and black pumps. All of the dancers' hair was pulled back into ponytails.

"You ready?" T. Bibby asked as he approached Sequoia in the backstage area.

"As ready as I'm gonna be," Sequoia smiled nervously.

"Look, you got this. Don't worry about nothing. Just go out there and kill it," Bibby told her with sincere confidence.

Her meeting with him had been very productive on all fronts. She discovered that she now had over five thousand spins a day on various radio stations throughout the country, including Chicago, New York, Los Angeles, Florida, Virginia, D.C., and Atlanta, but what she was most thrilled about was that she would be going on *106th and Park* with Rocki and Torrence J. to introduce the world premiere of her new video.

By now the Highline Ballroom was jam-packed, and the music that was thumping from the previous act (who was currently on the stage performing) had the whole place rocking.

Everyone, from wardrobe technicians, hip hop and R and B artists, audio and visual technicians, agents, and managers scurried about the arteries of the Highline Ballroom frantically.

When the preceding act ended, the stage coordinator that she would be going on next alerted Sequoia.

"Look," Bibby rubber her by the shoulders, "this is your moment. It's one of many more to come. It's what you've always dreamed of, and it's what you walked out on school for. Don't let it all be in vain. Time to show and prove," Bibby coached her. "You got it?"

Sequoia nodded, but inside she was beginning to feel her anxiety building. She quickly converted back to her routine therapeutic remedy and thought of a calming tide coming in from the ocean along the Costa Rican coast.

"Hello, Bibby," Desiree said as she approached them both.

"What's up girl? You ready to go out there and do your thang?" he asked jovially.

"I'm a little nervous, but I'll be good," Desiree admitted. "As long as my girl here has her game face on we'll be good." She placed her arm over Sequoia's shoulder. "You read to do this, Quoy?"

"As ready as I'm gonna be," Sequoia said unconvincingly. "Guess what though?"

"What?"

"I'm going to be on *106th and Park*."

"Really?" Desiree search Sequoia and Bibby's expressions for any hint of joking. "When?"

"Next week," Sequoia said.

"Quoy that's wonderful!" She hugged her.

"Sequoia, sweetie, you're up," the stage coordinator said.

"Okay," Sequoia shook her limbs loose and exhaled deeply. "Wish me luck."

"Good luck girl! You got this." Desiree was excited.

"Sequoia?" Bibby said. "Go out there and have fun. Don't worry about being perfect or none of that. Just remember your choreography and everything else will flow naturally."

Sequoia nodded attentively. "Okay."

She mounted the stairs that led to the stage, followed by Desiree and the two other dancers. When they received the cue, everyone took their position on the stage as the lights in the Highline Ballroom went off.

Sequoia said a silent prayer as she lowered her head. The audience was dead silent, and somehow, in that moment, Sequoia found peace. When the song started she sprang to life. A clip of her video played in bits on the large projector screen that was above her head.

The dancers, along with Sequoia, were in sync with the rhythmic beat, and when Sequoia crooned her song over the beat with one of the most unique and captivating voices ever to grace an eardrum the audience nearly melted. She ended her song to a standing ovation from the crowd. The crowd began to get so loud that Sequoia wondered if they were cheering for the song at all. At one point, Sequoia found herself inconspicuously checking to see if she had a wardrobe malfunction.

When she was able to rule that possibility out, she realized that it may very well be because of her performance. She bowed and blew kisses to the fans appreciatively before making her exit off the stage, where she was immediately greeted by an ecstatic Bibby.

"That's what I'm talking 'bout girl!" he exclaimed. "You killed that shit!"

"Didn't she?" Desiree hugged her from behind.

The rest of her dance crew, including Bibby, was congratulating her on a job well done.

"Thank you!" Sequoia said emotionally to everyone. "Thank you!"

"That was amazing Sequoia," Bibby said. "Tell you what; how about we catch the rest of the show and I'll take you and Desiree out to one of my favorite restaurants in New York?" he told her. "Besides, I need to discuss some things with you about touring and doing a few features with some good friends of mine."

"I hope y'all are talking about me," Famous said as he approached them. Bibby embraced him and him and Sequoia exchanged hugs.

Famous was sporting a custom leather Louis Vuitton outfit, with custom Louis Vuitton Air Force One gym shoes. His hair was low and tapered, and boasted a deep wave pattern. His smile revealed a chipped tooth, and his eyes were covered with dark Louis

Vuitton shades.

"I seen you killing it out there," Famous told Sequoia.

"Thank you!"

"And I seen the news, too," Famous said. "I'm sorry you had to go through that."

Sequoia nodded solemnly.

"But I wanted to know if I could get you on my next album."

"Tell you what," Sequoia said. "You help me with a single on mine, and I'll help you with one on yours."

"That's what's up," Famous said, looking at Bibby. "I see you're showing her the ropes."

"My apprentice," Bibby joked.

"Famous, you're up right now," the stage coordinator told him.

"Alright." He turned to Sequoia. "I'll have my people get with your people."

"Quick thinking," Bibby said, "but you may want to think about changing clothes. You're beginning to be a distraction to everyone around here."

"What? No I'm not." Sequoia looked around and noticed that everyone, from the audio technicians to the janitors, was derisively staring at her. "You know what, you're right. We'll be in my dressing room. Could you please tell Sean to guard my door?" Bibby nodded. "C'mon Desiree," she said.

"Gotcha," Bibby said as he watched her walk towards her dressing room. She turned around just in time to lock eyes with him. He was staring at her as she walked, she thought, but instead of being offended Sequoia blushed and offered him a warm smile before entering the dressing room behind Desiree.

CHAPTER 29

The boisterous applause from the *106th and Park* audience warmly ushered the hosts, Torrence J. and Rocki, onto the show. The two emerged from backstage with huge smiles and salutary gestures in some of the latest exclusive sponsored apparel.

Torrence waited for the crowd to simmer down before speaking. "Hello everybody, I'm your host Torrence J."

"And I'm Rocki," she chimed in.

"And you're watching *106th and Park* on B.E.T.," Torrence said. "We have a lot of things in store for you today."

The audience applauded.

Torrence J. continued. "Today we have some very special guests in the building," he paused. "We got my man T. Bibby." The audience applauded.

"He's introducing an up and coming artist by the name of Sequoia, who has gained a tremendous amount of notoriety from her YouTube video (which you may be familiar with). She will be introducing the world premiere of her new video, 'Caribbean Girl,' today in a little bit."

More applause ensued.

Rocki spoke; "But until then, we'll be kicking off the countdown with Ace Block coming in at number ten with 'Grind.'"

The video played as Sequoia endured the grueling process that was hair and make-up in her dressing room. "You have some of the most beautiful, evenly toned skin that I've ever seen," the plus-size female make-up artist of African descent said. "It almost seems like a sin to disrespect it with make-up," she joked.

"Thank you!" Sequoia exclaimed.

"I'm serious, girl," the woman said. "I've been doing this for fourteen years and I have never seen skin like this. And are those your real eyes?"

Sequoia blushed. "Of course."

"Wow!" The woman came within inches of Sequoia's face. "What color are they?"

"Depends on the time of the year," Sequoia said. "Sometimes they're green, but the natural color is aqua blue."

"That's amazing!" The woman shook her head jealously. "It should be a crime to look that good."

Sequoia sighed. "Stop it."

"I'm serious," she laughed. "Tell you what; I'll just use a little blush and eye shadow. Is that alright?"

Sequoia nodded. "That's cool."

A knock at the door interrupted her train of thought.

"Come in," Sequoia said.

"You ready to do this?" Bibby said as he entered the room. "What's good, Tiffany?" he spoke to the make-up artist.

"Hey Bibby."

"A few more minutes and I'll be good to go," Sequoia said.

"That's what's up," he said. "Just follow my lead, and don't worry about anything. Rocki and Torrence J. are excellent hosts so you'll have nothing to worry about. Consider this your new home," he said. "You got anything else you wanna know before we go out there?"

"As a matter of fact I do." Sequoia turned to face him. "Will they be asking me about the incident at school?"

"No," he said. "I spoke with the producers about it and we've agreed to just focus on the video today. But they wanted to know if you'd be interested in coming back to the show to discuss your attack to bring awareness to the seriousness of the issue of on campus attacks."

Sequoia pondered it for a moment. "What do you think?"

"I'd say it's a no brainer: do it," he responded. "It'll give you a chance to connect with your fan base on a more intimate level. It will show them that you're an actual human being that goes through real life events like anyone else."

Sequoia nodded as she digested what he was saying.

One of the female producers of *106th and Park* knocked on the door before poking her head in. "We're going to need you guys in five."

"Alright. Give us a minute," Bibby said. "I'll be outside waiting for you Sequoia. Try not to take too long."

Tiffany concluded her magic touch with one last stroke of the powder brush.

"You're all set," Tiffany said before picking her IPhone up off a nearby table and searching the options. "Is it alright if I get a picture of you?"

"Yeah, but we gotta hurry up." Sequoia posed beside her as Tiffany snapped a picture of them both with her phone.

"Good luck out there."

"Thank you!" Sequoia said as she gathered her things to leave.

The song from the previous video faded in the backdrop as Torrence J. got his cue from the producers to host.

"Alright, this next guest needs no introduction. He's a long time member of the *106th and Park* family. I'm talking about rapper, actor, producer, business mogul, oh MAN the list goes on," Torrence J. said energetically.

"Give it up for the one and only—" Rocki said.

"T. BIBBY!" They both said in unison as Bibby emerged from backstage to a roaring applause.

Bibby was dresses in an all black Deshawn Juan jogging suit and black Number Nine Air Jordan gym shoes. His neck boasted a platinum chain and Jesus medallion covered in diamonds. His ears were adorned with enormous rocks that looked like they were carved out of Arctic glaciers.

Bibby shook hands with various members of the audience as they gave him a warm, loud, cheering welcome.

"Man!" Torrence J. said in disbelief. "Feels like we got the president up in here!" he joked. The audience simmered down.

Bibby embrace Torrence and Rocki. "What's good, y'all?"

"I'm good," Torrence J. said, "and as always I see that you're doing big things."

"Yeah, but word Torrence J," Bibby said in his arrogantly authoritative tone while staring into the camera. "I want to focus on my new artist today. She's hot! She's beautiful! And she's about to kill the game!" he said confidently.

"And by new artist, Mr. Bibby is talking about the YouTube sensation Miss Sequoia Ariás," Rocki said. The audience applauded.

"And yo, if you haven't seen or heard this girl, you have obviously been living under a rock," Torrence J. said, gaining everyone's attention. "Aside from her beauty, this one may have one of the most epic and memorable voices of the 21st century."

"Torrence is right," Rocki chimed in. "I heard her voice, and this woman is amazing."

"So, without further suspense, we want to welcome Sequoia to the *106th and Park* family," Torrence said as Sequoia emerged from the backstage to an earth-shattering applause.

She strutted sexily on three inch heels into a deafening applause from the audience. Sequoia waved and smiled.

Sequoia took her position next to Bibby as the crowd continued on with their applause.

"Wow!" Rocki said shockingly as she surveyed the audience's reaction to Sequoia's presence. She stared at Torrence blankly as the crowd continued on.

The applause ensued for so long that Torrence J. had to interject to try to calm them down. When he was finally able to do so, he conducted his interview.

"Wow!" he exclaimed. "I don't think I've ever heard the audience this hyped up before. What about you Rocki?"

"Definitely not," Rocki laughed. "So first, let's start off by saying that we want to introduce you as the newest member of the *106th and Park* family."

The audience applauded.

"And of course I'm checking you out up here killing it. Your shoe game is crazy!" Rocki said as Sequoia modeled her black, open-toed, suede and leather with faux-fur trim, Salvatore Ferragamo pumps.

The shoes complimented the tight-fitted, black, suede and satin, Hermes dress that she was wearing, which rose four inches above her knee. Her long mane was pulled back into a pony tail and hung freely over her right shoulder in one large braid.

Torrence J. smiled at Sequoia mischievously. "Damn girl! You standing there looking like a sexy-ass margarita," he said, causing everyone to laugh. "So I hear that you're a Harvard law student?"

Sequoia nodded. "That's partially true," she said. "Unfortunately I've had to make some very tough decisions lately because of my work schedule, so I'm putting school off for awhile. But that does not mean that I encourage someone to do the same. Stay in school and get your education." She pointed at the audience and they applauded.

"So, this is your first time ever, well, second time, shooting a video right?" Rocki said.

"No, you were right the first time. This was my first video," Sequoia said.

"But what about the video on YouTube?" Rocki asked.

Sequoia laughed. "Believe it or not, I had no idea my best friend was going to do that. Unbeknownst to me, she had been compiling a serious of events together to make the clip, and posted it on YouTube without me knowing."

Torrence and Rocki laughed.

Rocki said, "And judging by you standing up here with me, everything worked out in your favor."

The audience applauded.

"Yes it did." Sequoia smiled. "Thanks to my girl, Jade, who couldn't be here with me today. So, if it's alright, I'd like to give a shout out to Jade."

"That's what's up," Torrence said. "And T. Bibby, when did you first hear about here?"

"I think the video was posted for all of three or four weeks, and she had over ten million hits, and a good friend of mine that works at the label put me up on her. And you know once I seen the video, the rest is history."

The audience applauded.

"So, going back to the video. You shot this joint in the Caribbean somewhere, right?" Torrence J. asked.

Sequoia nodded. "In Costa Rica, my native land. It's actually where I was born, but in reality it's only one of many." She laughed.

"One of many?" Torrence said. "Yo, I did hear that you were mixed with like three or four nationalities or something like that."

"It's four," Sequoia said. "I'm Costa Rican, Native American, Nicaraguan, and Filipino."

Torrence J. shook his head in disbelief. "Yo, I'm at a loss for words." He walked off the stage in a dramatic fashion, causing everyone in the audience to laugh.

Rocki laughed. "We're going to get back to the countdown while Torrence throws his tantrum. Go ahead and introduce your video, Mami."

Sequoia looked at the camera. "I'm Sequoia, and this is the world premiere of my new video, 'Caribbean Girl.'"

When the video ended, the expression on Torrence J. and Rocki's faces clearly said that it was a hit.

Torrence looked into the camera with a serious expression. "Look, we have to vote this video on the countdown. Text S-E-Q, seven, seven, two, nine, nine to vote it on."

"Like Torrence said," Rocki added, "you guys have to vote that on the countdown. Please!" she begged in a joking manner. "I love it!" She smiled.

"Uh, T. Bibby, would you like to say something before we go to break?" Torrence asked.

Bibby, with a blank expression, simply said, "Man, that joint speaks for itself. Y'all at home know what to do. Vote."

Torrence laughed. "You're right about that. And what about you Sequoia, you want to give a shout out to somebody?"

"Just my mother, Rosa, and best friend Desiree right there." She waved at them both.

"Oh, that's your mom right there?" Torrence asked, and Sequoia nodded. "Straight up? Yo, mom is fine as hell over there. Well, it's obvious that beautiful women roll together."

"Thank you!" Sequoia spoke into the mic.

"Absolutely, and I'm pretty sure that we'll be seeing your new video on the countdown soon. Just promise me that you'll make this your new home. Matter of fact, maybe sometime in the not-so-far future you can come host the show with me. Is that cool?"

Rocki shot Torrance a jealous glance as Sequoia spoke. "That's cool. I'll be looking forward to that."

"That's what's up," Torrence said. "Look, we're going to take a break, so let the fans know where they can find you on Twitter or Facebook."

"Okay, you can follow me on Twitter at Sequoia backslash."

"Alright, that message was for women only. I don't want no dudes contacting my wife's Twitter page," Torrence said ambiguously. "Now, I'm just joking. But it's been nice having you."

"Thank you," Sequoia cooed softly.

"We'll be back with the countdown after this break," Rocki said.

When the producers cut to commercial, Sequoia, Torrence J, Rocki, and T. Bibby exchanged warm embraces before parting ways. Sequoia and Bibby exited the stage.

"What'd you think?" Sequoia asked as they entered backstage.

"I think you're one step closer to being the hottest thing that ever happened to R and B and pop!" Bibby said. "And I just got a text from Famous, so we're about to swing by the studio to a writing session, and if we can, get some recording done."

"Let's do it."

CHAPTER 30

"How was that?" Sequoia asked Black One, a popular music producer, as she finished laying her vocals down over the track created for her and Famous.

"That was perfect, Sequoia," Black One said into her headphones. "You nailed it on the first take. You can come out right now if you want to, but try to stick around for a minute because I might want you to do a few ad-libs."

"Okay," Sequoia said as she removed the headphones and placed them atop the spit-screen covered microphone. She emerged from the booth to a satisfied crowd.

Bibby was at the boards, along with Famous and Black One, while Rosa and Desiree sat on a plush leather sofa picking over open boxes of Chinese take-out.

Desiree and Rosa smiled giddily at how good Sequoia sounded over the studio monitors. Rosa spoke with a mouthful of beef, broccoli, and white rice: "That was good."

"Mm hmm!" Desiree added, with her mouth filled with shrimp fried rice. "You killed it."

"Thanks guys," Sequoia exclaimed appreciatively.

"Yeah, you killed that, shorty," Famous added. "This record is gonna be a hit. I just wish that it was gonna be on my album."

"Aw!" Sequoia expressed compassion. "Don't worry. I promise to go extra hard whenever we hook up to do your record."

Bibby spoke, "Sequoia, don't know if I mentioned it, but Black One is one of the most prolific producers in this game, and he is a good friend of mine and has been for years. And it's not every day that he has something good to say about any artist, especially a new one.

"So, for him to compliment you on your skills the way he did when you was in the booth..." Bibby looked at Black one. "Just tell her what you told me."

"No doubt, no doubt," Black One said. "It's like this: you're the entire package. Your vocals is hands down some of the best I've ever heard, and trust me, I don't say that often." He paused. "You're extremely beautiful, and you're professional!

"You came in here a couple of hours ago with your game face on, and you finish an entire chorus and a verse. And you did it all before Famous could even write a single word. That's unbelievable!"

"Yeah, she definitely did that," Famous said coolly behind his Cavalli shades.

"I will say this too," Black One said, "I will definitely look forward to working with you in the near future, and if any one of my close friends or associates feels the need to ignore you, I'll be sure to let them know that you're the real deal!"

"Aw!" Sequoia said coyly. "I really do appreciate that."

"Don't mention it," Black One said in an even tone. "You deserve it."

"I don't know what it is, but I ain't feelin' it tonight," Famous said. "So I'ma take that beat to the crib and send you my verse some time tomorrow. I gotta go put some real thought into this one." Famous rose from his chair. "Can't let you kill me on our first song together." He smiled as he towered over her.

"Well, make sure you bring your A game playa, because I'm holding no prisoners," Sequoia said as she poked him in the chest flirtatiously.

Bibby rose from his seat awkwardly and interrupted Famous and Sequoia's moment. "So, are you and your peeps about to head out, or do you plan on sticking around a little bit longer?"

Sequoia had no clue what she was supposed to think about Bibby's public display of jealousy, but she figured for now she would simply pretend as if it never happened.

"I...uh... Actually, I don't know." Sequoia looked at her mother and Desiree for any signs of protest. "You know what, I think we'll just call it a day for the night so I can get my mother back home. Especially since they just insisted that we leave."

Rosa and Desiree frowned at her as they picked up on the hint and began gathering their things.

"Y'all gonna need a ride?" Bibby asked.

"Yup," Sequoia told him before retrieving her Marc Jacobs leather jacket from the coat rack.

Everyone exchanged their goodbyes as Bibby arranged for his driver to escort Sequoia and her party to their respective habitats. When he received the call that their ride was awaiting them just outside the building, the three began to make their departure.

However, as they exited the doorway of the studio on their way to the floor elevator, Famous derisively pulled Sequoia's arm, gaining her attention as her mother and Desiree continued on toward the elevator.

"Sequoia, I apologize for grabbing you like that, but I wanted to know if you'd let me scoop you up so we can kick it sometime?"

Sequoia was taken slightly aback by his abrasiveness, but she respected him and his talent, so on that strength alone she didn't want to disrespect him.

"And what exactly is your definition of kicking it?" Sequoia asked for curiosity's sake.

Famous smiled mischievously. "Shit, we're both consenting adults. I'm pretty sure we can come up with something constructive to do with our time."

Sequoia scoffed and rolled her eyes. "Aren't you engaged?"

"Something like that," he vaguely admitted in a hushed tone.

"And you have kids, right?" Sequoia shot him a noteworthy glance.

"One, actually," he corrected her.

"Right," Sequoia said dryly, "well, I'm sorry, but I have no desire to become a home-wrecker."

"Sequoia, I'm not asking you to get married. I just want to kick it."

Sequoia sighed heavily. "Look, I don't want to be disrespectful, but I don't want anything to do with you or any other man in this industry," she said curtly. "I think you're a very talented artist, and I appreciate you working with me, and I'll be looking forward to working with you again, but that's as far as that goes."

Famous nodded solemnly. "I can respect that. And I'ma tell you something." He took his shades off and stared into her eyes. "It's a lot of snake ass fuck niggas in this game that won't give a fuck about you. All they'll want from you is some pussy so they can brag to their niggas about you. And ain't nothing more worse in this industry than a woman that can't keep their legs closed.

"Protect your reputation. Without it, you'll never go far in this game."

Sequoia nodded.

"Be easy, girl," Famous told her, "and in the event that you change your mind, my offer's still on the table." He laughed. "I'm just fucking with you. I'll be finished with the verse tomorrow."

Sequoia smiled awkwardly as she locked gazes with T. Bibby over Famous's shoulder. The moment was short, but long enough for Sequoia to pick up on the envious undertone that lay beneath his sudden change in body language.

However, Sequoia didn't feel the need to entertain her assumption by staying long enough to find out what he was thinking. But one thing was certain; he needed to get a handle on the possessive drives he was handling her with before it compromised their business relationship.

Sequoia accompanied Desiree and Rosa into the open elevator car.

"What did he want?" Desiree asked immediately.

Sequoia looked at her plainly. "To remind me of something I already knew?"

Desiree waited for a brief moment, anticipating more details, and when they never came she inquired: "Remind you of what?"

"Not to trust these dudes in the industry," Sequoia said. "They're all the same."

CHAPTER 31

The Next Day

"So, how do you like your new place mom?" Sequoia asked Rosa as she dropped a two of spades on the couch before her and Rosa.

Rosa scooped the spade up with a two of diamonds. "I like it very much. Thanks for asking," Rosa said, and they both laughed.

They were playing a game of Casino, a game that they both had grown accustomed to playing with each other since Sequoia was a little girl. It was also one of the only things that her father had taught her to do before deserting them.

Sequoia dealt another four cards to the both of them and waited for Rosa to toss a card out. "So, how have you been feeling lately?" She studied Rosa for any attempt at downplaying the situation. "I mean, physically."

"Doctors say I'm expected to make a full recovery. He suggested that I stay in hospice so they could monitor me closer, but I told him that it wouldn't be necessary."

"You sure?" Sequoia asked with a knowing eye trained on her.

Rosa sighed heavily and trained her aqua blue eyes on Sequoia with an annoyed expression. "Yes, I'm sure Sequoia." She paused to consider Sequoia's body language, and wasn't convinced that she believed her. "Sequoia, I'm fine, really. Seriously, this is the happiest that I've ever been in my life. My little girl is all grown up and doing her own thing, and is actually taking care of me now. And I've got the operation that I needed.

"In all truth," Rosa wiped the tears that were fighting to emerge from her eyelids, "I don't want to think about how much worse my condition would be right now if it weren't for you."

Sequoia was now shedding tears as well. She hated to entertain the what-if's that had lain in wait outside of her mother's door if she hadn't stepped up to the plate when she did. She worked hard, saved, and stripped to provide any contribution that she could to get the bone marrow transplant that Rosa needed. Though the past life that Sequoia had lived seemed as if it were centuries old, the mental and emotional scars that still remain from that time were very relevant and alive at the present moment. Now that she was more financially blessed, she intended to do everything in her power to personally see to it that Rosa lived the long, prosperous life that she deserved.

"Come here," Rosa pulled Sequoia into her warm embrace. "Te amo! You hear me?"

Sequoia nodded as the tears cascaded down her face. "I love you too."

"Just us," Rosa said before interlocking pinky fingers with Sequoia. It was a gesture that they'd been doing ever since the divorce to display their loyalty and commitment to each other.

"Just us," Sequoia repeated with a weak smile. "Guess our little card game is done for today."

"I guess so," Rosa laughed as she wiped her eyes, "but look on the bright side: we're back living under the same roof, so we can play a million times more before you leave."

Sequoia had decided to stay with her mother until she was able to find her own place to stay. She appreciated the gesture that Bibby had extended to her by letting her take up residency in his condo, but she didn't want to send Bibby any wrong messages by being in such close proximity—even if he was 'barcly there,' as he incessantly put it. She also didn't want her mother to get the wrong impression either, because as painful as it would be to deliver the news to her, she had no plans to stay there with her either. The problem was, she now had to convey her feelings to her.

"Right," Sequoia said uncertainly. "About that. You do realize that I just signed a five million dollar contract, and that I'll be spending the majority of my time in the studio until my tour dates get set? Assuming that I don't decided to get my own place in between them."

Rosa frowned. "Well, I'm certainly not looking forward to that."

"Don't say it like that." Sequoia was feeling guilty. "You know I'd never leave you like that."

"I know, Sequoia," Rosa said.

"But you know what?" Sequoia asked. "I've been thinking. How would you like for me to get you a nanny?"

"No thank you," she said curtly.

"Could you at least think about it?"

Rosa pondered it for a moment. "Thought about it." She snatched up the cards. "The answer is still no."

"You're no fun." Sequoia pouted. "Think about it some more for me please. I need to know that you're gonna be taken care of whenever I do get on the road."

"Like I said, I'll think about it."

"Um hm." Sequoia rolled her aqua blue eyes and caught a glimpse of the TV screen out of her peripheral view. "Mom, look!" She fumbled with the remote as she raised the volume to *106th and Park.*

Rocki spoke. "Alright now, this next artist was just on the show a couple days ago and received so many votes from our viewers that her new video jumped straight to number six on our countdown."

Torrence J. said, "That's right. We're talking about none other than my lovely wife, Sequoia."

Rocki rolled her eyes and sighed heavily.

"I still haven't officially told her that we're getting married, and I hope that me telling millions of viewers first doesn't affect her decision when I ask her." Torrence J. laughed. "Girl, you know I'm just playing. But here's the new video by my wife, Sequoia: 'Caribbean Girl.' Hope you guys enjoy it."

Sequoia was so ecstatic that she forgot to breathe for a full ten seconds. Rosa and she embraced each other tightly as they jumped and screamed joyfully.

Sequoia had ascended to an astronomical height. She was high off of light right now! She'd always dreamed and fantasized about having a video of her own on B.E.T. and now that it had actually happened she was awestruck.

However, the blissful euphoria that she planned to dwell in forever, like most things, had its expiration date. Within the next five minutes, her phone was going so berserk that she was convinced that her expiration date had come. It was a text message from Jade, Desiree, and one from T. Bibby. Everyone was congratulating her on entering the countdown. Bibby also added that he would need her in the studio at her earliest convenience.

Sequoia looked at Rosa. "I'll need a rain check if you intended on celebrating. The boss needs me at the studio."

The disappointed look on Rosa's face clearly said that Sequoia's new field of employment would take some serious getting used to.

"I understand," she said dryly. "Just try to call before you come, so I'll know to expect you," Rosa said before retreating to her bedroom.

Sequoia found the situation to be a bit ironic. She maintained a 4.0 G.P.A. over nearly five years and somehow she couldn't quite interpret why Rosa was acting so clingy all of a sudden. Surely she had to know that no matter how much she would like to stick around and live with her, her life as they once knew it was changing. She would need her own space, possibly in multiple states at some points, and would undoubtedly be spending long stints away from everyone. At this point, she could only hope that Rosa could get with the program. If she didn't, there may serve to be some serious glitches in her system along the way.

CHAPTER 32

The passing weeks had taken a tremendous toll on Sequoia's eating and sleeping habits. Her schedule, after the premiere of her video on B.E.T., had gotten so hectic that she could hardly keep up. That was the reason why she'd just downed her third energy drink within the past twelve hours and was practically plotting on conquering her last one.

The mounting buzz surrounding the Sequoia brand throughout the music industry had sparked a controversial spike in the demand for her talents amid the elite producers and artists of the game. She largely attributed the demand to word-of-mouth, along with her guest appearance on B.E.T.

Nevertheless, it was a demand that she intended to meet with quality supply within a reasonable time frame. So, whenever she was granted clearance from her label to work with an artist, she always sent her chorus or verse back within the next twenty-four hours.

Her professionalism and hasty responses had earned her referrals from producers like Timberlake, Swiss Bangers, and Smooth and Trey, which resulted in more work and features on songs with artists like Chris Black, Rich Frost, and Gooch. Not to mention the top songwriters like Kory Hilton, Ricko Love, and Neon, who T. Bibby had personally arranged for her to work with on her first album. The high demand for Sequoia's talents allowed her to charge sixty-five thousand for a feature, something that was grossly atypical for a new artist.

Sequoia understood her position fully. She was blessed, and eternally grateful to T. Bibby for all the help that he was providing her with, and she reciprocated his generosity back by chaining herself to her office desk (so to speak), spending countless hours in the studio, sacrificing both her sleep and food as a means to show him that she was just as dedicated, if not more so, to the success of her career as he was.

It was an admirable gesture on her part, and certainly one that hadn't gone unnoticed by T. Bibby. Though, she had no idea of knowing this until he brought it to her attention.

Sequoia was fortified in Studio 101, in Brooklyn. The studio sat inconspicuously tucked between a Chinese food store and a nail salon in a strip mall. The location was a lot less sophisticated than the studio in the skyscraper, but something about it had a secret hold over Sequoia. The ambiance had a warm, homey feel to it that seemed to galvanize a creative side in Sequoia that she hadn't known existed. Plus, it was a whole lot cheaper.

One thing that it wasn't, however, was a safe haven from T. Bibby. His over-protective defenses had remained at an all-time high ever since the incident on campus with Dhuram. Any missed text messaged or phone calls immediately flipped his caution meter into panic mode, and unfortunately for Sequoia, today was no different.

One simple mistake, like failing to bring her phone charger along with her to the studio, which consequently led to her phone battery dying out, had gotten Studio 101 raided with three of Bibby's muscle-headed goons, with him in tow. It was a bit dramatic for Sequoia's taste, but she took comfort in knowing that someone genuinely cared about her personal safety.

"What's good, Ricko Love?" Bibby checked the producer out as he entered the room while suspiciously eyeing him for any signs of foul play.

Bibby was dressed in faded black denims, white Air Force One gym shoes, a black leather Pelle Pelle coat with fur along the neckline, and a gray designer sweater.

Bibby removed his designer shades and conspicuously scanned Sequoia's appearance as she sat on the leather sofa with her writing tablet.

"You alright?" Bibby asked Sequoia.

She smiled knowingly. "Yeah, I'm good." She held up her phone. "I forgot to bring my charger. My battery's dead."

"Ah," Bibby said. He was noticeably embarrassed, but played it off well. "I figured there had to be a reason why you weren't answering your phone."

Bibby looked at his body guards. "Give me a minute." He walked over to Sequoia and sat beside her. When he noticed the bags that were beginning to take shape underneath her eyelids he said, "You need some sleep."

Sequoia rolled her eyes. "Yes, dad," she joked, "as soon as I finish this song that I've been working on."

Bibby laughed. "Dad, huh? Funny." He removed his Blackberry from his hip and scanned his screen. "I've got forty-three dates scheduled for you, starting in the middle of June."

"That's nearly three months from now," Sequoia said.

"Exactly," Bibby responded. "So what we need to start going over is what songs we are going to do. Also, we have to schedule more choreography. And don't forget, you have a few more recent dates in Jersey, Philly, and here in New York."

Sequoia nodded.

"And usually the label would handle these types of issues, but I want you to have as much creative control over your own career as possible: that goes for your wardrobe, music, concepts, choreography, all the way down to your image. And considering how hard you've been working, we'll probably be having that conversation a lot quicker than I'd expected.

"That is why I'm going to need you to take a break from all of this and get some sleep. Your schedule isn't about to get any easier anytime soon.

"I talked to Famous yesterday about a video for that 'Chemistry' joint as soon as next week, and over the next few weeks I have you scheduled to do photo shoots for *Ebony, Essence, Esquire Magazine*, and modeling my tall line of women's wear, not to mention a few radio stations in the country."

Sequoia sighed. "Wow! That sounds... challenging. But I'm pretty sure I'll make you proud," Sequoia said confidently.

"There's no doubt in my mind," he said, suddenly adopting a more even tone. "Now, what I also want to talk to you about is your manager, Jade."

"What about Jade?" Sequoia didn't understand where he was going with all this.

"It's nothing bad or anything, I assure you of that," he said, "but this is a business, and I know that you may have a personal relationship with her, but I don't want you to let that get in the way of your opinion of what I'm about to say."

Sequoia couldn't comprehend his angle so she braced herself for whatever it was he may have to say.

Bibby picked up on her uneasiness and thought to reassure her before he continued on. "Sequoia, it's no big deal. Really," he said. "I just want to say that from a business standpoint, your girl Jade is not being very productive in the capacity of a manager's role."

"She's trying. I talked to her yesterday," Sequoia attempted to defend her. "She says that she keeps getting stone-walled, but she is trying."

"And I'm not knocking that," Bibby said, "but it's something that you need to take under strong consideration if you intend on being successful in this game.

"And one of the first things is that you realize that you're only going to be as strong as your team. Everyone from your accountant down to your daily stylist has to be for the best interest of your professional career, because if this is not the case, then I guarantee you, you will lose!"

"But Jade does have my best interests at heart? Things just aren't working out for her right now."

"That's because she lacks experience and connections," he told her. "Now, that doesn't mean that she isn't a wonderful person, but like I said before, from a business standpoint, your business relationship with her is not benefiting you."

"Now, you can continue to pay her ten percent of whatever you make from now on for doing absolutely nothing for you in a business sense, or you can make some much needed adjustments in your roster so that it benefits you in the near and distant future."

"Like what?" Sequoia asked timidly as she slowly digested his logic.

"Hire me as your manager," he said almost immediately. "Because, let's be honest, I've been functioning in that capacity for awhile now anyway. But, instead of the ten percent you were paying Jade, I'll want fifteen percent."

"I don't know..." she said skeptically as she ran her palm over the white headband that partially secured the ponytail she was sporting. She was wearing dark, Old Navy, blue jeans, blue and burgundy Old Navy sweater, and a pair of blue and white Number Five Air Jordan gym shoes.

"What's there to know, Sequoia?" he retorted. "I've booked all of your dates. I've arranged for multiple photo shoots, radio interviews, and you're working with some of the hottest producers and artists in the game because of me. I don't want to make it seem like I'm pressed for a bigger cut because we both know I don't need the money, but like I said before, this is business, and I'm providing a service that, frankly, I may as well get paid for." He chuckled. "Just think about it."

Sequoia was thinking alright. She was just finding it extremely hard to be objective about his proposition, though it made totally good sense.

Still, it was something about his timing, or the presentation, that wasn't sitting well with her. She had no intention of letting her personal opinions cloud her better judgment or steer her from the fact that he made several very valid points, none of which included the fact that her video had be a number one on the B.E.T., V.H.1, and M.T.V. countdowns for over two weeks, and that her hit single was steadily climbing the Billboard 100 while the single had over eight hundred thousand downloads on ITunes.

"I'ma leave you to get back to your work for now," Bibby said as he rose from her seat. "Kareem is gonna stay with you to make sure you make it back home safely," he said. "Just have him call me if you need me." He made his way toward the door after giving Ricko Love a pound. "Start keeping an extra battery with you. You had half of the world worried about you," he said, before making his departure.

Sequoia sighed as she watched T. Bibby and his entourage of goons file out of the room behind him. She wanted to feel some kind of way about their little meeting, and to some end, offer deep thought to what it was that he was suggesting, but deep down she knew what she had to do—and in the end it only made sense!

CHAPTER 33

"Well, well, well," Dr. Ming Lee said teasingly as Sequoia entered her office. "Look who decided to finally stop by." She closed the door behind Sequoia and embraced her warmly. "I almost thought that you were going to cancel on me again."

"I know, I'm sorry!" Sequoia said genuinely. "It's just been so hectic for me lately."

"I can imagine." Dr. Lee smiled. "What with you being this big new star now and all," she said dramatically.

"Stop it." Sequoia made her way over to the chaise lounge and sat her leather, black and cinnamon printed Versace purse down.

She was wearing a matching Versace jacket, Falke tights which looked more like stockings with black stripes, black Versace knit top, and a black leather skirt that was embellished with cinnamon stitching. Her attire was complimented with black and cinnamon Versace pumps.

"I did want to congratulate you and wish you the best," Dr. Lee said pleasantly, "and say that I never knew you were so talented. How come you never told me?"

Dr. Lee was dressed in a violet cowl neck knitted sweater, a long black skirt with a thigh-high split up her left leg, and calf-height leather boots.

Sequoia shrugged. "I don't know. Slipped my mind, I guess."

"Well, remind me to get your autograph before you leave." She laughed. "That way I can brag to my daughter when she's a little older and tell her that we're good friends."

"Alright," Sequoia chuckled. "How is she, by the way?"

"Aw, she's so smart," she exclaimed. "Which I personally

believe is a by-product of my genetic makeup, not Henry's."

They both laughed.

"How's your mother?" Dr. Lee asked.

"She's doing so much better, actually," Sequoia said. "Nagging me to death, but doing good nonetheless."

Dr. Lee sat on the edge of her desk. "And how about your attacks?"

"You know, it's funny you ask me that, because I haven't had any trouble out of it. I don't know if it's because I've been busy, or what it is."

"Well, have you been taking your medication?"

"Every morning."

Dr. Lee pondered her reply for a brief moment. "So what are you doing here?"

Sequoia's face contorted to a puzzled expression. "I don't understand."

"Okay," Dr. Lee said slowly. "What I mean is, I've been trying to get you here for over two months and you've cancelled all of your appointments on me. I even called to check up on you when I saw the news that someone on campus attacked you, and you never came. According to you, your mother is getting better, and I'm assuming everyone else is okay.

"So what would make you call me out of the blue and squeeze your little self into my schedule?" she asked, "unless, of course, there is something that is bothering you that you only feel comfortable talking to me about."

Sequoia shook her head in disbelief. "Am I that obvious?"

"Probably not to anyone else," Dr. Lee joked, "but don't worry about that. What's wrong?"

Sequoia sighed heavily before updating Dr. Lee about

everything from her new ambiguous business relationship with T. Bibby to the possible fallout that she stood to suffer with Jade when she advised her of her managerial changes. She even told her about the overprotective and seemingly possessive way in which Bibby dealt with her on a daily basis, not to mention her decision to put school off for awhile.

In essence, she was simply seeking sound advice today, not as a client but as a friend. Just as she had anticipated, Dr. Lee was not one to disappoint.

Dr. Lee walked over to Sequoia and sat beside her. "First, let me say that I think that putting school off temporarily to pursue your lifelong dream was a great idea, and it may be playing the biggest part in your ability to deal with your anxiety better.

"But, in regards to T. Bibby, I strongly feel that you should set some strict boundaries with him, and just let him know that his actions are making you uncomfortable. You also have to understand that that's a two-way street, because you don't want to do anything that may be misinterpreted as suggestive, or anything that will give him the wrong impression about your relationship."

"Trust me, I don't," Sequoia said seriously, understanding exactly what Dr. Lee was implying.

"Well, just be honest with him. Both of them, actually," Dr. Lee said. "Especially Jade. And you should do it quickly, because you don't want her to find out from someone else before you have a chance to tell her. Try not to look at it as if you're being disloyal, because from the way it sounds, she's not really good for that position. Considering that this is business, you have to be willing to make some tough decisions in order to do that."

"Funny," Sequoia said, "that's exactly what he said."

"So you agree that it's time," Dr. Lee continued before she could speak. "Nothing personal on your end. It's just business."

Sequoia nodded. "I understand. I'll call Jade when I get out of here and let her know what's going on," she said flatly. "It just seems wrong, considering that she was the one who put the film together and put it on YouTube, which led to me being discovered. Without her, there would be no me," Sequoia said honestly.

"Sequoia, I'm not saying sever all ties with her. I am more than confident that you can find many things for her to do and keep her in the fold of what you're doing, but when it comes to a manager role, you may have to replace her to get the job done correctly," Dr. Lee said. "Just think about it."

Sequoia nodded apprehensively.

"On another note," Dr. Lee said, "have you been meditating lately?"

"Actually, I have," Sequoia exclaimed. "About forty minutes a day."

"That's great Sequoia," Dr. Lee said as she walked over to her desk and searched for something. "Just keep at it." She located a card and handed it to Sequoia. "What do you think about that?"

Sequoia read the card. "An acupuncture specialist?" she said with great skepticism. "I don't know. What am I supposed to think?"

Dr. Lee shrugged. "I don't know what you're supposed to think, per se, but I will say that I have been to several treatments myself and it is truly a unique experience. I recommend that you try it at least once."

Sequoia studied the card as if it were a foreign object. "I mean, I heard about acupuncture and all, but what exactly does it do for you?"

"A number of things, according to different medical and mental health studies," Dr. Lee said as she pried her calf-high boots off and sat on a large throw pillow. "It relieves stress, helps strengthen the immune system, and gives your limbs and joints a lot more mobility, among other things."

Sequoia's eyebrow furrowed. "Sounds great! I'm just trying to wrap my mind around being a human pin-cushion." She chuckled.

Dr. Lee laughed. "It's not like that at all. In all truth, you can barely feel it."

"I'll think about it," Sequoia said, unconvinced.

"Please do," Dr. Lee said, "because in your new line of work it can get very easy to lose yourself with everything that's going on. You want to stay as grounded as possible."

"I definitely agree with you on that." Sequoia kicked her shoes off and walked over to the throw pillow that was adjacent to Dr. Lee's and took a seat.

Dr. Lee subsequently lit several incense sticks and filled the backdrop with a relaxing recording of a rainforest's waterfall.

The two then freed their minds into a meditative state and ascended to a peaceful state of spiritual bliss.

Though temporary, Sequoia basked in the aversion for as long as her conscious would allow, because she silently dreaded the idea of the reaction she would receive from Jade when she conveyed to her that her services would no longer be required. She was almost certain that the news would change the dynamics of their relationship. She only prayed that it would be something that they could get through...together!

CHAPTER 34

The visit to Dr. Lee's office had proven to be a beneficial one in more ways than one for Sequoia. Not only had she received sound advice on two key issues that she'd been struggling with lately, but she also had one of the most productive meditation sessions she had in months. Not to mention the referral to the professional acupuncturist, whom she was strongly considering calling within the next twenty-four hours.

She figured that a thousand needles being shoved into her epidermis would take her mind off of the verbal lashing that she was sure to gain from Jade once she delivered the blow.

Nevertheless, she wanted to get it over with as quick as possible, which was a huge surprise to her, figuring that she'd never been the confrontational type. Jade wasn't making it any easier by no answering her phone. She tried to call her a total of six times already and still no answer, so she called Desiree to see if she had heard anything from her.

Desiree picked up on the fourth ring and answered in a winded tone, "Hello!"

Sequoia looked at the phone. "Desi?"

"Mm hmm."

"Did I call at a bad time?" Sequoia asked apprehensively. "Sounds like you're working out."

"No, I'm good. What's up?"

"I wanted to know if you've seen Jade. I really need to talk to her about something important but she's not answering her phone."

"Actually, I have. She's right here in my living room."

"Oh, is she?" Sequoia said dryly. "That's strange. I didn't even know what she was coming to the city today," Sequoia said. "Tell you what; keep her there for me until I get there."

"Gotcha," Desiree said before hanging up quickly. Sequoia stared at the phone, baffled.

Sequoia was having mixed feelings about how chummy the relationship between Jade and Desiree had become. On one hand, she loved the idea that they both embraced each other as if they'd known each other their whole lives, but on the other hand, there was a suspicious amount of clandestine activity between the two of them that was perplexing to say the least.

The world as Sequoia knew it had changed so much over such a short period of time that she offered very little observation to the little things that had been ever-changing in her immediate circle. Things like Jade's attire, which was usually weird and abstract, but was now hip and sexy, and her timid demeanor, which had been replaced with a fierce attitude.

Not to mention the frequency in which they conversed and visited each other. Sequoia was beginning to hope that she had nothing to worry about with them too.

For the sake of her peace of mind, she wanted to give both of them the benefit of the doubt, but her more recent experiences with fame had conditioned her to believe in the worst case scenario— your best friend would be the one to stab you in the back.

Sadly, her suspicions weren't put to rest when she arrived at Desiree's apartment. Upon crossing the threshold, Sequoia immediately noticed a change in room temperature that had nothing to do with the thermostat, but had everything to do with the negative energy that was coming from the couch that Jade and Desiree were sitting on.

"What's up y'all?" Sequoia said apprehensively as she closed the door behind her.

"Hey," they both said dryly without looking up from the television.

The lack of enthusiasm didn't go unnoticed, but Sequoia decided not to address it. "Jade, I didn't know you were coming here today."

Jade scoffed but said nothing.

The gesture slightly irritated Sequoia. "Did I do something wrong guys?" she asked as she sat in Desiree's recliner chair.

Jade shrugged. "I don't know," she said curtly, "did you?"

Sequoia rolled her eyes. "What is this? Why are you treating me like this?"

Jade's body language morphed into a confrontational posture. "I don't know Sequoia. It probably has something to do with you throwing me under the bus as your manager, for T. Bibby."

Sequoia was floored. "Wha—It wasn't like that at all Jade, I swear!" Sequoia said, trying to figure out how Jade found out before she could tell her.

Jade folded her arms across her chest defensively while Desiree pretended that neither of them was in the room. "It wasn't like that, huh?" Jade asked. "Well, why didn't you at least call me to tell me about it instead of letting him do it for you?"

"Wait a minute. Who called you?" Sequoia asked, her angst continuously mounting for a certain someone she knew was responsible.

"Who do you think?" Jade said. "T. Bibby himself."

"T. Bibby," she said in total disbelief. "When?"

"Like four days ago, why?"

"Four days ago?" Sequoia searched her mind for a timeline. "But we only talked about the idea of him being my manager just two days ago, and we never agreed on anything. So why would he even call you and say that?"

"I don't know." Jade shrugged. "Maybe you should call him and find out."

"Jade, honestly, I only discussed the idea of hiring him as my manager two days ago, and I've tried to contact you today to tell you about it but you wouldn't answer your phone."

"So what?" Jade scoffed. "You were looking for me to tell me I was fired?" Jade asked.

"No, no! I only wanted to talk to you about it," Sequoia lied.

"Talk about it," Jade repeated nastily. "What do you think, I'm stupid or something?" Jade rose from her seat and advanced toward Sequoia slow and steady, with an air of aggression that she never knew existed in her. "You know I really don't believe you. I do everything in my power to see to it that you get noticed, and what do you do? You cut me out of the picture as soon as you get the first opportunity."

Jade was now looming over Sequoia menacingly, like an angry wolf, which made her extremely uncomfortable. She couldn't determine whether or not Jade was preparing to attack her, or if she was about to scream in her face.

"Jade it's not like that! I'm serious!" Sequoia was so emotional that she was nearly in tears. She couldn't believe that she had hurt Jade to this degree.

Jade pointed a stern finger in Sequoia's face. "I don't want to hear it, Sequoia. You knew exactly what you were doing, you cold-hearted BITCH!"

Sequoia was taken aback. She was speechless. She'd never seen Jade act remotely aggressive in all of the time that she'd known her, and to see her like this was downright scary.

Sequoia looked up to Desiree for help, but to her surprise she was cracking up laughing on the couch.

"That's enough Jade," Desiree managed to say in between laughing her lungs out. "Stop it!"

"Gotcha," Jade said to Sequoia before laughing violently.

"You should've seen your face," Desiree struggled to say.

Sequoia scanned their faces in confusion for answers. "Wha...

What's happening? What are you guys talking about?"

"She's just playing with you, Sequoia!" Desiree said.

Sequoia stared at Jade to see if there was any truth to what Desiree was saying. When she saw the expression that Jade was wearing, she knew it was true.

Sequoia smacked Jade's thigh. "That's not funny," she said with much attitude before laughing herself.

"I'm sorry Sequoia, but Desiree put me up to it," Jade said.

"Tattle-tale," Desiree teased. "Sorry, Quoy, but in my defense that laugh was well worth it. Your face was classic!"

"Yeah, I hope that me almost having a heart attack was really worth it."

Jade sat down beside her. "And don't worry about the manager position. I agreed with T. Bibby to step down, cause let's be honest, I could never do for your career what he could do," she admitted.

"How did you two even talk?" Sequoia fished. "Did he call you?"

"No, I called him actually, and we both agreed that if we could convince you to allow him to be your manager then I would step to the side."

"But what about your percentage?" Sequoia asked.

"What about it?" Jade asked. "I'm not worried about that. There will be plenty more opportunities for me, maybe in photography or film, which I'm strongly considering pursuing right now. So don't worry about me. Just focus on your career for now."

Sequoia exhaled a sigh of relief. "You don't know what that means to me," Sequoia said emotionally. "I thought you weren't going to want to have anything to do with me when I told you."

"Aw!" Jade advanced toward Sequoia and gave her a hug. Desiree followed Jade's lead, and hugged her as well.

Jade spoke. "Sequoia, I love you! I would never put anything or anyone before our friendship."

"Make that two of us," Desiree added.

"I love you guys too." Sequoia cried tears of joy. It was moments like this that no amount of money in the world could replace.

Sequoia knew that it would take the kind of genuine love and support that Jade and Desiree showered her with to keep her grounded throughout her thriving career.

CHAPTER 35

The prank was cruel, that's for damn sure, but not nearly as cruel as the idea of sacrificing her friendship with Jade over something as insignificant as a management position. Fortunately for Sequoia, fate had profoundly blessed her with one of the best friends the world had to offer, so not only was she able to avoid a Mexican standoff with her, she received her blessing to professionally part ways and figuratively get into bed with T. Bibby. Albeit, at the temporary expense of her sanity, thanks to the well rehearsed charade that Jade and Desiree put together.

What was more important was that she could now put the entire issue behind her and focus solely on her career, which, thanks to Bibby, was steadily gaining momentum.

Over the past several weeks, after the managerial issue, Sequoia performed at several shows in New Jersey, Boston, New York, and Maryland, along with a radio interview with HOT97, and several photo shoots and interviews with top magazine companies like *Ebony, Jet,* and *Esquire.* To her surprise, T. Bibby was personally playing chaperone to her along the way. He even allowed her to use his private jet for business trips to Atlanta and California to work with two of the top producers in the country (whom he had also arranged for her to meet and work with). In all cases, Sequoia wasn't one to disappoint. She showed up ready to work and killed it every time.

Her work ethic and the serious approach she took toward her career was both admirable and intriguing to Bibby, and Sequoia was able to measure her assessment by how well he treated her, and by the personal information he shared with her—not only about his personal life, but also about the intricate dynamics in which the music industry operated. He shared everything from image and marketing to the importance of networking and relationship building.

Sequoia didn't take a fraction of it for granted either. She sucked up the game like Kat stacks at a Souja Boy concert. She knew that she was in a position that most artists in the industry coveted. Most would never be privy to the information and knowledge that Bibby exposed her to, and she was very vocal to him about her appreciation for it.

At times, she felt as if he had taken her under his wing as an apprentice, as if he were preparing her for the future or something. It was something that she wasn't able to make good sense of at the moment, but it was something that she was extremely grateful for nonetheless.

To a small degree, T. Bibby's actions did come as a surprise to her, considering that the aforementioned behavior followed a serious discussion she had with him about maintaining a platonic relationship. It was a conversation that Sequoia felt was unavoidable, and was strongly suggested by Dr. Lee, but it was also one that Bibby had no desire to shy away from. He agreed to uphold their agreement with the utmost integrity.

Sequoia felt that the open line of communication that subsequently resulted from their agreement made it much easier to do business. They began to develop an impenetrable bond that set things into their perfect balance and prodded Bibby to pull some extra strings to keep Sequoia's plate full. As a result, Sequoia's schedule had gotten so hectic with photo shoots, concerts, and various other appointments that her writing sessions and compositions of her own choreography had become her primary sources of entertainment.

However, she was beginning to have mixed feelings about that, partially because the more she'd create, the more creative freedom Bibby would give her over her own career. The downside to her newfound freedom was that the boundless avenues of expression required hard work, and all of her hard work was making her a very dull person.

Sequoia, not being one to dwell in a dormant stat of boredom, quickly acquired two new friends to help her cope with the process: Twitter and texting, or "T and T" as she commonly referred to it.

She'd been stabbing away at the digital keyboard of her phone so much that her thumbs were beginning to develop the early stages of arthritis. Nevertheless, it provided her with the perfect distraction, for the moment, from the bustling occupants at the music video shoot she was currently at.

She had a lead role with the rapper Famous for the hit single "Chemistry" that they'd collaborated on. They'd been filming for the second day now in New York City and were beginning to do the 'money shot,' which would conclude the entire video shooting session.

The shot was taking place at Oai restaurant in downtown Manhattan, where Famous and Sequoia were arranged to have an intimate dinner by candlelight. The shot wasn't expected to last longer than two hours, which was great news to Sequoia since she'd been on the set for the past fourteen hours.

She was in dire need of a hot bubble bath and the Posturepedic mattress that she was secretly waiting to acquaint her Victoria's Secrets with. The only thing, or only one, who was slowing down the process was Famous. The sooner he arrived, the sooner everyone on the set would come to going home, and according to his stylist a few of his celebrity rapper friends had just arrived on set, so he was out back in his trailer giving them the royal treatment. By definition, that meant that they were getting stoned out of their minds—although Famous would generally argue that it was simply for medicinal purposes (something about stressing and insomnia and whatnot).

Sequoia couldn't care less either way. Her only concern was wrapping up the video shoot as soon as possible so she could peel off the tight fitting, strapless Gucci dress she was wearing. She feared that her head would pop if she didn't get it off soon—one of the many cons to being a celebrity.

Whether it was Famous's tardiness, or how uncomfortable she currently felt, it didn't change the fact that she was killing it!

She was wearing an eggshell and gold, strapless Gucci dress that boasted a cotton, knitted design with a gold, knitted, interlocking Gucci insignia just beneath her ample breasts. Her feet were adorned with a pair of eggshell and gold, three inch, Gucci, leather, calf-high heels. The heels of the shoe were metallic gold with a similar metallic hoop that encased her pretty, pedicure-adorned big toe comfortably. Her hair was straight-pressed down her back, and her face bore little to no make-up—only small traces of eye shadow and slight traces of glitter.

She knew that she could be facing murder (by the way she was killing it), but she was extremely uncomfortable and couldn't wait to get out of her costume and into a hot bubble bath, and then climb into her Harvard sweats.

The very thought had subconsciously set Sequoia's gaze on the door, awaiting Famous's unpredictable arrival. She sighed heavily as the fashion stylist fiddled with the wrap-around leather strap on her Gucci heels.

A short while later, Famous emerged through the door dressed in an all-black, leather, custom Gucci outfit with matching tennis shoes and Gucci shades. A brief surge of excitement shot through Sequoia when she noticed Famous, figuring that they could finally get on with the shoot, but it quickly dissipated at the instant she took in the sight of the entourage who was with him. She assumed the two were the cameos.

"Sequoia?" T. Bibby approached her with a skeptical look as he noticed her sudden change in mood. When she didn't respond, he called her again. "Sequoia?"

"WHAT?" she snapped, but quickly regretted it when she saw who it was. "I'm sorry, T. Bibby, I'm just... agitated."

"Somebody upset you?" Bibby asked, getting in protective mode while looking in Famous's direction.

"No, I'm good," she assured him. "I'm just ready to finish this shoot so I can get to a bed."

"Alright. I'll go get the director so we can get started." Bibby walked away and Famous approached her.

"You ready?" Famous asked.

Sequoia nodded as she stared at Jewels Santiago and Fat John coldly.

Famous took in her demeanor as he apprehensively introduced her to them. "Sequoia, this is Jewels Santiago and Fat

John. They're close friends of mine."

"I know who they are," Sequoia said with attitude while staring at Famous, utterly ignoring their presence. "It says a lot about you. The company you keep, and all," she said curtly, before rudely turning her back to them.

The female stylist noticed the sudden change in room temperature and began to busy herself with the wrinkles on Sequoia's wardrobe that didn't exist.

"Sequoia, huh?" Jewels Santiago approached her and spoke out of earshot of Famous and Fat John with an ambiguous smile as Sequoia turned to face him. "Or should I say… Vixen?"

Sequoia sighed irritably. "Never heard of her."

"Look, shorty," Jewels Santiago spoke softly, "your secret's safe with me." When he saw that she wasn't receptive to his small talk he lowered his tone and asked, "How's your friend doing?"

Sequoia stared him down. "What difference does it make?"

"Look," Jewels Santiago was growing frustrated, "just send her my most honest apology. I didn't mean for that shit to go down like that."

"I'm sure she'll be looking forward to hearing that," Sequoia said sarcastically.

"I feel you." Jewels Santiago rubbed his face while staring her down mischievously. "I will say this though. I believed in you from the very first moment I saw you, and I knew you was gonna be something special. Real shit, ma. So whenever you get ready to leave the past in the past, hit me up so we can make some music together… in more ways than one."

Sequoia forced an irritated laugh as she snatched his card out of his hand. "Don't hold your breath."

Sequoia was about to tear the card into shreds, but T. Bibby grabbed it from her. "Make sure you include me in this discussion if we're talking business," he smiled. "I'm her manager."

"Oh, word?" Jewels Santiago said before clapping and embracing Bibby.

"But I'm quite sure she'll love to work with you," Bibby spoke for her.

Sequoia didn't know what to think or say at the moment, so she kept her mouth shut in fear that she might reveal too much. She most certainly didn't appreciate the way in with Bibby rudely asserted his authority into the situation.

Jewels Santiago's eyebrows furrowed. "Well, let me think about that." He clapped Bibby once more before Famous and Fat John approached to show him some love.

Sequoia silently withdrew herself from the crowd, including the stylist who had been eavesdropping heavily but pretending not to. She scoffed to herself as she watched the birds of a feather flocking together.

"Industry niggas ain't shit," she said with disgust while mean-mugging the crowd.

"You alright, Sequoia?" video director Kenny Boomer asked her when he saw how standoffish she was, and how she was staring at the artists.

Sequoia shook off the feeling and smiled at the director. "I'm sorry. You might've caught me in a trance. I really am tired," she partially lied.

"Well, I'ma need you to drink a Red Bull or something, because I need you for this one last shot. The quicker we get this done, the quicker you can leave and go home."

Sequoia laughed. "Naw, I'm good. I'm ready when you are."

"Good. Let's get to it." He assembled everyone and appointed everyone else to their designated areas.

Everyone maintained a professional edge throughout the entire shoot, so they were able to finish within an hour and ten minutes.

The moment couldn't have come soon enough for Sequoia either. No sooner than Kenny Boomer yelled "cut" did she attempt to make her hasty departure. She was in hot pursuit of the dressing room, and would've made it without incident if Fat John didn't throw his humungous figure in front of her.

"Please, just give me a second to explain myself," he attempted to persuade her.

"Aren't you violating one, or several, implications of my restraining order against you right now?" Sequoia asked simply.

"Look, ma, I ain't trying to blow your spot up right now or none of that. I just wanted to come down here and apologize to you in person. My man told me that you were down here doing a shoot and I figured that this would be the best time, if any, to do it," he explained.

"It's just... ever since that night I've been feeling real shitty, ma, and I don't want you thinking of me as no dog ass nigga, because I'm really not like that. I was drunk and I didn't know what the fuck I was doing. And I apologize for that."

"That's comforting to know," she said dryly. "Now, if you'll excuse me." She tried to push past him but he grabbed her arm.

"Damn shorty, you foul ass shit!" he snapped. "A nigga opens up to you and you disrespect a nigga like that?"

Sequoia snatched away from him. "Get your hands off of me," Sequoia spoke in a muffled tone as she trained her eyes angrily on his. "And F.Y.I., you tried to rape me! You violated me! Now, I don't know if you think there's plausible explanation for your behavior from that night, but in my eyes you're nothing but a piece of shit coward who takes advantage of women.

"So, in case you were wondering, no, I don't accept your apology! You can shove it!"

"Is everything alright?" T. Bibby caught the end of Sequoia's onslaught as he approached to address the noticeable confrontation.

"I'm pretty sure your boy will fill you in on all the details. I'll be in my dressing room changing." Sequoia walked off before he could respond. She had no desire to remain in the company of a potential rapist.

Sequoia had always been big on watching the company she kept; her mother taught her that. T. Bibby apparently didn't share the same upbringing. The association itself drew Sequoia to wonder what type of person Bibby really was, what he would be capable of when he got a few drinks in his system. Her opinion thus far was that he was erratic and explosive, but unfortunately for her she would soon learn the true extent to what he was capable of.

CHAPTER 36

Sequoia had been practically coasting on a sea of heated fumes ever since her encounters with Jewels Santiago and Fat John at the video shoot. Two weeks had passed and she still couldn't believe the audacity of both of them, especially Fat John. He knew that he had violated the terms of the restraining order she had taken out against him by coming to the video shoot.

Though she could've easily gotten him arrested, she didn't want all of the attention that she was sure would come from it. She knew that it would create far more problems than it would prevent, so she opted for door number two and gave him a pass this time around. She concluded that next time, however, he wouldn't be so lucky.

Jewels Santiago was a completely different story altogether, carrying on as if he had done nothing wrong that night. He had literally ripped her best friend a new asshole at a time when they were supposed to be getting to know each other better, and he apparently saw nothing wrong with that picture because she consented to have sex with him. It was safe to say that she wouldn't be taking him home to meet Mamma.

Sequoia confided her experience at the video shoot to her dear friend Sasha. Of course, she had to fill in some very secretive blanks for her along the way, secrets that she promised herself she would never tell anyone. But, she rationalized in her mind that Sasha had earned the right to know, being that she'd been there for her when she needed her the most.

So, when Sasha pressed her to reveal the true details of the night that they'd both attended the Fat John concert, she told her everything from the quarter million dollar hush money that Fat John had given her via his lawyer to the way she spent the bulk of it to pay her mother's medical expenses and setting her up in a nice home.

They discussed the juicy details over lunch at a local sushi joint in downtown Manhattan. They wanted to get stuffed before meeting with a realtor that was set to show Sequoia some luxury condos at the Tribeca.

She knew that Rosa wouldn't approve of her wanting to move, but she needed her personal space, not to mention the security and privacy that could only be provided by a sophisticated high-rise condo like the Tribeca. It was somewhere that paparazzi and crazed stalkers couldn't get to.

The plan was to view four properties, but after Sequoia saw the second one she was hit with some purchase-altering information that gave her pause.

"This is one of the most coveted condos in the building," the older, Jewish realtor said as she strutted gracefully on the Brazilian bamboo wood floor. Her heels made a loud echo as she spoke. "And over here, we have floor to ceiling windows that come with an adjustable tint that can be accessed by the touch of a button."

The realtor, Mrs. Silverman, reeked of an expensive perfume in a three thousand dollar, royal blue pantsuit with enough make-up piled onto her face to audition for a circus. "Now, if I could turn your attention to the kitchen—"

"How much?" Sequoia was ready to cut through the red tape.

"Excuse me?" Mrs. Silverman wasn't sure if she'd heard her correctly.

"How much does it cost?" Sequoia retorted.

Mrs. Silverman clasped her hands together nervously before courageously spilling out, "I can let it go for an even thirty K a month."

Sequoia swallowed hard. "Thirty thousand a month?" she exclaimed. "That's ridiculous."

Mrs. Silverman expressed shock. "I beg your pardon Miss Ariás, but the Tribeca is one of our firm's most sought-after real estate but some of the most powerful and influential people in New York. Many A-list celebrities, from Justin Timber to T. Bibby, reside in this building."

Sequoia shot Sasha a troubled glance at the mention of T. Bibby's name.

"T. Bibby stays in this building?" Sequoia asked Mrs. Silverman.

"That's right," she responded.

Sequoia looked back at Sasha. "Why haven't you told me that before?"

"I didn't know," Sasha quickly defended herself. "I had no idea he stayed here."

Sequoia took a moment to think the whole thing over. "I guess that is kinda weird, right?" Sasha said. "Staying in the same building as your boss? But everyone knows that he has houses all over this town."

"True. And it's not like I would ever see him," Sequoia rationalized. "And knowing him, he's probably never here either. But I'm not really feeling the price so I think I'll pass anyway," Sequoia said. "Besides, I'm only looking for somewhere to stay for the next year or so anyway."

Mrs. Silverman looked visibly shaken by the idea of potentially losing out on a potentially significant deal. Mrs. Silverman had been having a hard time in the economy, and she knew that if she didn't sell a condo, and soon, she would be receiving a pink slip. So, she did was anyone in her position would do.

"Very well, you leave me no choice," Mrs. Silverman said. "Twenty-seven five."

"No, that's alright," Sequoia said as she began heading towards the door. "I'll just go call another realtor and see if I can look someplace else."

"Twenty-five," Mrs. Silverman said.

Sequoia opened the door as Sasha followed suit. "Bye-bye."

"Twenty-two!" she said desperately.

"I'll take it," Sequoia said, shocking both Mrs. Silverman and Sasha. She shut the door before she could exit, and hurriedly walked over to shake hands with Mrs. Silverman. "It's nice doing business with you."

Mrs. Silverman reluctantly shook her hand as she began to process what had just happened here. She had been in the business for nearly twenty-five years and could contend with the best of them, but today she had been outwitted by a young woman less than half her age.

It left a bitter taste in her mouth, but unlike most, she didn't hold a grudge. She respected the game, and therefore respected the player. So, instead of making a vain attempt at renegotiating the terms, she swallowed hard and gave Sequoia her best smile.

"Great doing business with you."

CHAPTER 37

According to Mrs. Silverman, the realtor, the condo would be ready for Sequoia within a week's time. That wasn't exactly what she wanted to hear after shelling out a staggering amount of money to secure the deal (something that she'd dare not disclose to anyone with good sense), but it would provide her with the amount of time that she needed to come up with a legitimate exit strategy from her mother's place. She wanted one that would minimize the risk of her suffering any significant physical trauma when she decided to tell her.

Sequoia knew that Rosa would blow a gasket when she found out that she was moving out, however, Sequoia also knew that she owed it to herself to bask in the spoils of her newfound wealth every now and again, and that's exactly what she intended to tell Rosa whenever she decided to work up the gall to actually tell her. She had been avoiding the conversation for the past three days.

Due to fear of confrontation, Sequoia gave her undivided attention to anything and everything that came to mind. She figured that a good distraction was all she needed, so when Bibby told her that he needed her in the studio A.S.A.P., she quickly complied. She'd spent the night at Desiree's apartment, which was in Harlem and closer to the studio, so she made it there within the hour. In that timeframe, Rosa called her three times, one of which she actually answered, but only to let her know that she was headed to the studio.

Sequoia was donned in a navy blue, Maison Kitsune, lamb's wool sweater; dark faded Seven jeans; and blue and white printed slip-on sneakers by Celine. Her hair was voluminous and curly, hanging freely over her shoulders. Her ears were adorned with sapphire and citrine earrings, which matched the sapphire and citrine pendant that hung freely from the small necklace that encompassed her gorgeous neckline.

Sequoia was actually surprised that Bibby allowed her to escort herself to the studio without sending a "Secret Service" team.

She wasn't fool enough, however, to believe that it would last, so she enjoyed her private space while she could. Though Sequoia had recently adopted new spending habits by purchasing her new condo, she was not ready to make the full commitment to make a universal upgrade to her wardrobe and car. Thus, she still possessed her blue Dodge Charger, but she promised herself that she would get a new Maserati if her next single did well on ITunes, and if her tour was a success.

New York, or the "Big Apple" as it is commonly referred to, had a long standing reputation that preceded itself as having the worst traffic in the country, but none of that seemed to phase Sequoia. Her only true concern was avoiding the paparazzi as she cruised the congested streets long enough to make it to the studio.

Considering that she didn't live in Los Angeles, paparazzi in New York weren't as bad as it good get, especially when the car was in motion, but the moment she stopped all bets were off.

Sequoia approached a red light like a minefield. Though her car was one of many amid a sea of commuters, she maintained a level of caution nonetheless. She figured that if she kept her head directly ahead, she could avoid eye contact with anyone in the cars next to her. When she unconsciously allowed her gaze to drift for a moment, she caught the eyes of a young girl who nearly jumped out of her seat with excitement when she locked eyes with Sequoia.

Sequoia reflexively focused her attention on the radio, fiddling with the buttons before stumbling on HOT97. A surge of adrenaline bolted through her anatomy when the sound of her song "Chemistry," which featured rap artist Famous, came pumping through her speakers. It wasn't an experience that she was completely unfamiliar with, but it was one of those things that would take some getting used to.

Just the sound of her voice over the neck jerking beat served as one of the many reminders that her dream had manifested into full fruition, and the feeling that came along with could not be measured in volume.

Sequoia arrived at Studio 142 a short while later, and was surprised when she was greeted with a warm applause. The room was packed with a plethora of familiar and not-so-familiar faces that were either producers or executive staff at Big Boy Records.

T. Bibby emerged from the crowd with a bottle of Siróc in his hand. He gave Sequoia a brief hug with his free arm. "I just wanted to say congratulations to Sequoia for officially topping the Billboard 100 chart, for having two hit singles on the charts at the same time—coming in at number one with 'Caribbean Girl' and number twelve with 'Chemistry.' I just wanted to tell you personally," Bibby said to Sequoia, "that we at Big Boy Records all wanted to congratulate you, and give you this."

Someone else emerged through the sea of people that were packed into the studio holding two huge plaques that commemorated her now historical position on the Billboard charts.

The plaques, the mood, and the love that she was receiving were both unexpected and one of the fondest memories that she would hold dear to her heart for years to come.

Topping the Billboard charts was an experience that very few artists have the privilege of achieving throughout the course of their careers, and Sequoia had managed to do it with her first and second single. The experience was indescribable! So much so, that she completely failed to noticed the person carrying the plaques until he spoke.

"Congratulations Sequoia!" Lil Will, who was arguably the best rapper in the rap game, said while holding both plaques. He placed both plaques alongside the wall before embracing Sequoia.

"Oh my God!" Sequoia exclaimed in a star struck manner. "Lil Will?" she said in disbelief. "What are you doing here?"

"I came to congratulate you," he said coyly, "and to see if you wanted to do a song with me."

Sequoia couldn't believe her ears. She had just been asked by the hottest rapper in the game to feature on a song with him. How blessed was she? Opportunities like these could single-handedly change the course of her career. She had no intention of turning him down.

"Of course!" Sequoia said ecstatically. "When do we get

started?"

"I was hoping today," Lil Will said, "if that's cool with you."

"Absolutely!" Sequoia hugged him again and smiled.

Sequoia released him before anyone got the wrong impression. It was just one of the many negative double standards that went along with the territory. The industry was tough, and everyone was always quick to judge, so women in the industry always had to be aware of their every move or it could be misconstrued as something it was not.

Though Sequoia would never have any lewd intentions towards Lil Will, she did have a great deal of admiration and respect for him. He was a multi-platinum selling artist, the C.E.O. of his own label Grown Currency, not to mention that he had confidence like none other.

Lil Will's dreadlocks were in five large braids to the back. His teeth were flooded with platinum and diamonds, and his body and face were covered in tattoos. His Southern drawl was courtesy of his Louisiana roots. His neck boasted seven chains, which adorned a striped V-neck over a pair of faded skinny jeans that were accessorized with a wallet chain. The wardrobe was complimented with a pain of Vans tennis shoes.

Lil Will looked more like he was about to attend an *X-Games* rather than record a song in the booth. That's what Sequoia loved about him, along with the rest of the world. He did his thing his way, and didn't give a damn what anybody thought about it.

T. Bibby poured Sequoia a glass of Siróc and offered it to her, but she refused it.

"You know I don't drink. Plus, I'm not even old enough," she said.

Bibby shrugged. "I won't say anything if you don't."

"Thanks, but no thanks. I don't drink," Sequoia said matter-of-factly. "But I do want to thank you for pulling this together for me. This is a dream come true."

Bibby took a huge gulp from the cup that he'd offered her. "Don't thank me. You earned every bit of this," he gestured around the room with his arm. "You got the number one videos in the country, you're getting over five thousand spins a week, and you're topping the Billboard charts," he said. "I told you I got you, but this is all you.

"Everybody, let's have a round of applause for Sequoia," Bibby said, drawing a huge round of applause from everyone.

Sequoia was nearly moved to tears. Within six short months she'd gone from being an undergraduate in Harvard to one of the hottest new artists who now shared a room with two of the biggest names in the music industry. In her eyes, regardless of what Bibby said, he was more responsible for her success than he cared to admit, but it was also that form of humility that she'd grown to love about him. Sure, he portrayed a tough guy, a business image to the world, but she learned long ago that deep down he was a teddy bear.

"Sorry to bring this celebration to an end, but can we get to it?" Sequoia told Bibby and Lil Will.

Bibby fixed his Prada-shade-covered glance on Lil Will in time to catch the surprised look that he was giving him. "I told you her work ethic is as crazy as yours," Bibby said.

"That's what's up," Lil Will said. "Let's get to it."

Bibby cleared the studio out so they could get to work, and after just two hours of work it came to everyone's surprise that they were able to give birth to a hit single titled "Sorbet." The song was so unbelievably good that Lil Will wanted to put a rush on its production to release it.

The lyrics to the song drew references from the frozen dessert, and its parallel to how decadently desirable they each were.

"We gonna have to make a video for this shit," Lil Will said as he bobbed his head to the song in its unfinished form. "She killed that shit."

"Thank you," Sequoia mouthed sexily.

"She's about to be big!" Lil Will said. "You definitely got a winner on your hands with her," Lil Will told T. Bibby.

"Don't I know it," Bibby said as he winked at her.

In that moment, Sequoia experienced a feeling in the pit of her stomach that she was vaguely familiar with. It was a feeling that she hadn't felt in awhile, but it was one that she knew well enough to ignore as well. She saw no sense in complicating her situation by giving her feelings even the slightest bit of acknowledgement. She knew how drastically their relationship would be altered if she were ever to act upon her feelings. She was also sure that if she did decide to reveal her attraction to him, T. Bibby would stop at nothing until he had her to call his own.

CHAPTER 38

The following weeks proved to be quite productive for Sequoia. Her career was gaining momentum at a pace that defied Einstein's law of relativity.

T. Bibby had arranged for her to conduct interviews and perform on all the popular night talk shows: Jay Leno, Jimmy Fallon, Conan, and Jimmy Kimmel. She also followed up her hit single with Lil Will with a video that she flew to Atlanta to shoot. Much of her other down time was either spent at the studio or with her mom, Jade, and Desiree as much as possible.

Keeping the balance was getting harder to do these days, especially when you factored in her work ethic, but she knew that all of her hard work would soon pay off, so it was all a matter of staying focused.

She had an appointment with T. Bibby in his office about a touring schedule in ten minutes, and she was only an elevator ride away from his office.

She was dressed to kill in a vanilla, Tom Ford dress, accessorized with a generous amount of jewelry around her ears, neck, wrist, and fingers. Her hair was in a long pony-tail as she strutted sexily in leather, vanilla, peep-toe, Tom Ford pumps.

Sequoia entered Bibby's open office door apprehensively and quietly, once she noticed he was on the phone. She knocked softly on the door and gained his attention. He signaled for her to come in and motioned for her to sit as he finished his phone conversation.

While seated, Sequoia allowed her eyes to wander to a picture on his wall of T. Bibby and his three sons. They were all handsome, and would undoubtedly break a lot of women's hearts one day. *Sons after their father's heart*, she thought.

Sequoia then turned her gaze on T. Bibby in a derisive manner that only a woman could execute. She noticed his faded gray True Religion jeans and white True Religion shirt, over a crisp pair of white, patent-leather Air Jordan gym shoes. His chain was flooded with diamonds and his earrings were the size of chandeliers. His pinky ring looked more like a piece of hail the size of a golf ball fell into the platinum encasement. It was also rumored to have set Bibby back a cool million bucks. His Caesar-style haircut looked like a tsunami hit it.

The two locked eyes briefly before Sequoia focused her attention on more important things, like the stitching on her dress, or whether or not the ashtray on his office desk was ceramic or glass.

When he ended the call he got straight to it. "What's good, Sequoia?" he said, with a hint of frustration in his voice as he rubbed his forehead.

"I'm good. How 'bout you?" she said, her words saturated with concern. Bibby noticed her tone.

"Oh, that," he motioned toward the phone. "A cargo ship headed to Thailand was hijacked by pirates, and unfortunately for me all of the fabrics that I ordered were on it, so now I have to push production of my new line back a couple months."

Sequoia was floored. "Wow!"

"Yeah, I know. Talk about the unthinkable," he said, "but I do have some good news."

"Oh, you do?" Sequoia began to grow excited.

"Absolutely. And by the way, you look great, as usual."

"Thank you," Sequoia blushed.

"Now," he said as he stacked papers into a neat pile in front of him. "You ready for your nationwide tour?"

"Sure am." Sequoia was beaming.

"Good, because I have you all set to start a month from now. Now, I'm not gonna lie to you, it's a very condensed schedule and it's a bit demanding, but I can promise you that if you can pull it off it will be worth it. So, you up for the challenge?"

"Of course," she quickly responded.

"Alright, we're going to do sixty-three dates in a hundred and twenty day period, including two radio shows in each forty-two stats. We'll do that during the morning and afternoon hours. Any questions?"

Sequoia exhaled deeply. "That sounds a bit overwhelming, doesn't it?"

"It is, I'm not gonna lie to you," he said honestly, "but with some extra time in the gym and choreography, not to mention some good rest and herbal tea for your voice, I think you'll be good."

"You think so?" Sequoia said, unsure.

"Of course, Sequoia. I told you I believe in you. I would've never put such a demanding schedule together for you if I didn't. And try not to worry about it. Just do it, and I'll do my best to be there with you every day."

"That's comforting," she said.

"You know I gotta be there for you, to walk you through the process," he said, "but before you leave, I want to go over some of the songs that you may use for your album."

"Oh, okay, cool," Sequoia said.

"Now, I've got one more thing."

"Shoot," Sequoia retorted.

"When were you going to tell me that we were neighbors?" Bibby said with a knowing smile.

Sequoia was shocked. "Who told you about that?"

"I can't reveal my sources," he joked. "You know, confidentiality and all."

"Oh, it's like that?" Sequoia pretended to be upset.

"Don't try to distract me," he said. "What floor are you on?"

"Wouldn't you like to know?" Sequoia teased.

"Oh, it's like that?" he shot back. "Well, check this out: I bought you a housewarming gift, but I'll give it to you only on one condition."

Sequoia frowned. "And what's that?"

"I get to bring it to you myself," Bibby smiled mischievously. Sequoia didn't trust the intent behind the façade that he tried to pawn off as a smile, and to a small degree she didn't really trust herself in close proximity with him.

Despite her suspicions, she replied, "What time?"

CHAPTER 39

The knock came at 6:57 PM, three minutes earlier than expected, which signaled T. Bibby's arrival. Sequoia knew that it was a bad idea inviting him to her place, and that she was practically playing with fire, but a huge part of her also didn't want to offend him by turning him down. Besides, despite her premature, prejudiced opinions about him, or the opinions from members of her camp to maintain a business relationship with him, she couldn't deny the affinity that they shared for each other that was growing stronger by the day. Not to mention the fact that he was the primary reason why she was currently having the success she was having in her career.

Not many artists in the history of the business had ever received the type of hands-on treatment that Bibby provided her with. Most executives would hold an artist back for months, if not years, until they were able to drop their first video, let alone album.

To Sequoia, that sort of dedication and belief in her career and talent from Bibby deserved to be reciprocated, which is why she didn't see the harm in expanding the boundaries of their personal lives a bit wider.

She figured that she'd give him a brief tour of the condo and chat for a short while before showing him the door, and for that reason she saw no need to get all dolled up in light of his presence. A mere pony-tail, gray sports bra over a loose-neck T-shirt that bore the word "Heartbreaker" boldly across the chest area, a pair of black leggings, and no makeup would suffice.

She opened the door for him and was greeted with a warm hug. Her nose was cradled into the hook of his neck, thereby making it impossible not to smell the generous amount of Izzey Miyaki cologne he was wearing—her favorite!

He was now wearing a white Gucci T-shirt with the Gucci insignia covering the seam of the shirt entirely, matching tennis shoes, and blue jeans. He ditched the bulk of the jewelry he was wearing earlier, bearing only his two carat earrings and diamond-studded watch.

Sequoia pushed the door closed and stared at his back, secretly checking him out. She couldn't believe that he was actually worth half a billion.

This man is a boss for real.

"Put some shoes on," Bibby said before turning to face her. "Ain't nothing more unattractive than a badass woman with some jacked up feet," he joked.

Sequoia sucked her teeth. "Please! That will never happen. I can easily be a foot model, and you know it." She raised her left foot and wiggled her toes.

"Yeah, whatever," Bibby said while slyly checking her feet out. "Anyway, what were you up to?"

"Nothing. Just working on a song to that track that Swiss Banger sent me."

"Always at it, huh?" Bibby seemed impressed. "That's what's up."

"Where's my housewarming gift at?" Sequoia asked. "You look like you came empty-handed."

Bibby brushed her off. "I got you. Just let me look around first," he said before giving himself a personal tour of her place. He drifted from the living room, surveyed the three hundred and sixty degree view of downtown Manhattan, and disappeared into the throes of her master bedroom.

"Wait—where are you going?" Sequoia asked growing agitated before reluctantly following behind him.

She discovered him in her bedroom, meters deep into her walk-in closet. Sequoia rested her palms on her hips in an offended manner.

"Um, do you have a search warrant? Because I'm almost certain that you're violating my privacy," Sequoia snapped.

"Girl, relax," Bibby said calmly as he emerged from the closet. "I gotta make sure you ain't got no niggas up in here."

"Whatever." Sequoia waved him off. "That will never happen."

"It better not," Bibby said seriously.

"Anyway," Sequoia dismissed his statement. "Could you please come out of my room so I can show you the rest of my place?"

"In a minute."

Sequoia rolled her eyes.

"Turn around."

"Excuse me?" Sequoia snapped.

"Turn around so I can give you your gift," he repeated. "And while you're at it, close your eyes and lose the attitude."

Sequoia sighed by complied with his wishes. "Don't be trying no funny stuff."

"Shhh."

"Did you just shush me?" Sequoia exclaimed confrontationally. She tensed up when she felt his hands caress her shoulders.

"It's just me Sequoia. Relax."

Her fears were put to rest when she felt a necklace grace her neckline. When it was clasped together, Bibby told her to open her eyes.

Sequoia did as told and immediately took notice of her reflection on the floor to ceiling mirror that was on the wall. What she saw nearly brought her to tears.

It was a platinum necklace flooded with huge diamonds throughout the entirety of the necklace. It was four times heavier and a least five times more expensive than the first one. She figured that the jewelry had to easily set him back two hundred thousand dollars.

Of course, two hundred thousand dollars is a drop in a bucket to someone like T. Bibby, but the idea of him splurging that much on her, in her opinion, wasn't something to be taken lightly.

Sequoia studied Bibby's reflection in the mirror and noticed that he was smiling.

"You like it?"

"Of course…" Sequoia exclaimed gleefully. "But—"

"Well, what else do you like?" Bibby said in a low tone as he planted soft kisses on her neck, completely ignoring her.

Sequoia tensed up and shot him a disapproving look through the mirror, but he didn't relent. To her surprise, her body slowly succumbed to his touch.

Sequoia knew that she would be lying if she said that she wasn't sexually attracted to him. She knew it ever since they first landed in close proximity with each other. But that didn't change the fact that he was her boss, and that meant engaging in any form of intimacy with him would drastically change the dynamics of their relationship. That was something that she wasn't sure that she wanted right now.

So, regardless of how bad their hormones were raging at the moment, or how great his kisses felt on the nape of her neck, Sequoia knew that someone had to be a responsible adult and put an end to their encounter before things got out of hand.

She reluctantly pulled away from him before turning to face him. "We need to stop."

"Why?" Bibby asked with a devilish grin. "And please don't tell me that you ain't feelin' me because we both know that that'll be some bullshit."

"It doesn't matter what I'm feeling. We both know that this will change things between us."

"Sequoia, you make it sound like that's a bad thing," Bibby

said as he closed the distance between them. He tilted her chin up with his left hand and stared into her aqua blue eyes. "Sequoia, I've thought long and hard about this too. About all of the questions that everyone will be asking: the press, our families. I've played every possible scenario out in my head for months now, and at some point, I just stop caring. I know what I want, and I don't care what people think. I've been dealing with criticism for years now and at some point there comes a time where you just have to stop thinking about that stuff and focus on what I want."

Sequoia digested what he said. "That's not my only concern." She slipped from his grasp.

"Well, what else could it be?" Bibby asked.

Sequoia considered her choice of words. "Truthfully?"

"Of course. Keep it one-hunnit."

"I don't want to get hurt." She led him out of her bedroom. Bibby stopped her in between the living room and kitchen area.

"How are you gonna get hurt?" Bibby was confused.

Sequoia folded her arms across her chest defensively. "You know exactly what I'm talking about."

Bibby sighed. "I'm not a mind reader Sequoia."

"Fine!" she said, annoyed. "You're T. Bibby! You're worth half a billion dollars. Women are always throwing themselves at you. I mean, I don't know about you but I'm looking for a long term relationship when I do decided to get into one," she said seriously. "I'm talking a ring, a house, kids, the whole nine! And no disrespect, I don't see that when I look at you."

"Really?" Bibby asked dryly. "And what exactly is it that you see?"

Sequoia rolled her eyes. "Can we please just drop it?" She tried to walk away but Bibby grabbed her—not in an aggressive manner, but in a manner that demanded she give him her undivided attention.

"Sequoia, I don't know what you see when you look at me, but when I look at you I see the most beautiful, intelligent, talented woman I've ever seen in my life. Any man would be a fool to let you go.

"So in case you were wondering, yes I would be interested in a long-term relationship with you. Yeah, the whole ring, house, and kids thing. The whole nine! But only—and I do mean only—if I can have that with you."

Sequoia wasn't naïve in the least bit, and she'd always prided herself on her keen ability to read people, but she could all but smell the sincerity coming from Bibby.

That was fantastic, but not enough to draw a solid commitment from her at the moment. Sure, Bibby was a modern-day Prince Charming in the flesh: a success story with the looks and personality to match his back account. But as it stood, it wasn't enough. She needed time to think.

Sequoia was about to make her proposal to him vocal, but she was silenced by a powerful kiss from him before she could utter a word. His tongue explored her mouth as if he were looking for gold.

Any protest or signs of reluctance were immediately dismissed from her mind at the feel of his touch. Suddenly, she craved and hungrily anticipated his touch.

They both partook in an extensive oral probing session while unconsciously drifting their way in the direction of the granite kitchen counter. Within seconds they were both shedding pieces of their clothing like dead skin.

Sequoia's loose-neck T-shirt was anxiously tugged over her head and cast to the floor. Bibby's Gucci shirt was the next to go.

Bibby picked Sequoia up by her rib area and placed her on the granite counter top. Their lust for each other intensified as they hungrily and passionately kissed each other. Bibby stripped Sequoia out of her sports bra and leggings and flung them to the floor. He licked her from her appetizing necklines to her ample breast, placing delicate kisses on her along the way.

Sequoia moaned softly while subduing her bottom lip with her top teeth while tossing her head back. Bibby teased her light brown nipples with the tip of his tongue, tantalizing her Hershey mound into an erect state. He sucked and nibbled at her nipple gently, drawing a small gasp from her.

"Um!" Sequoia moaned.

He set his sights on her other breast, giving it as much attention as he gave the first one. He then kissed her from her breast, down her stomach, to her inner thighs.

Sequoia's breathing intensified as he commenced to put hickies on both of her inner thighs. Her sexual juices began to saturate the crotch of her blue, laced, Victoria's Secret panties.

Though Bibby was driven by his insatiable desire for her, he somehow found the strength to pull himself away from his task long enough to examine the unique and captivating creature before him. Sequoia was truly a thing of pure beauty. Bibby noted that she looked even better in her birthday suit. Her 36C breasts were perfect and perky. Her stomach was flat and toned, and complimented her wide hips. Her thighs were shapely and toned, yet still creamy and soft enough to leave finger indentations on them. Her feet were small and had a meticulous pedicure, and so perfect that even the most prudish of men would develop a foot fetish after seeing them.

Sequoia used her palms to hoist herself up on the countertop, creating just enough leverage and slack to allow Bibby to pull her panties off. He tossed Sequoia's Secrets onto the floor as the arousal in his pants throbbed at the sight of her perfectly waxed, plump southern lips. A hint of her sexual secretions remained on her vaginal lips, which Bibby found to be decadently pleasing to the eyes.

He wasted no time lapping up the juices, making perfect use of the countertop as he dined on her southern cuisine.

Sequoia's neck snapped back reflexively as he orally pleased her. "Umm... aww!" she moaned.

Bibby snugly inserted two fingers into her while sucking her clit. Sequoia placed her hand on the back of Bibby's wave-patterned-head as he went to town on her.

Sequoia had never felt so much pleasure in her life. The oral dominance that Bibby was subduing her with was blowing her mind! He was licking and sucking all of the right spots. Sure, she had broken her virginity with her high school sweetheart, and engaged in sexual acts with him on a significant amount of occasions, but the things that Bibby was doing to her on the countertop had quickly put her ex's sex game to shame.

Sequoia's hips rocked synchronically to Bibby's hand job as she felt herself near an orgasm. She gritted her teeth as her eyes shuddered violently as an ocean of pleasure flowed onto Bibby's hand.

"Aww! Mm!" Sequoia's head was spinning as she wiggled her hips on the counter.

Bibby stared at her erotically as he removed his clothing, exposing a massive erection.

Sequoia nearly jumped out of her skin as she contemplated the pain that she would have to endure in order to adjust to his member.

Bibby read her mind. "Relax, baby. I'm not gonna hurt you. I promise."

His confidence provided her with very little comfort, so she used a legitimate distraction to prolong the inevitable. "Do you have any condoms?"

Bibby revealed a six pack of Magnums as if on cue. He ripped one out of the wrapper with his teeth before covering his erection with it.

He then grabbed Sequoia by the waist and navigated her hips towards the edge of the countertop. Her fear was evident to him, so he kissed her passionately to distract her momentarily. When he felt her body release a great deal of its tension, he inserted his magic stick; slowly, methodically, calculated!

Sequoia lay back and spread her legs far apart as Bibby slowly guided himself into her. His arousal was perfectly stiff as he watched his shaft penetrate her delicate, moist walls.

Her wetness allowed for her walls to contract and readjust to his girth, and within minutes the two had found a rhythm. Their pelvises clashed rhythmically, creating a muffled clapping sound. "Mm! Mm! Mm!" Sequoia moaned vocally. Bibby had never known a woman's folds could ever feel so good. He'd been with countless women throughout his life, and not one of them could hold a candle to Sequoia. She was the complete package, and the best he'd ever had!

While still inside her, Bibby lifted her off of the countertop and moved toward the refrigerator. He used the stainless steel Kenmore appliance to hold Sequoia up against as he plunged into her wetness in a long, deep, thrusting manner, which drew loud moans of pleasure from her.

"Oh! Please, don't stop!"

They sucked each other's lips as moans and grunts escaped their mouths with each powerful thrust. The elevated tryst was brief, and was followed by a hot pursuit of the couch, in which Sequoia's ankles found themselves by her ears as Bibby plunged inside of her.

"Aw! That's my spot!" Sequoia moaned. "Don't stop! Don't stop! Aw!" She came hard and long, saturating his pelvic area with her love fluids.

When Bibby felt himself nearing a climax, he immediately pulled out to prolong it. He allowed Sequoia to gather herself before instructing her to straddle him. Her rhythm was a bit off and out of sync. He could easily tell that she hadn't had much experience with being on top.

He watched her face contort into a painful expression as the length of his anatomy disappeared into the thick of her folds.

He used his hands as guides. "Go slow baby. And arch your back so you can glide on it and find a rhythm. Just try to emulate your dance move of riding." Sequoia complied and immediately noticed the difference. She felt the friction the front of his shaft was creating against her clit, and she trusted his hands to guide her hips to the beat of ecstasy.

She felt as if she were being taught how to ride a horse for the first time, except only different. As soon as she got the hang of it Bibby removed his hands and allowed her to coast on her own. To her surprise, within a few short minutes she had worked him into a climax. He dug his fingers into her fleshy derriere and grunted loudly as he came hard.

The both smiled in satisfaction while panting heavily as they kissed each other passionately.

"That was the best ever!" Sequoia said as she kissed him again.

"The absolute best," he corrected her. "You know I'm not going nowhere after you put it on me like that," he said seriously.

"Is it alright if we keep this a secret for now?" Sequoia asked. Though she felt as if she were in heaven, she didn't want to ruin it by bringing the world into their business so soon.

"Whatever you like," Bibby said. "Your wish is my command," he joked.

"Oh, you're a genie now?" Sequoia kissed him again.

"If that's what you need me to be," he retorted.

"Alright then. I got a wish right now," she said sexily.

"And what's that?" he asked.

"I'm ready for round two."

"Your wish is my command," he said before kissing her passionately.

They spend the next six hours making love, christening the couch, the shower, and the bed before collapsing, spent, into each other's arms. Bibby was fast asleep while Sequoia lay wide awake in his arms, as her mind began to process the gravity of what they'd just done.

She began to grow certain that her satisfied state was temporary, and would soon dissipate into a pool of regret. Even though she wanted him as bad as he wanted her, she found it hard to completely ignore the number of indicators, including the advisory from her close friends, not to get involved with him.

As startling as it was to admit, even though she factored it all into her decisive equation, she couldn't deny what she was feeling. It felt good! And there was no way she was about to stop anytime soon. For now, she could only hope that the skepticism that everyone had toward T. Bibby simply turned out to be projections of their worst fears, and not her. One day, her life may depend on it.

CHAPTER 40

It didn't take an astrophysicist to understand that the dynamics of Sequoia and T. Bibby's relationship would change dramatically after their sexual encounter with one another. However, their schedules were so hectic and conflicting with one another that they were deprived of the opportunity to fully indulge themselves in each other's company.

The time apart was just fine by Sequoia though. She felt that she needed the distraction that her thriving career provided to keep her mind off of him. It was a feat that had already proven to be challenging enough in itself, and was growing all the more complicated with each email, text message, and phone call he sent her way.

It wasn't as if she didn't want the attention. In fact, it was the total opposite. She loved hearing his voice and secretly craved his presence whenever they were apart from each other. She was also well aware of his long standing track record with women, and that gave her pause. She knew that it would be in her best interests to protect her feelings, regardless of how she felt on the inside.

She had no desire to rush things between them and end up getting her feelings hurt. At the rate that they were going, they'd be topping out at the speed of light by next week.

Then came the issue of anonymity: Sequoia wasn't ready to go public with their relationship, but Bibby couldn't care less.

What Sequoia wanted was exclusivity! She wanted boundaries and restrictions and lots of attention, not an ongoing fling that would end before it truly began, and would subsequently define her career. If T. Bibby couldn't promise her that, then she would end it all on the spot.

Sequoia was more than willing to have that conversation with him, and soon, but their schedules conflicted with each others' so much that they hadn't quite gained the opportunity to formally address it. Either he was out of state away on business, or Sequoia was in dance rehearsal or a writing session in the studio. In any event, their paths hadn't crossed for a substantial time period in nearly two weeks.

They both realized that some time had to be set aside to speak to each other, so they scheduled a date to do so. In between that time Sequoia had to revisit Boston for a court appearance, a follow-up for when she was attacked by Dhuram on the Harvard campus.

Sequoia also flew out to provide her gorgeous features as a cameo of Lil Will on another video he was shooting, titled "Ten Rounds." Bibby was also there, but he was only there for a short period of time so they never got an opportunity to speak before he had to leave.

After three weeks had passed, Bibby's calls, emails, and texts and dwindled and had become less frequent. Though Sequoia didn't want to jump to any conclusions, a huge part of her felt as if Bibby was beginning to purposely avoid her. A part of her doubted that was truly the case, but the idea itself would usually take on a life of its own inside her head and give birth to suspicions that were generally hard to put to rest. That's exactly what it did.

Sequoia, not being one to sit on her feelings, chose to take her concerns directly to Bibby as soon as the opportunity arose, and as luck would have it, the glorious day had arrived.

Bibby had just finished a meeting in his office, so Sequoia's timing was practically perfect. She waited for his assistant's cue to go on back before proceeding to his office, all the while wondering what kind of relationship Bibby had with the young, attractive intern.

It was the beginning of June, and the temperature had climbed to nearly ninety degrees, and the temperature reflected in Sequoia's wardrobe.

She was donned in an ivory-colored Banana Republic skirt and matching business jacket. She wore a pair of mocha, peep-toed Giuseppe pumps to match her silk, mocha-colored blouse. A pair of brown Gucci shades adorned her face and matched her brown Gucci clutch. Her hair was pressed straight to the sides and down her back, and her neck was adorned with the necklace that Bibby had recently given her, with two carat diamond earrings that resembled teardrops.

When she entered the room, T. Bibby was just hanging up from his phone call.

"There she is," he rose from his seat enthusiastically and approached her. He attempted to kiss her, but she moved away from him.

"We need to talk," she said curtly.

Bibby was taken aback by her mood. He closed the door behind her. "What's up with you? A nigga can't get no love?" He was confused.

Sequoia turned to face him and removed her shades. "Have you been avoiding me?" she asked with attitude, with her arms folded across her chest.

"Avoiding you?" Bibby repeated, bewildered. "What are you talking about? I've been fighting tooth and nail with both of our schedules for the past three weeks just to be able to get this opportunity right here. And this is what you're on? What's wrong with you?" Sequoia was unfazed by his response. His attitude meant nothing to her at the moment. What she wanted was answers, and justification for his recent behavior.

"Nothing's wrong with me," she responded. "I just feel that ever since we had sex you've been extremely 'busy,'" she emphasized with her finger quotation marks, "and I want to know if it's because you don't want anything to do with me."

Bibby stared at her compassionately, but said nothing. He retrieved his IPhone out of the pocket of his denim jeans and placed a call.

"Have my ride ready in fifteen. Thanks," he said before saying to Sequoia. "I want to show you something," he told her while staring into her eyes.

Twenty-five minutes later, they were in the back seat of his black Maybach Exelero only moments away from a huge storage facility.

When they arrived, they received clearance from the gate checkpoint and bypassed the property storage bins until they neared a storage warehouse. Bibby advised his driver to wait behind as he guided Sequoia into the warehouse.

Inside, the warehouse was a plethora of luxury cars, S.U.V.s, charter buses, yachts, off-road vehicles, and sports cars of all sorts. Sequoia counted forty-nine collective vehicles.

"Please tell me that these aren't all yours?"

"I wish I could," he said. "Let's just say I have a fetish."

"More like an addiction," Sequoia retorted.

Bibby smiled as he led her to a newly painted tour bus. He led her inside the new tour bus and showed her the décor. The inside was smothered in wood-grain and gold trimming. There was a mini-bar, 52" plasma screen, bunk beds, a master bedroom, studio, and two elaborately decorated bathrooms.

"What do you think?" Bibby asked her.

"It's nice of course. What do you want me to say?" Sequoia had no idea what any of this had to do with anything. "What does this have to do with us?"

"It took me over a week to find this," Bibby began a monologue, as if he were totally oblivious to her presence, "and over a million dollars to buy and supe up."

Sequoia had no idea where he was going with this, but her patience was running thin with him. Her little expedition to his office was supposed to leave her with answers, a sense of closure even, not a meaningless tour of his extensive car collection.

Needless to say, the gesture did very little to contest the egotistical, narcissistic, and selfish rumors that clung to him wherever he seemed to go.

"T. Bibby, could you please just answer my question?" Sequoia demanded.

Bibby sighed, frustrated. "Sequoia, this is the answer to your question. This is your bus. I bought it for you to go on your tour with. This is what I've been doing. I haven't been avoiding you; I've been working on this gift for you.

"Sequoia, I know that our schedules may've been conflicting lately, but that's just the nature of our careers. Truthfully, I love it, because the time apart makes me think about you that much more. It makes me want you even more, and when we're together it'll only make me cherish everything about you."

Sequoia's heart melted on the spot. She couldn't believe how thoughtful and considerate Bibby was. For weeks she had been trying to come up with the perfect way to attack him for not making any time for her, and here he was shelling out loads of money to accommodate her every need.

Bearing witness to his generosity and thoughtfulness first-hand put Sequoia in a shitty mood. She couldn't believe that she had doubted him. Confronting him about the true status of their relationship had only exposed her own insecurities, which were nothing more than the projections of her innermost fears. She was afraid she would be discarded and left alone, like her father had done to her when she was younger.

But Bibby's sense of awareness was like telepathy when it came to her, because he could always tell when something was bothering her, and that was something he couldn't live with. Bibby was old enough to know that communication was the backbone to every relationship, and without it they were nothing.

"Okay, it's obvious that you have a lot on your mind Sequoia, so just let me know what it is," Bibby asked.

Sequoia pouted in a childish manner. "I'm sorry! I've just been having some really crazy things running through my mind lately."

"Like what?" Bibby pressed her.

"Like..." Sequoia responded nervously. "Are we going to be exclusive or not?"

Bibby scoffed. "Girl, I just spend over a million dollars on this bus for you, and this is not out of our company budget. The only other women that I spend money on in my life are the mother of my children and my mother. So, how's that for an answer? Is that exclusive enough for you?" Bibby asked in an annoyed tone.

Sequoia was at a loss for words. She didn't want to put her foot any further in her mouth than it already was, so she did what any girl in her position would do: she gave Bibby exactly what he deserved, love and affection.

She wrapped her arms around his neck and stared into his eyes. "I'm sorry. I don't know what's wrong with me. I guess I just thought that what we had was just for one night."

Bibby smiled. "You're crazy, you know that?" he said. "Ain't no way in hell I'm letting you get away from me." He pecked her on the lips. "I'm crazy about you."

Bibby kissed her again, only this time he used lots of tongue. He began to kiss her neck while running a free hand up her skirt. Sequoia's eyes rolled in the back of her head as Bibby sucked her neck with simultaneously rubbed his fingers over her lace-thong-covered clit.

"Umm! That feels so good!" Sequoia moaned.

Bibby hoisted her skirt upward to her waistline and pulled her panties down.

Sequoia stepped out of them as Bibby kissed her beautiful thighs, north up to her southern paradise. He wasted no time with pleasing her, massaging her clit while delicately sucking and nibbling at it. Sequoia came within a few short minutes.

He then bent her over by the waist, staring lustfully at her Brazilian-waxed, puffy, moist opening that bore traces of her love secretions alongside her vaginal walls. He dug a magnum condom out of his pocket and dropped his pants to his ankles. He placed the condom on and entered her slowly.

"Aww!" Sequoia winced.

Bibby pulled out and entered her again, drawing another moan, and inserted more inches of his manhood. He repeated the process until her vaginal walls adjusted to the girth of his member.

He developed a mild pace, watching himself disappear and reappear in her wetness. The very sight of her blemish-free, apple-round bottom nearly made him explode prematurely, so he closed his eyes and paced himself.

By now Sequoia had relieved herself of her jacket and was moaning in intense pleasure with every stroke. The rhythm between them continued to build as the thunderous sound of pelvises colliding with one another echoed through the tour bus!

"Ahh! Ahh! Ahh! Ahumm!" Sequoia cried out as she felt herself about to cum.

Bibby grunted softly as he felt himself nearing a climax as well. "Aww!" he groaned when he came hard.

Sequoia's leg began to shake violently as she came with him. "Umm!" she moaned loudly while trying to catch her breath. She stood upright with Bibby still inside of her and arched her neck so she could kiss him passionately.

"How's that for an apology?" she joked sexily.

Bibby chuckled. "Let's just say I have to find more reasons to have a disagreement, because that was definitely worth it."

They both laughed.

"You know I'm never gonna let you go, right?" Bibby said as he planted soft kisses on her neck. "So whether you like it or not, you're stuck with me. 'Til death do us part."

Sequoia smiled at the thought of being with him forever. Although, deep down his statement rang an eerie octave of seriousness that was borderline psycho. But she didn't care, because to a huge degree she felt the same way—or at least that's what she thought.

CHAPTER 41

Five Months Later

The last five months of Sequoia's life were completely lost to her. They were a total blur, and not for lack of memorable experiences and moments. In fact, it was the complete opposite.

She had just completed a nationwide tour, headlined by two of R and B's most successful artists; Keisha Colb and Monikah. The experience was electrifying and inspiring, and she never wanted it to end.

Everything went so fast that she could barely keep up. A different city every night, sixty-seven dates in a one hundred and thirty day period, not to mention the countless radio interviews. And to everyone's surprise, Sequoia still wanted more! She had fallen in love with the stage and realized that she was an absolute natural for it. She felt that she was born to be an entertainer and was seriously looking forward to the international tour that T. Bibby assured her he would arrange sometime in the near future.

He also provided her with much needed support and guidance throughout the entire touring process. Between Keisha Colb, Monikah, and T. Bibby, Sequoia received all of the T.L.C. she needed to make popping her touring cherry as painless as possible.

However, touring, albeit extremely fun, wasn't the only cherry that she managed to bust on tour. Sequoia made perfectly good use of the tour bus that Bibby purchased her. They had sex every opportunity they were given, and as a result their relationship continued to flourish so much so that they began to publicly display affection for one another.

Within a short period of time, Sequoia no longer cared what anyone thought about their relationship. She felt as if she was living a fairy tale life alongside her Prince Charming, and she had no desire to get to the final chapter anytime soon.

Before long, time no longer held any significant value in her life. She only used time as a gauge to determine and anticipate her next encounter with Bibby. She was caught up in a rapture of love, which she displayed to him by letting the L word slip one night when they were together. She knew that by doing so the dynamics of their relationship could be dramatically affected in an unpredictable way, but she had taken a leap of faith and was surprised when he actually reciprocated her feelings by uttering those beautiful words back at her.

"I love you too, Sequoia," Bibby said before planting a soft kiss on her lips and sexing her up all night long on the tour bus one unforgettable night.

For once in her life everything was perfect! She had the man of her dreams, she was becoming one of the hottest new female R and B and pop artists of all time, and her mother was still around to see it all.

But, for all the pros she was experiencing in her new life, there was one con in particular that did make all of the fun she was having a lot harder to enjoy. That was her inability to spend time with her mother and friends.

On several occasions, Sequoia was fortunate enough to fly Desiree and Jade to a few shows, but neither of them could stay for the duration because of their schooling. Rosa couldn't come at all because her doctor had advised her to stay close so he could monitor the progress of her condition, which was something that Sequoia found to be strange considering how long ago it was that she had her transplant.

Nevertheless, Sequoia made it a top priority for all of them to meet once a week via Skype so they could do some much needed catching up with each other. Like always, Sequoia was the topic of discussion.

"Hey y'all," Sequoia waved excitedly at Jade, Rosa, and Desiree on her laptop screen.

"Hey," they all said, nearly in unison.

"How's the tour coming?" Desiree asked.

Sequoia shrugged nonchalantly. "It's tiring, but it's almost over with. Either way, it's definitely the highlight of my life. I really wish you guys could be here."

"We do too."

"I second that," Rosa smiled happily.

Sequoia's heart warmed. "So what have you guys been up to? And what did you do with your hair?" Sequoia finally noticed Desiree's new hairstyle.

"You like?" She struck a few vague poses, which made everyone laugh.

"Actually," Sequoia inspected her Halle Berry-style hairdo that was now a honey blonde and cinnamon hue, "I love it!"

"I told her chu'll love it," Rosa said in her thick Spanish accent.

"But enough about me, let's talk about these rumors I've been hearing," Desiree said.

"What rumors?" Sequoia said defensively.

"These rumors." Desiree held up a recent copy of *Hip Hop Weekly*, which showed Sequoia snuggled up with T. Bibby at a restaurant in Houston, Texas. "Is there any truth to this story?"

"Dag, nosey," Sequoia dodged the question while grinning criminally.

"I told you!" Jade said to Desiree.

"She didn't admit to anything yet," Desiree said. "Did you Sequoia?"

Sequoia pretended to be scratching the back of her head. "See, what had happened was..."

Everyone laughed.

Sequoia had become so distracted with her conversation that she failed to notice T. Bibby enter the room until he was kissing and hugging her.

"Don't tell me you're playing on the internet again?" Bibby said, until he noticed that she was on Skype with her friends and family.

Sequoia blushed at the awkward coincidence as Bibby tried to quickly remove himself from the webcam's view, but he was already spotted.

"I told you!" Jade exclaimed as Rosa and Desiree wore masks of shock on their faces. "I win! And I will collect my payment sometime next week."

"Yeah, yeah, yeah," Desiree said, mad at the idea of losing a wager to Jade.

Sequoia had yet to utter a word, and judging by her facial expression she was extremely embarrassed. "Don't clam up now Sequoia," Desiree said. "How long has this been going on?"

"About five months."

Everyone either sucked their teeth or shook their head disapprovingly.

"Sequoia? Call me later so we can talk in private," Rosa said in a motherly tone.

"Well, where is he? Where did he go?" Desiree asked.

"Yeah, tell him to come here so I can meet him," Rosa said.

Sequoia looked in T. Bibby's direction, who was standing adjacent to the cherry wood and pearl dresser, just out of eye shot of the webcam's view. "My mom wants to talk to you."

Bibby sighed before reluctantly surrendering himself for interrogation. He loomed over Sequoia's shoulder as he spoke.

"What's up everybody? Jade. Desiree. Sorry miss, but we haven't had an opportunity to meet until now. I'm T. Bibby."

"I know who you are. And it's also good to meet you," Rosa

said cordially. "I just have a few questions for you. How old are you?"

"I'm thirty-six."

Rosa shook her head. "Sequoia, he's old enough to be your father. What's wrong with you?"

"I know Mom, but I—"

"I love her," Bibby cut her off, drawing a surprised look from Sequoia and everyone else, "and I know I'm older than her, but to your credit, you've raised a beautiful, talented, intelligent woman who's wise beyond her years. And I intend to treat her with the most profound respect and love that a queen like her deserves."

Everyone was silent for a brief moment before Jade broke the silence; "Yeah, what he said."

Everyone laughed awkwardly.

Sequoia brought the conversation back to a more serious tone. "Mom, I don't want you to worry about me. Just trust me on this. I've put a lot of thought into it, and for once in my life, I'm happy. So could you just, please, give me your support on this?"

Rosa wasn't sold on the puppy dog look that Sequoia was giving her, but she wanted to be happy for her. She felt that she did deserve it, and if T. Bibby made her happy, then she would just have to support her.

"You have my blessing, Sequoia," Rosa said reluctantly before shifting a stern gaze to T. Bibby. "I'm trusting you with my daughter, so take care of her. I'd hate to have to come out there."

Bibby smiled while staring into Sequoia's eyes. "Trust me; you don't have to worry about that. I'm holding on to this one." He kissed her on the forehead.

"Aw!" Desiree and Jade said childishly, and Sequoia blushed.

Desiree said, "I do have one more concern. Do you think that this will affect your professional careers?"

"Not at all," Sequoia responded quickly. "If anything, it'll only make us more successful."

"Assuming there's no serious disagreements," Jade added.

"Disagreements?" Sequoia repeated. "What could we possibly disagree about? Listen, just try not to worry about me. I'm good. We're good. So don't worry about it. I'll be looking forward to seeing you guys soon in Chicago."

"How many more dates do you have left?" Desiree asked.

"Just three, I believe," Sequoia said, "but don't quote me on that, though. But hey, was I tripping, or did you guys place a wager on me?"

"Mm hmm," Jade said plainly. "And I won."

Sequoia's annoyed expression went unnoticed by Jade as she absent-mindedly gloated at her expense.

"We figured we'd make it interesting," Desiree added, "but never mind that."

"You're right," Sequoia said. "Well, I'll call you guys once I arrange the place tickets for you. Remember, it's in two days."

"Alright Sequoia. Call me soon so we can talk, you hear me?" Rosa said. "Te amo!"

Sequoia chuckled. "Okay mamma, but I am alright, trust me. And I love you too! I love all of you guys! Be expecting a call from me tomorrow."

"Okay. Be safe," Desiree said.

Everyone exchanged their friendly goodbyes before disconnecting from Skype.

Sequoia faced T. Bibby. "That went well," she said sarcastically.

"Ain't better than we expected," he said before wrapping his arms around her. "At least we don't have to sneak around them anymore. Now I can love you the way I want to. Just try not to worry about anything. From now on, you're all mine, and nobody can take us apart from each other."

"Aw!" Sequoia said as she embraced him. She was in a state of ecstasy; a high that she would soon find out would wane over time.

CHAPTER 42

Sequoia didn't receive any flak throughout the duration of the leg of her tour about her relationship with T. Bibby, but when the tour was over, all bets were off.

Jade and Desiree tore into her the worst, expressing their strong disdain for T. Bibby and their relationship. Their concerns ranged everywhere from his close association with various beautiful women in the industry, to rumors of his sexual relationship with R and B pop star Sassy. Jade's primary concern, though, was the history that T. Bibby had for swindling his artists out of their money. Desiree couldn't seem to get past the violent temper he was publicly known for.

Amazingly, Rosa hadn't given her any grief about her decision. She supported her, which to her was a complete surprise. In regards to Desiree and Jade, Sequoia thought that they were completely overreacting. She felt that they had no valid argument as it stood that could justify their contempt for their relationship. She defended her man, arguing that he spoiled her rotten and treated her like a queen. She concluded her argument by assuring them that they had nothing to be worried about.

However, Desiree's fears became her own one celebratory night when the mixture of alcohol and jealousy got the best of T. Bibby.

It was during Sequoia's album release party, which was taking place at the 20/20 Club in New York, that she received this rude awakening.

Jade, Desiree, and Rosa were also in attendance, and mingling with several celebrity figures while T. Bibby played chaperone to Sequoia, introducing her to the movers and shakers of the industry that she had yet to meet as a hit song from Sequoia's album played in the backdrop.

After making their introductions, Bibby excused himself from

Sequoia to speak with an associate about a pending business agreement.

Sequoia couldn't be more thrilled. The red, open-toe, spike Balenciaga heels were killing her, and the plush couch in the V.I.P. section couldn't have been more attractive that it was at the time. Her spiked heels accompanied the red sequin Salvatore Ferragamo gown and spiked bracelet and necklace she was wearing. Her hair was straight-pressed.

The comfort zone that Sequoia had sunken into made reconnecting with her entourage seem like a task, so she held up camp on the couch and did what anyone in the 21st century would do: she sent a text message, starting with Desiree.

Sequoia: Where r u?

Her phone vibrated a short while later.

Desiree: With the man of my dreams. LOL what about u?

Sequoia: Alone in the VIP. Wouldn't mind having some company... Hint, hint. :)

Desiree: U? Alone? Where's your prince?

Sequoia: Away on business. He'll be back. But I was hoping...

Desiree: I get it. B there in 60.

Sequoia smiled as she continued her assault on the digital keyboard on her phone. She barely noticed the man that was approaching her until he was just within arms' reach.

"Oh my God!" Sequoia nearly dropped her phone when she saw who it was.

"I hope I didn't startle you. I just wanted to take this opportunity to come over and introduce myself. We haven't had a chance to meet." Rap icon and business mogul Kay-G extended his hand for her to shake.

Sequoia quickly regained her composure and rose to her feet. She nervously smoothed out the wrinkles in her dress and accepted his hand.

"I'm sorry. I was just texting my friend." She beamed giddily. "But I'm such a HUGE fan of yours. I love all of your music and I think that you are one of the most talented M.C.s of all time."

Kay-G smiled. "Thank you. That means a lot. But I wanted to come and tell you that I'm also a huge fan of yours, and I wanted to know if you could lay some vocals down for me on my new album?"

Sequoia was speechless. She had just been asked to do a song by the most influential man in the industry. Usually, a manager would deal with this side of business, but only a fool would prolong a response to someone of Kay-G's stature. And one thing Sequoia was not was anybody's fool. She wasted no time with accepting his offer, figuring that she fill T. Bibby in on the details later.

Sequoia slyly took in his demeanor, taking note of the platinum tuxedo and open collar, white, button-up shirt that boasted platinum cufflinks with the initials "KG" engraved in them. His hair was low and was razor-lined. The soft leather coal-colored Prada wingtip shoes he was wearing looked as expensive as the humungous diamond earrings that adorned his lobes.

"Yes, yes, of course," she said. "It would be my honor and privilege to work with you."

"Great." He handed her a business card. "Call me as soon as you get available and I'll squeeze you into my schedule."

"Absolutely! How does tomorrow sound?" Sequoia saw no need to waste any time.

"That'll be perfect. I'll let you know which studio to meet me at when you call. Until then, enjoy yourself. And, oh, you look very nice today."

Sequoia blushed. "Thank you."

As he removed himself from her company, he snapped his fingers as if he was just hit with an epiphany. "I noticed that you don't have anything to drink. I'll send a waiter over here with a bottle of Spades." He walked off before she could tell him that she didn't drink.

Not only had Sequoia taken a vow of sobriety until her dying day, she wasn't legally of age to drink either way. She didn't want to offend him by turning it down though, so she figured it would be cool if she just went along with the flow.

T. Bibby eyed the transaction between Kay-G and Sequoia from across the room as he shook the hand of a close friend and business associate. He concluded the brief meeting abruptly as jealousy enveloped him.

"I'm sorry, Erv, but I gotta check on something real quick. I'll holla at you in a minute," Bibby said before storming off, not waiting for a response.

He snatched a drink from a tray that a passing waiter was carrying and downed it in one motion. He was furious. He couldn't believe that Sequoia would play him out in public like this. And Kay-G? He was supposed to be his boy. They had been cool, close friends for the past fifteen years. He knew full well what the rules of the game were: never come at your man's main girl.

Needless to say, he would be dealing with him at his earliest convenience, but for now he had tunnel vision and his sights were set solely on Sequoia. And he had some very choice words for her that he was certain she wouldn't like.

He walked into the V. I.P. section with her to see her drooling over Kay-G's business card.

"Hey baby," she beamed when she saw his face. "I couldn't—"

"What the fuck was you doing talking to that nigga, Kay? Hunh?" he snapped, cutting her off mid-sentence.

Sequoia sucked her teeth and looked at him as if he'd lost his mind. She had no clue where this was coming from.

"Excuse me!" Sequoia retorted angrily as the waiter came over and handed her a glass of Spades. The waiter offered Bibby a drink as well but he refused.

"Do I look like I want something to drink?" he snarled at the waiter. "And what...? What...? This nigga sending you bottles and shit over here. Tell me something, Sequoia, when the fuck did you start drinking?"

By now the waiter had withdrawn himself from the melee and alerted a nearby bouncer that a possible altercation would occur in the V.I.P. section.

Sequoia rose from her seat. "Look, you need to chill out. I can smell alcohol on your breath, and you're coming at me all crazy on some B.S.," Sequoia said as calmly as she could. She was trying to keep her voice low, but it had become utterly apparent to her that everyone within earshot could clearly overhear their conversation. And though that realization made Sequoia want to discontinue the conversation, Bibby had other plans.

Bibby closed the distance between them and spoke in a harsh tone. "What is it? Hunh Sequoia? You got yourself a little taste of fame, and some money in the bank, and now you've forgotten what we've built." He scoffed before removing his designer shades. "Let me guess: you're just dying to spread those pretty little legs of yours as fast as you can for the next industry nigga with some clout."

Sequoia was completely floored by his statement. Her blood was boiling. She'd done absolutely nothing to deserve such a verbal assault, and she wasn't one to play victim to anyone's abuse so she reacted.

She tossed the champagne drink in his face. "Don't you ever disrespect me like that!"

She attempted to walk away from him but he grabbed her arm aggressively. Sequoia snatched away from him. "Get your fucking hands off of me!" she snapped.

"Is everything alright?" a bouncer asked as he took in the view of T. Bibby drenched in liquor and Sequoia in heated contempt.

"What's going on?" Rosa asked as she noted the tension in the air between her daughter and T. Bibby.

"Yeah Quoy, what's up?" Desiree asked, ready to come to her defense.

Sequoia looked at Bibby with a mixture of disgust and disappointment in her eyes.

"Nothing. Let's go," she said before callously scooping up her red and black, studded, Salvatore Ferragamo clutch. "And for the record, Kay-G approached me about making a song together. But it's obvious that you have some serious issues that you need to work through. So, do us both a favor and lose my number until you learn how to treat me with some respect."

Sequoia stomped off as everyone looked on in a state of confusion. "LET'S GO!" she said to her entourage.

They followed suit, but Rosa felt that it was necessary that she speak her piece before leaving. "I ask you to take care of my daughter and this is how you treat her? You're crazy! I raised her right. You'll never find another woman like that. Trust me." Rosa shook her head disapprovingly as she exited the place.

CHAPTER 43

An entire week had passed since T. Bibby had showed his sass at Sequoia's expense during her album release party. The very public verbal lashing had cut a wound in Sequoia so deep that a simple recollection of the event stung as if it had happened yesterday. Sequoia couldn't believe the nerve of him, and to compound the problem, the tabloids wasted no time with printing the story, plastering the words "TROUBLE IN PARADISE" in bold red letters across the front page with a picture of Bibby and her that was split down the middle.

T. Bibby had been texting and emailing her like crazy, but she refused to answer. That, in a nutshell, was terrible for business because—being her manager—T. Bibby arranged and advised her of her appearances and obligations. The timing could not have been worse, considering that her debut album had just been released and the two of them needed each other to promote it. But, album or not, Bibby was completely out of line at her album release party, and that was something that she just could not tolerate, let alone get past.

Luckily for her, she was under the management wing of one of the most shrewd and prolific C.E.O.'s in the game who was all about his money. To ensure that his cash flow continued, Bibby emailed her entire schedule to her for the next two weeks. It was a crafty yet thoughtful gesture on his part, Sequoia thought, even though he almost screwed up her opportunity with Kay-G. Fortunately for her, Kay-G was an understanding person, who fully understood how the business worked and understood T. Bibby even better. So, he agreed to postpone their collaboration until it was convenient for the both of them when she called him. He also made it his business to advise Sequoia to be safe around T. Bibby, which she found to be extremely odd considering their fifteen year history as friends. One would think that his loyalty would be to T. Bibby, and not her.

Sequoia couldn't seem to evade the idea that the entire situation was beginning to creep her out. The mystery that lay behind his intent for giving her such a strong advisory practically introduced her mind to entertain a sea of other questions, with one primary question taking center stage: what was it that Kay-G knew about T. Bibby that would make him feel compelled to give her such a stern warning?

It was nothing that she intended to waste good energy on though, because as that point they were done as far as she was concerned.

Sequoia thought Desiree, Jade, and her mother would pounce on the opportunity to keep Bibby and she separated for good, but they were a lot less vocal this time around. That was a shock to Sequoia, considering all of their positions on the relationship when she made it back from tour. She figured that neither of them wanted to rub it in by saying, "I told you so."

But, it was exactly what she needed at the moment. Their presence alone spoke volumes, and no words were actually needed. As far as she was concerned, outside of her tribe of three, her career was the only thing of significant importance at the moment.

Sequoia's schedule was jam-packed, even considering that she had to make a few selective cancellations to avoid being grilled by detail-seeking editors and journalists. But, as the old showbiz adage goes; "The show must go on."

Within the course of a day's time, she made guest appearances on *Good Morning America,* two radio shows, and *106th and Park.* It was seven o'clock at night and to some degree, her day was just beginning.

Sean, her bodyguard, accompanied her, along with her stylist Corrine. Corrine was one of a team of stylists that Bibby appointed to her months ago. Corrine was very professional and didn't talk much, which made her more effective at her job. She was twenty-four years old, had a chestnut complexion, and a curvy figure. Her maroon colored hair was braided into a Mohawk.

Neither of them ever pried into her personal affairs, which Sequoia greatly appreciated, thereby making them some very cool people to chill with in between taking care of business. They were practically friends, and Sequoia loved the fact that she was able to relax and be herself while she was with them.

"I'm starving. Do we have enough time to get something to eat before the flight?" Sequoia asked Sean from the back seat of the late model Suburban.

Sean examined the time on his Hublot wristwatch. "Not really. We'll probably have to grab something on the plane."

"On a commercial flight," Sequoia pouted in a whiney, childlike manner. "First class or not, that food sucks. I've gotta get something now."

"We're not taking a commercial flight," Sean replied curtly, hoping that Sequoia wouldn't press him for details.

Sequoia immediately picked up on her reserve and spoke to him in an even tone. "So how are we going to get there, Sean?" she said curiously.

"Let it go, Sequoia," Sean said simply, while staring out the window of the S.U.V.

Sequoia was fuming. "Let it go." She rolled her eyes. "Tell you what; drop me off at the airport."

"That's not gonna happen and you know it," Sean responded firmly.

Sequoia wanted to incite a protest, but she decided against it. She folded her arms across her chest. The pre-orchestrated transport had T.Bibby's DNA all over it. He obviously couldn't take a hint. She wanted nothing from him. Not even an apology would suffice at this point.

She felt her anxiety building, which was unusual considering that she hadn't had many complications with it lately. *Breathe, Sequoia, just breathe.*

Sequoia relished in her moment a while longer before stumbling upon an epiphany. She had no desire the let her disdain for T. Bibby get in the way of her enjoying herself. Besides, what could she possibly have to complain about? She was about to collect seventy-five thousand dollars by simply making a guest appearance at a popular nightclub in Miami.

Not to mention that she currently had the number one album in the country, which sold more than eight hundred thousand copies in its first week. As it stood, she had produced five number one hit singles from a single album, which set the record for one of the highest selling and most number one hit singles off of a debut album by an artist of all time.

"You alright Sequoia?" Corrine asked from her left.

"Yeah, I'm good," she said. "I'm just going to enjoy myself and have fun with you guys."

"That's what I'm talking about," Sean said energetically. "That's the Sequoia I know. Tell you the truth; you was starting to scare me there for a minute. Getting all diva-ish on me."

Sequoia and Corrine laughed.

"Well, I'm sorry if I was," Sequoia said animatedly. "But the more I sat back and thought about it, the more I thought about how blessed I am. I have nothing to complain about. So I'm just going to sit back and enjoy the rest of the day and take it all in like a grateful person is supposed to."

"That's what's up." Sean was glad that she dropped it. Corrine smiled approvingly at Sequoia's maturity.

They arrived at a private airstrip fifteen minutes later. T. Bibby's G5 jet was already fueled, so within twenty minutes they were in the air and on their way to Miami.

They touched down three hours later on a private tarmac that was a stone's throw away from the Atlantic Ocean. Sequoia had eaten a small chicken breast with scallops smothered in gravy. It was nothing to brag about by her standards. It was just enough fuel to get her to the next venue.

Sean, Corrine, and Sequoia loaded into a black Suburban and were driven a mile away where they filed into a helicopter.

"Oh!" Sequoia exclaimed enthusiastically. "I never been in a helicopter before. And is it just me, or does it seem as if going to the club in a helicopter is a bit much?"

"You can say that," Sean said simply, hoping that Sequoia wouldn't ask him any more questions.

Corrine didn't respond, which was normal for her. She just sat quietly as if she were awaiting instructions.

Sequoia was so excited at the idea of her first ride in a helicopter that she failed to notice the course of the helicopter's direction until she was nearly two miles out over the Atlantic Ocean.

"Sean, where are we going?" she yelled over the noise of the helicopter's turbine and propellers as she watched the shoreline fade out of sight.

"We're almost there!" he replied.

Sequoia looked at Corrine for answers, but she shrugged her shoulders as if she hadn't had a clue. So, she began to get mad.

"Somebody better let me know what's going on right now! Because I'm only seconds away from contacting someone to inform them of my whereabouts!"

"Chill girl, damn!" Sean said as he turned around to face her. "You know I got you. It will never be like that when I'm around. So just chill. Someone wants to talk to you."

Sequoia got the hint as soon as the words left his mouth. Sean didn't need to spell it out, it was evident. Her suspicions were confirmed moments later when the sight of an elaborate yacht grew bigger in sight before they descended onto a helipad atop the yacht.

T. Bibby was at the bow of the ship with his arms extended welcomingly, with an arrogant smile on his face.

"Let me guess; he's the someone?" Sequoia said with attitude. "But thank you, Sean. Thank you for letting me know who your loyalty lies with."

"Sorry Sequoia, but he's the boss, and I'm just following orders," he said as the helicopter made its landing. "So, you quit frontin' and go see what he wants. Because you know you want to."

Sequoia didn't respond. She just looked out of the window at the vast ocean as she secretly tried to conceal her excitement. She knew that Sean was right, but she wouldn't dare let her expression betray her.

CHAPTER 44

Sequoia rolled her eyes at Sean and Corrine as they both waved goodbye from the fleeing helicopter. They'd ditched her on the yacht with T. Bibby and had taken off; leaving her in the middle of the Atlantic Ocean with the man she currently had mixed feelings about.

The blaring sound from the helicopter's turbine grew fainter as its propellers launched an assault on the sky and crept nearer to shore. Sequoia watched the helicopter until it resembled a dot in the sky. She felt that she needed something to fix her gaze on to distract her from the emotions that had been galvanized by T. Bibby's presence. So, when the helicopter had completely vanished from view and she was forced to digest the fact that she wouldn't be going anywhere anytime soon, she permitted her emotions to carry her to the bow of the ship so she could over look the sea.

Bibby was obviously avoiding her for the moment. He vanished into the massive cabin on the yacht for unknown reasons, and to some degree, Sequoia appreciated it. She needed time alone to digest the events of the day, time to clear her head and collect her thoughts. A bird's eye view of the still ocean was the perfect distraction, and the backdrop she needed to assist her with her thought process.

The tranquility that Sequoia received from the sight and smell of the ocean was intoxicating. She closed her eyes and inhaled the salty mist that escaped from the sea and imagined being back in Costa Rica.

Before long, she'd lost all sense of time, problems, and unresolved conflicts that currently existed in her life. Time flew, and before long a full moon was staring Sequoia down. The night sky was filled with a plethora of stars—stars that resembled haphazardly scattered prisms in a dark room. The sight was captivating!

Sequoia had no idea how long she'd been there, but she figured it had to be at least a few hours because her legs and feet had long since fallen asleep. She had to shift her weight periodically to each foot to take away the pain. Not that she was complaining though, because truthfully, she wanted to bask in the moment for as long as possible before she had to come face to face with the elephant in the room.

But, Sequoia was smart enough to know that the state of peace that she currently resided in would soon be tested, and her curiosity wouldn't allow her to let T. Bibby off the hook. She secretly wanted to pick his brain to see why it was that he had behaved in such a disrespectful manner towards her the night at the club. She knew that he had been drinking and had spoken out of jealousy, but that did not excuse the way he treated her.

The ordeal had provided her with a lot of perspective on their relationship, but she was still having a problem coming up with a solution to their problem. She knew in her heart that he was a good man that loved her, but she also knew that he was extremely insecure about his position in her life. On one hand, she wanted to be with him, and on the other hand, she wanted to run to the furthest corner of the earth and hide.

Although Sequoia wanted to relish in the breathtaking view of the ocean, the idea of the imminently approaching conversation between them was dominating her thoughts. She managed to push the thoughts out of her mind temporarily and allow her attention to linger on the idea of the phenomenon that was sea, moon, and stars. But no matter how hard she tried, her reality was right there, wrapping his arms around her waist while gently planting kisses on her neck.

Sequoia flinched from the initial contact, startled, but she quickly calmed her nerves when she realized that it was none other than T. Bibby. When the initial shock began to wane, a million thoughts began to inundate her mind.

"Beautiful, ain't it?" Bibby said softly into the nape of Sequoia's neck.

Sequoia sighed. "Isn't it," she said with attitude.

Bibby stared at the back of her raven, long, cascading curly hair with confusion. "You lost me."

"It's beautiful, 'isn't' it. Not 'ain't' it," she curtly corrected him.

Bibby chuckled. "Well, excuse me Miss Ivy League."

"Whatever." Sequoia waved him off.

Bibby frowned. "I see that you're still mad at me."

Sequoia didn't respond. In all truth, she wasn't as mad at him as she was letting on, but she had no desire to make this easy for him. If he wanted her forgiveness, then he was going to have to put on his hard hat and Timberland boots because he had a lot of work to do.

Bibby chose to remain silent to give Sequoia the time she needed to calm down, but he never released her from his arms.

After a long, quiet moment, Sequoia spoke, "It is beautiful."

"I wasn't talking about the sky, Sequoia." Bibby craned his neck so he could look in her eyes. "I was talking about you."

Sequoia sucked her teeth and said with a sneer, "That was so cheesy."

Bibby smiled. "I thought you liked cheese."

Sequoia shook her head and faced the ocean, and Bibby took that as his cue to keep talking. "I know what else you like. Well, besides me."

Sequoia scoffed. "And what's that?"

"Well," he kissed her neck, "you like being near the ocean. It reminds you of the time when you were back home in Cost Rica. It always gives you a sense of serenity and peace. That's why I arranged for you to be brought out here like this. I know my tactics are a lot less subtle than what you may be used to, but I figured that you probably wouldn't have come if I asked you. Plus, I kinda needed a little help from my ocean buddy over there to set the mood, so I can keep you from kicking my ass.

"I figured that the distraction of the ocean would give me enough time to come up with the perfect apology for the way I treated you the other night."

Sequoia giggled but said nothing. She wanted to stay mad at him, but as always, he knew exactly what to do and all the right words to say. Sequoia hated to admit it, but he was becoming her kryptonite. Her superpowers held no authority in his presence. He was making her weak, dependent even. That unsettling truth was a reality that she wished she could escape, because emotional vulnerability to someone like T. Bibby was not only an Achilles heel, it was bad for business.

They both remained silent a long while before Sequoia decided to turn and face him. "So you remembered all of that, hunh?" Sequoia stared into his eyes intently.

"I remember everything you ever told me Sequoia."

"If that's the case, why would you front on me like that the other night? You know I would never cheat on you, or even fix my mind to disrespect our relationship like that. I'm not some groupie chick that opens her legs for anyone, let alone an industry nigga. And you know that."

Bibby rubbed his hands up and down her arm nervously. "I know baby. And I'm not gonna sit here and make excuses for myself because you don't' deserve that either. You deserve better.

"You deserve someone who will take care of you, respect and trust you, and treat you like the queen you are. Not someone who questions your intentions and is insecure, or who jumps to conclusions before he even gets his facts straight. And I know that I've been all of these things lately, but I'm here to tell you that I'm here today. I'm the guy you need me to be and I don't want to lose you for nothing in the world. I love you."

Deep down, Sequoia knew she should've ended it all right there and established sensible boundaries that lay strictly within the realms of a business relationship, but when she opened her mouth to speak the complete opposite came out.

"You're only saying that because you know I want to kick your ass," she said, and they both laughed and shared a hug and kiss.

"I love you Sequoia! You're the only woman for me," Bibby said emotionally.

"I love you too!" Sequoia kissed him. "Just try to do me a favor—trust me."

Bibby nodded. "I do, baby."

When Bibby concluded that he was in the clear and that she was no longer mad at him, he allowed his gaze to shift predatorily to the outfit she was wearing.

She was clad in a smoke gray and yellow Christian Louibiton dress and matching sling-back heels, not to mention a smoke gray and yellow Christian Louibiton suede timepiece clutch and yellow embellished Plexiglas collar and wrist accessories.

Bibb was sporting white Polo khaki shorts, white short-sleeve button-down Polo shirt, and white Casual Polo shoes with no socks.

"You looking amazing! As usual." Bibby eyed her.

"Thank you."

He grabbed her hand and led her toward the cabin of the yacht.

The yacht was one of the top of its class. It had every amenity imaginable; marble tile, Jacuzzi, wood grain and gold trimming, flat screen television, kitchenette, master bedroom and guest room, whirlpool tub and standing shower, satellite cable, G.P.S. tracking, and four on-board jet skis.

When Sequoia entered the cabin she immediately noticed the candlelit dinner set on a dining table with an adjacent mobile food tray that was covered with a plethora of exotic foods and fruits.

Bibby pulled her chair out for her and poured them both a glass of vintage wine.

"This is romantic," Sequoia was beaming, "even though you know I don't drink." She shot him a skeptical eye. "But I'll make an exception today since it is wine."

"Don't worry, boo, I got you." He kissed her on the cheek. "We're just getting started. I promise, you ain't seen nothing yet."

"Ooww!" Sequoia said excitedly.

Bibby removed the silver lid from their plates and introduced Sequoia to the main entrée: wild salmon smothered in gravy and diced asparagus with cream covered scallops that were sprinkled with bell peppers, thyme, tomatoes, and onions.

The meal didn't stand a chance. They both devoured their dishes before sinking their teeth into a generous slice of red velvet cake.

Sequoia was stuffed and was physically drained. She only wanted to take a warm bath and spoon with Bibby until she fell asleep, but he obviously had other plans.

Bibby drew her a hot bubble bath, then helped her undress before helping her into the tub. He fed her chocolate covered strawberries while she sipped champagne. Sequoia was in heaven!

Bibby then lathered a sponge with Dove body wash and washed her entire body, foot to head. Sequoia reclined back and bit her bottom lip seductively as she stared at Bibby with pure lust in her aqua blue eyes.

Bibby returned her glare as he planted a wet kiss on her luscious lips. They both tongue-probed each other's mouth while the candles flickered a wavering silhouette on the tiled walls.

Bibby dipped the sponge in the water between Sequoia's legs and squeezed the soapy remnants onto her perky, ample breast. Sequoia was in ecstasy. She cocked her head back, inviting Bibby to her succulent neckline, which he took as his cue to suck.

A soft moan escaped Sequoia's lips as Bibby brought the sponge down between her legs and began massaging her clit with it. He ditched the sponge after a short while and began fingering her. Before long, she was cumming all over his hand underneath the water and moaning loud enough to be heard back on shore.

By now, Bibby's erection was throbbing painfully inside his white Polo khaki shorts. He let them drop to the floor and exposed his massive erection. He removed his matching button-down shirt, wife beater, and shoes, and climbed inside the tub.

He pulled Sequoia to her feet and kissed her passionately while palming her soft, large, fleshy bottom. He cradled her left leg in the crook of his arm and entered her slowly, drawing out a loud moan. He moved at a slow, rhythmic pace until he felt himself nearing a climax. He withdrew his member from her love tunnel before he reached the brink and turned her around. He placed one of her pretty, pedicured feet on the side of the whirlpool tub and bent her over. He entered her slowly.

He groaned.

She moaned.

Sequoia was wet and tight as a virgin with a womb that was even more attractive than she was which made it hard for Bibby to last long. He felt himself nearing an orgasm again and decided to just go with it, figuring that he'd get the first one out of the way so he could last longer the second round. He pulled out and came on her back.

"Am I dreaming, or is that shit really that good?" Bibby was astonished.

Sequoia smiled wickedly as she faced him. "Does this feel like a dream?" She kissed him while massaging his member.

Bibby was sensitive to the touch, but he didn't dare tell her to stop. Sequoia discovered the sponge, and after lathering it up she washed him clean.

She then did something that totally surprised Bibby: she took him into her mouth. Sequoia had adamantly stated in the past how she wasn't a big fan of oral sex, and her first time administering fellatio several months ago was a testament to that. In fact, it was so terrible the first time around that he had to force her to stop to give her a few pointers so she could step her game up.

But today was completely different. She was a totally different woman with the skills of a pro. Bibby couldn't believe his eyes, let alone the feelings she provided him with as she worked her magic mouth on him. She licked, slurped, bobbed, and spit on his member while simultaneously stroking him and training her aqua blue eyes seductively on his. Within moments he was back to life and ready for round two.

They took their next sexual bout to the bathroom floor, where Sequoia straddled Bibby as he lay on a towel. She rode him slow and calculated, making him groan and cry out in pleasure. After five minutes or so, Sequoia noticed Bibby's breathing intensify and took it as an indication that he was on the precipice of another climax. So she dismounted him and turned her back to him, giving him a front row view of her perfect, shapely backside.

Sequoia placed her small, pedicured feet on his thighs and bounced on his pogo stick like she was trying to prove a point. Within moments she could feel his pulsating dick swelling inside her, coupled with his throaty grunts and groans. They both came in unison, and hard!

Sequoia panted heavily as she stared back at Bibby, who was also breathing hard. "Mamma's learned some new tricks."

"I see," Bibby said. "You sure you haven't been… practicing?"

Sequoia slapped his thigh. "Stop playing with me," she turned to face him, "but let's just say I think I may be addicted to porn now."

They both laughed.

They soon after retired to the master bedroom, where they made love until the sun came up before falling asleep in each other's arms.

CHAPTER 45

Sequoia was awoken by Bibby sometime later in the afternoon by gentle kisses being placed all over her face.

She grimaced. "What time is it?"

"Time for you to refuel. You burned a lot of calories last night," Bibby said devilishly.

Sequoia frowned. "Funny," she said before returning his kiss. "I never knew you were such a comedian."

He tickled her and watched her squirm and laugh uncontrollably underneath him. "Yeah, I know just how to make you laugh."

"Uncle! Uncle!"

He stopped long enough to take in her beauty. He was totally mesmerized by her. Even after countless hours of love-making and sleep, she still looked more beautiful than the brightest star in the galaxy.

He loomed over her on all fours, like the four-legged king of the Safari Desert who was moments away from sinking its teeth in the next meal.

"I made you breakfast," Bibby said in his wife beater and powder blue Polo pajamas.

He cooked her an egg and cheese omelet with green and red bell peppers, turkey bacon, and buttered toast on rye bread, with a glass of orange juice and milk to wash it down.

"Aw, thanks babe!" Sequoia said as he set the tray before her. "I think I need to get mad at you more often, especially if it means that I'll be getting this type of royal treatment." She popped a piece of bacon in her mouth.

"Well, fortunately for you, I intend on doing this as often as possible whenever we're together." He kissed her but quickly stopped when the annoying sound of his cell phone began ringing.

"Sorry, babe," Bibby said. "That's the Bat Phone. I've got to get it." He went to retrieve the cell phone that was on the nightstand. "Only a few people have this number and they only call in case of emergency. Let's just hope that there's nothing wrong." Sequoia crossed her fingers.

After a few seconds of eavesdropping on the conversation, Sequoia was able to detect that the news that Bibby was receiving had to be anything but bad.

She heard her phone ring and pointed in the direction of her purse for Bibby to retrieve. She watched as he sifted through the purse for her phone before unintentionally stumbling across three full bottles of her medication. He stared at the three bottles inquisitively with an ambiguous scowl.

Sequoia hurriedly scurried over to him and snatched the bottles out of his hand. Bibby looked at her, puzzled, as Sequoia morphed into an anxious wreck right before his eyes.

She couldn't believe that she had been so careless. She was sure that they weren't going to be able to get past this. She feared that he would now think that she was a crazed psycho.

She suddenly wanted him to spend as much time as possible on the phone with his assistant, so she could have enough time to think of an escape route. Unfortunately for her, he had other plans.

He ended the call. "You alright?" He studied her for a reaction.

Sequoia nodded, though it was clear that she was shaken.

"You're not sick or anything, are you Sequoia? Like, physically?" Bibby asked with genuine concern in his voice.

Sequoia shook her head. She remained silent with her eyes fixed on one of the three bottles from her bag that was in her hand. She felt a strong sense of dread enveloping her, which usually gave way to an anxiety attack.

"Sequoia?" Bibby called out to her.

Sequoia looked at him apprehensively with body language and eyes that mimicked defeat.

"Mind telling me what those are for?"

Sequoia sighed. "They're for anxiety...and depression," she lowered her gaze once more, " ...and Bipolar Disorder."

Bibby said nothing as he processed what she was telling him. He sat on the bed with his back facing her. "How long have you had these problems?"

Sequoia pulled the sheet over her naked breasts. "Since I was thirteen."

Bibby shook his head. "And I had to find out like this." He paused. "Do you think that's fair to me, Sequoia?"

She began to cry. "No."

"Then why wouldn't you tell me?" he pressed her.

"I don't know." She wiped her eyes. "I was scared, I guess. I didn't want you to think I was some type of psycho!" she sobbed. "I didn't want you to break up with me."

Bibby wiped Sequoia's face free of tears. "Break up with you?" he said, confused. "Sequoia, is that what you thought? That I would break up with you?" Sequoia nodded as she wiped more tears from her eyes.

"Sequoia, I love you!" he said sincerely. "Why would you even think something like that?"

Sequoia said nothing.

"Sequoia, there's nothing too big for us to tackle together. I want to be there for you whenever you're going through anything in life. But you have to be honest with me. Don't ever shut me out of your life like this again. Do you hear me?"

Sequoia nodded.

"I know this may be a lot for you right now, so let's just drop it until you feel like talking about it again. Alright?"

"Alright. Thank you," Sequoia said somberly.

They embraced each other and kissed.

"Now," Bibby said, "you ready for some good news?"

Sequoia fingered the loose strands of hair on her face behind her ears and exhaled the fleeting anxiety. "What's up?"

"First, we got clearance to shoot the 'Full Package' video in the Dominican Republic for next week. But I must warn you: what I am about to tell you may be a little difficult to process. So try to stay calm."

Sequoia mentally braced herself as she cut a slice of omelet and ate it.

"Kresha, the pop star, had to drop out of the world tour with Lady Goo Goo because she broke her leg during a dance rehearsal. And lucky for you, Lady Goo Goo personally requested that you open up for her on the world tour."

"Oh my God! Are you serious?" Sequoia exclaimed excitedly. "That's amazing!"

"So does that mean yes?" Bibby asked, as if he was unsure.

Sequoia nodded her head in disbelief. "Yes! Of course the answer is yes! This is an opportunity of a lifetime!"

"Absolutely. But I will warn you, it's an international tour, so you'll probably be on your own for nearly eight months."

Sequoia considered what he was saying momentarily before responding. "It'll be tough, but I don't want to miss an opportunity like this. So, I'll just have to make some adjustments."

"You sure this is what you want to do?" Bibby asked. "You know you're not going to see anyone; your mother, your friends, me."

"You're not coming along?" Sequoia was confused.

"Sequoia, I would love to, but my plate is too full right now. I have an acting gig that I'll be doing in a few weeks and countless projects in the making."

Sequoia suddenly understood why he kept asking her.

"Look, I'm not trying to make this hard for you. You should definitely go. I just want you to know that things could be real lonely out there, and that you may need to prepare for it. I'm pretty sure I'll be able to work something out so we can see each other in between times, but as your manager I will definitely advise you to do this.

"Lady Goo Goo is the biggest pop star since Madonna. You'll never have another opportunity this early in your career to that type of fan base. So we're just going to have to tough it out until it's over with."

Sequoia couldn't believe her luck. Lady Goo Goo had requested her to fill the void that Kresha left behind on her world tour. It was certainly an opportunity of a lifetime—one that she wasn't about to squander for anything in the world.

"You have two months until the tour starts, so let's focus on the video you're about to shoot for right now, and we'll work everything else out later. Deal?"

"Deal." Sequoia was elated.

"Good. Not that that's out of the way," Bibby said. "I'ma need you to pop a few of those pills for me. Don't want you transforming into no crazy person on me." He laughed.

Sequoia hit him with a pillow before playfully punching him. She knew he was just teasing her, but she intended on making him pay for it with a few rounds of toe-curling sex before going back to shore.

Sequoia took the prescribed dose of pills from each bottle and washed them down with the orange juice.

CHAPTER 46

The months that led up to Sequoia's departure were a couple of the toughest months she'd been through in her life. They left her physically drained, emotionally exhausted, and socially destitute.

She had no idea of the task that she signed on for when she first accepted the tour. At times, she found herself wanting to abandon the idea and take a break, but that wasn't the legacy she intended to leave behind. She wanted to inspire young women to work hard and chase their dreams, not to quit when the ride began to get rough. So she toughed it out and, in retrospect, it was well worth it.

In two months, she'd managed to film four videos, record over thirty songs, do two commercials, the cover of *Rolling Stone Magazine*, and attend countless dance rehearsals. She loved the fact that she was able to keep most of her dancers that were with her national tour with Keisha Colb and Monikah. It made the rehearsals so much easier, figuring that they would use some of the same routines. But nothing good came without its share of sacrifice, which showed in Sequoia's social life (which was nonexistent at the moment). She hadn't seen or spoken to any of her friends for over two weeks, and though they expressed their disdain for it via Twitter and emails she had yet to find a way to return their calls.

Her mother, however, was a lot more understanding. She had become extremely flexible when it came to sharing Sequoia with her demanding schedule over the past few weeks—which, by Sequoia's count, was a total of three times in the last twenty-four days. Not exactly numbers that she was proud of, but she fully understood that the level of success she was reaching for was going to come with significant sacrifices. Anyone who bitched about it along the way would simply have to get over it, she thought.

Of course, she was too much of a cream puff to ever make such a statement publicly, so in true non-confrontational fashion, Sequoia opted to throw a going away party with attendees ranging from D- to A-listers in the entertainment, corporate, and athletic world to distract everyone long enough to break to proverbial ice.

T. Bibby allowed her to use his mansion in the Hamptons to throw her party, and the turnout couldn't have been better.

Rosa wasn't feeling up to it, saying that she wasn't up to dealing with a crowd of people. So, Sequoia made her a promise to spend as much time as she could with her before leaving to go on tour. But Jade, Desiree, and Sasha were able to make it.

Jade was practically antisocial by genetic trait, and Desiree and Sasha were the complete opposite. So, as Sasha went off to mingle with the patrons, Desiree—in a genuine attempt to appease Jade—vowed to not leave her side until it was time for them to leave.

The two carved themselves out an invisible cubicle on the patio deck of the large mansion and practically waited there until Sequoia decided to return.

Sequoia, on the other hand, was completely oblivious to the compromises that were made on her behalf while she played hostess on the hip of T. Bibby. Neither Jade nor Desiree approved of their relationship, especially since the night at the 20/20 Club where his jealous tirade led to a night of embarrassment for everyone involved. But they were supportive enough to tolerate him being with her, even though deep down they knew that she deserved better.

"You look beautiful tonight," Bibby said as she slowly strolled through the living room and into the gourmet kitchen.

"Thank you!" Sequoia beamed.

She was wearing a black, knee-length, Versace dress that was embroidered with leather and studs around the seams and hem. She had a matching purse, leather and studded earrings, leather and studded bracelet, leather and studded choke chain, and a pair of open-toed, leather and studded Versace boots. Her hair was pulled up in a feathered Mohawk, which made it possible to see her new, first tattoo of three music notes behind her ear.

Bibby was clad in an all black silk and polyester Versace pantsuit the color of a baby seal, with matching Versace shades embellished with gold insignias and black Versace loafers. He had long since allowed his wave pattern to grow into a small tapered afro that boasted three small parts to the side. Four massive gold chains with diamond-encrusted Jesus faces adorned his neck.

"So you wanna tell me why you're avoiding your friends?" Bibby asked her as they navigated through the throes of guests who were in the kitchen and into the den.

"Is it that obvious?" Sequoia was shocked that he noticed.

Bibby nodded. "And it's unnecessary."

"I know, but..." She paused. "I haven't exactly been the best friend these last couple of months."

"Well, you can explain that to them," Bibby said.

Before Sequoia had realized it, she was standing on the patio, just feet away from Desiree and Jade. Sequoia cut Bibby an annoyed look.

"That's not right," she said.

He shrugged. "I'll talk to you later." He kissed her on the cheek before vanishing back into the house.

"We don't bite, Sequoia," Desiree said as Sequoia reluctantly joined them.

"Are you guys made at me?" Sequoia asked.

Desiree scoffed. "For chasing your dreams and getting the success you deserve? What, are you crazy?" Desiree said. "We could never be mad at you."

"But doing it while not answering our calls and not at least giving us an explanation or making time for us is a bit unnerving. But we forgive you." Jade smiled.

Sequoia embraced them. "I'm sorry guys! I've just been so busy lately," she said as they released each other.

"Where's Sasha?" Sequoia looked around the patio deck and spotter her near the north end of the pool exchanging information with a player from the New York Knicks. "Oh, there she is," Sequoia said dryly, "just being Sasha."

Sequoia turned to face them. "Anyway. You guys look great by the way," Sequoia said as she eyed them impressively.

Jade was donned in a tight-fitted cream and forest green, stretch rayon blend dress by Bebe. Her ears boasted a pair of opal, chalcedony, and diamond drop earrings; black and patent leather pumps by Manolo Blahnik were on her feet. She was wearing a pair of forest green Nina Ricci prescribed eyeglasses.

Desiree was clad in a sand-colored silk and lace Jill Stuart dress and a pair of sand-colored mesh, peep-toe boots. She was carrying a sand-colored, snake skin and leather clutch that matched the highlights in her hair, and leather and suede J. Brand jacket.

"Thanks, Quoy!" Desiree exclaimed with a bright smile. "And you look amazing! As usual."

Jade nodded. "You do."

"Thanks." She smiled. "I wish you guys could come with me on this tour. It's gonna be lonely."

"Me too," Desiree said.

"I'd second that," Jade said, "but that's too long. I couldn't possibly miss that much school."

"Wait." Desiree claimed the floor to speak. "T. Bibby's not going with you?"

Sequoia frowned. "Unfortunately, no. He promised that he'll be there as much as he can, but he has a lot of upcoming projects, so..."

"Well, hopefully he behaves himself while you're away," Desiree said sarcastically.

"Desi?" Sequoia didn't want to get into this with her now.

Desiree shrugged. "I'm just saying..."

"So what about your mother? Is she gonna be alright while you're gone?" Jade asked.

"She's fine. She's my biggest fan." Sequoia laughed. "She wants me to go for it. I promised her you guys will check on her and that I'll call her every night," Sequoia said. "And that reminds me, I have six more months left on my lease in the condo, and I wanted to give you both keys to it.

"I know that you'll be in Cambridge most of the time," Sequoia said to Jade, "but now you'll have somewhere to go hang out when you come to New York. And Desi, I want you to take my car."

"Sequoia, you're talking like we're planning your funeral," Desiree said and they laughed.

"No, I'm not," Sequoia said, "but there's no sense in having all this stuff just lying around. I never cared for it that much to begin with, and I'm pretty sure there will be a lot more in the near future, so have fun. You know I love you guys. And when I really get my affairs in order I intend to set you both up real nice."

"That's what I'm talking about," Desiree said, hugging her. "A girl sure could use it." She was all smiles.

Jade hugged her. "Thanks Sequoia!"

"Oh, shit," Desiree said frantically. "Check your six, Sequoia." Sequoia turned to see T. Bibby approaching. He kissed her on the cheek and spoke to Jade and Desiree.

"You two enjoying yourselves?"

They both nodded.

"I love your house," Jade said.

"Yeah, you have great taste," Desiree said, meaning every word of it.

"Thank you!" he said.

"T. Bibby," a woman's voice called him from behind.

Everyone turned to see Korrine Stevens, the video vixen-slash-porn star, who a great bulk of the industry dubbed "Superdome" for her unique talent of performing fellatio.

"Yeah?" Bibby said coolly.

"I just wanted to tell you that we're leaving," Korrine Stevens said.

"Alright. Hope you guys enjoyed yourselves," he said.

"Oh, we did," she said with a mischievous grin. She smiled awkwardly at Sequoia and waved. "Hey Sequoia. Love your music. And I know that your tour will be a success." She waved before leaving.

Sequoia rolled her eyes and shot Bibby a glance that could kill as she aggressively released him. "What the fuck was that?"

Bibby seemed unsure of what was agitating her. "Excuse me, Sequoia, what's wrong?"

She tugged at his arm violently and pulled him out of earshot of Desiree and Jade. "First, what is she even doing here? I didn't invite her."

"I did," he said plainly.

"And you don't see a problem with that?" Sequoia was getting heated.

"Sequoia, you're acting as if I cheated on you or something."

"Babe." Sequoia brought her voice down to an even tone so he could get it. "This woman is a known industry hoe. Everyone has fucked her. And here she shows up at my going away party waving goodbye to you like y'all have history or something."

"And your problem is...?"

"You know what, don't worry about it." Sequoia tried to walk off but Bibby stopped her.

"Sequoia?" He grabbed her arm. "Did you take your

medication today?" he asked seriously.

Sequoia was hurt. She couldn't believe that he had just said that. She snatched away from him.

"You know what? Fuck you!" She stormed off.

"Let's go," she said to Jade and Desiree without acknowledging his request to stop.

Sasha saw the heated exchange from across the deck and hurriedly dismissed herself from his company to be with her friends.

"What did he say, Sequoia?" Jade asked as Sasha joined them in time to eavesdrop.

"Enough to end a relationship," she said curtly as they made their way out of the mansion, drawing the attention of everyone in attendance.

Jade and Desiree looked at each other with an ominous glare. Sequoia informed the valet to get her car. Bibby materialized from inside the house before the valet could return.

"Sequoia, wait," he said as he closed in on her.

By now her car had arrived and she asked Desiree, Jade, and Sasha if they could wait in the car while she talked to him. They all reluctantly complied.

"What?" Sequoia turned to face him with an attitude.

Bibby searched for the right words. "Sequoia, I know you're upset right now, but I got something to say and I'ma really need you to hear me on this."

She folded her arms defensively and listened.

"Okay, I said this before, but I don't think you heard me clearly. So I'm gonna repeat myself." He grabbed her hands gently. "You're the only woman for me. Nobody else matters. Please believe that. You should never have to question my loyalty to you.

"I wanted this night to be special—for it to be one of the most memorable nights of our lives. Not for us to be fighting." He sighed as he reached in his pocket. "And to prove to you how I feel about you. I wanted to know," he pulled out a red leather ring box and opened it to reveal a twenty carat diamond engagement ring, "...if you'd do me the honor of being my wife?"

Sequoia gasped as her lungs suddenly seemed to be deprived of air. She couldn't believe what was happening. She had dreamed of this day since she was a little girl, and now that it was here she didn't know how to respond.

She gazed at the humungous stone that he managed to put on her ring finger with mixed feelings. She digested the look of dread that was coming from Jade and Desiree before turning to see the ecstatic expression on Bibby's face. By now various attendees that were in the party had filed outside to see what was going on.

"So what's it going to be, Sequoia?" Bibby asked. "You gonna make me out to be an honest man or what?"

Sequoia smiled awkwardly as her mind raced at warp speed. She looked up at the crowd of onlookers and back and Jade, Desiree and Sasha. She had made her mind up. She knew exactly what she wanted, and she saw no sense in prolonging the situation any longer.

CHAPTER 47

Nottingham, England

Two Weeks Later

Sequoia sank her talons into the plush armchair of the first class seat as the plane's tires made contact with the tarmac. She didn't necessarily have a fear of flying, but it was something about the way a plane landed that always sent her anxiety meter through the roof. She couldn't seem to resist entertaining the notion that the plane would somehow crash during landing and burst into a ball of flames. It wasn't exactly practical thinking on her part, but it was her struggle and she owned it.

Nevertheless, she had landed safely, and that was something to be grateful for. She smiled nervously at the white, middle-aged man in the seat next to her, who was probably reserving his judgment of her for fear of her response as he prepared to unload.

"You okay Sequoia?" Sean asked as he retrieved her bags from the overhead compartment.

Sequoia beamed. "Yup."

"Miss, excuse me for butting in," the white passenger who was next to her said in a strong English accent, gaining Sequoia's attention, "but you're Sequoia, right?"

"Yes." She gave him a once-over. "You've heard of me?"

"Of course I have." He was suddenly enthusiastic. "I had no idea that I was sitting next to you this entire time. I'm Steve, by the way." He offered to shake her hand.

Sequoia reluctantly accepted it. "Hi Steve." She wasn't sure what to say.

"My kids love you. And I might say, you're a very beautiful woman," he stated eagerly.

"Thank you sir."

"Sequoia, I hope it's not too much to ask, but my kids would kill me if I didn't at least get a picture of you."

Sean moved in closer. "Sequoia, you okay with that?"

She shrugged. "Why not?"

"Oh thank you," Steve said anxiously as he extracted his phone out of his platinum-covered Calvin Klein suit jacket pocket and set it to photograph before handing it over to Sean.

He reluctantly accepted it. "I don't recall reading this in the fine print."

"Be a good sport," Sequoia said as she posed with Steve.

"Yeah, yeah, yeah." Sean took the picture and gave Steve his phone back.

"Thank you." Steve smiled. "Are you touring here?"

"Yes. I'll be in town for a few weeks before heading to Germany."

"Oh, that's great!" he exclaimed. "I have to get my daughters some tickets. That is, of course, assuming that they don't already have them." He laughed. "Well, I don't want to hold you up any longer. Thanks for the picture. Can't wait to tell everyone that I saw you."

"Well, tell everyone that I said hello."

"Will do." He retrieved his briefcase from the overhead compartment and exited the plane.

"That was fun." Sequoia smiled as she passed Sean on the way off the plane.

"Yeah. Fun," he said dryly as he followed her lead, toting her bags, along with her personal assistant Ebony and her stylist Corrine.

Sequoia, Sean, Corrine, and Ebony navigated through the terminal until they met with the prearranged chauffer of a black S.U.V., courtesy of T. Bibby. They managed to keep a low profile as they exited the terminal, even considering that they were toting enough luggage to contain travel gear for a hundred people.

The frigid February air demanded multiple layers of clothes, so everyone in Sequoia's camp was cloaked in their winter gear. Sequoia was wearing DKNY cashmere sweatpants with a matching hooded sweater that was the color of a dolphin, and a pair of dolphin-colored UGG boots. She had a navy blue DKNY down coat over her sweat suit and a navy blue DKNY skull cap.

Sean was wearing a black leather Belle Belle coat over an all black Polo set and wheat Timberland boots, and a black skull cap. Corrine was wearing a designer tan-colored blazer with unique gold stitching and dark H&M jeans with Prada gym shoes. Ebony was donned in a rust-colored Dior pantsuit, cream pea coat, and cream suede Dior boots.

They rode in a convoy of S.U.V.s to a nearby hotel. Jet lag was doing its number on Sequoia, so she retired to her room for the rest of the evening. When she awoke, she contacted everyone via text and webcam to let them know that she arrived safely.

Her first show wasn't until a week from that day, and her dance crew members weren't supposed to be arriving until tomorrow night. She had a strong urge to go sight-seeing and find a foreign diner with deliciousness that she could stuff her face with, but the stage director presented her with an opportunity of a lifetime that she didn't want to pass up.

Lady Goo Goo was doing her sound check and dance rehearsal at the Capitol FM Arena in Nottingham, England, and considering that Lady Goo Goo had personally requested for her to open up for her, not to mention the fact that she was an international superstar! Not only did Sequoia want to meet her, but she was hoping that she could have an opportunity to meet her to pick up a few pointers.

Sean, along with her personal assistant, Ebony, and her stylist, Corrine, who couldn't seem to discontinue recording the entire experience on her camera phone, came along. They all set a few rows from the front and silently watched Lady Goo Goo conduct her rehearsal.

Lady Goo Goo's act included a culmination of suspended wires, suggestive dance moves, and blood! Yes, blood! Nevertheless, it all came together perfectly in a desirably morbid fashion that only she could pull off.

After a lengthy dance routine, Lady Goo Goo informed her dance crew to take fifteen while she talked with the stage director and sound technician. However, midway through the conversation she spotted Sequoia in the audience chairs and frantically motioned for her to come over.

Lady Goo Goo respectfully ended her conversation with them both and greeted Sequoia with a warm, sisterly hug when she came within arm's reach.

"Oh my God! I'm one of your biggest fans!" Lady Goo Goo exclaimed seriously with a smile.

Sequoia blushed. "You don't have to do that."

"Sequoia, I'm serious," Lady Goo Goo was adamant. "I love your music. I love your dance moves. And I think you're the most beautiful woman in the world."

"You're going to make me cry," Sequoia wipe a tear from her eye.

"Aww!" Lady Goo Goo embraced her.

"I can't believe that I'm in Lady Goo Goo's arms," Sequoia said into her chest.

"Well, believe it, sister." Lady Goo Goo released her and gave her a warm smile.

Sequoia took Lady Goo Goo in for the first time and noticed that she was a lot shorter than she looked on screen. Sequoia figured that she was about 5'2", and that was being generous. She was very thin, with an athletic build and palm-sized breasts, and a surprisingly large butt. She may've weighed 110 pounds, maybe. Her blonde hair was pulled back into a ponytail. Her skin was pale and her nose was pointy, but she was cute nonetheless.

She was sporting a white halter top with black stretch pants and Nike tennis shoes.

"You're so beautiful," Lady Goo Goo said. "It's almost unrealistic. I heard about it, but it's something seeing you in person. Anyway," Lady Goo Goo continued, "I know you hear that all the time. So, can we get to know each other better? My treat."

Sequoia smiled annoyingly wide. "It would be my pleasure."

An hour later, they were digging into chicken salads in Lady Goo Goo's dressing room. An assistant of Lady Goo Goo's retrieved the meal from a nearby McDonald's, per her orders, and it was just fine by Sequoia. She wasn't in the mood to be gawked at, and the privacy that the dressing room provided inadvertently created an environment where they could both speak as openly and candidly as they wanted.

"So, I hear that you're in a relationship with T. Bibby," Lady Goo Goo said with a trace of cynicism before stabbing her salad with a plastic fork and devouring it. "And I hear that he proposed to you and you turned it down."

"Something like that," Sequoia uttered unenthusiastically. "I just feel that I'm not ready for that kinda commitment."

Lady Goo Goo's eyebrows furrowed in a sardonic fashion. "You know, usually I would hold my tongue on things like someone's relationship, but I'm team Sequoia! So I just have to ask; why would you jump into something so serious so soon into your career? And with someone like T. Bibby?" Lady Goo Goo asked with genuine concern. "Okay, granted he's very attractive and very rich, but I've met him—several times actually—and he's tried to have sex with me each time."

"Really?" Sequoia was shocked. "When—when was this?"

"Sometime last year," she said casually.

"Oh, well, we weren't together then," she said, somewhat

relieved.

"Sequoia, that's not the point," she told her, staring directly at her. "He's the owner of the record label you work for. He produces the majority of your music, and I hear that he's managing your career."

"Wow!" Sequoia was shocked. "You heard all that, hunh?" she said sarcastically.

Lady Goo Goo placed her salad onto the countertop and did the same to Sequoia's. She then took Sequoia's palms into her own and looked her squarely in the eyes. "Sequoia, I've been in this industry for several years now, and I've long ago conquered the goals that I set out for myself. I've made some mistakes along the way, but thanks to my management team and my family I was fortunate to spare myself a lot of public humiliation.

"Now, I'm not trying to tell you what to do. I'm just giving you advice. You are very talented and very beautiful, and you have one of the most promising careers in the making, but all of it can be thrown down the drain with poor deals, bad contracts and management, and the inability to find a peace of mind.

"That relationship that you're in is toxic. And though I'm one that believes a person can change, I also have to be honest with you: you're an enigma, a sex symbol, a heroine. You're every man's fantasy, and even some women's." Sequoia scoffed. "I'm serious!" she exclaimed. "T. Bibby has a reputation that precedes him. Everything from misogyny to bogus business practices, and whether you know it or not he's extremely jealous and possessive. At some point your personal relationship will compromise your business relationship. Trust me.

"So I guess the real question is; what are you in this industry for? An unstable relationship, or a successful career as an entertainer?"

A knock at the door garnered both of their attention before Sequoia's assistant, Ebony, spoke from the other side. "Sequoia, I have T. Bibby on the phone out here. Says he needs to talk to you. He says it's important."

"Speak of the devil," Lady Goo Goo said before grabbing her salad and sitting Indian style in her chair. "You should probably get that." She took another bite of her salad before speaking. "We'll have plenty of time to talk over the months to come. Just promise me you'll at least consider what I'm saying."

Sequoia arose from her chair reluctantly. "I promise." She walked over to the door and turned to say, "Lady Goo Goo?"

"Humph?" she answered with a full mouth.

"Thank you!" Sequoia said seriously. "I really do appreciate it."

"Anytime doll." She smiled.

Under normal circumstances, Sequoia would've brushed what Lady Goo Goo was telling her off as another frivolous opinion of someone who was simply nosey, but not this time. This time it was different. Her intuition was beating up her insides and giving her the most ironic gut feeling, one that would certainly make her reevaluate her situation more thoroughly and put things into their proper perspective. Suddenly, she felt that she needed to, before something happened in their relationship that neither of them could take back.

CHAPTER 48

Berlin, Germany

One Month Later

A little over a month had elapsed since Lady Goo Goo had voiced her strong opinions about the way in which she felt about T. Bibby and Sequoia's relationship should go, and already the rumors were starting to pour in.

Sequoia was in gray sweatpants, a gray sleeveless shirt with a white halter top underneath, and white ankle socks. Her hair was pulled back into a pony tail. She was sitting Indian-style on the white comforter that was atop her massive, king size bed inside her hotel suite, perched over her laptop with her ear glued to her phone.

Sequoia wanted reassurance. She wanted to give T. Bibby an opportunity to formally address the incessant yet disturbing rumors that dominated every blog site, social network, and tabloid. Though she held her tongue while he went through great lengths to defend his stake in their relationship, he had yet to lay out a strong enough defense on his own behalf that could convince Sequoia of his innocence beyond a reasonable doubt.

"Why are you constantly beating around the bush?" Sequoia basked into the phone. "ARE YOU FUCKING HER OR NOT?"

"NO, I'm not fucking her Sequoia," T. Bibby said into the phone. "We were only out for a business meeting."

"At Joshua's?" Sequoia said, referring to the popular, exclusive restaurant that Bibby owned that was named after his son. "You take your ex-girlfriend to your restaurant while I'm away and pawn it off to me as a business meeting? And you don't see why I would have a problem with that?"

"Correction," he said, "she's not my ex-girlfriend, just an

artist on the label that I—"

"Had sex with in the past," Sequoia finished his sentence for him.

Bibby spoke after a lengthy pause. "You know, for someone who refused my proposal, you sure do feel entitled to put in your two cents about the way I conduct my business affairs."

"WHAT?" Sequoia was shocked. "So that's what this is? Payback for me not accepting your proposal?"

"Of course not," he said. "It's simply business."

"Well, since it's all 'business,'" Sequoia enunciated the word, "tell her to stop posting pics of herself laying next to you while you're asleep in your bed. And posting comments on my Facebook wall about how good it feels to be back in your bed."

"SHE SAID WHAT—"

Sequoia hung the phone up on him and turned it off before he could get another word in. It was painfully obvious to her that his argument was baseless. He apparently hadn't covered his tracks as well as he thought.

And his partner in crime, Sassy, was obviously operating out of a completely different playbook. A playbook that seemingly contained no confidentiality clause, because she had been advertising details of their sordid affair to anyone with ears or a laptop ever since Sequoia set foot in Europe.

The reality of the situation that her relationship with T. Bibby currently confined her to gave merit to the wise words of wisdom that Lady Goo Goo shared with her over a month ago; that their personal relationship would eventually compromise their business relationship.

The narrative all played along to the tune that Jade and Desiree had been singing in Sequoia's ear since their relationship began. The two had all but climbed through the forty-third story window of her hotel suite to comment on the rumors that were permeating the industry about T. Bibby's infidelities. But Sequoia had heard enough, and had no desire to entertain anyone else's opinion of how she should handle her affairs. So for now, she simply decided to just stay off of her phone and off of the internet.

Sequoia had entered the music industry to build a career as an entertainer, not to be in a committed relationship. She'd suspended her scholarship to chase her dream and had made countless sacrifices thus far to ensure that her dreams could manifest full circle. And even though she loved T. Bibby and really wanted to be with him, she felt that it was time that they should take a break. She needed to focus on her career and enjoy the experience that her world tour had to offer.

Thus far, she had performed in front of sold out crowds in the U.K., New Zealand, Nottingham, England, and Manchester, England at Manchester Arena.

Her friendship with Lady Goo Goo continued to flourish, even in spite of their conflicting schedules, as did her relationships with Sean, Corrine, and Ebony. The reality of being thousands of miles away from home in foreign terrain had practically caused them to grow closer to each other. Because, as it stood, even though Sequoia was transitioning into an international star who was recognized anywhere she set foot, inside she simply felt like an American. Those stark realities made her homesick and, in some ways, subconsciously gravitate toward what she was most familiar with—Americans!

The tour was not only providing her with an experience as an entertainer, but a diverse cultural experience as well. She quickly understood how proximity in the world strongly influenced one's religious beliefs, philosophies, language, ideals, customs, and physical attributes.

As she traveled from region to region, or country to country, she also understood the importance of learning about the customs before engaging the townspeople to ensure that she didn't offend anyone with her Westernized, American way of doing things.

Nevertheless, the cultural learning experience would serve as the perfect distraction that she desperately needed to keep her mind off of her relationship with T. Bibby for the moment. Figuring that she had two days until her next show in Berlin, she decided to call her mother, check her emails, get dressed, and assemble her team so they could take to the streets of Berlin to go sight-seeing.

CHAPTER 49

Geneva, Switzerland

Three Months into Tour

"Coming!" Sequoia unnecessarily yelled at her ringing cell phone from the bathroom, as if the caller on the other end could hear her. "Just one second." She wrapped a huge dry towel around her curvaceous nakedness as she climbed out of the shower and dashed to the phone.

"Hello? Hello?" she repeated frantically into the phone's speaker until she realized that the caller had already hung up before she was able to answer.

She searched the caller I.D. for the last incoming call and discovered that it was Desiree. She hadn't spoken to her in nearly two months, and not for lack of trying. It was simply one of the many downsides to being away in another country on tour. Finding free time was almost impossible!

Outside of ongoing discussions and consultations with various musical directors at each venue, or tour and production managers about everything from stage props to visual and audio equipment, not to mention public appearances, autograph signing, exercising, and sight-seeing, it was simply complicated managing her career while maintaining some form of a social life. She only hoped that Desiree understood that.

Sequoia was milliseconds away from hitting the redial button on her phone when a disturbing image on the television filled her peripheral. In that split second she discarded the phone, completely forgetting why she pursued it in the first place, and desperately tracked down the remote. When she discovered it on her mahogany wood nightstand, she raised the volume and listened to the *E-News* reporter.

"Sources say that the sex tape depicting R and B singer Sassy and business mogul T. Bibby was leaked intentionally by R and B singer Sassy. This all falls in the wake of the alleged rumors that T. Bibby was stepping out on his girlfriend, Sequoia, with Sassy, while Sequoia is away on tour. Both R and B singers are signed to Big Boy Records, a record label that T. Bibby has owned for the past fifteen years."

Sequoia turned the television off and flung the remote. She began to cry frantically as she retrieved her phone and began stabbing away at the digital keypad.

She phone T. Bibby, but he didn't pick up. So she called a second, third, fourth, and fifth time. She sent him several text messages, voicemails, and even emailed him, but he refused to accept her calls or return them.

"Aagh!" She threw her phone into a nearby dresser, cracking its screen on impact. She sobbed emotionally at the thought of Bibby being with another woman.

She collapsed weakly onto the memory foam mattress and sobbed into her hands. Sure, she had no desire to get married to him at that point in her life, but they were still in some form of a relationship. They never officially separated, and even if they did, how could he continuously subject her to the type of embarrassment that his infidelities were subjecting her to? And so soon after they'd been apart?

She'd only been away from him for a three month period, and in that time frame he'd managed to betray her trust, publicly humiliate her, and—according to the blogs and the more recent sex tape scandal—apparently commit a disturbingly unknown amount of infidelities while she was away.

Now all she wanted was answers. All she wanted was for him to tell her that none of it was true, for him to convince her that the love they shared was real.

A light rap on the door momentarily drew Sequoia away from her thoughts.

"Go away!" Sequoia yelled in a childlike manner.

"Sequoia, it's me," Corrine said. "Open up."

Sequoia reluctantly willed herself to her feet and sluggishly sauntered to the door. She wiped her face free of tears before opening the door.

She tried to be brave, to act as if she had no idea of the reporting of Sassy and T. Bibby's sex tape on *E-News*, but any attempt to conceal the pain that she was currently masking when out the window when she locked eyes with Corrine.

It was apparent, that she knew, and the house call that she was paying Sequoia had nothing to do with styling or wardrobe, or socializing, or even the broad range of being career-oriented. She was there as a friend. She was there because, despite the façade that Sequoia was attempting to display to her, Corrine knew that Sequoia had heard the news, and she was there to provide her with a shoulder to cry on.

Before Sequoia could speak, Corrine pulled her into her warm embrace as the tears poured onto Corrine's shoulder.

"Don't cry, Sequoia." Corrine drew back to stare into Sequoia's eyes. "You're a beautiful woman, inside and out, and you can have any man you want on this planet. Please try not to get caught up on him. You deserve better."

"I know Corrine," Sequoia sobbed, "but it hurts so bad!"

CHAPTER 50

Tokyo, Japan

Month Four

Sequoia tried to suppress the pain, to contain it as best as she could, but everywhere she looked there were reminders of the extreme lengths that T. Bibby had gone to ensure that her heart would shatter into a million pieces. Though Sequoia was able to mask her pain with forced smiles and carefully-scripted interviews, deep down her insides were tormented.

She didn't want to think about him. She only wanted to focus on her career, to bask in the experience of her tour, and to continuously top the Billboard charts and sell out shows; for her fans and reporters to focus on the fact that she had currently sold more than eight million albums, and have over 1.4 million downloads on ITunes, not to be grilled at every venue or public outing about her relationship with Bibby or to get her opinion about the incessant rumors of his infidelities to various women of the industry. Sequoia simply wanted people to focus on her as an artist!

She hated it! And she hated the scrutiny, but as T. Bibby had once schooled her in the past about working free publicity, whether good or bad, to her own benefit, a huge part of her had to admit that the driving force behind her records sales didn't solely rely on her good looks and talent. It also lay with her controversial relationship with T.Bibby.

It was a hard truth that she had a problem digesting, a truth that she wanted to convince herself went unnoticed by the rest of the world. But the more she traveled to different countries for her tour, the more she was faced with the harsh reality that there was no escaping the rumors.

Even in Tokyo, where over nineteen million people were crammed into a space that was no bigger than Manhattan, and the customs, language, and traditional values were a stark contrast to that of American culture, Sequoia still couldn't seem to evade the rumors that surrounded T. Bibby.

Sequoia, along with her entourage, attended an autograph signing at a popular music store in Tokyo for thirty minutes to give some of her Japanese fans an opportunity to meet her in person.

Local news reporters, journalists, bloggers, editors, and local authorities were packed to the acrylic paint on the drywall as Sequoia conducted her signing. The sea of multi-racial fans, who were predominantly Japanese, not only filled the music store to the brim, but they also formed a single-file line outside of the store that spanned the length of two city blocks.

Sequoia was comfortably dressed in faded Derion jeans, black suede number five Michael Jordan gym shoes, a black knitted Chicago Bulls sweater, and a red and black Chicago Bulls snapback hat. Her neck bore no necklace and on her wrist was a red G-Shock wristwatch.

She smiled and secretly marveled over the idea of the turnout at the signing as she signed an autograph for two young Japanese girls on the cover of her album. The two teenage girls giggled feverishly as they received their CDs before graciously walking off.

The next to approach was a slightly overweight Japanese man with designer lens glasses and short spiky hair. He was dressed in a colorful, button-down long-sleeve shirt, extremely tight-fitted Levis, and leather open-toed sandals with no socks on his feet.

He spoke with a level of enthusiasm and femininity that betrayed any secret he had to keep about his sexual orientation.

"O! M! G!" he exclaimed animatedly. "I am your biggest fan!" he handed her twelve copies of her album that he wanted her to sign, which Sequoia stared at in confusion. "You are the epitome of a super woman, and you look even more beautiful in person."

"Thank you!" Sequoia was slightly annoyed by him, but she loved his energy nonetheless.

"Sequoia, I admire you. You're strong. You're fierce. And you're beautiful. And from me to you," he looked around suspiciously and brought his voice to a whisper, "to hell with that T. Bibby. You can do better. If he wants to go off and get industry trash pregnant then—"

"Pregnant?" Sequoia repeated in confusion, before realizing that her countenance would reveal how delicate a topic the situation truly was to her to a complete stranger. She forced a smile before carrying on with the signing, and said nonchalantly, "Well," she shrugged, "I've moved on. So, if he and Sassy want to—"

"I'm not talking about Sassy," the man stopped her. "I'm talking about that industry hoe, Korrine Stevens. Superdome!"

Sequoia's heart dropped to the pit of her stomach. She seriously doubted that the rumor had legs to stand on. T. Bibby would never be so reckless as to have sex with an industry whore like Korrine Stevens. And without a condom! It just simply didn't make sense.

The idea alone of Bibby having unprotected sex with a woman like Korrine left a bad taste in her mouth, like shit on her taste buds, and that reality must've shown in her expression.

Sequoia turned to Corrine and asked her, "You heard something about T. Bibby getting Korrine Stevens pregnant?"

Corrine suddenly wore a worried expression as she apprehensively spoke. "I didn't want to tell you. I—"

"So it's true!" Sequoia snapped as her new phone began to ring. "I need a break."

Sequoia rose from her seat, ignoring her phone and the mob of fans that were anxiously waiting for her to autograph their CDs and memorabilia.

Sequoia rushed to the wash room and locked herself inside and began crying into her palms. She was on the brink of a breaking point. She needed time to think; time to collect her thoughts, time to finally face her true feelings head-on so she could put them to bed.

But, the unfortunate truth was, she had only witness a

fraction of the true pain that T. Bibby was about to put her through.

Manhattan, New York

The Tribeca

Desiree stared at her IPhone with mixed feelings. She had yet to get in touch with Sequoia for the past three months. Sure, she understood that she was busy and that her career was demanding, but she couldn't wrap her head around the idea that Sequoia was shunning her to the degree that she was, and at a point in her life when she apparently needed her the most.

Desiree knew that Sequoia was hearing about T. Bibby and his infidelities, and she knew that she was heartbroken. All she wanted to do was be there for her, but she insisted on pushing her away.

Desiree loved her, and as it stood, she would still do anything for her, but the last thing she would do was kiss her ass. So, if she wanted to tough it out by herself, then that was fine by her. She only hoped that when she did decide to return her calls that she understood that she would not be conquering an obstacle course for her as quick as she normally would.

Desiree's thoughts were interrupted by a trail of light kisses that unexpectedly graced her neck. She spun on her heels to see a stark naked Jade, who was staring at her lustfully through her black designer frames.

"Hey, baby," Desiree said unenthusiastically before planting a peck on Jade's lips.

Jade picked up on her change in mood. She stared at Desiree in her black, laced Victoria's Secret bra set. She casually admired Desiree's features, from her size six, multi-colored pedicured feet, to her shapely mocha-colored thighs, petite waist, wide hips, flat stomach, perky 38B breasts, and honey and cinnamon highlighted, Halle-Berry-style hairdo.

"What's wrong?" Jade closed the distance between them and trained her jade green eyes intently on Desiree's gray eyes. She kissed Desiree on her chin and waited patiently for her response.

"It's Sequoia," she said sadly before callously tossing her phone on Sequoia's king size bed. "She still hasn't answered her phone."

"I know," Jade huffed as she rubbed Desiree's arms affectionately. "I tried to call her a few times today too. She's just going through a lot right now and—"

"I want to be there for her, Jade. She's like a sister to me," Desiree said emotionally. "We don't know where she is or if she's alright, or even if she's on her meds or not. I—"

"Shh!" Jade silenced her with her index finger. "I know, babe. But try not to worry about her. She's a really big girl, and I trust her decision making. Just... just focus on us right now. Tonight is supposed to be special for us. It's our anniversary." Jade smiled sensually.

"You're right," Desiree said. "Sorry 'bout that."

"Don't worry about it." Jade kissed her. "Just... make it up to me." She made a head gesture in the direction of the bed.

Desiree smiled seductively. "With pleasure." She locked lips with Jade as they made their way to the bed.

Desiree understood how important tonight was for Jade. It was Jade's turn to play a dominant role in the bedroom for the night, and she had been looking forward to it for a week now. So, Desiree stripped to her birthday suit and submitted to her will while she pleased her for the next three hours.

CHAPTER 51

San Diego, California

Sasha Guiliani sniffed the line of coke off the rapper Torrey Guns's stomach before licking up the near invisible trail of residue that the coke left behind. She then pursued his erection with vigor, taking his full length and girth up to her tonsils before gagging and nearly choking.

"Fuck!" Torrey Guns exclaimed as his eyes rolled into the back of his head. He grabbed a fistful of Sasha's hair as she began to develop a rhythm on his shaft. "Damn girl!" He bit his lip. "You a beast."

Sasha sucked his bone dry and plopped it out of her mouth. She kissed his helmet before expelling a glob of saliva onto his erection. She gobbled his testicles, sucking them both individually before taking his shaft back into her mouth. When she was satisfied with the coating of saliva that she applied to his shaft, she mounted him with her fleshy backside facing him and her pedicured feet on his boney thighs.

She took him in her ass slowly, and placed her palms on the silk sheets of the custom-made bed on either side of him before gyrating her hips methodically.

"Mmm! Uugghh! Uhh! Uhh!" Sasha moaned as she rhythmically plopped down on him.

Torrey Guns made vocal grunts and groans as he palmed both of her ass cheeks and spread them as far apart as he could.

After several minutes of snugly penetrating Sasha's tight rectum, Torrey Guns exploded his love seed into her.

"Aaggh!" he exclaimed while panting hard.

Sasha dismounted him and took him back into her mouth, cleaning his member of any traces of residue and swallowing the remnants of his cum.

"I ain't know Italian bitches was boss freaks like that," Torrey Guns said as he stared lustfully at Sasha.

Sasha's tanned skin and large 34D breasts glistened with sweat. She worked her shoulder-length hair out of her face and negotiated it behind her ears. She climbed beside Torrey Guns and lay beside him, while sensually rubbing his tattoo-covered torso.

Sasha had met Torrey at one of Sequoia's concerts in New York City on a backstage pass. They hit it off instantly and had been having sex ever since.

Sasha had invited him to her father's beachfront house in San Diego for the weekend. The house was a seven million dollar terra-cotta and stucco designer mansion that contained every possible amenity one could dream of: indoor and outdoor pools, Gazebo, gym, basketball and tennis courts, gourmet kitchen, five bedrooms, four and half bathrooms, and a theater room.

Guns was a talented lyricist whose career had yet to fully find traction, but Sasha wasn't with him for his money. Her father had plenty of that. She loved his personality and ambition, not to mention his confidence and ability to make her cum.

They started out as a fling, but the more time that they continued to spend together, the more he grew on her. Even though she knew that he secretly had a thing for her friend, Sequoia. That was understandable by anyone's standards, considering how beautiful she was, but it was also becoming extremely annoying to have to hear every time they were together. Today was no different.

"Sasha Guiliani," Guns said as he gazed at her with a satisfied smile. "The best friend of Sequoia Ariás." Sasha rolled her eyes. "You think she got you faded on the head game?"

Sasha sucked her teeth. "Hell no! That prude," Sasha said with conviction. "Don't get me wrong, that's my girl and all, but she's too uptight." Sasha reached over onto the bamboo wood nightstand and grabbed a marble-glass weed pipe and lighter and sparked the

Blue Dreamer Kush. She took a strong toke of the Kush and coughed violently before passing the weed pipe and lighter to Guns. "Like the time when she pressed charges on Fat John for allegedly—"she emphasized with finger quotations—"attempting to sexually assault her."

Guns coughed incessantly when he took the news. "Sexual assault?" he repeated, dumbfounded. "I remember that night. They said that he was charged with a gun and some drugs."

"That's because he paid her a quarter million dollars for her silence." Sasha chuckled. "But all of this is supposed to be confidential so you have to promise to keep this between me and you."

"Hunh?" Guns was already contemplating how to use the information to benefit his career. "Oh, I promise. Your secret's safe with me." He flashed her a winning smile.

"Good." Sasha grabbed the book that she was just pages away from finishing and began to read.

"What's that you reading?" Guns asked. "That new book, *Candid Affairs* by Korrine Stevens?"

"Yup. And let me tell you," she shook her head slowly in disbelief, "this girl is exposing everybody in the industry, even T. Bibby. I know Sequoia is gonna flip when she reads this shit."

"Yeah, that's fucked up," Guns said. "I hear he's been doing her real dirty while she's been on tour. Got the girl pregnant and ere' thing." He tried to grab the book from her but she pulled away.

"What are you doing?"

"You can read this shit later," he said with a smile. "It's our time."

"I know." She trained her eyes on the book. "I just want to know if your name is in here too."

He laughed. "Naw, my shit ain't in there shorty," he said as he secretly contemplated how much money he could sell the information about Sequoia for.

Sydney, Australia

Sequoia had read the book *Candid Affairs* three times and still couldn't seem to accept the assertions and claims that Korrine Stevens was alleging. It all seemed so appalling and unbelievable. To think that one woman could've possibly had sex with so many women and men in the industry was, to her, far-fetched.

But what was even more disturbing was that not one person who she allegedly had sex with had actually come forth to challenge her assertions, not even T. Bibby. And the allegations of their secret rendezvous were as disturbing as they were countless. The most disturbing of the lot being that she allegedly had sex with T. Bibby during Sequoia's going away party at Bibby's mansion in the Hamptons, while Sequoia was in another room. The same night that Sequoia and Bibby engaged in a lightweight altercation over Korrine Stevens attending her going away party. According to Korrine, it was the sexual tryst that she'd engaged in with Bibby in the Hamptons that had led to her pregnancy.

The thought alone was sickening! To think that Bibby could actually have sex with another woman, Korrine Stevens at that, while she was in the other room was causing her insides to do summersaults. A part of her felt that no one, especially Bibby, was capable of such a treacherous act, but an even bigger part of her knew that it was true.

Sequoia tossed the book onto the vanity dresser of her trailer and wiped the tears from her eyes. She extracted her cell phone from her Prada bag and pulled up her Facebook app.

Despite all of the rumors that she had heard that were both alleged or substantiated, she had yet to actually change her Facebook status. A small fraction of her heart wouldn't allow her to. Somewhere inside of her, she wanted to believe that he still loved her, that they could make it right, that she would someday wake up and find out that the bad parts of the past five months were actually a dream.

Not anymore. She could no longer pretend. Simply put, things were what they were. There was no sense in avoiding the obvious any longer. She needed to formally sever any personal ties that she had with him. If for nothing else, she intended to get closure.

She updated her Facebook status to "single and ready to mingle," a statement that she personally felt was extremely misleading on her part because she had no desire to mingle with anyone anytime soon.

The updated posting was more of a calculated strike, a strategic attack to combat the series of strikes that had been inadvertently launched on her heart while she was away on tour.

Sequoia was at war, and not by a formal declaration. She had been prodded into it, goaded into it, practically dragged into it, and her natural instinctive response was to defend herself—to defend her heart!

It was terrain that she had never traversed, and the battlefield was lonely. She had no formal training and as it stood, countless casualties decorated her landscape. She was losing, but she was also a fighter, and the warrior inside of her refused to expose her neck to her vicious enemies and admit defeat.

So she relied on her strengths, which was her ability to think. Her first instinctive thought was to consider the first rule of war: know thy enemy. Sequoia knew that T. Bibby was possessive, controlling, misogynistic, and to a large degree, manipulative. He also had a serious thing for Sequoia, and though he had lost all right to voice his opinion about any personal relationship decision she decided to make in reference to scouting new "talent," Sequoia knew that the idea alone of her involved with another man would drive him crazy.

A light rap on the trailer door demanded that Sequoia shift her focus back to the reason why she was there in the first place. Her beauty had caught the eye of every major magazine editor and photographer, north and south of the equator. The world had fallen in love with her. They were fascinated with her and her beauty.

Editors were practically lining up at her feet to get her to grace the cover of their magazines. The demand for Sequoia's image and physical attributes had only compounded the upward surge in her stack, thereby making her extremely exclusive. Exclusivity dwelled in the same department as costly, not to mention associations with the best brands in the world—like *Sports Illustrated*!

Sequoia had landed the cover page of *Sports Illustrated* magazine, along with an eight page layout for the summer season swimsuit issue. To bring the photogenic magic to the stands as hastily as possible, *Sports Illustrated* decided to make use of Sequoia's geographic proximity to Sydney, Australia to conduct their shoot in between her tour dates.

A team of photographers, wardrobe technicians, hair and makeup artists, and journalists were provided courtesy of *Sports Illustrated* to use a mixture of the natural beauty that Australia's elements provided coupled with Sequoia's beauty.

The photography crew had apparently arrived, and was now anxiously awaiting Sequoia's arrival onto the sandy beach of Sydney, Australia's coastline.

Sequoia's IPhone rang simultaneously, so she scooped it off of the vanity dresser as she headed toward the door. She was in a sapphire colored silk robe and flip-flops.

"Hello," she said while opening the door for the makeup and hair crew to enter. "Oh, hi mom... Yeah it's kinda bad timing right now... I know Ma, it always is," Sequoia chuckled. "I'll be done in thirty minutes or so... Yeah, I read it," her attitude quickly changed. "I don't want to talk about that know. I'll call you back in a little bit... I love you too."

Sequoia sighed heavily as she ended the call with her mother. Everyone knew about the book, even her own mother. She wanted to launch a full-scale attack on Bibby's email and Twitter accounts, but her conservative nature wouldn't allow it. Instead, she abandoned all thoughts pertaining to the subject that was T. Bibby and set her focus on the upcoming photo shoot she was minutes away from.

New York City, New York

Rosa placed her phone back inside her purse and waited patiently for the doctor to return back to his office with the results of her tests.

She had been secretly frequenting his office for the past seven months without anyone's knowledge. The visits began with symptoms of anemia, high fever, and cold sweats. As it stood, the symptoms were becoming more progressive.

Rosa had an idea of what it could be, but she had never been the type of person to jump to conclusions. With all that was going on with Sequoia and her career, Rosa deemed it best to keep everything under wraps until she was absolutely certain of what the true origin of her symptoms were.

Rosa was dressed conservatively in a two piece business suit that was the color of ashes by Michal Kors, an ash-colored calf-suede cap, and black Manolo Blahnik, metallic leather pumps.

Her neck was adorned with an emerald and diamond necklace by Van Clefandappels, a white gold diamond ring, and a stainless steel watch on a leather strap by Cartier.

Rosa had long since abandoned the life of luxury when she and Sequoia's father split up. Her priorities shifted dramatically. She only wanted for Sequoia to succeed in life, so she forked over everything she came across to provide her with all of the opportunities in the world, and as it stood, it was the best investment she could ever make. Now, Sequoia was practically insistent that she have the best, and only the best, until her dying day.

The office door opened and Dr. Drake entered and closed the door behind him. Dr. Drake was tall, 6'3" of height, mid-forties, with a full head of dark hair, clean-shaven, and perfect teeth.

He was donned in his usual white lab coat, black slacks, and patent leather shoes. In his hand was a clipboard. He forced a weak smile before finding his seating behind his desk that was cluttered with paper. He sighed heavily as he clasped his hands together on top of the clipboard—not a good sign by Rosa's judgment.

He avoided eye contact for as long as he could before apparently working up the courage to say the most devastating words that Rosa would ever hear in her life.

"I'm sorry that I have to say this, but Rosa, you have six months to live."

CHAPTER 52

Johannesburg, South Africa

Month Six

Sequoia panted heavily as the crowd of twenty thousand plus awarded her performance with a thunderous applause and standing ovation. She smiled widely in appreciation as her eyes frantically examined the beautiful South African crowd of people erratically.

She wished she could dwell in that moment forever. The stage was where she belonged. She was built for it. She found a small piece of heaven every time she set foot on stage.

The stage had become her new sanctuary, her beach alongside the Atlantic Ocean off the cost of Costa Rica. It was a place where all of her troubles, fears, issues, and anxieties could be cast into the crowd.

In a weird, unexplainable way, Sequoia felt a sense of vulnerability when she performed in front of a crowd, and strangely, she noticed the same sense of vulnerability in the eyes of each member of the crowd. They needed her just as much as she needed them. She was their escape, and they were hers.

The probability of an innate level of dependency being a natural human reaction to abandonment or rejection was a theory that never seemed to evade Sequoia's curiosity. Maybe it wasn't just her. Maybe the world was hurting. Maybe, just maybe, everyone at some point just needed an escape, a place where they could temporarily escape from the pain. Maybe!

The unfortunate truth that everyone eventually had to come face to face with was that the escape was temporary, and that soon the pain would return.

Still, in all, it was something indescribably magical about

bearing witness to over twenty thousand fans from foreign terrain reciting the lyrics to her song verbatim in a language that was not their native tongue.

Sequoia interlocked her fingers with her dancers, who each did the same with dancers who were standing adjacent to them and took a bow before the audience.

Sequoia, along with the dancers, exited the stage and was greeted with celebratory applause and cheers by the stage director, audio technician, video technician, and her tour manager.

Everyone was beaming in a feel-good mood. Sequoia searched the face of everyone who was in the throes of the congested backstage area as she entered and witnessed every form of expression from joy to exhilaration to envy and lust.

Sequoia spotted Ebony, her assistant, who intercepted her before she could make it to the dressing room.

"What's wrong?" Sequoia asked when she took in her troubled countenance.

"I got some...," she made a pained expression, "not so good news."

"What is it?" Sequoia said dryly. "And if it has anything to do with T. Bibby then you—"

"No, no, no," Ebony assured her. "Trust me. This has nothing to do with him."

"Well, can it wait until I get out of this thing?" Sequoia was referring to the aqua blue satin and lace cat suit she was uncomfortably stuffed into with a pair of aqua blue suede, tassel-covered, open-toed Guiesseppe heeled boots.

Her fingernails were aqua blue and her hair was raven-colored, with several single braids that contained decorative aqua blue, African-inspired hair ornaments.

"Not really," Ebony said honestly. "It's your lawyer. Says your being sued."

Sequoia stopped in her tracks and sighed as her face metamorphosed into a scowling mask. "Sued? Sued for what?"

"Something about violating a confidentiality clause," Ebony said with eyes that were a mixture of confusion and curiosity.

"Confidentiality clause?" Sequoia's brain raced as she tried to deduce where the true nature of the suit derived from. She had only signed one confidentiality clause in her life, but she had never told anyone about the "hush money" that she had been given—nobody except for Sasha.

"Yeah, confidentiality clause," Ebony stated. "It's all over the internet. Supposedly, some underground rapper…," Ebony snapped her fingers as if it would jar her memory, "Torrey Guns said that you told him about an incident with you and Fat John, where he supposedly tried to… assault you."

Sequoia quickly deduced that Ebony was making an attempt to bait her for information, so she quickly decided to bring their conversation to an end.

"Is he on the phone right now?" Sequoia asked, referring to the phone that she held covered over her chest.

"Yeah. Here." She handed the phone over and watched Sequoia as she made a hasty retreat into her dressing room.

Sequoia knew exactly who Torrey Guns was, and besides a few brief interactions with him in passing, she had never dealt with him on a personal level—especially to the extent that she would ever divulge secret information to him that would compromise the confidentiality clause that she agreed to. Considering that no one outside of Sasha was privy to the vital information about the incident in question, she had a pretty good idea where Torrey Guns got his information from.

If so, Sasha had just officially severed any bond that they were able to re-solidify after the Fat John incident. For the second time in her life, she began to contemplate seriously hurting another human being. Sasha Guiliani was well within the range of her crosshairs.

Two Weeks Later

E-News *Studios*

"And how long was she stripping before she became an entertainer?" the female *E-News* reporter asked.

Desiree reluctantly answered, "It wasn't that long, maybe six months or so."

A small part of Desiree felt as if she was betraying her best friend, but an even bigger part of her was convinced that Sequoia had written her off in exchange for a newer, more exclusive crowd of friends.

Desiree accepted the idea of Sequoia being very busy early on in her tour, but it was over six months into the tour and Sequoia has only managed to contact her a total of three times.

Desiree felt as if Sequoia had let the fame and the money change her, and in her opinion, the primary catalyst that had prompted the change in her was T. Bibby! She had never approved of their relationship, and had gone out of her way to communicate her feelings with Sequoia about that relationship that she had with T. Bibby, but she disregarded the advice at every turn.

Now, though no one had officially come out and made a public statement about it, Desiree felt that a large portion of the industry felt as if Sequoia was now the laughing stock of it.

The fusion of the reports that Sequoia supposedly compromised a confidentiality clause, and was now being sued by Fat John, mixed with the allegations of Bibby's infidelities with Sassy and the industry whore Korrine Stevens, which led to her getting pregnant inadvertently, kept Sequoia's name in the headlines simply by association. That was excellent for record sales, because, as it stood, Sequoia had sold over seventeen million records worldwide, and had over twenty-one million downloads on I-Tunes, but it all came at the expense of her personal life.

Desiree was convinced that Sequoia was nothing like the person that she remembered growing up with. It pained her to her core to think that things between them would never be the same. It was a hard truth to swallow, but Desiree had already digested it. In her eyes, Sequoia had practically set the tone of their relationship by not disclosing the details to her or Jade about the situation between her and Fat John over a year and a half ago. Sure, it was none of her business, but guarded, decisive moves like that, in her opinion, only confirmed to her that they were not on the level that she thought they were on.

That was why she felt justified in her resolve to disclose intimate details about Sequoia's past life as a stripper to the highest bidder. As it stood, the highest bidder, *E-News*, was willing to fork over half a million dollars for her story. They'd also agreed to keep her name and identity anonymous. To show her appreciation, she handed over a few risqué pictures of Sequoia while posing and dancing suggestively.

"I only have one more question Miss James," the reporter said. "What was Sequoia's stripper name?"

Desiree hesitated for a brief moment before mustering up the courage to say, "Vixen. Her stage name was Vixen."

CHAPTER 53

Toronto, Canada

Month Seven

Five hundred thousand dollars is what Fat John was demanding of her for breaking the confidentiality clause between them, and in all truth, she didn't blame him. He'd paid for her silence to guard the vital information that she had on him that could ultimately define him and ruin his career, and because of a leak that she was solely responsible for, the same information that he'd paid her to guard with her life was now plastered across every tabloid, blog site, and entertainment news network in the world!

Information was everything, and Sequoia was learning this lesson the hard way. People paid top dollar for information every day. Governments have established entire countries simply because they were privy to esoteric forms of information. Corporate investors have made billions in the stock markets because of the correct information.

Intelligence agencies like the C.I.A., Interpol, M-16, and the K.G.B. simply existed because of their ability to acquire bevies of information for national security's sake, and she made a fool's mistake by casually spilling the informative beans to someone as sloppy as Sasha at a time in history, and in her life, when it mattered most. This was the information age!

But, she decided to take it on the chin and chalk it up as a learning experience. So for that reason, she would simply pay the money and sever all ties with Sasha after she put her foot in her ass.

Besides, according to Forbes, she was one of the top earners in the entertainment business, coming behind Lady Goo Goo with an estimated forty-six billion. Corrine was the one that brought it to her attention, and truthfully, she had been so focused on her tour and other work-related expenditures that she never found the time to actually sit back and verify whether or not their calculations were correct.

In any event, she was more than sure that she could easily cover the five hundred thousand dollar bill. Figuring that she was only weeks away from the end of her tour, she thought that it would be best if she started to focus on all of the wonderful things she wanted to do for her mother, Jade, and Desiree—starting with Desiree!

Desiree had been her best friend ever since they were young, and they had never spent more than a month apart from each other since they were twelve. She felt extremely bad about the demands that her career placed on her life, and how it made it nearly impossible for her to talk to her, but she intended to spoil her rotten when she made it home.

For now, she had to consult with her accountant that T. Bibby had provided her with over a year ago to see what her actual net worth was so she could clear her debt with Fat John.

Sequoia's ear was pressed against the phone as she casually strolled through the aisle of a Walgreens with a foot-long Twizzler dangling from her mouth. Sean, Corrine, and Ebony were each raiding the junk food section of the convenient store, per her orders. Sequoia was patiently waiting for her accountant to give her the balance on her account. She was comfortably dressed in a Havana-printed silk-satin top, pink Splendid drawstring cotton shorts, and rubber gladiator sandals by Jimmy Choo. She accessorized her outfit with a powder milk-colored Llano Panama fedora by Pachacuti, clubmaster half-frame acetate Ray Ban sunglasses, a pink Nixon time teller rubber watch, and a mint green and pink, leather-trimmed, woven Dolce and Gabbana tote bag.

The convenient store was practically empty, which Sequoia greatly appreciated. She needed the break from the autographs and paparazzi harassment that she'd been subjected to over the past year or so, even if it was only temporary.

Sequoia thumbed through a magazine selection and nearly had a heart attack when she stumbled upon the cover of *STAR Magazine*. She stared at the magazine in shock for an indistinguishable amount of time. She didn't realize that her mouth was hanging wide open until her foot brushed against the Twizzler that once hung from it and now was on the floor. She disregarded the Twizzler's entire existence as she slowly extracted the magazine from the assortment.

She stared at the cover befuddled. Her mind could not process one single thought. Confusion enveloped her. She wanted to pinch herself to see if she was dreaming, but there it was, in black and white. In bold letters: "INTERNATIONAL SUPER STAR EXPOSED!! Anonymous source reveals the former life of pop star Sequoia Ariás as a STRIPPER!!"

Sequoia flipped over to the page where the article continued and nearly collapsed as she read through the article. She could tell instantly where the details came from, and the three pictures that were meticulously placed in choice areas throughout the article were a blatant confirmation of that theory. Only one person in the entire world was in possession of the pictures, and it would be needless to say that she no longer had a desire to do anything good for her. In fact, she had just earned herself a top slot on Sequoia's shit list— right next to Sasha!

The most disturbing part of the article that felt like twenty miniature chainsaws slicing at her heart was that she allegedly did it for an undisclosed amount of money. Sequoia knew what she had to do. She began stuffing the entire rack of printed *STAR* magazines into her tote bag until her accountant's voice seeped through the phone's receiver and startled her. She accidentally dropped several of the magazines just as Sean and Corrine were simultaneously rounding the corner of the aisle.

"Hello? Larry?" Sequoia frantically spoke into the phone while trying to manage the fiasco of a predicament that she found herself in.

"Yes Sequoia," her accountant Larry said, "I have your balance."

"Sequoia, you need some help?" Sean said, with two hands full of tote baskets that were stuffed to capacity with junk food.

"Hunh, no," she told Sean as she forced a weak smile while trying to scoop the magazines up.

"So you're not ready to hear it," Larry the accountant said as he assumed she was talking to him.

"What?" Sequoia said, confused. "Oh, I'm sorry Larry. I wasn't talking to you. Go ahead."

"Okay," Larry said. "Your total net balance is three million, four hundred, and sixty-three thousand, two hundred and forty-two dollars and seventy-three cents."

Sequoia froze in her hunched over position as if her sudden change in posture was impeding her ability to hear properly.

"Excuse me Larry, but did you just say forty-three million? Right?" Sequoia was completely oblivious to the expressions of astonishment that had claimed both Sean and Corrine's faces as they took in the cover of the *STAR* magazine. By now, Ebony had discovered them all in the aisle and was now walking over to see what they were looking at.

"What are you guys do—" Ebony stopped dead in her tracks as she took in the cover as well.

"No Sequoia, I said three million," Larry corrected her. "And I know it doesn't make any sense, so I checked into it, and discovered that Big Boy Records hasn't cut you a check in over nine months. So you have to call T. Bibby at the label and straighten it out."

Sequoia was so infuriated that she could barely think straight. She ended the call without offering Larry the accountant so much as a goodbye.

Suddenly, the questions that she was sure that Sean, Corrine, and Ebony was practically waiting to barrage her with meant nothing to her.

She dialed Bibby's personal line and told them, "Do me a favor and buy every copy of this magazine. I'll explain later."

Sequoia had been so preoccupied with her career that she'd failed to pay attention to the primary reason why she was working so hard to begin with, but now that her eyes were wide open she was ready to take the gloves off.

Relationships failed all the time, and marriages ended in divorce at a rate that could potentially deter any "I do"-sayer from even entertaining the thought. So, accepting the idea that her relationship didn't work out the way that she had planned it with Bibby was a large pill that she painfully had to swallow. What she refused to accept was that T. Bibby was maliciously playing God with her finances.

If it was one thing she wouldn't tolerate, it was someone playing with two things: her time and money! Manipulations of either were viewed as a cardinal sin in her eyes, and would be dealt with accordingly—in the most extreme fashion! Her shit list seemed to be growing longer by the day, which, in some cases, would make administering punishment to each recipient a thing of priority. But not in this case—in this case she knew exactly who she was targeting first, and his name started with T and ended with Bibby.

"Hello beautiful," Bibby's voice came through the receiver. "I've been waiting for you."

Sequoia was fuming. Just the sound of his voice was causing her blood to boil. "WHERE THE FUCK IS MY MONEY?" she said as she stormed out of the Walgreens in pursuit of the rented S.U.V. outside, completely forgetting to get her prescription filled.

"You want your money?" Bibby arrogantly teased her. "Come and get it."

CHAPTER 54

Manhattan, New York

Three Weeks Later

September 30, 2011

"Come and get it!"

The eerie statement that T. Bibby had arrogantly taunted her by saying had been ringing a dark tune in her head for weeks, and now that her tour was over she was more than willing to take him up on his challenge.

Bibby's office was the first stop that Sequoia was making, and she was only an elevator ride away. She was donned in a lacquered lace coat with ruffled lace peplum slit, and a lacquered lace corset that was the color of fog by Alexander McQueen. Her feet rested snugly in a pair of fog-colored Alexander McQueen, patent-leather pumps that matched her fog-colored, lacquered lace, Alexander McQueen handbag. Her ensemble was completed with a pair of teardrop diamond earrings and matching necklace and pendent that was of a lavender hue. Her hair was straight pressed.

She exited the elevator to T. Bibby's office floor and immediately took in the change in social climate that undoubtedly hinged on her presence. There were seven people in total in the waiting area, and Bibby's new receptionist was parked behind her receptionist's desk. Everyone was wearing either a look of prejudice on their face, or skepticism.

"Hey Sequoia? T. Bibby's in a meet—Sequoia? Sequoia!"

Sequoia disregarded his assistant and stormed in the direction of Bibby's office. She was on a mission, and anyone who intended to get in her way would essentially become a casualty of war because at the present moment, she felt like a walking landmine.

Sequoia barged into his office, utterly disregarding the presence of the two well-dressed, middle-aged, white man and woman in his office as she callously barked, "WHERE THE FUCK IS MY MONEY?"

"I....," Bibby's new receptionist, Bridget, said while panting, "I tried to stop her."

"You're fired," Bibby said simply with anger in his tone before directing his attention to his colleagues. "I apologize for the inconvenience, but can you please give me a brief moment with Sequoia?"

The two respectfully complied, both apprehensively speaking to an angry Sequoia who simply nodded in their direction with her arms folded defensively across her chest as they left.

Bibby closed the door behind them before fixing his lustful gaze on Sequoia. "You look wonderful today."

"FUCK YOU!" Sequoia spat, heated. The mere sight of him had resurrected a series of emotions in her that she'd worked so hard to suppress. "Where's my money?"

"Whoa!" Bibby animatedly stated. "Calm down, Sequoia." He strolled over to his desk casually before saying in a seemingly mocking fashion, "I've never seen this side of you before." He loomed over his desk, searching until he found the copy of *STAR* magazine that displayed her on the cover page. "Then again, I've never seen this side of you before either." He held the paper up so she could see the cover. "A *stripper*?" he said dramatically before placing the paper back on top of his desk. "Not Miss Ivy League."

"My money?" Sequoia was in no mood to play mind games with him. "Where is it?"

"Your money," he repeated mockingly as he slowly walked around to the front of the desk and leaned his backside against it. "Funny story. One that I know you're just dying to hear. You're welcome to sit if you like." He motioned toward his guest office chair.

Bibby was sporting a Tom Ford suit that was the same color as a blue-nose pit bull with black leather Salvatore Ferragamo loafers. His white button-up shirt was open around the collar and bore no tie. His hair was Caesar style with a bold wave pattern. His wrist bore a brown leather band, Frank Muller watch, and on his pinky finger was a huge diamond ring. His ears were adorned with huge diamond earrings.

"You know what?" Sequoia snapped. "Fuck you! I don't have to deal with this shit. You'll be hearing from my lawyer."

"And what are you going to tell him? Hunh Sequoia? What are you going to tell him?"

It was something about the way that he spoke that gave Sequoia pause. She halted in her tracks to see where he was going with this.

"What are you going to tell him? That you signed a management contract that compromised the initial recording contract that you signed?" Sequoia turned slowly on her heels to search his face for any traces of perjury. She found none.

"Uh... What are you talking about?" Sequoia's voice quivered as she spoke. "I only agreed to give you fifteen percent."

"Yeah, verbally," he said, "but on your contract that you signed, you agreed to give me one hundred percent of your publishing, one hundred percent of your record sales, and eighty-five percent of your touring."

Sequoia felt as if her heart had somehow gotten stuck in her throat. She could barely breathe. She wanted to believe he was lying, but as she recalled back to the night in question when she signed the management contract, she had no recollection of ever reading it—a novice mistake that she was now paying for.

Her eyes fluttered as tears began to fill them. "But I trusted you. I... I loved you!" she cried. "How could you do this to me?"

"I only did what you allowed me to do, Sequoia," he said honestly. "And whether you know it or not, I only want what's best for you. Though it may not look like it now."

"Want the best for me?" Sequoia repeated, dumbfounded. "You cheated on me! You got a girl pregnant while I was away! And now you stole all of my money!" Sequoia sobbed. "Why? Why me? I love you!"

"Well, when you say it like that it does sound pretty fucked up," he casually said, "but I only did that so you would learn never to trust anyone in this business."

Sequoia's facial expression betrayed any attempt she made to conceal her confused mind. "I... I don't understand what you're saying."

"What I'm saying is, I don't want your money Sequoia." He closed the distance between them. "I want you."

The pain and frustration was visibly noticeable in Sequoia's eyes and face. Tears cascaded down her face as she tried to contain her mounting anger. It took every microscopic fiber of her will to keep from slapping him as she slowly spoke in a frustrated tone. "You... hurt... me." Her eyes were beet red. "I would've done anything for you."

"And I'm sorry about that." Bibby eyed her intently. "And I understand that you may never be with me again," he said, seemingly as if he accepted it. "So all I'm asking you for is one night. Spend one night, tonight, with me, and I'll tear up your management contract and put every penny that is owed to you in your account."

Sequoia couldn't believe what he was asking of her. She hated him! She despised everything that he stood for. She wanted nothing to do with him. There was no way she was going through with his request.

"I can't do that." She stood her ground.

"And why not?" Bibby walked back over to his desk. "Because of your morals? Because of my past... indiscretions?" Bibby sat in his chair behind his desk and spoke in an arrogant tone. "Sequoia, we're talking about your future here. Everything that you worked so hard for all hinges on this one night."

Sequoia felt defeated. Bibby had played her like a fiddle. He held all of the cards that could make or break her as an entertainer.

She wanted to be moralistic, to exude a fierce and admirable level of pride and integrity, but her good common sense wouldn't allow it. There was simply too much money and too much at stake to throw it all away because of her pride.

"So what's it gonna be, Sequoia?" Bibby asked, wearing a smug look on his face. "I don't have all day."

"What time?" Sequoia said in a low tone.

"Excuse me, I couldn't hear you. What'd you say?"

Sequoia was fuming. His arrogance and management of the situation was both disheartening and upsetting, but Sequoia knew she had to comply so she reluctantly said, "What time?" a little louder than before.

"That's more like it." He stared off as if he would find the timing that would be most suitable on the ceiling. "Make it seven o'clock, but not at the Tribeca. Come to my house in the Hamptons."

"Okay," Sequoia said weakly. "Is that all?" she asked sarcastically.

"Actually, no." He rose from his chair and retrieved two large bags off of a large file cabinet and handed them to her. "Wear this when you come." He dug inside of his pocket and extracted an elongated, velvet jewelry case and gave it to her. "And put this on with it."

Sequoia tossed the jewelry case in the bag without looking at it. She stared at Bibby with eyes that were filled with a bitter mixture of confusion, pain, anger, and love.

Bibby lowered his tone to a more gentle and honest level.

"Sequoia, I'm sorry for all of the pain I caused you. I really do love you." He shrugged. "I guess I just don't know how." He kissed her on the cheek before slowly returning to his seat, leaving a staggered and perplexed Sequoia standing alone to sift through her mind that was now cluttered with a plethora of distressing thoughts.

She turned to leave once more and Bibby thought to add one more thing: "Oh, and Sequoia?" Sequoia sluggishly turned to face him. "Happy Birthday," he said simply.

CHAPTER 55

Think of the beach, Sequoia!

Sequoia had managed to contain her mounting anxiety attack when she was in T. Bibby's office, but all hell broke loose inside of her at the moment that she stepped out of his office.

Now, she was in the restroom with her back pressed against the door trying unsuccessfully to control her breathing.

Breathe Sequoia!

She clutched her chest as she tried to clear her mind of all aggravating factors, but the idea alone was starting to feel like an insurmountable task.

Think of the beach!

Her emotions wouldn't let up. Her thoughts wouldn't let her rest. She was swarmed with emotions. They were bullying her, teasing her, taunting her at every turn.

Think of the fucking beach!

Sequoia was hyperventilating, but it was beginning to wane. Her anxiety was starting to flee. After a few more minutes, her breathing was practically under control. She was able to stand erect.

She pursued the sink to splash some water on her face. As she wiped her face free of the water, she caught a glimpse of her reflection in the mirror. She wasn't impressed. In fact, she was actually disappointed. She looked weak—broken; everything that she wasn't. She was the epitome of what every young woman wanted to be: strong, fierce, and fearless. It was about time that she starting acting like it.

It was no one's fault but her own that she'd gotten involved with Bibby in a relationship. She'd compromised her rule of not dating industry men and now she was paying for it for not sticking to her guns. She'd invited a snake into her house and now seemed surprised that it had actually bitten her.

There was no sense in crying about it. She knew what she had to do. She had a seven o'clock appointment and she intended on making it.

However, that was nearly eight hours away, which, in her opinion, was more than enough time to make several pit stops along the way. And Sasha Guiliani was well within the range of her crosshairs first.

Sequoia was chauffeured to the Tribeca. Coincidentally, Sasha had an epiphany that convinced her to take up residency in New York, in the Tribeca, on Sequoia's birthday. She apparently figured that because Sequoia's tour had ended that she was going to go all out and "do it big," as she put it, and spare no expense in doing so. But, she would soon find out that an extravagant birthday bash was the last thing on Sequoia's mind.

Sequoia had instructed the chauffer to wait outside of the Tribeca as she went upstairs to Sasha's condo. She had no desire to stay long.

Sequoia coped with the rigorous red tape security measures before gaining access to Sasha's floor. Being in the building gave Sequoia a bittersweet feeling. She had only taken up residency there for a collective time of two months, and had not been there to have the experience of allowing her lease to run out. But within the short two month period so much had happened.

It was there that she had actually signed her first lease and officially stayed by herself; it was there that she truly experienced the exclusive treatment that the rich and famous are afforded daily; and it was there that she had her first sexual experience with Bibby. They were nothing that she was necessarily proud of at that point in her life, but it was, however, perfect justification for never wanting to step foot in the building again.

She knocked on the door and listened closely as Sasha approached the door from the other side.

"Here I come, Sequoia!" she said in an elated tone as the sound of locks being unhinged annoyingly echoed throughout the hallway. The door swung open and Sasha exclaimed excitedly, "Happy Birthday Seq—"

Sequoia struck her in the face, busting her nose before she could complete her sentence. Sasha fell to the floor, whimpering while nursing her bleeding nose. She peered up at Sequoia with a mixture of fear and confusion in her eyes, wearing nothing but a gray Harvard T-shirt and blue silk and satin panties.

"Stupid ass bitch!" Sequoia angrily stated as she loomed over her. "Yo loud mouth ass cost me half a million dollars!"

"I'm sorry Sequoia!" Sasha's lip quivered. "I— I didn't know he was going to tell someone. It—It was an accident!"

"Well, accidentally lose my fucking number, 'cause I'm done fucking with yo ass! You're too fucking sloppy! And yo ass is always high or drunk. So don't fucking call me again or I swear to God I'll..." Sequoia flinched as if she were about to hit Sasha again and Sasha balled up into a fetal position.

"I'm sorry Sequoia! Please!" Sasha begged for her to relent. "I never seen you like this before!"

The fear in Sasha's tone struck a chord in Sequoia. She managed to contain her mounting anger long enough to process what she was actually doing. This wasn't her. She wasn't the violent type.

Sequoia had yet to conclude that the true premise behind her sudden change in mood and violent rage lay with her inability to take her medication.

She stared at Sasha with contempt. She had done what she came there to do. She saw no sense in compounding the assault with anything else. Their eyes locked for a brief, silent moment before Sequoia vehemently stated, "Remember what the fuck I said, bitch!" Sequoia stormed off, already contemplating the last, and final, person who she had to confront that was on her shit list.

CHAPTER 56

Brooklyn, New York

Sequoia had no clue about the direction in which her conversation with Desiree would go, but she was sure that it wouldn't end well. Desiree had betrayed her to the ultimate degree, and the motive that prompted her betrayal continued to elude Sequoia's line of reasoning.

Sequoia had yet to determine whether or not her timely hiatus away on tour had somehow compromised their communicative relationship so dramatically that Desiree would jump to such an extreme act of betrayal, or if she was simply jealous of her success.

In either scenario, Sequoia was finding it extremely difficult to even consider finding a way to mend their broken relationship. The thought alone of Desiree's treacherous act of disloyalty angered Sequoia so much that she strongly considered severing all ties with her and never speaking to her again, which would be an extreme case scenario considering how long they'd been friends—a term that Sequoia was learning not to use so loosely.

Friends would never abandon their sacred, informal pledge of loyalty to one another, especially for an "undisclosed amount of money." Friends had each other's back, particularly in times of adversity. Friends protected one another, whether it is one's reputation of personal well-being. Most importantly, friends selflessly attended to the state of one's convalescent mother during their time of absence.

The fact that Desiree had practically abandoned and trampled upon her obligatory duties as a friend to Sequoia had all but drawn a line in the sand and declared war! Now, Sequoia was amped up beyond measure about their imminently approaching confrontation.

She arrived at Desiree's apartment forty-seven minutes after she'd departed from Sasha's place. She instructed the chauffer to wait outside until she returned. Sequoia knew that Desiree was inside because the Dodge Charger that she had given her was outside.

Sequoia saw no sense in knocking; figuring that she still possessed a key. She braced herself for the inevitable confrontation that was sure to ensue and entered the apartment.

"Ahh!" Mmm ahh!" Jade practically screamed at the top of her lungs as she neared her third orgasm. She loved it when Desiree shoved her tongue into her ass while simultaneously massaging her clit with the rabbit vibrator.

The sexual feat would prove extremely challenging to pull off for a normal person, but Jade was flexible as they come. Her contortionist demonstrative efforts made it all the more easy for her to twist her frame into an awkward position that would allow Desiree the easy access that she desired.

Desiree and Jade were in the middle of Desiree's queen-size bed. Jade was upside-down with her ass toward the ceiling and her back against Desiree's bare chest.

Desiree licked around the rim of Jade's tight anal opening before spewing a mouthful off saliva onto Jade's asshole. Desiree shoved two fingers into Jade's rectum and continued to simultaneously galvanize her clitoris with the vibrator.

Jade began to buck wildly, rolling and gyrating her hips erotically as she reached her peak.

"Ahh! Oh shit! Ahh! Eww!" Jade yelled as cum oozed and squirted out of her, creating cascading trails of cum down her stomach region and onto her breasts.

Sequoia approached Desiree's bedroom door with apprehension as she overheard the ear-piercing moans and wails coming from the other side of the door. She found her luck and timing to be equally terrible, figuring that she'd made a house call during Desiree's sexual rendezvous. Needless to say, there would be no confrontation between the two of them that night.

Sequoia decided it to be best that she leave before her unexpected and unannounced arrival was discovered as weird, unexplainable behavior. She trained her mind to leave, but something about the way that Desiree was moaning had given her pause.

She'd been around Desiree in the past when she was having sex before, and she had never been that vocal before. In fact, she wasn't the vocal type, and when she was vocal, Sequoia was one hundred percent sure that she sounded nothing like the person who was screaming at the top of their lungs on the other side of the door.

Whether by sheer curiosity or the desire to satisfy her own insatiably mounting arousal, Sequoia found herself within eight feet of Desiree's bedroom door. The closer she got, the more it seemed practically impossible to resist the urge to take a peek into Desiree's slightly ajar bedroom door.

Sequoia chipped away at the eight feet inch by inch, until she could feel her breath coming off of the door. She peeked into the slightly ajar door and nearly fainted when she took on the sight of Desiree and Jade's live girl-on-girl porn scene.

Sequoia's mind drew a blank as she stared in a befuddled fashion. Suddenly, the idea of Desiree and Jade's secretive sexual relationship put a lot of past anomalous occurrences between the two of them into perspective. Now, she understood why her and Jade had gotten so close. She understood why Jade's taste in fashion and word usage had changed so dramatically. And she fully understood why Jade had developed a habit of frequenting New York whenever her schedule permitted. They were... lesbians.

Sequoia had no idea how she was supposed to feel, but she began to feel as if Jade somehow aided Desiree's betrayal. Be it knowingly or unknowingly, she was still guilty by association, which made the very thought alone seemingly compound the pain and anger that she'd previously developed in her heart toward Desiree. Now both of them were on her shit list, and considering that she was literally within video and audio range of them, she saw no sense in prolonging the inevitable.

She stormed into the room abruptly and began launching her verbal assault.

Jade and Desiree immediately sprang from their awkward sexual position to their feet and began searching for lone clothing items that they'd discarded haphazardly onto the floor while in the heat of the moment. They both wore astonished and embarrassed looks on their faces.

"Gay ass bitches!" Sequoia exclaimed vehemently. "In here lickin' on each other asses and shit!" She spoke to Desiree: "So this is what the fuck you two sneaky bitches been up to?

"And why the fuck would you tell *E-News* that I was once a stripper, Desi? Hunh? Why the fuck would you do some stupid shit like that?"

"Because," Desiree said curtly as she pulled a T-shirt over her head.

"Because what, Desiree?" Sequoia folded her arms across her chest defensively. "Hunh? Because what?"

"Sequoia, I'm sorry!" Jade said in a tone just above a whisper as she slowly approached her with tears in her eyes.

Sequoia sucked her teeth before training her hate-filled eyes on Jade. "Fuck you Jade! You're just as guilty as her!" she snapped. "And don't even think about touching me, you nasty bitch!"

Jade was hurt, and it showed on her expression, but Sequoia couldn't care less. She had made her bed and now she would have to lay in it.

"Don't talk to her like that," Desiree jumped to Jade's defense.

Sequoia chuckled. "Bitch, please!" she scoffed. "Worry about defending your damn self."

"Defend myself from what?" Desiree said with an arrogant tone that was beginning to annoy Sequoia. "From you?" She laughed. "Sequoia? Miss Celebrity Princess? Miss know-it-all goody little two-shoes. F.Y.I. Sequoia, you may be a lot of things, but a threat you are not."

Desiree closed the distance between them, coming so close to Sequoia's face that she could smell her cherry Mac lip gloss, as she spoke with hostility. "So yeah," she shrugged nonchalantly, "I told the *E-News* reporter that you used to be a stripper. So what? And they paid me half a million dollars to do it. We both know that you ain't gonna do shit. So why don't you do us both a favor and knock off the charade. In fact, why don't you do me one better," Desiree continued as she brought her voice to a calmer, seductive tone. "Unless you're trying to strip down to your birthday suit and join us, I suggest you GET THE FUCK—"

Sequoia unleashed a barrage of blows to Desiree's face, catching her off guard and causing her to stumble backwards onto her bed. Sequoia then mounted her and proceeded to choke her.

Blood covered Desiree's face as she struggled to wiggle free from underneath Sequoia's weight and firm grasp. She tried to pry Sequoia's hands from around her neck, but discovered it to be in vain. She tried to claw at Sequoia's face, but she wouldn't allow it.

Desiree began to feel her air supply deplete. She slowly felt herself losing consciousness. She began to wonder what had come over Sequoia. Out of all of their years as friends, she had never seen Sequoia so violent...so angry! She was convinced that Sequoia was going to kill her. She searched Sequoia's eyes for any sign of remorse, of compassion, and found none.

Sequoia's eyes reflected that of a maniac. She was lost in the moment, completely oblivious to her surroundings. Desiree began to plead for her life as tears rolled down the sides of her face.

"You fucking bitch!" Sequoia said through clenched teeth.

Jade had watched all that she could. "Sequoia, stop!" she screamed frantically as she approached her from behind. "You're going to kill her!"

Sequoia turned her attention to Jade and pointed a threatening finger at her. "Don't you fucking touch me." She mashed Desiree's face into the mattress as she rose to her feet. "Stupid ass bitch!" She panted heavily. "I would've done anything for your stupid ass! Both of you." She stared at both of them. "And you betray me like this? Me!" She began to cry. "With the whole world against me I just knew that I could count on both of you to have my back," she walked over to the door, "but I guess not, because apparently our friendship had a price."

The tears continued to fall in torrents from Sequoia's eyes. "I loved you guys! I did what I did for us. FOR US!" she repeated loudly. "And this is how I'm repaid?" Sequoia shook her head as she struggled to speak. "You two will never find another friend like me... Remember that."

Sequoia exited the room without looking back. Jade ran to Desiree's side and hugged her tightly as she cried onto her shoulder. They both knew that Sequoia was right, and that she had every right to feel how she felt. Even more so, they would never find another friend on the earth like Sequoia, for she was one of a kind.

CHAPTER 57

Hamptons Gated Community

7:03 PM

The graphic images of Jade and Desiree's sexual tryst were etched into Sequoia's brain; practically boring holes into her memory bank, and the fact that her memory was photogenic meant that she had the unwanted privilege of reliving the experience every time she blinked her eyes.

Five hours and thirty-three minutes had elapsed since she'd stormed out of Desiree's apartment, and she still couldn't seem to shake the disturbing images from her mind.

Her two former best friends had been engaged in a clandestine sexual relationship behind her back for God knows how long. Who would've thought? Her only defense for the moment to seemingly rid her mind of the utterly disturbing memory was to concentrate on the mission before her.

Since the odds highly favored the idea that she would leave T. Bibby's place wearing a blended aroma of guilt, shame, and sex had prompted her to pay her mother a visit first. She was only able to stay a total of thirteen minutes before reluctantly convincing her that she would be back in a few days.

She figured she'd need the extra time to herself when the night was over, so she rented a luxury presidential suite at the Waldof-Astorian Hotel to retreat to when it was all over.

She felt a strong sense of gloom envelope her as the chauffer entered the wrought-iron gate of T. Bibby's mansion. They drove the lengthy, paved driveway at a moderate pace before making it to the front door.

Bibby was standing out front holding a bouquet of red roses.

He opened the rear passenger door for her and told the driver, "I'll take her from here."

He handed Sequoia the roses, which she reluctantly accepted. "Happy Birthday again!" he said with a wide smile before lustfully giving her the once-over. "You look good Sequoia," he said seriously.

"Thank you," Sequoia said with no emotion.

Sequoia was donned in a soot-colored V-neck dress with fish-line detail by Alexander Wang and black suede and Plexiglas pumps that were also by Alexander Wang. She bore no other jewelry besides the amethyst necklace and garnet ring with diamonds—all gifts from Bibby.

Bibby was clad in a black and gold, silk, Versace shirt, black Versace trousers, and black velvet Versace loafers that bore a gold Versace insignia.

He motioned for Sequoia to lead the way into the house, which she reluctantly did. Once inside, Sequoia immediately took in the ambiance. The entire house was littered with rose petals, and lavender scented candles were meticulously scattered and burning in every crook, crevice, ledge, and table. Smooth jazz filled the backdrop, as did the tantalizing aroma of an exotic dish.

To her own surprise, Sequoia was impressed. She hadn't received any romantic attention from anyone but Bibby, and that was over eight months ago. The extra mile that he had taken to commemorate her twenty-first birthday was not only flattering, but it also reminded her of all of the amazing times they shared together in the past.

"Let me get that for you." He took the roses and set them on a nearby table.

"You really didn't have to do all of this," she said as her eyes simultaneously probed the layout.

"What, are you kidding?" Bibby exclaimed. "This may very well be our last time together, so I figured," he shrugged, "why not make it a night to remember?"

That made perfectly good sense to Sequoia, especially

considering that this would definitely be their last time together. That she could assure him. In any event, she did need the temporary distraction from the traumatic experience that she suffered at Desiree's apartment earlier—even if it was only for one night.

Bibby led Sequoia to the mahogany wood dining table where their food waited. Underneath a silver cover was a grilled sirloin steak, steamed vegetables, a baked potato that was smothered in butter, sour cream, and onions, and a side dessert dish of strawberry shortcake that was smothered with strawberries and whipped cream.

Sequoia wasn't much of a drinker. In fact, the only drink that she was actually able to stomach was wine—merlot to be exact— which Bibby knew and had taken the liberty of providing. It was a gesture that Sequoia greatly appreciated because she needed something to take the edge off. She downed the first glass and poured herself another from the bottle that was adjacent to her glass.

"Slow down, Sequoia," Bibby said in a fatherly tone. "No sense in rushing. We have all night."

Sequoia rolled her eyes and responded to her statement by taking another huge gulp from the second glass. Apparently the idea of having all night with him required a heavy dose of alcohol for her to bear through it.

"Sequoia, are you alright?" Bibby was starting to get concerned. "You haven't eaten your dinner yet."

"I'm not hungry," she curtly stated before downing the rest of her drink. She tried to pour herself another glass but Bibby stopped her.

"C'mon, Sequoia," he grabbed her hand, "that's enough."

Sequoia snatched away from him, which accidentally caused the glass in her hand to fly across the room and onto the marble-tiled floor.

Sequoia completely ignored the glass shattering in the backdrop as she spoke with contempt; "What is all this? Hunh?" She motioned around the room. "Jazz. Candlelit dinner. Rose petals. Why do all this?"

"Because you deserve it," he said.

Sequoia scoffed before laughing in a deranged fashion. "Because I deserve it?" she repeated in disbelief. "Did I deserve to be cheated on? Hm? Did I deserve to be disrespected and publicly humiliated? Hunh?" She closed the distance between them. "Did I deserve to be manipulated into signing that fuck up management contract you made me sign?"

"I told you I don't want your money, Seq—"

"BULLSHIT!" she snapped, cutting him off mid-sentence. "Better yet," her tone was now even and calm, "I know what you want." She grabbed his crotch and kissed his cheek.

Bibby drew back from her. The nerve of her was slightly unnerving. He had never seen her like this before. He couldn't determine if the woman before him was a woman scorned, or something a lot more... mental!

"Sequoia, I just want to have a nice time with you," Bibby said.

"So let's do it..." Her speech began to slur as she suddenly felt her head spinning. She began to feel overwhelmed and light-headed.

"Sequoia? Are you alright?" Bibby asked as he watched her brace her weight against the mahogany table.

Everything became a blur to her. She couldn't form one clear thought. She couldn't distinguish if she was experiencing an anxiety attack or something... else.

Suddenly, Bibby's voice took on the sound of a P.A. system that was submerged in water. She couldn't understand a word that he was saying. She shook her head violently as if it would shake off the sudden effect that she was feeling and only succeeded in becoming dizzier. The floor beneath her seemed to have vanished, and without any idea of how she made it there, she was laying face-first on the floor.

Bibby helped her to her feet. "Sequoia, I think you need to lie down. You might've had too much to drink." He carried her to the guest room that was on the first floor of the mansion and delicately laid her on the plush queen-sized bed. He meticulously removed her pumps from her feet and placed them onto the floor. He then carefully placed her head onto a pillow before staring at her compassionately. She was an angelic being. Her beauty was inside and out. She was a rare jewel that had practically fallen into his lap, and he abused it.

A huge part of him strongly regretted the way that he had treated her, but an even bigger part of him knew that their relationship would end the minute she realized that she was too good for him. So, he had to create a way to keep her dependent on him, to keep her tied to him until death do they part. Now that he was sure that he had succeeded in making her distrust every man on the planet, he was certain that she would never be with another man. He would ensure it.

Sequoia peered at Bibby in confusion through her blurred vision for a split second before losing all consciousness.

CHAPTER 58

Sequoia awoke the following day with a mind-splitting headache. Her eyes fluttered incessantly as she struggled to regain her perception. When her vision was fully restored, she gazed about the room and couldn't distinctively recall how she had gotten there. She sluggishly removed the comforter from her body and noticed that she was wearing one of T. Bibby's Polo shirts and her laced thong.

Suddenly, it all began to come back to her. She had been carried into the room by Bibby last night after she began to feel ill after having too much to drink. He had obviously undressed her and tucked her in, a noble gesture on his part, especially considering that her unconscious state and undoubtedly deprived him of the highlight of his night. She knew that he preferred his women alive and sentient.

A small part of her felt guilty about it, until she considered the reason why she was there to begin with. She was there for one thing: to pay a ransom, and her body and dignity were the asking price. They were two bargaining chips that she found to be extremely disturbing to even entertain parting with.

Yet still, she was slowly digesting the idea that Bibby would be looking forward to collecting what is owed to him, so she figured it best that she attend to her hygiene before that time came.

Bibby was nowhere in sight, which Sequoia was more than certain wouldn't last for long. She made an attempt to sit upright and felt a surge of crippling pain shoot through her anatomy.

Her head was spinning and her body was extremely sore. Her stomach felt as if it had been hit with a sledgehammer. She was cramping like crazy, which was odd, because 'Miss Period' wasn't expected to grace her vaginal doorstep until the following week, so she figured that she could rule that out.

Sequoia found the pain to be even more intense when her

feet settled onto the floor. She had never had alcohol poisoning before, but she was beginning to wonder if it was the explanation for the pain that she was feeling. She was strongly considering going to the emergency room. She visually scanned the room for any sign of her purse or phone, and noticed a paper that was ripped in half. She picked up the paper and realized that it was her management contract. She was free!

Apparently, Bibby really didn't care about the money, because with the severing of the contract she would now receive all of the money that was owed to her.

The thought alone nearly made her forget about the pain— nearly. It hurt like hell when she walked to the shower. She had frequented his house countless times in the past, so she helped herself to fresh towels and toiletries that were stored in the guest closet.

The shower head felt like pellets on her skin as it hit her body. She gritted and bore through the pain as she lathered her body with Dove soap. She rubbed the soap over her delicate, light brown nipples, and grimaced as she discovered them to be extremely sensitive. She washed her southern gourmet and found it to be extremely raw. She was puzzled, because she had no recollection of Bibby and her having sex last night.

She exited the shower a short while later and was surprised to see that she felt ten times better. There was no sign of life in the house. Sequoia had no clue if Bibby was upstairs in his room asleep, or if he was away on an errand, so she decided to call him before making preparations to leave.

She dried her hair with a plush, thick, white dry towel before stumbling across the cordless phone that rested on a glass table in the living room. She plopped down on the expensive couch that was before the coffee table and intended to reach for the cordless phone until she noticed a DVD with a post-it sticker attached to it that read "PLAY ME" in bold letters.

Sequoia looked around suspiciously to see if Bibby had somehow materialized out of nowhere. When she deduced that the coast was clear she hurriedly inserted the DVD into the DVD player. She frantically retrieved the remote to the 62" flat-screen television and thumbed the television to life.

A short while later the DVD sprang to life and a rail-thin man was on the screen having face time with the camera. The man spoke with sincere emotion.

"If you're listening to this Sequoia, I just want you to know that my name is Eric Rolling. I'm a former porn star who contracted H.I.V. As it stands, I currently have full blown A.I.D.S., and according to the doctors I only have two weeks to live." The man paused for a lengthy moment as he struggled to speak.

Sequoia was only twenty-two seconds into the DVD and she was already freaked out by it. She had no idea who the man was or why he was speaking to her so... personally. But she listened intently as he continued on.

"I just want you to know that I'm sorry." He began to cry. "I really needed the money for my family. I—I just couldn't leave them with all that debt." His eyes were moving erratically. "Just... please... please forgive me."

In a split instant, the scene flipped to one of the most disturbing and disheartening footages she'd ever seen in her life. It was footage of her unconscious body from the night before. She was completely naked, and Bibby was having sex with her.

He wasn't having sex with her, or making love—he was punishing her. He pounded her like a maniac, flipping and twirling her unconscious body in spine-bending positions as he drilled her.

Fear and shame overcame Sequoia as she watched him take advantage of her. When he had finished with her, and had obviously cum inside of her, he rose and stared at her in an indecisive fashion.

After a few long seconds of deep thought, Bibby motioned for someone to come in his direction. It was then that Sequoia's heart sunk into her foot. She didn't realize that she was holding her breath until she had to gasp for air.

She watched as Bibby instructed the former porn star, Eric Rolling, to climb on top of her and have sex with her. With no condom!

"I see you found the birthday present I made for you," Bibby said in a nonchalant tone from behind Sequoia. "Hope you enjoy it."

Sequoia was filled with so much anger and rage that she spun around with neck-breaking speed and flung the remote at him. Bibby just barely ducked the blow that the remote would have surely caused. The remote landed on a nearby wall and shattered into pieces.

Sequoia hopped over the back of the couch and began viciously punching and kicking Bibby. He suffered through the first thirteen seconds of her assault before striking her powerfully across her face. Her jaw broke instantly on impact, making a loud cracking noise. The blow was so devastating that Sequoia lost all footing and, before she could catch herself, her face had collided with the marble-tiled floor, breaking the bone that encompassed her eye socket.

"Hiyelp!" Her broken jaw wouldn't allow her to form the word 'help' properly.

Bibby's countenance had shifted dramatically. Seeing her wounded and injured seemed to have galvanized a sadistic and violent side of him. He grabbed Sequoia by her hair and brought her to her feet.

"Bitch, you was gonna leave me?" he asked in a maniacal tone. "Let's see you take yo A.I.D.S.-infested ass and fuck with one of them industry niggas now."

Sequoia clawed at the death grip he had on her hair while pleading. "Why? Why ME?" She tried to claw at his face, but Bibby jerked her head back with one hand and punched her in the mouth with the other.

Sequoia fell to the floor. Her lip split in half and three of her teeth were now loose. Blood covered her face and mouth as she began to crawl weakly into the kitchen.

Bibby continued with his rant as she entered the kitchen. "Stupid ass bitch!" he yelled. "I'M THE MOTHER FUCKER THAT MADE YOU! I'M THE MOTHER FUCKER THAT BELIEVED IN YOU!" He began to cry. "I LOVED YOU! WE COULD'VE BEEN TOGETHER FOREVER! BUT YOU DIDN'T WANT THAT!" He followed her into the kitchen. "NAW, YOU DIDN'T WANT THAT." He tossed a chair out of the way that sat before the granite island, causing her to peer back at him in plain fear.

He grabbed her by the hair again and hoisted her up to her feet, slamming her back against the granite island. Sequoia winced and grimaced in pain.

He stared at her, deranged. "GET YO ASS UP HERE."

Sequoia's tears blended with the blood that covered her face as she stared into the face of the man that she once loved. Her hand fished desperately for the butcher's knife that she discreetly noticed was on the granite island behind her.

"Look at you," Bibby said judgmentally. "You ain't so hot no more are you?" He laughed before shaking his head. "All this good pussy, gone to waste." He reached underneath the Polo shirt that she was wearing and caressed her southern folds gently before shoving his middle finger inside of her aggressively.

Sequoia winced while still frantically searching for the knife. When her finger brushed against it, she desperately clutched it within her grasp.

"How 'bout I put a condom on and take you for another round? Hunh? For old time's sake." He smiled devilishly.

"IN YOUR DREAMS MOTHER FUCKER!" Sequoia yelled before stabbing him repeatedly in the chest. "TAKE... THAT... MOTHER... FUCKER!" she shoved the knife into his chest and watched as blood began to pour from his mouth.

The confused and panicked glare in his eyes indicated that he knew he had drawn his last breath. Sequoia moved out of his way as he fell face-forward onto the knife, driving it further into his heart.

Sequoia collapsed to the floor next to him. She felt herself losing consciousness. She tried with all the energy that she could muster to dig through his pants' pockets. She found his phone and began to dial 911.

"911, what's your emergency?" a female operator said.

"I... I..."

Sequoia lost consciousness before she could finish the sentence.

EPILOGUE

Present Day

Sequoia's eyes shifted back and forth erratically as her mind processed the events of that day. The experience was traumatic. The pain was raw, and her heart sagged underneath the weight of the burden. Thanks to T. Bibby, she was now a walking disease.

She avoided eye-contact with the webcam's eye. She felt as if the world was watching her, judging her, mocking her.

She glanced at the number of viewers that were tuned in for her live stream in the corner of the computer screen, and wasn't moved in the least bit that the number topped out at over forty-three million viewers.

She spoke dryly. "The doctors say they found rohypnol in my system, the date rape drug commonly referred to as a roofie." She shrugged nonchalantly before breaking down and crying dramatically. "He gave me A.I.D.S!" She wiped her eyes aggressively before forcing an ambiguous smile. "Or, the 'death sentence,' as I refer to it." She used finger quotations to illustrate her point as she laughed, deranged.

Sequoia suddenly wore a blank expression. "Am I mad?" She nodded her head. "I suppose so," she said in an even tone. "Do I regret killing T. Bibby?" She scoffed. "I mean, I'm remorseful about taking another human being's life, but no, I don't regret killing him.

"I learned a lot from T. Bibby." She wiped a torrent of tears from her face with her hand. "It was him that made me realize that there are a lot of evil people in this world... in this industry.

"It was him, along with a few of my former close friends, that taught me to never trust another person."

She wiped her nose. "And I know what you're thinking. If I

knew I had A.I.D.S. all along, why would I continue on living my life in the fashion that I chose to without telling anyone?" She paused. "I'll tell you why," she said matter-of-factly. "Because on behalf of me and every other woman like me, who's been abused, betrayed, manipulated, or taken advantage of, I did what I felt was necessary to… level the playing field.

"And I know I hurt a lot of people along the way," she wiped her face once more, "but something had to be done, and someone had to do it." She paused to consider her emotions. "So… So I.. I got even. For me and everyone like me. And I understand that because of what I've done, the industry will never be the same, but ask yourself, what would you have done if you were me?" Sequoia paused as if she were waiting for a response. "But I know you guys are waiting for me to finish the story, so I won't keep you waiting any longer.

"So brace yourselves, because I can assure you that if you thought what I've already told you was something, you are going to flip when you hear the rest. And some of you may not like me after I finish this story," she shrugged, "which is understandable. Some of you may even want to kill… which is also understandable. But I want you to know something." She stared intently into the camera. "I wasn't always this way. T. Bibby made me like this. Sasha made me like this. Desiree and Jade made me like this. The industry made me like this."

Sequoia wiped her tears once more. "So, without further adieu," she smiled mockingly, "here's the rest of my… the rest of my… confession."

To Be Continued…

CPSIA information can be obtained at www.ICGtesting.com
Printed in the USA
LVOW08s2358180815

450605LV00002B/343/P